THE Lady AND THE ROBBER BARON

THE KINCAID FAMILY SERIES

JOYCE BRANDON

DIVERSIONBOOKS

Also by Joyce Brandon

After Eden

The Kincaid Family Series
The Lady and the Lawman
The Lady and the Outlaw
Adobe Palace

Diversion Books
A Division of Diversion Publishing Corp.
443 Park Avenue South, Suite 1008
New York, New York 10016
www.DiversionBooks.com

For more information, email info@diversionbooks.com

First Diversion Books edition July 2015.
Print ISBN: 978-1-68230-246-0
eBook ISBN: 978-1-62681-904-7

This book is dedicated to my daughter, Suzanne, and the men, women, children, and grandchildren who have loved her. And to Brenda Firestine and Hilda Brandon. Thank you for your patience as I slowly evolved into a mother, mother-in-law, and grandmother.

CHAPTER ONE

October 1880

The theater was packed. The house lights had been turned down, and the stage lights had not yet been turned on, so Jennifer could still make out a few of the faces in the front rows. She didn't see her brother Peter anywhere.

This was opening night for *La Fille du Danube*, a ballet she had never before danced in public, and she could feel the nervous energy vibrating through her. Peter had promised to be here.

Simone stopped beside her and peered at the audience. "Ooooh, I have never seen him before," she purred.

"Which one?" Jennifer asked, scanning the faces of the crowd.

"That one, in the third row. He is so gorgeous!" Simone said, sighing dramatically.

Jennifer scanned the third row until she saw the one Simone was excited about. Ballerinas lived in their heads and worked in their bodies, so they spent a lot of time inventing fantasies they had no time to live out. The man was inches taller than the people around him. And more handsome than anyone she'd ever seen before. But his commanding presence would have drawn attention even if he were not so gorgeous.

"I should have known you'd notice him," Jennifer said, struck by his dark hair, rich olive complexion, and deep-set eyes that sent a tingle up her spine. His wide, square jaws were clean-shaven, a rarity in this day and age.

"Dance for him," Simone whispered.

"Oh, Simone, he's probably taken," Jennifer said.

"How would you know?" Simone asked, giggling.

Jennifer conceded the point. She had almost no experience with men, except for her dance partner, Frederick, who had worked very hard to seduce her last year. She'd learned very little from the experience, except that he was as confusing personally as he was on the dance floor.

Besides, being a ballerina left no time for romance. And even when there was time, she'd always been too tired or too busy—except for Frederick, which had probably been a mistake.

"Men can be untaken," Simone said firmly.

Real men, as the girls called nondancers, admired ballerinas, but the first thing they did when they got one was try to take her away from the theater. Falling in love with Frederick had been a gradual, easy thing to do and had not threatened to change her life. In Jennifer's mind a ballerina, herself included, was a butterfly. She could not go back to being a caterpillar, any more than she could be happy in love with a man, no matter how gorgeous, who would take her away from the theater.

Some women managed both careers and children, but she knew instinctively she couldn't. She knew how marriage had been for her parents, and she didn't consider herself experienced enough to carry off such a complicated relationship. Her mother had seemed to know how to handle a great many odd situations. Jennifer knew only the theater. In real life, too many things could come up that she wouldn't be able to handle. And she had chosen to become a ballerina—there were no other choices after that.

A girl in the back yelped, and someone cursed. Sounds of a scuffle followed, and Jennifer imagined two girls slugging it out over stolen tights or something equally trivial. It would be a great night or a terrible night. Perhaps both. Generally when energy and tempers ran this high, something extraordinary happened. Last time, they had performed magnificently in spite of more injuries than ever before. It hadn't seemed to matter that injuries sidelined girls faster than their names could be crossed off the lineup. Or that almost none of the girls mentioned on the program would actually dance tonight. The ones who did dance would absorb the general hysteria and be energized by it.

Jennifer was accustomed to seeing her fellow dancers do the impossible—dance numbers they had not rehearsed or did not know or performed in the wrong costumes or with hair flopping wildly because hair pins had fallen out. The wildness of their emergencies added a feeling of danger that created its own energy.

The orchestra ended the overture and the conductor raised his arms, preparing to begin the adagio that would carry her out onto the stage. From the prompter's box Bellini, the owner of the dance company, caught her attention and nodded. She straightened.

The music began softly and slowly rose to a crescendo. Across from her, all four wings were packed with eager faces. At a cue from Bellini, twelve girls pranced joyfully on stage. Simone would be next, then Jennifer.

Alone in the wings, Jennifer stepped all the way to the back to get momentum for her entrance. Her calf bumped against a box someone had placed in exactly the wrong spot. Without looking back, Jennifer eased the box farther back with her foot so she had the room she needed.

Simone made her entry and executed a perfect *pas assemble*; the audience applauded. The music shifted into a *sarabande* and the director gave Jennifer her cue. She leaped forward, sprang into the air, and threw her legs wide apart *à la quatrième*. In spite of her nervousness, her body performed the movements with energy, with verve. She landed noiselessly and swept regally toward her place in front of the troup.

The concerted gasping of a dozen girls sent Jennifer's heart plummeting. She rechecked her placement. Unless Bellini had instructed her incorrectly, which was unthinkable, or unless she had completely forgotten where she was supposed to end the *écart* and begin her *pas ballotte*…Of course, in her present state that was completely possible…

As Jennifer stepped toward the supporting dancers to correct her position, the line, usually as perfectly positioned as an English hedge, broke into a dozen fragments. The girls drew back from her in horror.

In that instant Jennifer knew she had done something unspeakable, something for which Bellini would surely fire her, throw her out of the company in total disgrace. Bellini roared something she could not understand. Panic engulfed her. Forgetting her part, she straightened and looked askance at the ashen faces of the girls who were backing away from her, cowering in fright. She would correct her error at once, if they would only help her. She would start over. She would—

Simone screamed. Surely Simone would tell her what she needed to do to make it right. But Simone only screamed and pointed at her. Wild hope leaped alive in her. Perhaps Simone was pointing at someone else. Perhaps this terrible moment could be blamed on someone else. Then she would not have to leave the ballet forever. She would not be disgraced, deprived of her chosen career.

Praying it was so, Jennifer turned to face whatever was behind her causing such commotion and fear. But she saw nothing, except more horrified faces. The audience gasped and murmured.

"Fire!" someone from the audience yelled. A man bounded up the steps and ran toward her. She recognized the dark man from the third row running at her, and she backed away in terror.

"No! No! Stay away from the curtain!" Simone screamed. The sensation of heat behind her caused Jennifer to turn. Too late. She saw that her long tulle skirt was in flames. By backing up, she had caused the flames to spread to the curtain. They flickered at waist height for a moment, then, quick as a rat, the crackling yellow and blue flames rushed toward the ceiling.

Still, Jennifer could not grasp how this had happened. As the handsome stranger reached her, he ripped off his jacket. She turned to run, and the faces in the audience, barely more than a blur to her, reflected fascination, horror, and expectation.

The man grabbed her around the waist, pulled her down, threw his coat over her burning skirt and beat at it with his hands.

"Are you all right?" he asked. His voice was deep and tinged with an upper-class drawl. His eyes were green as the ocean.

Jennifer's head was spinning. "I...I don't..."

People screamed. Flames licked at the ropes holding the curtain, paused a moment, then spread across the support timbers.

People leaped to their feet and stampeded toward the exits. Overhead, fire crackled. Smoke billowed and filled the top of the theater. The smell of burning rope and dusty curtains stung Jennifer's nostrils. She couldn't believe how quickly the fire had spread.

The handsome man turned to the dancers, who appeared frozen in their places. "Go out the alley exit. *Move!*" he yelled.

Grabbing Jennifer's hand, he pulled her toward the nearest exit. She wanted to ask him a question, but people were screaming and yelling so loudly she knew she wouldn't be heard over the terrible din. The back exit was blocked by a throng of people pressing so hard against the door that no one could move. The stranger cursed loudly enough for Jennifer to hear him.

"Stay here," he said to her. "Step back!" he yelled at the backs of the terrified people, who were pushing vainly against people wedged so tightly they couldn't move through the doorway. "Give the people in front some room, or no one will get out!" he shouted.

They ignored him. He pulled a redheaded man off the back of the throng and shook him. "Get a grip on yourself! Or we'll all die here!"

"Sorry," the redheaded man said, seeming to come to his senses.

"Help me," her rescuer ordered the man. "Help me clear this doorway!" Together the two men methodically pulled people one after another off the back of the pushing throng, and then enlisted their aid. Slowly, order was restored. Those at the front were freed up enough to begin moving through the doors.

With the crush relieved, the dark stranger came back for Jennifer. "Quickly," he said, taking her hand.

Someone screamed. Jennifer looked up in time to see an overhead beam, fully engulfed in flames, falling toward them. The man pushed Jennifer out of the way and followed her, falling and rolling as the flaming beam crashed between them and the door. Then he crawled to her side and lifted her up. "Are you hurt?"

"I don't think so."

Smoke stung her eyes. Most of the fire was overhead, but it was creeping down the walls. Above and behind them a piece of the ceiling fell. The tall stranger sheltered her with his body. Sparks from the falling debris ignited new fires.

One of the long, heavy beams that supported the curtains crashed past her shoulder and through the floor behind them, sending out a shower of flames that ignited a small fire on her bodice. Jennifer screamed. The man slapped out the fire with his hands. She heard the crack of something breaking overhead, and he jerked her out of the way as another flaming beam fell in front of them, completely blocking their escape.

Jennifer screamed and tried to get away from the heat, but the fire had trapped them. It had only taken a moment, but she realized with amazement that she was going to die in this fire. The thought stunned her. She had never once considered dying.

Peter Van Vleet heard the clang of the fire engines and looked skyward. In the west he saw an odd brightness glowing against the overcast sky. He nudged his horse into a run. The fire could be at the Bellini Theatre. He had intended to be early tonight because he hadn't wanted to miss any of Jenn's performance, but his supervisor had kept him late.

Peter worked as a stockbroker at Walter and Company on Wall Street. He hated his job, and it took all his determination just to keep showing up for work. By the time the market closed every day, he was exhausted. Tonight, shortly after closing, his supervisor had tracked him down and asked him to stay for a special meeting. After the meeting, he'd been offered a promotion to trainer. Peter could tell by his supervisor's jovial expansiveness that he fully expected him to be highly pleased. Peter tried not to show his lack of enthusiasm, but it had felt like another bar in his prison.

A block from the theater, Peter reined in his horse. Fire engines blocked the street in front of the burning theater. The roar of the fire was deafening. Men manned hoses and passed water buckets hand over hand. People huddled in groups, watching in horror.

A hard knot of fear formed in his belly. He dismounted and ran to a group of women sheltered against the freezing drizzle that had begun to fall. They were staring at the fire with big, luminous eyes. "Have you seen the ballerinas?" he shouted.

A woman shook her head.

Panic stirred in Peter. He had worried about any number of things happening to his sister, but he had never entertained the idea of her burning to death in a fire. At the thought, his mouth went dry as a stone. He pushed through the crowd, searching for Jenn. At last he saw a costumed ballerina and made his way toward her.

"Where are the other dancers?"

The girl turned. Simone. Of all the girls he knew, he least wanted to see Simone. His mind flashed a picture of Simone and his father kissing. He felt flooded with shame and sick inside, as if he had eaten rotten meat.

"Where's Jenn?" he shouted over the noise.

Simone's great, dark eyes filled with tears. "I don't know," she whispered. "She was still inside…We got out the back entrance, but it was blocked by a falling timber right after…" She gestured helplessly at the building, which was a solid sheet of flame. "I didn't see her again…"

The smoke was thicker here. Behind them fire engulfed the stage and the north side of the theater. The man had led her back onto the stage, looking for another way out. Now they were almost where they'd started from. She hoped he hadn't been disoriented by the smoke and fumes. Her own head felt light and dizzy.

The man lowered Jennifer over the edge of the stage and dropped her into the orchestra pit, then leaped down to join her. Fires burned all around them. He started cautiously forward. The smoke was so thick she could no longer see the ceiling.

"Keep your head down," he yelled, pushing her head down with his hand. She stayed low, where she could still breathe, but she was terrified that the fire would soon cover them completely. Then what would they do?

An explosion in the back shook the theater. Fires around them flared into new brilliance. Ropes burned through, and flaming curtains dropped, showering sparks and starting fires in the first ten rows of seats. The blaze had become a roaring inferno. From backstage new explosions added to the racket. People screamed in the distance. Coughing, the man pushed Jennifer toward the front exits.

Smoke stung her eyes. She couldn't see where she was going. She bent forward and clung to his hands, which were tight around her waist. She stumbled and almost fell, but strong arms picked her up and carried her the rest of the way.

As they reached the doors, cold air filled her starved lungs. The sudden change from hot to cold made her lurch forward in a spasm of coughing. Behind them the roof fell with a tremendous roar.

Bells clanged as more fire wagons arrived. Jennifer had never seen so much confusion. Men yelled and women screamed. The man put her down, caught her hand and pulled her through the crowd and out into the open. Even then he didn't let her stop or catch her breath. Away from the smoke and noise it was windy, and the thin drizzle had turned to freezing rain. But she ran beside him, feeling weightless, energized with sudden joy that she was alive.

Another fit of coughing made Jennifer realize that her lungs were burning and she needed to sit down and rest. But the man kept moving with such determination and energy that all she could do was follow in silence. After knowing him for only a few minutes, she had already learned to trust him.

Behind them firemen yelled over the general pandemonium. But the man pulling her along ignored everything and continued eastward, glancing at the tangle of carriages, surreys, and cabriolets as if looking for something specific.

Finally, when she was about to give up and beg for rest, he stopped beside a dark mahogany brougham. He threw the door open and lifted her into the carriage, then spoke to the driver and climbed in beside her.

Peter was frantic. He hadn't found Jenn. The roof of the theater had caved in, and she was still missing.

He ran from group to group, searching for her face.

People were starting to leave. He felt sick, and sagged momentarily against a carriage. Someone tugged on his arm. He looked up to see Simone standing beside him.

"I saw Jennie! She got out!"

His knees went weak with relief. He covered his face with his hands and stifled the sobs that threatened to betray him. Moaning in sympathy,

Simone reached out and touched him. Peter leaned away from her hand; he didn't want her pity.

"Do you hate me so much?" she whispered.

"I don't hate *you*. I hated what you and my father did to my mother."

Simone started to cry. Fat tears welled up and spilled over, making shiny tracks on her dirty cheeks.

Her tears surprised Peter. He wanted to find Jenn, but he couldn't walk away with Simone crying. He waited for her to stop, but she cried harder. He heaved a sigh. Without warning Simone hit him in the chest with her fist. She hit him again and again.

He caught her arms and pinned them behind her. She was strong for such a small, delicately made woman. She squirmed against him so hard he almost laughed, but he knew better than to laugh out loud.

She glared at him, hating him suddenly. "You don't care about anything, do you?" she said, panting as if she had run a mile.

"I care about finding my sister." Simone's dark, tear-wet eyes reproached him. His mind flashed a picture of her lying naked beside a swimming pool at sunset, her slender back pink and delicately curved in the reddish evening glow.

The summer he was sixteen, Simone had lain naked beside the pool half a dozen times at the Van Vleet family's summer resort house in Martinguas. His friend Edwina had teased him about Simone, claiming the girl was posing for him and him alone. Edwina had said that Simone might be the mistress of the father, but she pined for the son. At sixteen, Peter could not possibly have imagined himself approaching his father's mistress.

In the fiery glow from the burning theater, Simone's full, trembling lips glistened with her tears. Without thinking, Peter bent his head and kissed them. Her sudden indrawn breath caused him to realize he'd made a terrible mistake—kissing a girl who didn't want to be kissed.

He tried to straighten, to correct his mistake, but Simone's mouth surged upward, twisted into his, and heat pounded into his loins with surprising strength. His arms seemed to be taking orders from his swelling manhood. He pulled her roughly against him and pinned her hips against his. He kissed her hard for a long time, and she sagged in his arms. He continued to kiss her, pouring in all the energy and passion he hadn't been able to contain at sixteen, until at last he remembered where they were and what he was supposed to be doing. He wrenched his mouth from Simone's.

"I have to find my sister." His voice sounded thick.

Simone's eyes widened and she gasped, "Oh, *mon Dieu*, you must go. Yes."

Peter was suddenly aware that others were staring at them, that he was doing something out of the ordinary. He wanted to turn Simone loose, to walk away, but his body needed to feel her there, needed her softness and warmth, and groped toward it.

Carefully, he lowered Simone down until her feet were planted firmly on the wet sidewalk. Her hands fell away from him. A sense of loss moved into him, but he let go of her and walked toward the front of the building to find his sister.

CHAPTER TWO

The raindrops that had fallen on her while she ran to his carriage cooled Jennifer's hot face. The darkness inside the coach was dank and cold, but the contrast felt good. The coach began to roll. She leaned back and took in a cautious, nervous breath, deeply aware of the heavy masculine energy of the man beside her. Ordinarily she would not think of getting into a stranger's coach, but for some reason she had become accustomed to following his lead. Besides, he was a respectable ballet fan. He would take her home, be sure she was safe, and that would be the end of it.

The carriage took the corner a little too fast, and Jennifer was thrown against his shoulder. He lifted his arm out of the way and pulled her close to him. She started to protest, but she craved closeness and protection. She gave in to the feeling and pressed her cheek and nose against his damp shirt. In spite of the smoke that clung to everything, the scent of his warm, wet skin mesmerized her.

"Are you hurt?" she asked, lifting one of his hands. In the darkness his hand looked big and square and beautifully made. She had always admired strong, capable-looking hands. This one was endowed with a magnetism that made her want to keep touching it.

"I don't think so," he said.

"I'm sorry...?" she asked, puzzled.

"You asked if I was hurt. I said I didn't think so."

"Oh, of course," she said, unwilling to admit that she'd been so engrossed in the feel of his hand that she'd forgotten her question. "I meant that you must have burned your hands, putting that fire out on my costume..." Something dark and sweet pooled low in her belly and distracted her, so her words trailed off.

"No," he said. "I'm fine."

Unable to stop herself, she lifted his hand close to her face and peered at it in the near darkness of the carriage. "Is that a burn spot?"

"It's dirt," he whispered, his mouth so close she felt the warmth of his breath tingling her cheek. She shivered. His voice seemed thicker and his breath came quicker. She wondered if her fascination with his hand was affecting him as much as it was her.

Jennifer caught sight of a building in the opposite direction of her home, and she suddenly snapped to her senses. "Where is he taking us?"

"Nowhere." The man's voice was husky. In spite of the darkness, she could tell he was looking at her intently. His lips were only inches from her own. Her lips tingled, and she wet them. He groaned softly and lowered his mouth to within a hair's breadth of hers.

"He must be taking us somewhere," she said, horribly, painfully aware of the thumping of her heart. She'd never felt so aware of herself or of any man before.

"No."

"No what?" she asked in helpless confusion.

Her head spun—who was this man? What did he want from her? She searched his face. All she could see was his eyes sparkling with silent humor.

Slowly and deliberately, he lifted her chin, looked into her eyes for a long moment, and kissed her. Lightly at first, just a simple brushing of lips against lips.

"I knew it would be like this," he whispered. "I even knew how you would taste." Then he lifted her onto his lap and turned her so that she was fully available to him. She knew she should say something to stop him, but she couldn't. Neither her brain nor her mouth seemed to work.

The second kiss was soft and sweet. Just a little more adhesive and tingling. His mouth tasted smoky on the outside and like warm, sweet figs on the inside. Her mouth opened to his probing lips, and his kiss deepened.

As if some switch had been thrown in her, she was suddenly overcome with a desire to feel and taste him. Her body strained against him. His body felt hard and hot and hungry against hers. Her head spun in tight circles. He, too, seemed to go out of control, kissing her as if he couldn't stop. Finally, when she was so breathless she felt faint, his lips burned a trail to her throat.

"He must...be taking us somewhere," she panted, struggling for control, fuzzily aware that she needed it, but no longer sure why.

"I told him to drive." His voice was thick with desire.

His lips found hers again, and his kisses became more demanding. She sucked his bottom lip into her mouth and bit it. He groaned and deepened his thrusting. That satisfied her mouth, but it did nothing for the rest of her body, which was putting up its own wild clamor. The fire that had almost taken their lives seemed to have lit its own fire in her. Moaning, she pressed against him.

He groaned and his strong hands pulled her hips against the swell of his hardness. "You are so beautiful," he whispered. He kissed her mouth, her throat, and finally, when he had reduced her to gasping, trembling need, he kissed her breasts. The feel of his hot mouth on her sensitive, naked skin startled her, and she cried out. Somehow her costume had been pushed down around her waist. His strong hands held her still and helpless while his hot mouth sucked at one breast, then the other, causing such a burning in her that she let her head drop back.

Then, as if he were determined to torture all of her at the same time, his mouth moved down to her belly and slowly up to her mouth. He kissed her so hungrily and so hard she forgot everything except his mouth, his warm body, and the heavy throb of desire between her thighs.

"I want you," he whispered.

A spear of heat stabbed her. She realized she was trembling all over. And only seconds away from being taken in a darkened coach by a man she'd never seen before tonight. "I must go home," she whispered, struggling to free herself from his grip.

"No...please...I can't let you go." He kissed her again, bringing her to such heat and madness that she knew that in one more second he wouldn't have to do anything. She would do it for him.

"Take me home," she whispered.

Reluctantly, he let her go.

She felt deprived. Her skin seemed to ache for his touch, which had been so incredibly warm and sweet and dark...it created such a hunger within her.

He glanced down at her naked breasts, which she had forgotten. "You should never be allowed to wear anything that covers such beauty," he whispered. "They're sweet and tender and perfectly shaped." Regretfully, he pulled a carriage robe around her and nestled her close. "So you don't catch your death," he whispered.

She sat on his lap, and she was still painfully aware of the swell of his hardness pressing against her left thigh. "I doubt I could die here," she said, feeling as if she'd never be cold again. He had an odd smile on his handsome face, and he was peering through the darkness at her with such intent interest that she felt a wave of sudden shyness. She put her head against his shoulder, closed her eyes, and listened to the heavy throb of his heart.

"We mustn't kiss anymore," she said softly. "This was...I don't know what came over me."

"Shocking," he agreed affably.

"Are you making fun of me?" she demanded suddenly, straightening so she could glare at him.

"Absolutely not. I'm agreeing with you."

"I'm not sure I like the way you agree with me."

He chuckled softly. "Would you prefer I disagree with you?"

His deft fingers unfastened the pins she'd put in her hair to hold her bun in place. Hair fell down around her face, silky against her shoulders and back, soft against the swell of her breasts above the blanket she clutched.

"I don't know," she admitted, puzzled.

Her head was awhirl. This man had the ability to confuse all of her at once. She'd known men who could confuse her mind, and a few who could confuse her body, but never one who confused all of her. Bellini said dancers were different from other people. They learned their movements with their muscles, not with their heads, and so they were more divided. This dark stranger had somehow united her body and mind, and conquered both. Obviously a dangerous man.

She wiggled around and pulled up her costume. "Check my buttons," she said firmly, presenting him with her back.

His warm hands lowered the blanket and fumbled with the fabric of her costume for a moment. "Ahhh," he whispered, then leaned down and pressed his warm lips to the back of her neck. Chills raced down the length of her spine. She felt her body arching as if it had a will of its own, which of course it did, but that was supposed to be only for dancing. His warm hands slipped around and cupped her breasts, and her body turned of its own accord so that his lips could reach her suddenly hungry mouth.

His tongue teased her lips. Moaning, she turned in his arms and let him kiss her for a long, slow time.

"You have the most incredible skin," he whispered, pushing her costume down once again and running his hands over her breasts and waist and hips.

She felt hypnotized by the feel of his hands on her. She knew she had to stop him, but her body urged her to wait just a few more seconds. There was no hurry. He was only touching her...

"What a beautiful, charming, seductive little witch you are." He leaned forward and brushed his lips over hers. The soft underflesh of his bottom lip tasted as sweet and intoxicating as smooth red wine, leading her on, making thunder in her blood. She wondered if there was such a thing as fig-flavored wine.

He kissed her again, and her head spun in tighter circles. After a time she heard a soft mewling sound and realized it came from her. The handsome stranger lay atop her, taking most of his weight on his arms and kissing her as if he were as mesmerized as she. She didn't remember how they had come to be lying down.

Slowly, while he continued to kiss her, his thigh wedged itself between her legs, and she felt the swell of his hardness pressing against her pelvic bone. An odd thing happened. Her body flooded with warmth, and her heart felt as though it opened all the way down to her loins.

Over the years, Bellini had told her a dozen times or more that in classical ballet, the dancer turns out the entire body, opening from the heart. She had never known what he meant by that. To her, a turnout started at the pelvis and was reflected in the legs and feet.

But somehow even without entering her, just from the feel of his manhood pressed against her pelvic bone, her body had opened from the heart. She wasn't sure how she knew, but she did. Tears flooded her eyes. She blinked them back, but he had seen them, or his lips had tasted them.

"Oh, God," he said, groaning, kissing her eyes, her lips, her throat.

She felt crazed with need. Her hands tore at his shirt and finally found the warm, adhesive flesh she'd been aching to feel. His broad back was strong and damp and heavily muscled. His hand slid down and slipped between her legs. The shocking touch sent a spear of heat shooting through her. Startled, she felt her loins flush with fiery heat and then herself spasming. She'd touched herself for relief before, so she knew what was happening, but she prayed to God that he didn't know. Panting, she waited until the spasms subsided. He was still kissing her with great urgency, but slowly she opened her eyes.

"I can't do this," she whispered.

He opened his eyes, and they were still dazed by desire. "What?"

"I can't do this."

"I can't *not* do it."

"I'm sorry," she said regretfully.

He groaned, sighed, shook his head as if to clear it, and sat up. "Don't tell me. Out of all the ballerinas in New York, I got the one who isn't wild and abandoned."

Jennifer's eyes clouded for a moment, then she laughed nervously. Something flickered in his eyes, a warning. But before it fully registered in her, he'd pulled her hard against him, and the laughter caught in her throat.

His mouth covered hers. He kissed her hard and hungrily, doing with his lips and tongue what he could not with his body. Dizziness overwhelmed her, and even though she had gotten her own release, heat rose up in her, and she could hear her blood roaring through her temples.

Abruptly, he released her. His eyes reflected none of the confusion she felt. He looked like a man who knew exactly what he wanted and how he would get it. "I'll let you go this time, bewitching ballerina," he said, his voice a low growl of desire, "but next time…"

CHAPTER THREE

Slowly and carefully, Jennifer opened the front door to the Van Vleet town house. To her chagrin, Peter was sitting in a chair in the entry hall, his head in his hands. As she closed the door softly, he looked up. The despair she saw on his face sent a hot flush of guilt and shame stabbing through her.

"Jenn!" he cried, leaping to his feet.

"Peter," she said, praying that he wouldn't notice that her lips were swollen from the stranger's kisses.

Peter rushed forward, his face haggard. As he reached her, relief and then joy washed over his handsome features. "God, Jenn!" he whispered, the words half strangled. He clasped her in his arms and hugged her so tightly she nearly couldn't breathe. "I thought you'd died in that fire." His voice shook. "Simone told me you got out, but I couldn't find you."

"I'm sorry, Peter. I had no idea you'd know about the fire."

He loosened his hold on her and looked down at her. "How did you get out? Where were you?"

"Just lucky, I guess. Did anyone die?" she asked, trying to change the subject.

"A few...God...I've never been so scared in my life. It was... amazing how quickly that theater went up. Like a bonfire," he said, pulling her into his arms.

"Any dancers? Any of my friends?" she demanded.

"No, not that I heard."

"I got out safely, thanks to...God," she ended lamely.

"I should have been there. How did you get home? I looked everywhere for you."

She looked down so he wouldn't see the lie in her eyes. "I shared a cab with Simone. She was so distraught...she needed to talk."

She told him about the fire, but omitted any mention of the dark stranger. When she finished, Peter shook his head, frowning. He had a wonderful frown. His blue eyes narrowed down to slits, and his handsome brow seemed to cling more tightly to his skull. The ridge of his eyebrows seemed more prominent, more glowering and formidable.

"Do you suppose that fire was set deliberately?" he asked.

"Who'd do such a thing?"

"The owner of the theater, for one." Peter looked at her as if gauging whether to share some important news with her. "I probably shouldn't bother you with this tonight, but…I found out yesterday that Chantry Kincaid the Third bought the Bellini Theatre three days ago. He has plans, secret plans, to raze the theater and rebuild on that site."

"Build what?"

"Derek wasn't sure, but we think cheap housing. Commodore Laurey owns the whole next block and is planning an extremely expensive development. Kincaid's plans will destroy the value of the Commodore's project. So Laurey will have no choice but to buy Kincaid off—at an extravagant price, no doubt. It's blackmail, and would be criminal if there were any justice at all."

Jennifer frowned. Sudden, hot anger rose up in her. She didn't know which she hated more—Peter still being friendly with Derek, who was lower than pond scum, or that her life was once again being disrupted by this robber baron Kincaid. She had never met the man, but she hated him almost as much as Peter did. Chantry Kincaid was totally unscrupulous. Both she and Peter believed he'd had their parents killed three months ago. The two of them had gone to the police with their suspicions, but Kincaid had covered his tracks exceptionally well. The police investigated and found nothing tangible to use against Kincaid in court, and he'd had an alibi, but Peter claimed he had bought off the police. Given the widespread corruption on the force and in other departments of city government, it was probably true.

Chantry Kincaid III was one of the wealthiest men in New York. According to Peter, Kincaid had taken money inherited from his grandmother—and a total lack of scruples inherited from his grandfather—and created a holding company that bought up and controlled untold other companies. He was a millionaire many times over, and he still had not reached his thirtieth birthday.

His grandfather, Chantry Kincaid, known as "Number One" in the tabloids, was even more unscrupulous, if that were possible.

Peter must have seen the confusion and anger on her face. "Look, Jenn, I shouldn't have brought this up tonight, of all times, but dammit—" He paused, and raked his strong fingers through his blond hair. "—I can't help myself. That bastard killed our parents, so—" He choked, and a muscle in his smooth-shaven jaw bunched and writhed.

"What, Peter? You know you can tell me anything."

"I...approached Kincaid on your behalf," he said defensively.

"What do you mean?" Jennifer felt the blood rushing to her head.

"You were tied up in rehearsal, and Bellini and I met with Kincaid. Bellini agreed to sell him the theater and move the ballet company into Kincaid's new hotel, the Bricewood East." Peter took a breath, eyed her for a second, and said, "I acted as your manager, since Sammy's out of town—"

Jennifer stared at her brother, unable to speak.

"—and signed contracts for you to star in three ballets at the Bricewood."

"Peter!" She couldn't believe he'd practically sell her into bondage. She could tell by the look in his eyes—half miserable and half defiant—that he knew he'd had no business doing it. Only his hatred for Kincaid could have allowed him to even consider it. She clamped her jaws shut to hold back the angry words.

"Dammit, I know it's not fair," Peter said, reading her reaction correctly. "But if we don't do something, he's going to get away with murder. You've got to spy on the man and find some evidence against him!"

"I'm not an investigator. I don't know anything about trapping a killer," she protested.

"Jenn, haven't you ever looked at yourself? Don't you have any idea what a potent weapon you are? God, Jenn, he would be putty in your hands," he said, pulling her close and hugging her. She buried her face against his pounding heart, and her eyes filled with tears.

Peter was as blond as she, but without any trace of softness. His skin was richly tanned and smoothly refined. Women were drawn to his powerful, masculine energy like cats to catnip, and men responded like tomcats protecting their territory from an invader. She'd seen him walk into a room and, within seconds, some man would feel an overwhelming need to challenge him, even if he had to pick a triviality to do so.

Peter was cool and steely under pressure, just as their father before them had been, and Jennifer hated not to match his courage and determination, but she had to stand firm. She didn't even know Kincaid, and the man terrified her.

"Look, I won't let him hurt you," Peter said. "All you have to do is go to the Bricewood. He'll take one look at you, and it'll be all over but the shouting."

"What if—"

"Don't try to think about it tonight. Rest now. We'll talk again tomorrow, before we go to the Bricewood."

"Go to the…"

Peter held her at arm's length and stared into her eyes. "It's just a simple appointment to meet him, discuss the fine points of the contract, and get your foot in the door."

Jennifer had the terrible feeling that it had all been settled. Peter was not a man to change his mind.

"You wouldn't have to do much," he said, scowling. His scowls were formidable. Generally, she could not withstand them—but this was different. "I'll take care of you. Please, Jenn." Peter never said please. She could see by the pleading look in his eyes that this was extremely important to him.

She dragged in a frustrated breath. "What exactly would I have to do?" she asked.

"Not much at all," Peter rushed to assure her. "Just keep your eyes and ears open for anything that might be helpful. I want to know what he's doing as soon as he knows."

"But I'm a dancer. I'll have no contact with him…"

"You will," Peter said. "Once he sees you, he'll drop Latitia Laurey like a red-hot horseshoe."

"Who's Latitia Laurey?"

"The Commodore's granddaughter, and one of the finest business minds in this town. According to Derek, she learned all her lessons at her grandfather's knee. A female robber baron, if you can imagine such a thing. I don't think there's any love between her and Kincaid, but they're two of a kind. She may be in love, but he's not. Derek says…"

"What?" Jennifer asked, suddenly intrigued.

"I don't know if this is true or not, but Derek said a Frenchwoman, I can't remember her name, ripped the heart right out of Kincaid a few years back. He's never been the same."

"I can't believe you did this to me," Jennifer said, bringing the subject back to what was bothering her. "Before I'd agreed to anything."

"Jenn! Kincaid killed our parents. To hell with his alibi. He killed them as surely as if he pulled the trigger himself. Doesn't that mean anything to you?"

Jennifer boiled with sudden anger. "Only that you've sold me to one of the most unscrupulous robber barons in New York—"

"Not exactly sold. Leased…"

"Whatever you call it, you know as well as I do that there isn't a theater owner or manager in this country who doesn't *expect*, as a God-given right, to sleep with his female entertainers. You know that's why I've stayed at the Bellini."

"Jenn!" Peter whispered tensely. "He's only a man, for Christ's sake. You're an accomplished dancer and actress. You've played parts that have had me in tears, and I knew what to expect ahead of time. You can do anything you set out to do. I'll do the dangerous parts. Kincaid doesn't resort to rape—he doesn't have to. I promise you'll be safe."

"So I'm just supposed to pretend to carry on with this man? Just pretend to be having a flirtation? Leading him on?"

"That's all. If he touches you, I'll kill him," Peter said grimly.

Now it was clear to Jennifer what Peter really wanted—any excuse to tear into Kincaid with at least a slim hope of pleading self-defense. She could see her brother standing before the judge, waiting to be sentenced for the murder of Kincaid. "I was just defending my sister, Your Honor."

Jennifer knew what she had to do. She shook her head. "I can't be part of this."

"Jenn, it's not like you to be so—" Peter stopped in frustration.

"Cowardly?" she demanded.

Peter shook his head. His gaze wavered and dropped. He loved her too much to use a derogatory word like that, but she could see the disappointment in his eyes.

Jennifer glared at him until his warm hand dropped away from her arm. Then she turned stiffly and stalked up the stairs to her bedroom.

Later, lying in bed and too tense to sleep, she wished she hadn't been so hard on Peter. He was twenty, two years younger than she, but at times he seemed worlds wiser. She admired everything about him, especially the way he had responded to the complicated circumstances surrounding their parents' deaths. And yet, part of her was almost relieved to be rid of them. She was still so angry at them. She hadn't even called them "Mother" and "Father" since she was twelve. In her mind they were always Reginald and Vivian Van Vleet. They had been difficult parents, with their volatile, flamboyant personalities. It was common knowledge that her father had kept mistresses—some less than half his age. Jennifer had hated it even more than her mother had. Stunningly handsome, even in his fifties, women had adored Reginald Van Vleet, including her and her mother.

Vivian had spent a good deal of time yelling at Reginald and complaining to her friends. She claimed she couldn't keep a young maid in the house because Reginald was always climbing into bed with them. The practice was not all that uncommon; many men expected to sleep with their female household help. But Vivian refused to put up with it. Finally, she had taken to hiring only old women, some barely able to get around.

Then, when Jennifer was sixteen, there had been a terrible scandal about her father and a fifteen-year-old girl. The tabloids had had a field day, but they never named the girl, who had apparently committed suicide over Reginald. That was a time marked by more yelling and even greater bitterness between her parents. The authorities had refused to prosecute her father over the girl's death, so it probably was clearly a suicide.

But the papers carried on so about it that Reginald had taken the family on an extended tour in Europe to let things die down. During those two years, Jennifer had studied ballet in Russia and France. She perfected her technique to the point where she was hired as the prima ballerina of the Bellini Ballet Company when the family returned to the States.

Now both her parents were dead, and Peter thought Chantry Kincaid III had been responsible. She and Peter had argued about Kincaid's involvement any number of times in the last three months. One of the tabloids had claimed his grandfather was to blame. They'd implied a Machiavellian plot in which the deaths somehow increased the Kincaid fortune. Peter swore that Number One was too old, and that the grandson, Chantry Kincaid III, was the real brains and destructive force at the helm of the Kincaid empire. Peter had almost convinced her that if the grandson hadn't personally killed her parents, he'd hired someone to do it.

She'd heard very little that was positive about either of the Kincaids, and she was sure the grandson would be nothing but trouble for her. Young and rich and handsome, Kincaid probably thought he could spin women around his little finger with charm alone. Jennifer clenched her fists. Well, it wouldn't work with her. She'd learned that game, watching the way her father operated.

She would keep the meeting with Kincaid tomorrow. But only to tell him that she was not going to honor the contract her brother had signed without her permission. Kincaid would have no choice but to accept her refusal. Powerful he might be, but she would not be bought, not at any price! She was a ballerina first, a woman second.

Night sounds lulled her. A bird cried out, as if a cat had gotten it. The sound did not come again, so maybe one had. That's the way her parents had died. Totally unexpectedly. One day she'd come home from ballet practice and found police carriages surrounding the house. She had run inside to see what was wrong, and had been met by their housekeeper, Augustine, who was hysterical.

Slowly, the story had emerged. Augustine and Malcomb, their butler, had taken the day off. Peter had returned home from his job at the brokerage house at four o'clock to find Reginald and Vivian lying on the floor of the second library. Reginald had been shot through the heart and had died immediately. But Vivian, who had been shot in the stomach, crawled the full length of the room. She left a bloody trail, and died with her face twisted in terrible agony against the carpet.

Jennifer closed her eyes tightly against the bloody image that still haunted her. She had not seen it herself, but the tabloids' lurid descriptions made her feel as though she had been right there in the middle of it. Jennifer cried softly until the pain eased.

Her mother had had a painful life from beginning to end—all because she'd married the wrong man. Jennifer vowed that she would not make the same mistake. She had no idea how Vivian had met Reginald, but she imagined a passionate courtship, driven by lust. A sudden flash to the handsome stranger in the carriage made Jennifer shiver. She didn't know what had come over her. Had the fire made her delirious? Well, at least she'd never see that man again. Her mother might make a mistake like that, but she would not.

Slowly, Jennifer unclenched her fists and forced herself to relax, one muscle at a time, until her mind was clear. But it was only a brief respite. Soon, thoughts were racing through her mind again. Peter was right. She owed it to her parents to try to bring Kincaid down. She would go to the Bricewood and meet him. And she would see what happened, and follow it as far as she safely could. Just thinking about it made her whole body tense again.

She sat up in bed and went through a series of stretches—paying special attention to those places where her muscles were sore and tired and achy. Stretching had always helped, and it didn't fail her this time. As she closed her eyes she could feel the energy flowing unobstructed through her body once again. Just before her consciousness closed down to a pinpoint, she had a flash of insight that she'd come to regret even going near Kincaid.

Perhaps Peter was wrong. Perhaps there was no safe way to approach a robber baron.

CHAPTER FOUR

Ahead of Jennifer's carriage, the wheels of hansom cabs carved delicate slits in the sun-glistened snow on the road curving off into the distance.

Reluctantly, she had decided to confront Kincaid and try to undo the damage Peter had done to her career. She glanced past her brother's handsome profile at three children knee-deep in a snowdrift, packing snow into balls.

The unexpected storm late last night had dumped over a foot of clean white snow on the city of New York, leaving the streets momentarily clean.

Her carriage glided to a halt and Jennifer leaned forward and peered up at the Bricewood, the jewel of the hotel and casino circuit and Chantry Kincaid III's pet project.

The Bricewood, on lower Fifth Avenue, near the elegant neighborhood of Washington Square Park, was five stories high and a block long. In an era of gingerbread and rococo flamboyance, the tall, white, gleaming structure was notable for its clean lines and simple style. A lofty colonnade overhung by a hip roof made it look more like a Mississippi River plantation house than a hotel.

Peter leaned forward, his expression grim and impassive. "It's beautiful, isn't it? Even if it does belong to a bastard like Kincaid...I heard he built it for just under a million dollars two years ago. Now it'd sell for three, easily."

"Do you suppose the illustrious Mr. Kincaid allows his hired help to enter by the front door?" she asked. Peter scowled, and Jennifer softened. "Sorry. It's just that—"

"I know, I know, Jenn. I had no right. I realize that now. You're entirely justified in being upset with me."

His taking full responsibility made her miserable. She leaned over and put her head on her brother's chest. "I wish things were like they used to be..."

"When we had money?" he asked, putting his arm around her.

"Innocence," she whispered, and immediately regretted it.

"I can't remember that far back," he said, looking away. He gazed out the window, ostensibly watching a young woman walk past, but she knew from the way the muscles bunched in his jaw that he was fighting his emotions. Jennifer felt a deep sense of sadness. Somehow their relationship had been tainted. She didn't know whether it was a residue from their parents' deaths or from Peter's obsession with Kincaid and getting revenge. She was terribly torn. Part of her felt that anything she had to do to end this stalemate would not be too much. But another part was angry and frightened and wanted desperately to walk away from everything.

Peter stepped out of the carriage and turned back to her, arms uplifted. She gathered her voluminous skirts and moved to the step. Peter grasped her waist and lifted her across the gutter and onto the red brick sidewalk of the *porte cochere*. The carriage entrance smelled of cedar and pine—a surprisingly woodsy fragrance. She stopped, breathed its pleasantness deep into her lungs, and caught a glimpse of the elegant lobby through the biggest windows she'd ever seen. Smiling attendants bowed as they opened the wide double doors.

On Peter's arm, Jennifer swept past more than a dozen salons to reach the registration desk, where an attendant in white uniform with gold braid waited. The main lobby, which gleamed like a gold-and-white jewel, opened onto a profusion of parlors, salons, reading rooms, smoking rooms, dining rooms, and bars, all elegant in gold and white beneath glittering crystal chandeliers.

"We're here to see Mr. Kincaid," Peter said stiffly.

"Your name, please?"

"He'll be expecting Miss Jennifer Van Vleet."

"One moment, please."

The man disappeared into the back. A few moments later a portly gentleman emerged from the back of the hotel and stopped in front of Jennifer. "Miss Van Vleet?" he asked politely.

"Yes."

"I'm Mr. Monroe. Come with me, please."

"Want me to come with you, Jenn?" Peter asked.

Monroe shook his head no. Peter touched his hat in a small salute and angled toward one of the salons. "I'll wait in there," he said over his shoulder.

Jennifer picked up her skirts and followed Monroe toward the elevators. Mirrors on all sides of the lobby told her she looked fine, but she felt overdressed in her late mother's gold satin gown and white mink muff, hat, and coat—the first she'd ever seen with the fur turned to the outside. These clothes, and everything else she and Peter owned, however temporarily until the estate sale next month, had been bought when her parents were alive and thought themselves rich. Next month it would all go on the auctioneer's block.

That thought alone set her against Kincaid. If it hadn't been for him and his grandfather, her parents would not be dead and she and Peter would not be losing everything they owned.

Monroe stepped back to let her enter the elevator. As it began its slow ascent, Monroe nervously licked his wet, pink, cupid's-bow lips. In the harsh electric light, his eyes appeared to glitter. Grateful for the presence of the elevator attendant, Jennifer tucked her hands into her mink muff as if that would protect her from Monroe's eyes. She was glad she wouldn't have to be alone with this man.

Finally, the elevator clanked to a halt. The attendant opened the door, and Monroe waved Jennifer out ahead of him. He took her elbow and guided her to a door marked MANAGER. He opened it and stepped back to motion her inside. The room was small and cluttered, not exactly what she had expected for Kincaid. Perhaps it was an anteroom.

She stepped inside, and Monroe closed the door and locked it. "Wanna drink?" he asked, loosening his cravat.

"No, thank you," she said, feeling slightly alarmed that he had locked the door.

"Take off your coat. I'll be a minute."

"I'll keep it on, thank you."

Monroe opened a drawer of the desk and lifted out a bottle. He poured amber liquid into a dirty water glass and held it out to her. "Sure you won't join me?"

"Positive."

"Suit yourself." He took a sip and sighed. "Now, tell me about yourself. What's your specialty?"

"I'm a ballerina."

"That's a new one. Ballerina, huh?" He finished his drink, put the glass down, and rubbed his pale hands together. "You gonna take 'em all off in the Baron Room or the Grand Salon?" he asked.

Jennifer's heart started to pound as she realized her mistake. This wasn't Kincaid's office at all. "I'm here to see Mr. Kincaid," she reminded him, willing herself into an icy calm.

"Mr. Kincaid's busy. Anyway, this is my bailiwick. I'm the theater manager. I'm the one you have to deal with."

"No. There's been some mistake."

She turned and started for the door, but Monroe grabbed her by the back of her coat and jerked her around.

Her pulse racing, she swung her elbow like a fist and hit him as hard as she could in the soft part of his stomach. As he doubled forward, she lifted a knee into his face. The effect was muted by her gown, petticoats, and coat, but it was enough to infuriate him. He cursed and grabbed her by the hair, pulling her down with him as he fell. Fortunately, he fell hardest and first, and she used his bulk to soften her own landing. Before he could recover, she leaped up and ran for the door, grateful that the physical demands of her calling gave her the agility to defend herself, even against a man as big as Monroe.

"You like it rough, do you?" he growled. Jennifer reached the door and jerked hard on the handle, but it did not open. Monroe grabbed her and pushed her toward a lumpy horsehair sofa against the wall. Jennifer screamed and lashed out, trying to kick him, but her legs got tangled in her gown and coat.

Staggering toward the couch, she screamed again. "Shut up!" Monroe bellowed, with a glancing blow to the side of her head.

She got one foot loose and kicked him in the shin. He cursed and forced her down onto the couch, his weight pressing her into the lumpy mattress. She screamed again. He hit her across the mouth, and they both fell silent for a moment, eyeing one another and panting. Over the sound of their heavy breathing, she thought she heard a key rattle in the lock. Monroe must have heard it, too, for he looked toward the door. Suddenly, it swung open.

"What's going on here?"

Jennifer blinked in disbelief. The handsome stranger from the carriage completely filled the doorway.

Monroe's face turned gray with fear as he scrambled to his feet. Jennifer struggled into a sitting position. Her rescuer stepped into the room and eyed her briefly, taking in everything with a glance—the tangled state of her gown, the hat that had fallen off, probably even noting the fear and anger on her face.

His expression hardened into fury, and he lunged forward and slammed a fist into Monroe's soft, doughy face. As Monroe staggered toward the wall behind him, the man followed, hitting him twice more before he banged hard into the wall and slowly slid down it. Jennifer couldn't tell if Monroe was faking or if he was just too smart to get up again.

The man walked over and took her by the arm, lifting her up into a standing position. "Are you hurt?"

Jennifer shook her head. He smiled in relief, his green eyes shining like sea glass in a sunny pool. She'd never thought green a particularly warm color, but, when he smiled, something primitive and vital shot through her.

Jennifer's mind reeled in confusion. "What are you doing here?" she asked. "Do you just follow me around, standing ready to save me?"

The man laughed. "Something like that. Aren't you glad to see me?"

"Wonderfully glad. But—"

"I work here."

"Doing what?"

"This and that."

He took her gently by the arm and helped her to her feet. "You look even more beautiful in the daylight," he said, his voice dropping into that huskiness she remembered so well. He pulled her close to him. "You're shaking," he whispered. "I should have killed him," he said grimly, "but you're safe now."

"I am?"

He grinned. "Yes. Don't you feel safe?"

Jennifer stepped out of his embrace and patted at her hair, which felt in disarray. "My mother taught me not to feel safe unless I was reasonably sure it was justified," she said, smiling.

He grinned. "Would you accept a compromise? I think I can guarantee your safety from everyone but me," he said, his eyes twinkling with amusement.

Jennifer laughed. "And," she asked, "you are?"

"Chantry Kincaid the Third. Please call me Chane. And I believe we have an appointment." A smile etched grooves on either side of his mouth, leaving a deep dimple in his right cheek and shadows in the hollows of his wide jaws.

Jennifer blinked in growing horror. Her mind struggled to take in the full meaning of what he had said. This man who had saved her twice had just introduced himself as Kincaid, the man who...Her mind refused to finish the thought. She didn't know whether to bolt out the door and run for her life or just sit down on the floor and cry.

Fortunately, the jangling of a telephone saved her and distracted him. He strode to the telephone and barked into the mouthpiece,

"Hello," his tone impatient and husky, more a command than a question. "No, Steve, you're not interrupting me. How on earth did you track me down here?"

He laughed at whatever was said. One heavily arched black eyebrow shot up and then lowered. He laughed again. "No," he said more quietly. "I don't want to see or speak with Laurey. Stall him." He listened for a moment, then chuckled. "Tell him I'm meeting with contractors this afternoon. That should give him something to worry about." Pure mischief sparkled in his eyes. He winked at Jennifer, obviously enjoying himself.

Jennifer felt a flush spreading over her entire body. She had no idea how to react. And for the first time in a long time she had no idea what part she was supposed to be playing.

"Oh," he said into the phone, as if it were an afterthought. "Yes, you can do something for me. Send two men from security here to pick up Monroe. Then get Tom Wilcox to find out who hired Monroe. I want to see that man in my office in an hour."

He hung up the telephone and looked intently at Jennifer. "We'll give Monroe what he deserves." Shaking his head, he sat down beside her. "Now, Miss Van Vleet, tell me about yourself."

It was an effort to keep from asking him how he knew her name. But, of course, he'd been at the theater last night. Everyone in the audience knew her name, and they had an appointment.

"Don't you know how famous you are in New York?" he asked, seeing her confusion. "You don't get out much, do you?"

Chantry Kincaid felt her presence the length and breadth of his body. She had blushed, and somehow this made her even more pleasing to look at. In the light of day, her eyes really were purple and her mouth really was as soft and kissable as it had felt last night. She had skin as creamy as carnations, with just a hint of warm plum in her cheeks echoing the amethyst fire in her momentarily confused eyes.

"Does it show?" she asked ruefully.

"A little," he said, smiling again. "But we'll change that. Starting with dinner, tonight."

"I can't."

"Your mum doesn't allow you out after dark?"

She didn't tell him her "mum" was dead. Was he callously tactless, or hadn't he put her together with her parents yet? She certainly couldn't tell him that she suspected him of having them murdered.

"I...work."

"Not tonight you don't. Remember, the theater burned down last night. I'll pick you up at seven," he said with finality, taking her arm and leading her toward the door.

"I came here to discuss my contract."

"I only discuss contracts with beautiful women over dinner," he said firmly.

This man really did think he owned the world, Jennifer thought, anger beginning to rise in her. Well, she was *not* the rest of the world!

"Then pretend I'm a man. I demand the right to discuss my contract now, this moment."

"Okay. The answer is no."

"You don't know the question."

"Doesn't matter." His tone was firm and final.

Her anger boiled, but it only added to her frustration. She was so confused she couldn't think of anything to do or say. She needed time to think, time to figure out how she felt about Kincaid being the stranger who had saved her last night and again today. Once she figured that out, everything else would fall into place.

"All right. I'll have dinner with you, but only to discuss my contract."

"Thank you. I'm honored," he said, bowing low before her.

Jennifer felt a momentary jolt of fear. But then she calmed down as she realized that she was doing exactly what Peter was asking of her. She was wooing Chantry Kincaid III in the best way she knew.

CHAPTER FIVE

Chane walked Jennifer to the lobby, where her brother was waiting. The young man glowered at him, and Chane realized that Peter Van Vleet might not consider him a friend. With regret, Chane watched the two of them leave the Bricewood.

"Mr. Kincaid." A voice at his side interrupted his thoughts.

"Yes?"

"There's a note for you."

Chane took the note and read it. It was from his grandfather. "Call for my carriage," he said, folding the note and putting it into his pocket.

Chane strode to his office to tell his lawyer and business confidant Steve Hammond how he wanted to handle the details of Monroe's dismissal. By the time he returned, the carriage was waiting. He climbed inside, rapped on the underside of the mahogany roof to let his driver know he was ready, and settled back against the richly upholstered seat. He was curious and a little concerned. The last time his grandfather had sent for him, he'd found himself knee-deep in the intrigues of high finance and a railroad war.

This peremptory summons had to be business. Number One considered social life a waste of time, even with his grandchildren.

His father, Chantry Kincaid II, called Chantry Two by friends and family when they needed to distinguish between the generations, was nothing like Number One. He, too, was wealthy and worked too hard, but he nevertheless managed to make time for a modest family and social life.

His father said Number One looked down on him for that failing. Number One didn't think he personally had any weaknesses, but he saw fault all around him. He took great pleasure in the fact that he was eighty-five years old now and as sharp-witted as he'd ever been, while the Commodore at eight-four was bedridden. Laurey's granddaughter Latitia ran most of the Commodore's businesses, though he didn't acknowledge it publicly.

Number One's wealth and reputation could be traced back to the early 1800s, when he had first become associated with Laurey. Their first joint venture had been starting a small construction company to help build the Erie Canal in 1817, when they were both in their early twenties.

By 1825, when the canal was finished, their Erie Estuary Company had somehow increased its net worth to well over a million dollars. Muckrakers claimed that Laurey and Kincaid had milked off that much by making illegal contracts to deliver goods that were never actually delivered. Government purchasing agents and equally crooked building inspectors filled their own pockets in the process. Everyone benefited except the state of New York, which paid the bills.

Using the million dollars they got from that venture, Laurey and Number One opened a hole-in-the-wall bank in 1832. Laurey was a handsome young man accustomed to living the good life. The second son of an English lord, Number One knew very well that he'd have to work for everything he got. And work he did, hard and diligently. Under his aegis, the bank prospered. If Number One's version of the story was to be believed, Laurey began relying on him more and more to take care of the business while he indulged himself in fast women, good liquor, and slow horses.

New York was experiencing an unprecedented period of growth, with investors coming from Europe in droves seeking profitable opportunities in the rapidly expanding markets of the New World. Number One funneled his proceeds from the bank into other fast-growing industries.

He was fully ready in the 1860s when the city commissioned the building of a new courthouse, to be situated behind City Hall, its cost not to exceed $250,000. Number One formed a conglomerate of construction companies and entered the low bid. In 1872, when the new courthouse was finished, the elder Kincaid had somehow acquired a large portion of the eight million dollars that the finished structure "cost." One newspaper reporter claimed that between Number One, Tammany Hall and its venal leader William Marcy "Boss" Tweed, and crooked city purchasing agents, the city had lost its shirt. No one speculated how much of it had gone into Number One's pockets, but if there was any truth to the story, the amount must have been sizable.

In the 1870s the city of New York decided to build an elevated railway system to connect all parts of the island so every place in Manhattan was within easy reach. Seeing his opportunity, Number One decided to take over the bank. This way, he wouldn't have to share the coming profits with Laurey, who he felt wasn't pulling his own weight.

No one knew exactly how it happened, but Laurey's personal fortunes diminished to the point where he was forced to sell the bank and other assets. Kincaid, thanks to his recent profits, was able to buy out his partner. When Laurey heard about the El, he sobered up and realized that the bank he'd just sold was in a position to make many millions of dollars from the city.

The Commodore tried to get Number One to void the sale, offering a full partnership in the assets he had left, but Kincaid categorically refused. Laurey then filed suit in court to void the sale, charging that Number One had taken advantage of him. In particular, he charged that Kincaid knew about the city's intent to build the elevated railway system at the time of the sale and he had kept it secret.

Kincaid fought the Commodore and won—although some said it was because he'd bought more jurors than the Commodore could afford. But the real reason the Commodore lost was because everyone of any consequence in New York had known the city was going to build the El. Laurey was out, and Number One became the sole owner of the bank just in time to turn the biggest profits of his career.

Laurey managed to cut himself in on the El profits by forming another conglomerate to compete with Number One. So the hard feelings between the two men escalated. Number One claimed that Laurey's competition had probably cost him millions of dollars.

The El took ten years to build and cost the city another fortune—far more than it should have. By the time it was finished, the two robber barons had turned a dying friendship into a bitter enmity. They now spent a good part of their time and energy trying to ruin one another.

If they'd been younger and had had more energy, Chane might have worried about them. But despite Number One's protestations to the contrary, his grandfather was falling apart almost as fast as the Commodore. Chane didn't see his grandfather often, but the reports he got through the family were that Number One was suffering from the ravages of old age. He had complained that his plumbing had gone out first, and then everything else had started to crumble. "Nature has a mean streak a mile wide when it comes to old men," he'd said. "No wonder we all die mad as hell."

The carriage rocked to a halt at the corner of Fifth Avenue and Thirty-seventh Street, in front of his grandfather's enormous two-story, granite house, dubbed the "Mausoleum" by the Kincaid children. As an architect himself, Chane appreciated the intricacies of its Romantic Classicism, but the windows were so small and so far apart that the house was indeed as dark inside as any mausoleum. He remembered telling ghost stories in the turret to his brothers and sisters.

His grandfather was a true robber baron—a wealthy, powerful man whose methods were reputed to be less than scrupulous. He was regularly labeled a blackguard, a thief, a cheat, and a liar by the muckraking press. When Chane was young, he'd asked his father what "robber baron" meant. Chantry Two had assured him that any man who could earn a million dollars had more enemies than friends, and that his grandfather was no exception. Chane had grown up suspicious of his grandfather, and yet, the old man had been good to him more than once. He'd taught him to peel an orange and to trust his own judgment above everyone else's.

Suddenly loath to find out why his grandfather had summoned him, Chane leaned out of his carriage and glanced at the row of tall, narrow windows on the first floor.

Another carriage was pulling up from the opposite direction, and Chane recognized it as his father's. Anxious to know what was happening, Chane leaped out of his carriage just as his father was running up the front steps.

"Dad! Wait up!" Chane called out.

His father whirled around, startled. "Chane! What are you doing here?" he asked, grabbing onto his hat against a sudden gust of cold wind.

"Grandfather sent for me. What's going on?"

"He's had a stroke, or so I've been told."

They climbed the stairs in silence. Number One's butler opened the door and nodded solemnly.

"How's my father?" Chantry Two asked as they entered.

"Not too good, I'm afraid, sir."

They took the stairs two at a time. Chane couldn't ever remember being inside his grandfather's bedroom. It was enormous. Only the lamps nearest the bed were lit, leaving the rest of the room in darkness. Number One hung onto everything he had, whether it was money, oil, or electricity, which had just recently become available to those few who could afford it. Nothing was wasted. He hadn't even allowed the upper floor of the house to be electrified because he was afraid it would cost more going uphill.

As they entered, the doctor looked up from taking his patient's pulse. "How is he?" Chantry Two asked.

"I'm not dead yet, so don't start talking about me as if I'm not here," Number One rasped. "Leave us," he said, waving to the doctor, who straightened, raised his eyebrows at them and walked to the door.

"Don't tire him," he warned.

"Don't tire him! Damnation! What the hell is he worried about? I'm dying. I'll have all the time in eternity to rest."

"Father—"

"If that charlatan is right, I don't have long, so be quiet and listen. I've got some irons in the fire that need to be pulled out, or I'll lose everything." He frowned. "I know that doesn't make sense, because I can't take it with me, but I don't want Laurey to get it. And you," he said, pointing to Chane, "are the one who has to keep him from it."

"Me?" Chane asked, glancing at his father in surprise. Chantry Two nodded in agreement.

"Yes, you! You've been living off the fat of the Kincaid land long enough! It's time you earned the right to call yourself a Kincaid, dammit!"

"Father!" Chantry Two said, trying to calm the old man.

"Don't 'Father' me. I wouldn't have to depend on your son if you weren't going off to Europe chasing that pretty face you married against my advice."

Chantry Two scowled but remained silent. His father had never forgiven him for marrying Elizabeth. He said she was as empty-headed as a gourd, which wasn't true. The old man didn't trust any woman who could remain beautiful past the age of twenty-five. He considered it the work of the devil.

Number One glared at Chane. "I need your help." A surge of warmth and apprehension filled Chane. As a boy he'd dreamed of hearing his father or even his grandfather say those words. But he knew from experience what providing that help could cost—all his time and attention for months, perhaps years, on end. His own plans and projects would have to be put on hold.

"What kind of help?" Chane asked cautiously.

"You know we're only weeks away from starting construction to extend the La Junta railway line along the Santa Fe Trail from Colorado through New Mexico."

"Yes, sir."

"Yesterday I got a telegram saying my superintendent had been killed. Bastard fell off a damned train, right under the wheels of the car following the coal bin."

"Rotten way to go," Chane said.

"Yes, it bloody well was." His grandfather panted for a moment, breathless from the exertion. "I've never asked you for anything before, but I need your help. I need a man I can trust. This railroad is too important. I have too much riding on it."

Chane understood. His grandfather's empire was as flimsy as most empires. The majority of his vast holdings were lined up like dominoes. One wrong move could bring down every domino. His own budding empire was like that as well. The problem was, Chane wasn't really interested in railroads—he'd done that already. What he wanted to do now was build a chain of luxury hotels from one end of the country to the other.

"I need you to take over my railroad project."

"There are ten men in New York who'd do a better job than I—"

"Save your breath. I've thought of all the men you're going to name. For one reason or another, they don't have what I need in the way of executive ability."

"Father's got that. All your super needs is the know-how to marshal a couple thousand men."

"He won't be available. He's taking your mother to Europe to see a specialist."

"Colorado and New Mexico will still be there when he gets back. And," Chane turned to his father, "what's wrong with Mother?"

"They will, but my money won't," his grandfather said, ignoring Chane's question to his father. "I've made certain commitments. My scouts have already recruited Chinese laborers who have boarded ships in Hong Kong headed for Los Angeles, men I've agreed in writing to pay by the day until the railroad is finished." Number One leaned forward, fixing his piercing green eyes on Chane. "Alive, I'd find a way to keep them from collecting against me. But dead...the damned probate officer will take great delight in paying them every cent they claim they have coming. Bastards! And the Commodore has designs on the route I've surveyed. If his men get to Raton Pass first, I stand to lose everything I've invested. I'll be the proud owner of Colorado's longest stub line going nowhere. And your inheritance won't be worth a plugged nickel."

"My inheritance?"

"That's right, my boy. I'm leaving you everything I own, if you promise to keep that bastard Laurey from taking it away from you."

"But what about Lance and Stuart and the girls?"

"They're of no use to me."

Chane glanced at his father. "We'll take care of them," his father assured him.

Chane was too stunned to speak. His grandfather didn't wait for a response. "I'll call my attorney as soon as you leave and tell him to put everything in your name. The Texas and Pacific, all my holding companies—everything—in your name. Whatever you need will be at your disposal, whatever I have. But you've got to save that railroad." He sagged back and scowled, his eyes glittering with challenge. "You might as well be warned. Laurey said I'd take Raton Pass over his dead body."

"That's acceptable to me, sir," Chane said. They laughed together. Too late, Chane realized his mistake. Now, thanks to that quip, his grandfather assumed he had agreed.

Suddenly, Number One looked weak and tired, his smile forced. "The railroad's your first priority, but there's one other condition. You cannot marry anyone by the name of either Laurey or Van Vleet."

Chane stiffened as Jennifer's lovely image floated before him. "Sorry, sir, but my future is not for sale. Not even for ninety million dollars."

"Bloody hell!" shouted the old man, shaking a feeble finger at Chantry Two. "Talk some sense into your son!"

A knock sounded on the door. "Come in!" growled Number One.

The doctor poked his head in. "Halbertson is here."

"Send him in."

Number One's right-hand man stepped inside and walked diffidently across the room, looking unusually timid in the face of his employer's impending death. Halbertson was tall and lean, with a stern face. His official title was secretary to Number One, but he was far more than that. He was more like a chief executive officer who carried out his employer's policy decisions.

"We'll be going, Father," Chantry Two said, taking Chane by the arm and steering him out of the room. He paused at the door to say, "I'll be back with Elizabeth."

"I doubt you can tear her away from her society friends for the death of an old coot she doesn't like anyway," Number One called after them.

Chantry Two closed the door, and Chane asked, "Why is Mother going to Europe to see a specialist?"

"Female problems."

"Serious?"

"It seems so to us."

"I'm not going to sell him my right to choose my own wife," Chane said stiffly.

"Why make a fuss? He's not going to last long enough to impose that condition on you, now is he?"

"I don't know."

"How could he make it stick?"

Chane shrugged. "Why am I being given all this? Don't you want your father's estate?" Chane asked incredulously.

"To me it's just that much more work to do. With your mother sick…"

Chantry regretted the need to lie to his son, but last night Elizabeth had pulled the rug out from under their marriage. And the truth was worse than the lie. He knew Chane had his own problems, but he didn't have anyone else to turn to. His middle son, Lance, had never been a businessman and probably never would be. He'd passed the bar, only to end up as a lawman in a remote outpost in Arizona. He'd even married a young woman the family had yet to meet. Stuart was fresh out of Harvard and wet behind the ears. Chane was his father's only immediate hope.

"We're leaving for Europe as soon as we can get passage after the funer…" His words trailed off. "You'll be on your own, but you'll be fine."

Chane had the awful feeling that he'd be anything but fine. Maybe his grandfather wouldn't die after all, or maybe he could find a superintendent to build the railroad for him. Or maybe he should just refuse the inheritance. But the thought of ninety million dollars…

The eldest Kincaid shook his head. "I never thought it would come to this," he said, touching his left side with his good hand. There was no sensation to let him know that the left side worked anymore. "Hell and damnation!"

Halbertson cleared his throat, obviously at a loss for words to comfort him. "I don't need your comfort," Kincaid growled.

"No, sir."

"Sit, dammit! I can't stand the sight of you towering over me like some damned vulture."

Halbertson pulled up a chair and sat, his pencil poised over a stenographer's tablet.

"I want you to see to it that my grandson doesn't marry the wrong woman and end up dumping my estate into the hands of my enemies."

Halbertson frowned. "But sir, I'm a businessman, not a marriage broker! How can I—"

"Just listen!" Kincaid interrupted. "You'll be given all the help you need. Call Noonan. He has the contacts and the knowledge. Ask him to recommend someone." Sudden weakness assailed him, and he closed his eyes and gasped for breath.

"Sir?" Halbertson asked. "Are you all right? Shall I call the doctor?"

"No, I haven't much time. My son will be back here any moment with the whole damned family." He paused, panting, wiping at his forehead, which was suddenly perspiring. "I don't want my grandson to marry a Laurey or a Van Vleet. Do you understand that? Under no circumstances is he to give my hard-earned money to anyone by those names."

"Yes, sir."

Halbertson was not surprised. Kincaid had good reason to hate both families. The Van Vleet man, whose name he could never remember, Robert or Roland or something starting with an R, had seduced Kincaid's granddaughter, Annabelle, when she was fifteen. Shortly after that, the unfortunate girl had entered a convent. And within three months she had managed to starve herself to death. Her body had been such a horrible sight, they'd had to close the coffin to spare family members undue pain. Kincaid believed to this day that his granddaughter's death had hastened the death of his much-loved wife by a good five years. Mrs. Kincaid had absolutely doted on Annabelle.

As for Laurey, everyone knew he was a scoundrel. He'd sent his first wife to an early grave with his philandering. The children from the first marriage were all married and settled, but there was that granddaughter from the second union who was still available. Still, Halbertson wondered why Mr. Kincaid was so worried about that. The grandson knew his grandfather's wishes, and surely he could find another eligible young woman to suit his taste. Perhaps this would not be such a difficult assignment after all.

"I know what you're thinking," Kincaid growled. "But Noonan tells me Chane is at this very time having an affair with one of them and preparing to court the other."

"Goodness!" Halbertson said softly, cursing silently to himself.

Jason Fletcher stepped out of the cabriolet and turned back to the cabbie. "You sure you brought me to the right place?" he demanded in his tinny tenor voice. He wondered if the man had taken advantage of him because he could tell he didn't know his way around the city.

Sometimes Jason's dishwater-blond hair, pale eyes, and drab appearance led people to misread him. Usually he could turn that to his advantage.

"This's the place all right, mister. No mistakin' it," said the driver in a flat monotone.

Jason couldn't imagine what a man who had enough money to build a house as big as a city block would need with his services. But he brushed off his new, already rumpled city-bought suit coat, stomped his boots on the sidewalk, and started up the steps that led to the massive front door.

"Hey, mister, ya gotta pay me."

"Wait for me."

"I don't wait for nobody, mister. Pay me now."

It was cold and dark, and Jason had no idea how soon another cab might come along this street. It was the kind of neighborhood where every man owned several carriages. He pulled out a twenty-dollar bill and ripped it in half. It was one he'd taken in a bank robbery last month in Kansas. There were plenty more where that had come from. He handed half to the cabbie and stuck the other half in his pants pocket.

"You'll wait for me now, won't you?"

The cabbie grinned. "Yeah, sure."

Jason climbed the steps and rang the doorbell. A small man in a black monkey suit opened the door. "Yes?"

"I'm here to see Mr. Kincaid."

"Is he expecting you?"

"Reckon so."

The man motioned him inside and closed the door. Without another word to Jason, he started up the stairs. Jason paced the entry hall, which was as big as most houses he'd been in. He couldn't imagine why his cousin had recommended him for this job, or even what the job might be. But he figured he'd find out soon enough.

The little man stopped and looked back at him, irritated. "Follow me, please," he said finally. Jason followed him up the stairs and into a bedroom that was dark except for one small lamp burning beside the bed. An old man lay in the bed.

"Mr. Fletcher?" The old man didn't look too bad until he tried to talk. Only half of his face worked. It was strange the way part of it moved and the other part didn't.

"Yes, sir."

"I'll get to the point, Mr. Fletcher. You've been highly recommended to me because you have a certain finesse in sensitive matters, and because you are unknown in this area."

Jason held back a grin. Latitia was right. Money could buy anything. "I have a job I'd like you to do," the old man continued. "It may entail your going out West. I understand that would not be out of the question for you."

"For a price," Jason said.

"You're a man of few words, Mr. Fletcher. I like that. My investigators tell me that you are very good at what you do."

Jason shrugged. If only the old bastard knew what he was really good at! Latitia had planted good information about him in the enemy camp. That impressed him almost as much as the fact that these city men spent a great deal of their time and energy trying to outsmart one another. Himself, he just preferred to work as little as possible. That way he could spend the rest of his time doing what he liked best—tracking down slim, blond, blue-eyed girls, toying with them for as long as he wanted, and then killing them long and slow in his favorite way. Nothing else compared to that.

These city men liked to sneak around and trick people into killing themselves. Probably some sort of satisfaction there, but it escaped him what it might be. Jason liked to see the blood flow. He didn't want to read about it in the newspaper. He wanted to see it and smell it.

"I'll be quite blunt with you, Mr. Fletcher. I do not want my grandson marrying Jennifer Van Vleet or Latitia Laurey. Do I make myself clear?"

Jason nodded. Very clear. Now he understood why Latitia had chosen him. "Yes, sir."

"I pay well, young man. You'll be put on salary, and the money will be wired to you every week, as long as you are doing the job. You just have to keep Mr. Halbertson advised of your whereabouts. Is it agreed?"

There would probably be an even bigger salary from Latitia. Jason nodded. "Agreed."

Kincaid smiled. "Good. Now I think everything's in place."

"'Pears to be," Jason agreed, smiling.

CHAPTER SIX

After her bath, Jennifer dried her hair before the blaze crackling in her bedroom fireplace. She was impatient with the drying, the combing, the slow and careful removal of tangles. But once she had smoothed her mane of silver-streaked blond hair to perfection, it was like a silky curtain highlighting her flawless face. Her mother had loved her hair. She'd said it was a glory and a wonder to everyone who saw it.

Jennifer squared her shoulders. "Mr. Kincaid," she said, glaring at the full-length mirror beside the fireplace. "I not only will not work with you, I will never see you again."

She tried to imagine his response, but couldn't.

"I'm sorry if this seems rude, Mr. Kincaid, but I am a prima ballerina. I have no time in my life for…" She paused. He hadn't asked her for anything except to work for him. Flushing, she began again. "You may have gotten the wrong impression of me. Ballet comes first. All those rumors you hear about dancers aren't true. We don't even have time for love affairs."

There was no telling what response he would have to that. She was glad Peter wasn't home. She needed the time to figure out how she felt about Kincaid being the handsome stranger who rescued her twice, this robber baron, Chantry Kincaid.

Even Peter would have to concede that the man must have some redeeming qualities if he was willing to risk his life to save someone else's. But even a terrible blackguard could do the right thing occasionally. As her grandfather used to say, "Even a stopped clock is right twice a day."

On the other hand, was she frightened of him because he seemed to want something only she could give? He could have any woman he wanted, why would he choose a ballerina? She glanced at the mirror and wondered what had come over her in the carriage to allow Kincaid so many liberties. Had the fire rattled her so badly that she'd lost all her inhibitions?

Her lips tingled with the memory of his kisses. Could a man whose touch felt so right be so wrong? Her body seemed to have already made up its mind. Only her intellect was still resisting.

Jennifer chose a red satin gown that emphasized her white shoulders and lifted her small breasts. She rang for Augustine and posed with the gown in front of the mirror. It was cut low in front and nipped in at the waist. Her bustle—one of the higher, smaller ones—provided an elegant fall for the pannier.

While she was waiting for Augustine to come help her into the gown, she chose a black velvet choker and her grandmother's antique cameo pendant for her throat, and cameo studs for her ears.

"Time to get ready, mademoiselle?" Augustine asked, sticking her head in the door.

"Yes, please."

Augustine tightened Jennifer's corset stays, buttoned the gown, arranged Jennifer's hair elegantly atop her head, and wove red silk roses through the shiny curls. As she smoothed the last tress into place and stepped back to admire her handiwork, Jennifer assessed herself in the mirror.

Her face looked different. It seemed to glow with an inner radiance, as if her fears and confusion had coalesced into light. When Kincaid walked her to her door after the fire, he'd called her "princess." In her mind she could hear the smoky baritone of his voice, turning the word into a caress, *princess*.

The grandfather clock in the downstairs entry chimed seven times. Her pulses throbbed in anticipation. The front door knocker sounded. A surge of energy like a bolt of lightning jolted through her, leaving her light-headed.

She heard men's voices downstairs and then the sound of footsteps climbing the stairs. Jennifer scrutinized herself in the mirror again and suddenly decided the silk roses in her hair looked tawdry. She was determined not to give Chantry Kincaid the impression that ballerinas were loose women. She closed her eyes and covered her face. She couldn't go through with it.

The footsteps stopped in her open doorway. Without looking up, she said, "Malcomb, please tell Mr. Kincaid that I've taken ill and will not be able to keep our appointment."

Augustine coughed and gripped her arm as if in warning.

Jennifer opened her eyes. Kincaid stood at the door, his face clouding over. He lifted one dark eyebrow, and heat flushed through her from the center outward until her whole body was on fire.

"Sorry," Kincaid said softly. "I know I shouldn't have been so bold, but your butler's arthritis seems to be bothering him, so I showed myself up." He stood so still it seemed as if a force were gathering within him.

Jennifer gazed into Kincaid's intent green eyes and realized there wasn't anything on this earth he couldn't have—if he wanted it badly enough. "Please leave us, Augustine."

Head down, Augustine scurried past Kincaid.

"I can't...go with you," she said.

He shrugged one broad, powerful shoulder. "Look, this isn't easy for me, either." His husky voice stirred emotions in her. She felt like crying or running away.

"I can't work for you, either," she said.

"We'll talk about it over dinner."

"No. It will just get more complicated."

"Maybe not. Besides, you like a challenge."

"How do you know that?"

"How many women, especially women of your station in life, reach the exalted level of prima ballerina?"

"I'm not like other women," she said softly, miserably.

"You're not limited the way they are. That's one of the things that draws me to you. When you dance, you defy the limits. When you kiss..."

That wasn't what she'd meant, but she was too mesmerized by his eyes to explain. She wanted to reach out and touch his warm, smooth-shaven face. The urge was so strong that her palms began to tingle.

Kincaid lifted his left arm slightly, and she knew he expected her to step forward and slip her right arm into the crook of his elbow. She had never been so torn in her life. She still didn't trust him, but she felt dizzy with confusion.

Oh, God. Shaken, but unable to help herself, Jennifer took his arm, surprising herself as much as him.

"I'm only going with you to get out of my contract," she said, her throat so tight that the words were barely more than a whisper.

"I know. I'll take anything I can get," he said softly.

Jennifer was puzzled by his need. He didn't sound like a robber baron who rode roughshod over anyone in his way. Unless, of course, this was part of the deception.

Kincaid took charge of her as if he were accustomed to doing so. He led her down the stairs and, brushing Malcomb aside, helped Jennifer into her coat, turning her with firm hands and slowly buttoning each button. Jennifer's eyes tried to evade his, but couldn't. Something sparkled in his eyes. In a dancer she would have labeled it desire, intensity, the sheer guts to attempt the impossible. In a dancer she would have admired it. Seeing it in Kincaid made her tremble like a caught bird. Yet some part of her quivered with a strange exultation.

Jennifer had watched actresses with their important lovers. It was impossible to live a sheltered life in the theater. And she knew that, without taking any liberties—unless it was in the way his warm hands touched her or the proprietary gleam in his eyes—he handled her as if he had already made love to her. Which, of course, he almost had.

"Good night, mademoiselle," said Augustine from the library door. She smiled, and Jennifer saw that she, the woman who had guarded her as fiercely as a tigress through childhood, earning her the nickname Mamitchka because she was so much like the fierce Russian women who guarded their daughters against lecherous men, had succumbed to Kincaid's charm.

"Good night, Mamitchka."

Kincaid opened the front door and held it for her. His driver swung the door to the carriage wide, and Kincaid helped her inside and then settled his tall frame beside her. The cushioned seats, the smell of the carriage, and the nearness of Chane brought back images of the night before. Her body tingled with awareness.

Kincaid tucked the lap robe around her, and the coach rolled forward almost imperceptibly on well-oiled springs.

"How long have you been a dancer?"

Jennifer struggled to regain her composure. "We're here to discuss my contract, remember?"

"I told you, I never discuss contracts with beautiful women except over dinner."

Jennifer struggled to remember his question. "I have always been a dancer."

Kincaid laughed. "I'm seeing this beautiful blond toddler in toe shoes."

Jennifer decided to shift the conversation to him. Maybe this rendezvous would prove useful, and she'd glean some information for Peter. "How is your grandfather?"

"My grandfather? How did you know about that?" he asked, peering through the semidarkness of the coach at her.

"I have friends."

"He's hanging by a thread."

"I'm sorry to hear that. And how's Latitia?" she asked, willing to be reckless.

"My God," Kincaid exclaimed. "How did you—"

"Did you think you were the only one with connections?" she asked, glad she had shaken his composure.

"Latitia is a friend."

"Do I look naive?"

"Obviously not," he said grimly.

"I grew up in the household of Reginald and Vivian Van Vleet, hardly a monastery, wouldn't you say?" Jennifer waited for his reaction to her parents' names.

"I'm afraid I haven't been in New York all that long. I spent most of my adult life in Texas and England."

"Doing what?"

"School in England."

"Which one?"

"Oxford."

The thought suddenly occurred to Jennifer that perhaps Kincaid hadn't even been in the States when her parents were killed. "That explains your slight British accent. Well, I'm not at all compatible with you, Mr. Kincaid. The only thing I know is ballet."

"I know everything else, so we'll do just fine."

Jennifer laughed in spite of herself. "So tell me when you and your friend are going to be married."

"We're not."

"I think she's set her cap for you."

"Latitia and I are friends—"

"The best, I'm sure," Jennifer interjected, smiling.

"I assure you I'm not interested in her in that way."

"I don't suppose you've mentioned this attitude to her."

"You're a feisty one, aren't you?"

The driver brought the team to a halt, and Jennifer was surprised to see that they were in the Bricewood's *porte cochere*. One of the bellmen opened their carriage door. Kincaid stepped down and reached up for her. Reluctantly, she moved to the door.

"Besides being feisty, you're the most beautiful woman I've ever seen," he whispered as he lifted her down and into his arms.

"Thank you," she said, laughing to cover her breathlessness. He pulled her so close to him that she feared he was going to kiss her right there. His manly scent—a musky fragrance so faint and, she suspected, so purely his—reminded her of the kisses they'd shared last night.

Kincaid guided her through the gaslit, half circle of the red brick carriage entry adjacent to the lobby of the spacious, high-ceilinged hotel. The brick drive was wet, and in the lamplight, plants in the atrium sparkled with dew.

"I thought we were going to the theater."

"Why should I share you with my competition? Dinner, the theater, gambling, they're all here," he said, smiling, taking her cold hand in his warm one. "Even the *New York Times* has conceded that the Bricewood East is more than a hotel. Sanzian, king of French chefs, rules the kitchen of the Sangaree Room. Even Thackeray has paid homage to his Wellfleet oysters. They're the best in the country."

"The Bricewood East? Are there other Bricewoods?"

Kincaid smiled. "You're quick," he said, guiding her through two doors that opened as they approached, the two doormen smiling and bowing as he swept her past.

"Not yet," he continued, "but there will be. Before I'm done, there'll be hundreds of them." He swept her through the Bricewood's lush main lobby, which looked even richer and lusher at night, and into the dining room where a dozen couples waited in line behind a thick maroon rope. Kincaid bypassed the waiting area and guided her to a reserved table for two. The maître d' appeared at once.

"May I order for you?" Kincaid asked.

"Please do."

"The princess special," he murmured.

The maître d' left, and Kincaid slipped her coat off, gave it to a passing waiter, and led Jennifer onto the Sangaree Room's smooth marble dance floor. From a cotillionlike raised portico next to the dance floor, the chamber orchestra played a Brahms waltz. Most men were intimidated by the knowledge that she danced for a living. Not Kincaid. He held her with authority, his warm hand pressing against her spine, guiding her firmly.

Waiters in gold and white moved noiselessly among gentlemen in glossy black evening coats and diamond-clad ladies in laces and ribbons as Chane spun her around the room. Jennifer glanced at the diners seated at the elegantly laid tables encircling the dance floor and saw faces she recognized: friends of the family, ex-friends who had snubbed her after her New York debut with the Bellini Ballet Company, others who had thrown themselves at her feet when her reviews were smashing, and still others who were cool no matter how good her reviews. Almost every gaze seemed riveted on her and her partner.

"Are they usually so attentive?"

Chane chuckled. The crowded room, which had buzzed with

conversations on their arrival, had indeed fallen silent. "Only when one of the dancers is a world famous *prima donna assoluta*."

"And the other is their host."

Glancing at her and then around the room, he smiled, and dimples appeared on his craggy face. His hand tightened around her waist. Just the feel of his hand—so warm and strong and insistent—made her body flush with warmth.

"Why did you choose dancing?" he asked.

Jennie laughed. "To irritate my mother." He looked startled. Aware suddenly that she had slipped into dangerous emotional waters, she continued softly, "Or because I'm a masochist. Or because I love it. I can't remember now. I think it was one of those."

Chane laughed. "Your mother didn't want you to dance?"

"She hated my bleeding toes, my bruises, and my aches and pains. She begged me to quit a hundred times. No one could understand why I would put myself through such torture when I didn't have to."

"Why did you?"

"Well, why do you work? Is your father broke?"

"No, but..." She lifted her eyebrows at him, and he nodded reluctantly. "So what do you do when you're not dancing?"

"For sheer enjoyment, I stay in bed all day. But if I absolutely must get up, I like to window-shop, drink coffee in French cafés, gossip with my friends."

"You have time for friends?"

"Only ballet friends. I don't have time for outsiders."

"What will you do next?"

"Next?"

"When you stop dancing?"

A frown marred the perfection of her smooth brow. "I shall dance as long as I'm able. And when I can no longer dance, I will become a choreographer."

"What about life?"

She shrugged. "Life beckoned, and I said no." She felt strangely bemused, as if her head were floating above the room. She knew she was showing off for him, flaunting her most cosmopolitan attitude, but she couldn't stop herself.

Without a break, the music had changed. Now it was a swift, colorful mazurka. They danced well together. She relaxed and let the music carry her along, let his arms and his body lead her. Kincaid held her close, but they danced so well together she felt no strain, no desire to protest.

He leaned down and whispered against her hair. "Jennie, love, why don't you save us both a lot of time and just tell me what I have to do to win your love?"

Caught off guard, she laughed nervously.

Chane's eyes were not smiling. They were intent and purposeful.

"Why should I tell you?"

"Wouldn't you like to see if I *can* win your love? Don't women enjoy setting up impossible requirements and watching men make fools of themselves trying to satisfy them?"

Jennifer stopped smiling. "Do most women do that?"

"One way or another, yes."

"How...demeaning." She must have stiffened in his arms. He flushed. It might have passed unnoticed, but for a split second his eyes were like a pond in which the water cleared for a moment, giving her a glimpse of the bottom.

"Do I sound cynical?" he asked ruefully.

"Not really," she said teasingly, her laughter bubbling easily to the surface.

To Chane her soft, sultry laugh sounded as though it was fresh from lovemaking. A tingle of pure pleasure raced down his spine.

"Why are you smiling?" she asked.

"Would you like to see me frown? I've been told I have a very impressive frown. People unlucky enough to be frowned at by me have been known to jump off tall buildings."

"Oh? Really?"

"I've had a couple of failures, but I'm working on it."

"King Midas in reverse."

Chane loved her soft, cultured voice, the way her easy laughter sounded like a song. He wanted to do outrageous things like throw himself on the dance floor and kiss her ankles, but he knew he couldn't tell her the truth. Easy conquests were boring, especially to a woman like Jennie, who undoubtedly had princes and czars at her feet.

"Sort of a Jay Gould of the emotional world," he said, grinning. "Everything he touches wilts."

"But he's fabulously wealthy."

"Does fabulous wealth impress you?"

"Yes. Do you have fabulous wealth?"

"Absolutely."

"And are you dashing and heroic?"

"Incredibly."

"And have you ever slain a dragon?"

"Not since last week."

"How did you do it?"

"Checkbooks at thirty paces."

Jennifer laughed. She had a way of tossing her hair that reminded him of a young Thoroughbred—sleek and spirited. The soft, shadowy candlelight emphasized the strong, graceful curve of her creamy throat. His lips tingled with the need to press against that slim column.

"I love the way you laugh," he said.

"Is that what you were doing? Trying to make me laugh?"

"No, this is an act. I'm trying to convince you I'm a harmless fool so that when I lure you upstairs I'll have the element of surprise on my side."

"Are you going to lure me upstairs?"

"A good general never gives away information that would destroy his advantage."

She laughed again, and the sound, like tantalizing wind instruments, made his loins ache.

The orchestra, upon his secret command, shifted into a Strauss waltz. "Does the music go on forever?" she asked, noticing. Kincaid smiled, and light seemed to dance and shimmer in the emerald depths of his eyes. Jennifer looked away, astonished at what was happening to her. She had somehow forgotten why she was here. As if Chane sensed her confusion, his hand touched her chin, and she couldn't keep herself from looking into his eyes.

The music rose to a crescendo. Kincaid swung her around and his hands guided her with the firmness and power of a trained dancer. Realizing she was out of step, she groaned in confusion. It wasn't like her to lose track—that was her job.

Kincaid's hand guided her back into the flow of the music. "I love it when you get confused like that. Who knows what else you might be lured into doing?" His voice was low and intense with possessiveness, his eyes caressing.

The pulse in Jennifer's throat punched against her skin as she flashed back to the carriage ride after the fire, when his eyes had devoured her exposed breasts.

"I hoped you wouldn't notice."

"It's very feminine, and less goddesslike," he said. Jennie laughed and tossed her hair.

An ache spread through Chane until it encompassed his entire body. As if she had guessed his distress, Jennie's eyes widened. The look in them was so curious and innocent, she looked ten years old suddenly, the epitome of a little girl ballerina, all pink muslin and tender white arms and face. He felt stricken.

"Mr. Kincaid?" Jennie asked softly, letting her hand rest on his jacket over his heart.

Chane groaned. "Do you notice everything?" Possessive and intimate, his rough, masculine voice made her tingle.

Jennifer slid her hand under Chane's jacket. The muted thud of his heart tingled her fingers. He felt magnetic and warm beneath her hand. She felt more alive than she had in years. "Please don't fall in love with me," she whispered. "I can't think of anything worse."

One of Chane's strong hands supported her from the waist. The other lifted her chin. He seemed to have forgotten that they were dancing in a roomful of people. He gazed deeply into her eyes. "How about my *not* loving you?"

The small pulse in her throat moved downward into her loins. She had no answer for Kincaid. His eyes reminded her that she had evaded his question, but he didn't push it.

The dance ended, and he led her back to their table. The maître d' appeared immediately, followed by a flock of uniformed waiters bearing plates heaped with thin, steaming, savory strips of hickory-flavored chicken and three kinds of melon. It was delicious, but Jennifer picked at hers, and Chane barely touched his. Instead, he asked about her childhood, her schooling, her dreams, friends, and family.

She waited for an opening to discuss her contract, but somehow Kincaid kept control of the conversation. Before she realized it, Chane waved the waiters away, took her by the arm and guided her out to his waiting brougham.

He spoke to the driver and then joined her inside. A nearly full moon silvered the unusually quiet streets. Jennifer leaned against the heavily padded seat back and let the chill night air cool her hot face. The carriage traveled south, skirting Washington Square Park, over to Broadway, then down Canal Street and through the heart of Chinatown, which had grown enormously in the past decade and was now crowded and noisy, and even at that hour, smelled of incense and exotic foods.

She'd been so bemused she hadn't realized until now how far out of their way the carriage had come. Her home was far uptown, in the other direction. She should be upset about that, but she wasn't.

"Where are you taking me?" she asked finally.

The carriage rolled to a halt. Kincaid flashed her a smile. "Here," he said, opening the door, stepping down, and holding out his arms for her.

The carriage stood next to the roadblock that kept traffic off the recently completed stanchion of the Brooklyn Bridge. Jennifer stepped down and into his arms.

"Isn't it magnificent?" he asked, turning so they could look at the half-finished bridge jutting out over the turbulent East River. "You know how difficult it is to span a river this wide?"

About a hundred yards out the bridge construction had halted. It had been stalled here for months, and perhaps would never be finished. Rumor had it that Roebling, the son of the original architect and builder, was ill, perhaps dying. His father had been killed in an accident on the bridge. The son had also been injured in a separate accident on the bridge and would probably die of his injuries as well.

"Maybe this bridge is only a dream," she said.

"Roebling thinks he can build it, and I agree with him. He's a remarkable man, but weakened now. He'll be lucky to live to see it completed. But he's training his assistant and writing everything down for him. It will be finished."

Chane gazed at the bridge, his profile strong against the clear, star-filled sky. "To think, a few years ago, it was only a vision in one man's mind. Now he's infected hundreds of men with his vision, and it's taking shape. Someday, carriages will traverse this span, and Brooklyn's days will be numbered. They've lived sheltered lives out there, but it will be very different once Manhattan reaches out with her Bessemer arms." Kincaid seemed to be in a trance as he stared across the river, littered with chips of gray ice floating on the dark, oily-blue water.

Jennifer fought back a sudden impulse to kiss Chane. For a long time they both stood still, staring out at the water until a uniformed policeman strode purposefully up to them and peered at them suspiciously, until he recognized Chane. "Oh, good evening, Mr. Kincaid."

"Evening, Withers. The young lady wanted to see the bridge."

"Well then, it's a good thing I didn't come by here just now, isn't it? Have a nice evening." Smiling, he turned and walked toward the far side of the bridge, where he gazed out over the water, his back to them.

Chane lifted aside the chain meant to keep traffic off the bridge and guided her onto the bridge approach.

Hand in hand they walked to the end of the first stanchion, where they could look straight down at the river below. The wind blew harder over the water. Jennifer felt both frightened and safe. The water was so far below, it seemed she was flying. She didn't trust herself not to plunge forward.

Chane must have sensed her thoughts, for his strong hand tightened its grip on her hand. "I won't let you fall."

Cold wind whipped around her skirts, sending chills up her legs. The broad wide band of water sparkled like diamonds, blazing in the moonlight. Jennie was mesmerized by the light—she could have stood there forever. But without warning Chane turned, pulled her into his arms, and kissed her. Just like that first time in the carriage after the fire, his lips were chilled on the outside and hot inside. He kissed her until a fire ignited deep inside her belly and she was sure her knees would collapse. Finally, reluctantly, Chane relinquished her lips and held her close.

A heavy gust of wind reminded Jennifer where she was and what was happening. "It's late," she whispered against his chest, suddenly afraid of his intensity.

"I don't want to take you home," he said, turning her and walking her back toward his brougham. He helped her in and called up to the driver, "Fifth Avenue and Thirty-second Street."

Jennifer rode beside Chane in silence through street after darkened street. She had expected him to try to kiss her again, but he appeared deep in thought.

It was a long trip back uptown, but somehow the time flew. Too soon, the carriage stopped in front of the Van Vleet town house. Chane helped her down, leaned against the carriage and turned with her in his arms. The streetlight carved new hollows in his craggy face.

"Good night," she whispered. Part of her wanted to reach out and touch his cheek. Even if she never saw him again, she had been touched by him. His passion for the bridge meant that in his own way he was an artist, too. This created a deep bond between them.

"Good night," he said softly, bending down as if he were going to kiss her.

Her heart pounded. She drew back, fearful she wouldn't be able to stop herself this time. "No more kisses."

"No more kisses," he repeated solemnly, sudden merriment twinkling in his eyes.

She pushed his arms away and walked toward the front porch. Kincaid made no effort to follow her. Jennifer stopped on the top step.

"I can't work for you," she called back to him.

"You signed a contract."

"No. My signature was forged."

"By your agent, who undoubtedly has the right to sign contracts in your name. It's standard procedure. If you are at all trustworthy, you are honor bound to keep the terms of the contract."

"Well, I'm not," she said stubbornly.

"Any court in the land would insist you honor that contract."

"Only if you pursue it."

"Why shouldn't I?"

"Because I would hate you."

"For how long?"

"Forever."

He laughed. "You think you can hold a grudge that long?"

"Longer."

"You give up on everything else. What makes you think you can hold a grudge at all?"

Jennifer walked quickly down the steps to his side. "I do not—I never give up."

"Maybe at work," he said, shrugging. "This is life. Maybe you only give up on life."

Jennifer frowned at him. The jut of his brow cast shadows that hid the expression in his eyes. But she was sure he was laughing at her. "You don't think I can handle life?"

He shrugged. "I suspect you can handle anything you want to handle." He took her by the shoulders and shook her gently. "I'd give up, Jennie, but you keep letting me back in."

"I don't mean to," she said ruefully, feeling much younger than her twenty-two years.

"As long as a woman keeps answering my questions, I can't walk away, especially if she's as beautiful and desirable as you."

She shook her head in confusion.

"Maybe you really aren't interested in digging into life. Personally, I like to get dirty every now and then."

"Get dirty?" she asked. She knew she needed to walk away from him and never look back, but something held her there.

"Work with my hands. Slam a hammer onto a railroad spike, rope a steer and brand it."

"You've done all that?"

"And more. Let me tell you about it tomorrow over dinner while we discuss how you're going to get out of that contract."

"Fine," she said. Somehow, by not kissing her, not even trying to kiss her, he'd thrown her off guard again.

Jennifer was in her bed, dozing off to sleep, before she realized she'd made another date with Kincaid. "Drat!"

She sat straight up and punched her pillow. "What have I done? Drat! Drat! Drat!"

CHAPTER SEVEN

The next day a note from Latitia was waiting for Chane, asking him to take her to the opera. He called her home, and while he waited for her to answer, he sorted through his mail.

"Hello," she said, sounding thoroughly comfortable with the telephone. There were fewer than four hundred telephones in the city, and most of them were in offices. The few people who had them in their homes spoke on them as if they had no confidence that anyone could actually hear them. Except Latitia, of course.

They talked for a few moments before he said cautiously, "I've got an appointment in one minute. This week is, uh..." He loosened his cravat, which seemed suddenly tight. "This week I'm busy. I'll be lucky if I even get to bed."

"And luckier still if it's with me," Latitia purred with a throaty laugh.

Silence stretched out while Chane struggled to think of a reply that didn't betray the fragile alliance he was trying to form with Jennifer.

"So," she said, sounding a little peeved. "How about next week? You're going to the Madisons' party, aren't you?"

"I don't know. My grandfather's ill, so I've taken on a load of extra work. Don't count on me."

She was disappointed, but he held firm. At last he hung up the receiver and breathed a sigh of relief. That would do for this week, but what about next week? If his luck held, he would be courting Jennie full-time, from now until they pitched dirt on his grave.

At ten o'clock Chane met with his grandfather and two attorneys. In the afternoon, he returned to the Bricewood East and stopped by Steve Hammond's smoke-filled office. Steve was a brilliant, restless man who smoked one cigarette after another and could talk circles around anyone.

As Chane's right-hand man, he worked so hard he rarely had time for relationships. Despite his awkwardness around them, women found Steve appealing. His deep-set, blue-gray eyes complimented his fair complexion and sandy-brown hair.

Steve stood up, but Chane motioned him down. "Sit," he said, dropping into the chair across from Steve's desk. He stretched tired muscles and leaned back.

"How'd the meeting go?"

"I told my grandfather he could find another sucker for his inheritance."

"Ninety million dollars? Something must have smelled," Steve said, frowning.

"Everything was up to my grandfather's usual high standards," Chane said grimly. "Unfortunately, I had the gall to want to survive with my skin and reputation intact."

Shaking his head, Chane continued. "Not only did Number One sign contracts with the Chinese agents, he also bought a steel foundry, a quarry, and six other companies to sell goods and services to the railroad, all at exorbitant prices, all highly illegal. Number One was proud of the fact that he was all set to fleece both his stockholders *and* the U.S. government."

Steve raised his eyebrows, then laughed, his voice gravelly from years of cigarette smoking. "Your only choice, as I see it, would be whether you want to go to jail or hang."

"That's the way it looked to me."

"So you walked out."

"I'm not going out West," Chane said, his gut twisting at the thought of leaving Jennie behind. In the past, he'd always thought of himself as a coolheaded scientist, but what had happened to him when he met Jennie was far from scientific. He was on shaky ground and he knew it. What his next move would be, he had no idea.

His mind flashed an image of her pale blond hair pulled back from her face, her strong neck and graceful arms curved over her head. She was a picture of pristine elegance and loveliness. That, and the heat of her kisses...

"So you declined their offer?"

Steve's question jolted Chane back to reality. "But they declined my decline," he said, grimacing at the amount of work ahead. "My grandfather promised to divest himself of the illegal companies. I have one more meeting with him this week. If all goes well, and he can prove certain things to my satisfaction, I'll…damn, I guess I'll end up building his railroad." How could he do that and still court Jennie? Maybe the combination of unlimited money and the most fascinating woman in the world was warping his mind.

Steve fished another cigarette out of his pocket. He bought the ready-made cigarettes, but he didn't keep them in the package. He stored them in different pockets, so when he was in a business meeting and couldn't smoke, he could fondle them. "If you're too honest, you could lose your grandfather's shirt for him," he said.

"If that's all we lose, I'll be satisfied."

"Well, as long as you know you're not getting me on any trains," Steve warned. He had a deep fear of train wrecks. Everytime there was a train wreck, the newspapers printed the gory details—describing six-foot splinters that impaled men, women, and children, flames burning trapped people to cinders, and fully loaded passenger cars that careened off collapsed trestles.

"How's Number One's health? Any chance he'll pull through this?" Steve asked, striking a match, holding it under the tip of his cigarette and taking a long drag. "If he recovers, we won't have to worry about any of this."

"The doctor is cautious, but he didn't expect Grandfather to live this long. The fact that he has could mean he'll be with us for a while. My parents have decided to assume he will. They're leaving for Europe tomorrow."

"I hope your grandfather has arranged a line of credit for *his* railroad."

"Not exactly. He wanted to leave us something to do."

Steve's head spun with all the things he had to do in a few short weeks. "I'll get right on it."

Chane walked toward the door. "Thanks, Steve. Hopefully, you won't have to ride any trains," he said, grinning.

Steve followed. "I'll have you sign that statement tomorrow. I'll want it notarized with witnesses."

Chane laughed.

Rehearsal seemed to go on forever. Late in the afternoon, Jennifer saw Kincaid slip inside, find a comfortable place along the back wall of the new Bricewood Theatre, and lean back to watch. Her heart beat faster. Without admitting it to herself, she realized she'd been waiting for him all day. Of course, she had resigned herself to his presence. Unfortunately, it was his absence that had been bothering her.

The Bricewood Theatre was almost as big as the Bellini Theatre had been. But it was newer and more modern. The footlights were electric instead of gas, making them safer and brighter. For that, she was glad—one fire was enough.

Jennifer and fifty young men and women were on stage, seated at Bellini's feet. He finished his instructions, moved his stool back to the wings, and motioned the dancers to their places. Jennifer walked into the first wings to wait for her cue.

In the pit below Jennifer's eye level, the director tapped his stick on the music standard, and the orchestra played the first strains of the theme for the *Blue Bird*. The glorious sounds of the music rose and fell in the huge empty space of the theater. Bellini's voice counted the beats, and when her cue came, Jennifer pranced out onto the stage *en pointe*.

In spite of the sudden inner turmoil caused by Chane Kincaid's appearance, she felt she danced well, but she could not be sure. It was unfortunate that people saw only her image, but could not sense the wonderful sensations she felt within while dancing. She wondered what Chane observed.

Bellini kept them later than usual. Finally, he dismissed them by rapping his cane on the floor and saying, "Eight o'clock tomorrow morning, ladies and gentlemen."

Jennifer glanced at Chane. He nodded to her and motioned for her to join him. Suddenly breathless, she nodded back.

In the private dressing room she'd been given, she quickly stripped off her practice clothes, scrubbed herself with the water in her pitcher, and dried off. Even so, the others left before her, and the theater felt unnaturally quiet. She combed her hair, dusted herself with Gillyflower talcum until the whole room smelled like carnations, and put on the lavender *peau de soie* gown she'd worn to the Bricewood that morning.

Jennifer walked down the dimly lit, narrow hallway, past the large, communal dressing room, which already smelled of sweat, greasepaint, sour socks, and hot glue from steamy ballet suppers. She must have taken longer than she'd thought, for even Pops, the stage door manager, had left. Perhaps Chane had gone, too. She didn't see him at the back of the theater.

Strangely disappointed, she hurried past the stage, down the steps, and through the darkened theater. But halfway up the aisle she sensed another presence and slowed her steps. She stopped and peered into the semidarkness.

"Don't be frightened. It's only me." She recognized Chane's slightly accented voice.

"May I?" he asked, stepping out of the shadows to push the door open. Deep within Jennifer's chest something quivered. Her knees felt weak, as if she had practiced to the point of exhaustion. He must have sensed her weakness; his warm hand cupped her elbow.

She walked beside Chane through the lobby to the outer door. Two bellmen swung it open. Jennifer breathed deep of the woodsy atrium and sighed, feeling the tiredness in her shoulders.

"You dance beautifully," Chane said, motioning for his carriage.

Outside, the sun was setting. Cold wind whipped around the corner of the building and blew tendrils of Jennifer's hair out of its bun. The morning's snow had melted into mud, which was now being spattered by heavy traffic that rumbled past on Fifth Avenue.

She captured the stray strands of her hair and looked up at Kincaid. His features—the most angular she'd ever seen—were not handsome by ordinary standards. His jaw was wide and square. A ruler placed along the sides of his face would square off perfectly until it reached the alignment of his mouth, where it angled inward toward his chin. The bottom of his chin was as flat and wide as his mouth. It pleased her that he looked so ruggedly masculine.

Chane seemed quite comfortable with her steady perusal. His sea green eyes, heavily and darkly lashed, smiled into hers.

"My buggy…" he said softly, motioning toward what she thought of as a doctor's buggy—a two-seater with a black top cupped overhead—a Stanhope. Two thoughts skittered through her confused mind. She was glad to see it was not the carriage he'd nearly seduced her in, and she was glad because her father had occasionally driven a Stanhope. She'd loved riding beside him. She knew she should refuse to ride with Chane again, but he'd found another weakness of hers, and his warm hand was exerting a slight pressure on her elbow.

"I—" Jennifer stopped. It seemed ridiculous to resist. Part of her had already surrendered. "My driver and carriage are waiting," she said weakly.

"Send them home," he said, now clasping her elbow with a firm hand. Before she could protest, he guided her to the only other carriage and waited while she told Langdon she had a ride. Langdon peered suspiciously at Kincaid, who slipped him a five-dollar bill. Langdon beamed, flicked the reins, and headed toward home.

Jennifer allowed Chane to help her up onto the high seat. The driver who'd been seated in the dickey behind the cab handed the reins over to Kincaid, scrambled down, and joined the bellmen greeting new arrivals.

On the busy street, horses galloped, men yelled, and whips cracked, but no one slowed to let them squeeze in. Kincaid waited for an opportunity. In the southern sky the gibbous moon flowed pale and ghostly overhead. In the west, high clouds caught afire from the sun setting behind the rim of buildings.

"We should have walked," Jennifer said, impatient with the heavy traffic.

"We'd never have made it across this street on foot." He laughed softly. Then, seeing his opportunity, he shook the buggy whip lightly and deftly, flicked the reins, and crowded the buggy into the flow of traffic.

His shoulder brushed hers, and he glanced down at her. "You're beautiful, princess."

His low-pitched voice set something fluttering within her.

In the near dusk, shadows darkened the hollows of his cheeks. His eyes seemed to burn into her skin, but she couldn't look away. At last he turned his attention back to the traffic and the slow trot of his team. Wind rumpled his black hair. Locks had blown across his straight black eyebrows, and she wanted to reach up and lightly brush the hair back into place.

Kincaid drove in silence, occasionally looking over at Jennifer, who felt no need to speak. He turned down a street she didn't recognize, then another. Just as she was beginning to worry about going off with him alone, he stopped the buggy in front of a large circular glass building.

"The German Winter Garden," he said, wrapping the reins around the brake handle and jumping down. "Have you been inside?"

"No." She knew from theater gossip that the German Winter Garden was a fancy speakeasy to circumvent the Sunday blue laws. People formed private clubs where they could buy beer on Sunday. Since she didn't drink, she'd never been there.

"Good. Come. You'll be glad you did."

The interior was a revelation. The entire ceiling of the enormous circular room was a domed skylight. The last rays of sunlight lit the uppermost dome, turning it golden. Halfway up the vast hall, tiers of balconies encircled the main floor. Men and women strolled arm in arm along the upper balconies or leaned on the white wrought-iron railings, watching the people below and across from them. A small orchestra on a raised dais played Strauss waltzes. In the center of the enormous room, couples at small round tables nibbled on cheese and radishes and drank beer. A few danced.

"This dome," he said, sweeping his arm upward, "was built about 1855. It's one of the earliest ever built with cast-iron rib framing."

"Is that good?"

"They used to think so. Until the Glass House burned to the ground, leaving only melted iron."

She had seen pictures of the Glass House in its prime, but she'd never been inside it.

"You know a lot of odd facts," she said.

"I'm an architect. I'm supposed to know odd facts about buildings. Would you like something to eat or drink?"

"No, thank you."

Chane guided Jennie into a cluster of deserted tables sheltered by ficus plants in waist-high wooden tubs, pulled her close, and gazed deeply into her eyes.

"You're the most beautiful woman I've ever seen," Chane said, his voice husky with desire. "Your eyes command attention. The beautiful curve of your chin, your hairline, the arch of your slim neck… architecturally, you are as perfect a woman as I've ever seen."

Jennifer wanted to say something, but her mind wasn't working.

As he brushed her cheek with his warm fingers, her heart fluttered. Lowering his head, bringing his lips within an inch of her mouth, he whispered, "You can always stop me."

Jennifer knew she should stop him, but her chin seemed to lift on its own, and her lips parted slightly. His kiss was chaste, merely a warm touching of smooth lips.

Then he sighed and stepped back, tugging at his cravat, his expression one of ecstasy and torment. A shadow of beard stubble darkened his angular jaws. In the fading light from the glass dome, his eyes narrowed as if he were trying to solve a weighty problem. At last he said, "It's going to be difficult."

"Yes," she agreed, not sure what either of them were talking about. All she knew was that a force was gathering inside her, and she wasn't certain she could stop it—or that she wanted to.

"This is going to upset a lot of people," he said, searching her eyes.

"You have no idea how many," Jennifer breathed.

As they emerged from their hideaway, Chane's attention was caught by hands waving at him from a nearby table.

"Yoo-hoo! Chane! Over here."

"Chane, who's that waving at you?" Jennifer asked.

"Oh, my God, it's Nathan and Edmée. No quick getaway for us

now." Chane sighed. "Come on, you can't help but like them," he said, taking her elbow and guiding her over to their table.

Edmée Brantley looked like a lovely, *haut monde* Gypsy with slanted green eyes, a fine bone structure, and a willowy body that was more elegant than voluptuous. Nathan was as blond as Chane was dark. He had sandy hair, tawny eyebrows, bushy blond wisps of muttonchop sideburns, and soft, gold-sheened, light-brown eyes. Every inch a king, Jennifer thought as Nathan smiled into her eyes.

Chane and Nathan shook hands warmly. Chane handled the introductions with easy grace, fairly beaming at his friends, leaving no doubt that he was truly glad to see both of them. His happiness produced an answering warmth in Jennifer. Edmée went up on tiptoe, kissed Chane's cheek, and smiled warmly at Jennifer.

"You are such a vision, love! It's no wonder our friend is smiling again," Edmée said, lifting an elegant eyebrow and giving Chane an arch smile.

"You lovebirds look like you're on your way out," Nathan said. "We won't keep you."

"Not this time," Edmée said, "but you must promise to dine with us soon. Why not make it a whole evening and go on to the opera?"

"It's a date," Chane said, giving Jennie a quick look, and smiling as she nodded her agreement.

After a round of good-bye kisses, Chane led Jennifer out the door to the buggy, still parked at the curb where they'd left it. He lifted her up onto the seat and walked quickly around to climb up beside her.

He flicked the reins, and the horse stepped forward.

Entranced, Jennifer rode in silence for a time. Stars blinked in the navy-blue sky. Kincaid put his arm around her. "Are you cold?"

"No." The air felt cold against her skin, but she was impervious to it. She closed her eyes. His arm felt warm and protective around her shoulders. She was enjoying the ride through the gathering dusk, pressed against his warmth.

"How long have you known the Brantleys?" she asked, breaking the silence at last.

"Nathan's father owned the house next to our house in London. Edmée was the cousin of a woman in Paris I used to…know."

Chane's voice had gotten huskier and more gruff at the end of that sentence. Jennifer looked at him sharply. *A woman he had loved, no doubt.*

"What was her name?" she asked.

"Colette." The huskiness came again. Chane cleared his throat.

"When did you last see her?"

"Not for years."

"How many years?"

Chane laughed. "What is this? The Inquisition?"

"No. I'm just curious. How many years?"

"I don't know. Ten or so."

"You must have been a baby."

"I was twenty-three." He frowned. "Six years ago."

"So what happened six years ago?"

"What makes you think something happened?"

"Because you're not with her. If something hadn't happened, you'd probably be married to her."

Chane laughed. "That's quite an imagination you have there, Miss Prosecutor."

"I'm a Van Vleet, remember? The women in our family understand liaisons. Why didn't you marry her?"

Chane shrugged, suddenly defensive. His scowl matched Peter's for signaling manly displeasure. He stared off into the distance, as though he were reliving something. His voice seemed to come from very far away. "Because there are some things I don't forgive."

"Chris Chambard, a friend—actually more like an uncle—has often said to me that it doesn't pay to have too many things one absolutely will not forgive. It's bad for the digestion."

"Your 'uncle' is right. But, unfortunately, there's one thing I don't seem to have any choice about."

"Well, since I've risked my fragile reputation to go out with you, I think you owe it to me to say what that is."

"Fidelity," he said gruffly.

Chane drove through a series of backstreets until he reached the river. Then he stopped the buggy, tied the reins around the brake handle, put his arm around her, and relaxed. The smell of the dank, fishy, river mud in her nostrils, the feel of him against her side, the sight of the gibbous moon silvering a wide band of the river's rippled surface, all combined to overwhelm her senses. For a moment they sat in silence, just listening to the sounds of distant traffic, the low, mourning whistle of a river barge floating past, and a few birds that hadn't yet settled down for the night.

Chane turned Jennie's face so she had to look at him. She shook her head and looked away so he couldn't kiss her. But she knew she wasn't strong enough tonight to save herself. Within seconds she felt his warm lips nibbling at her neck, then her cheek, then her chin. She resisted as long as she could, then finally, with a sigh, she gave in to his warm insistence and raised her lips for his kiss.

He groaned deep in his throat and kissed her as if there was no way he could stop. Heat flushed from some dark center into all her limbs. Breathless, she ended the kiss and hid her face against his chest.

"What a treacherous little trifle you are, smelling of carnations and looking like an angel," he said, his voice thick with passion and pleasure. "I want you, Jennie. I want you so much it scares hell out of me."

She shivered and hugged herself for warmth. "You'll be sorry. We'll both be sorry when it's over, Chane."

"It will never be over. Marry me, Jennie."

"No...Please don't do this," she cried, moving as far away from him as she could manage.

"Why not? I've never felt like this before. I love you."

"You don't even know me."

"I don't have to know you. I feel you—in every cell of my body."

She knew he wanted to make love to her, but he didn't. He wrapped the carriage blanket around her and held her close. She reveled in the chill of the night air, the beauty of the moon-silvered river, the warmth of his arms around her. She felt alive and well and happy, but she feared it would all end badly. She wanted to ask him if he had been responsible for her parents' death, but she couldn't think of any way to open the subject. Just the thought of it made her shiver.

"You're cold," he said. "Time to go. But I don't want to take you home. Stay with me tonight."

"I can't do that."

"Why not?"

"I just can't."

"Are you afraid for your reputation?"

Jennifer laughed. "It is assumed that ballerinas are loose women with absolutely no morals. And coming from the family I did, how can you even ask that?"

"You are not your family. I'm not my family. I'm an individual. If you don't label me because of my grandfather, why should I label you because of your parents?"

Jennifer sighed. Chane was too reasonable. Everything he said made such good sense. "But other people think we are our parents."

"To hell with other people. Marry me. We'll make a new family with new rules."

"I can't marry. I'm already wedded to the dance."

"Don't be silly. Dancers marry all the time."

"Then they become mothers and leave dancing. I couldn't do that."

"Why not?"

"I don't want to."

"Well, if you aren't the marrying type, then spend the night with me. You have to be one or the other."

"No, I don't."

"You respond to my kisses. You want me the same way I want you. Can you deny that?"

Jennifer shrugged. "It doesn't matter. I don't have to be loose or married. There are other choices."

"Celibacy? What kind of choice is that?"

Jennifer lifted her chin and stared out at the river. At the moment it seemed an unacceptable one, but she would never admit that to him.

"Look, maybe you don't love me at the moment, but can we assume that you at least like me?"

Jennifer shrugged.

"Great. Can we assume that you don't despise me?"

Jennifer shrugged. She wasn't ready to give in to the man who might have murdered her parents. Compelling as he was, she couldn't shake Peter's and her suspicions.

Chane frowned and fell silent. His feelings were hurt, but he didn't want to show it. He wasn't accustomed to being rejected by women. The combination of his family name, his outgoing personality, his appearance, and his money, had always worked before. He had far more women interested in him than he could ever find the time to court, even if he were so inclined.

But Jennifer Van Vleet, who was broke, with no good reputation, and without the benefit of family connection, would not give him the time of day, even though she responded quite passionately to his kisses.

Jennifer saw the look on his face and let out a small, stifled cry. "Oh, Chane. I'm so sorry. I never meant to hurt you."

Chane started to lie and deny it, but the sudden softness in her eyes made him shrug and look away. He was not above using any advantage, however pitiful, if it helped him to win her. Damn her! he thought to himself. Damn those lips, those eyes, that angelic face.

Jennifer felt awful. It had never occurred to her that she might hurt his feelings. She had been proceeding as if he had none, as if all the terrible things Peter had told her about him were indisputably true. Of course, they could still be. His having feelings did not negate other rotten tendencies, but at least now he seemed human to her. With the proof of his vulnerability still pinching Chane's strong, handsome features, Jennifer writhed with self-reproach.

"I'm sorry," she said quietly.

"I don't need your pity," he said stiffly.

A spear of heat shot through her loins. She lifted his arm and slipped under it to press herself against his warm side. "I might need something, though."

Kincaid looked down at her. "What?"

"A…kiss?"

"I don't need your charity, either."

"Fine. Then take me home."

Chane heard the stiffness in her tone and realized that now he had hurt her feelings. Cursing himself for a fool, he lifted his arm from around her shoulders, grabbed the reins and tugged on them, to turn the horses. At one level, he realized they didn't have room to maneuver, but he didn't care. The horses stamped their reluctance to be forced into unexplored territory on a dark night, but he urged them forward.

Without warning, one of the horses went down, as if it had either stepped into a ditch or lost its footing. The other horse panicked, and the buggy tilted, lurched, and began to roll over. Jennie screamed. Chane cursed and tried to catch her, but there was little he could do. The angle of the tilt was too steep. The Stanhope went over, and Chane did the best he could not to fall on top of Jennifer.

They rolled free of the carriage and ended up in a marshy area a few feet away from the overturned carriage. The horses tried to regain their feet, but the trace chain held them pinned. Chane crawled over and grabbed their leads to calm them before they broke their legs thrashing around.

"There, boy. There, there," he crooned, slowly settling them down as he unhitched them from the overturned Stanhope. He tied their bridles to the nearest wheel and turned back to Jennie.

"Are you all right?" he asked.

"I think so," she said, groping for the blanket.

Chane fished in his pocket for a match. He lit it and saw that her face, hands, and gown were smeared with mud.

Jennifer looked up at Chane. His face and jacket were muddy. "Every time I get near you, disaster strikes."

He looked so funny, she began to laugh.

Grimacing, he helped her up. "I'm just going from one high to another, aren't I?" he asked ruefully.

She could see that he was truly upset that he'd almost gotten her hurt. His obvious despair touched her heart, and she sobered. "So what do we do now?"

"Thought I'd trip you and break your leg or something."

"I mean about the carriage," she said, motioning toward the overturned Stanhope. "Can I help?"

"No, thanks. I think I can fix it." He used the horses to help get the Stanhope righted, then inspected the horses and hitched them back into their traces. Back on the roadway, he helped her in and turned toward a main street. The sound of traffic had died down. It was absolutely quiet, as if everyone in the city were home eating dinner. Jennie's stomach growled loudly, and she was suddenly sorry she had refused to eat at the Winter Garden.

"Hungry?" Chane asked.

"Starved."

He drove toward the Bricewood. As soon as she realized where he was going, she said, "I can't go there. My gown is a mess."

"I'm not taking you home hungry. And we don't have to eat in public," he reminded her.

He drove to a back entrance and turned the carriage over to a bellman who pretended he saw nothing wrong with their mud-spattered clothing. They took a private elevator to the top floor, where the carpets were even thicker and the view breathtaking. Below, the whole city sparkled with light. Chane unlocked an unmarked door and ushered her inside.

"What is this?" she asked.

"My home," he said.

The apartment was richly furnished. The walls were white, the furniture light oak, and the carpets gold. Even the draperies were white and gold. The overall appearance was lighter and more open than most Victorian homes. Jennifer loved it.

"Are there other people here?"

His eyes narrowed slightly. "Would you prefer to have other people here?"

"No."

"Good, because there are none. I could ring for someone to bring us dinner, or we could rummage around in the pantry for our own dinner."

"I'd rather do that."

They found cheese, bread, butter, and wine. He opened a can of peaches and found plates and silverware. On the floor before the fire, they ate ravenously.

"That was so good," she said, sighing, when they were through.

"Now I know the way to your heart. A little wine, a few peaches," he said, smiling and raising his glass to toast her.

They fell silent for a time, both gazing into the fire as if hypnotized. "Call your brother," Chane said, glancing at her, "and tell him you've decided to stay at the Bricewood tonight."

Jennifer's pulse raced with excitement. "I can't do that," she said, knowing she'd never be able to resist him.

"I promise I won't make love to you. I just want to spend some time with you," he whispered.

"How do I know I can trust you?"

"I give you my word."

"Hmmm," she said teasingly. "I have no idea what your word is worth."

"Well, if you spend the night, and in the morning you realize that I've kept my word, won't that give you some measure of my trustworthiness?"

"I suppose so." She frowned. "But I think I should have good reason before I entrust myself to a man."

"Trust has to be based on something. Do you trust me now?"

"No."

He grimaced. "Didn't anyone ever teach you how to lie politely?"

"No."

"I was afraid of that. Well, since we have to start somewhere, why don't we start from where we are?"

Jennifer knew better than to take such a risk, but the thought of leaving him seemed unbearable. He showed her the telephone and left her alone to make the call.

Peter was out. Relieved, she told Augustine not to worry, she'd be back in the morning.

As she walked back to the fireplace where Chane had stretched out on the floor, she felt suddenly self-conscious. She had no idea why she'd agreed to stay or what she'd do here.

Chane reached up, took her hand, kissed the palm, and tugged lightly until she knelt beside him. His skin glowed in the firelight and his deep chest dropped off sharply beneath his ribs. Her hands ached to touch him, but she resisted.

"You look like an angel," he said huskily. "You're probably the wildest thing in New York with everyone except me."

Jennifer laughed softly. "Is that your greatest fear? That I'm sleeping with everyone but you?"

"Why not?"

She shook her head in exasperation. "Wouldn't it be easier to assume that if I don't sleep with you, I'm not sleeping with anyone?"

"Easier perhaps, but less likely to be true. That would be assuming that I'm the best and the luckiest, when in fact I'm not that arrogant."

"I heard you were shamelessly arrogant."

"About some things maybe, but my ability to win the most beautiful woman in New York is sadly lacking, as you can see."

"How do you know I'm worth winning?"

"I don't. But I want you, and I trust my instincts…most of the time."

"Not this time?" she teased.

"Not completely," he admitted.

"Why not?"

"I don't know. Maybe because I've never known a woman like you."

"Why am I so different?"

"Most young women come out at sixteen, and from that moment on it is apparent that they and their hapless mothers are locked on a treadmill from which they cannot escape until they catch a suitable husband. You probably didn't bother to attend your coming-out party, or if you did, you danced alone."

Jennifer shrugged. "I didn't have one. We were in Russia at the time, and I was being pursued by a Russian count who also could not believe that I was turning down his offers of marriage."

"See. I rest my case."

"I've seen what happens to women who get married. They're usually miserable. They work like slaves. Then they die in childbirth, or they survive and have to put up with the drudgery of running a household and being a mother. It's a terrible life. Even my mother's life was terrible. Despite all that money and servants, she was hopelessly bound to a man who ran around with every woman he laid eyes on."

"There are very few terrors of that sort that money cannot solve, aside from your mother's problem, of course."

"I don't have money anymore."

"But I do."

"I have more problems than you have money," she said solemnly.

"Tell me your biggest financial problem."

"My family home is about to be sold to settle my parents' estate. My brother is working at a job he hates in order to keep us from having to turn out our old family servants. I feel like a leech, because my contract with Bellini doesn't even cover the basics of life. I could go on and on, but I won't bore you with these things. You shouldn't have asked," she said, feeling miserable.

Chane nodded. At last, something he could understand. Perhaps she'd only been holding out until he named her price. Now, he knew how to proceed. He felt suddenly better and worse. She could be bought, and of course he'd known this all along. Everyone had a price, but it was sad to know hers. He'd rather she be the one person on earth he couldn't have at any price.

"What are you thinking about?" she asked softly.

"Nothing."

"Yes, you are. I can see it on your face."

"What would you like me to be thinking about?"

"I'd rather know what you were actually thinking about."

"I was thinking about us."

"Is there an us?" she asked, raising an elegant eyebrow.

"Come here."

"I am here."

He reached up, caught her hair and pulled her face down so his lips were almost touching hers. A small ache started in her loins. "Now," he growled, "now you are here." His hand lowered her head down until his mouth covered hers. His lips were warm and searching. He kissed her for a long time, and she felt somehow judged and found lacking. At last he released her.

Chane ached for more of her, but part of him felt angry and spiteful. He wanted to hurt her, to let her know in some way that he resented knowing her price. She looked confused by the kisses, and he was glad.

He stood up, pulled her up into his arms and carried her to his bed. In the bedroom, he lowered her feet onto the floor, jerked the covers back, and started to undress her.

"You promised," she said softly.

"I think I promised not to make love to you tonight."

"Yes."

"I'll keep my word. I always keep my word."

"You sound angry."

"Do I?" He sighed. He had no business being angry with her. She had a problem, and he had the solution. There was no need to get upset just because she was human.

"You can't go to bed in a muddy gown," he said reasonably.

She turned so he could unbutton her gown. Surprised, Chane slowly undid the buttons. He felt he was beginning to understand the pattern with Jennie. She protested, then she allowed. Perhaps it was important for her to be on record as protesting. And once she had, she was free to do as she pleased. He'd known other girls like that…

She slipped out of her gown. He was surprised to realize that she did not wear corsets or stays, only a thin cotton slip. She untied the bustle and dived under the covers. He undressed down to his underwear and slipped in beside her. "I'm cold," she said, sliding into his arms.

It was ecstasy and torture holding her while she warmed up. He loved the feel of her against him. His whole body ached for her, but he restrained himself.

It was she who kissed him first. She who deepened the kissing, she who began caressing his back. Her hand on his waist was driving him wild. He finally pulled her hands between them and held them while he caught his breath. "Would you stop that, or I'm not going to be able to keep my promise."

"What promise?" she whispered, eyes closed.

"The one I made to get you to spend the night, remember?"

"I release you from your promise."

Chane laughed. "What a little witch you are. You trick me into breaking my promise, and then you declare me untrustworthy. Nope, sorry." Determined to turn the tables, he buried his face against her throat and kissed it until she squirmed with need. Then he moved lower to kiss her breasts.

"Are you sure this is not considered making love?" she asked, panting.

"Of course I'm sure."

"Thank goodness," she said, sighing. He felt heavy and hard against her belly, and it seemed odd to feel safe with such a thing between them. It didn't make sense. She was in his bed, alone with him in his apartment, but the sensations coursing through her were the most delicious she'd ever felt.

"Was that another complaint?" he whispered, his fingers starting at her shoulders, stroking down her arms to bite into her hips and pull her against him. It was getting harder to think of witty responses.

The sound of his breathing was heavier now. His words were thicker. The game was more difficult for him as well. She pulled his mouth down to hers and kissed him hard. He was devouring her, and it was not enough. She wanted him to hurt her. She wanted him to take her, and yet he only kissed her.

"Oh, God," he said, groaning.

She could hardly think. "I know," she said, her own head spinning. He mumbled something, but she couldn't reply. She let him slip down and kiss her breasts. The sweet darkness in her belly was spinning in tighter circles. Her back arched, and the fever he'd created in her seemed to coalesce in one blinding second. She cried out.

"Jennie...love..." Chane pulled her tight against him and held her while she spasmed in silence. When the heavy throbbing in her belly stopped, he released her and rolled over to lay beside her. His hand found hers and squeezed it.

Jennifer drew in a heavy breath. She felt both guilty and wonderful. She'd gotten her release, but Chane must be in agony. "Are you okay?" she asked.

"Is a burning torch comfortable?" he asked, patting her thigh.

Jennifer snuggled close to him and nestled into his back. Chane lay there all night, unable to move away from her magnetic skin. He felt like a man on fire with the ecstasy of love and longing. He knew he had to be crazy to have asked for this sort of torment, but he knew he'd do it again in a second. He only hoped that this earned him some respect as a man of his word. If it did, it would be worth it. If not, he could always slash his wrists.

Chane slipped out of bed at six o'clock. He washed and dressed and was at his desk working when Steve came in at seven. "I want you to do something for me this morning."

"Sounds serious."

"It is." He told him about Jennie's financial problems and ordered him to solve every one of them. "And rewrite her contract so that she's getting what she deserves. I want her to be the best-paid prima ballerina on the planet."

"Yes, sir."

Jennifer woke to find sunlight streaming in the window and Chane looking down at her. "'Morning," she whispered.

"Good morning, beautiful."

"I'm a mess," she said, reaching up to cover her face. Chane pried her hands away from her face and stroked her cheek. "You're wrong. You are incredibly lovely. Your skin is so smooth, it doesn't look like it even has pores."

He kissed her, and his morning mouth tasted musky and wonderful. His kiss was intense and burning, and she got caught up in whatever was driving him, responding wildly to his blizzard of kisses, as if she, too, were someone else entirely.

Chane groaned and pushed himself away from her.

"No," Jennifer said, moaning.

"I promised."

"You promised for last night."

"And thanks to my incredible self-control, I made it through hell for you. I'm not going to ruin my reputation now," he said, gaining strength as he put some distance between them.

Jennifer knew she should be grateful, but that was only one of the thoughts she had on the subject.

Her body ached all morning, and no matter how hard she danced, all she thought about was Chane.

CHAPTER EIGHT

Chane pulled his gold watch out of his vest pocket and glanced at it. Seven-twenty. Almost twelve hours since he'd seen Jennie. He'd been trying to break away all day to seek her out, and hadn't made it yet. Frustrated, he straightened his cravat, took a deep breath, tapped lightly on the closed door of his grandfather's bedroom, and waited. Footsteps crossed the hardwood floor, and then the door opened.

"Come in. He's expecting you."

Chane crossed the darkened room to the bed, which was lit by two kerosene lamps.

"I don't appreciate tardiness, young man."

"I've been held hostage by your attorneys all day," Chane replied, feeling testy.

His grandfather scowled at him, but only half of his face worked, making it more pathetic than fearsome. "Well, sit down!" he growled.

"Yes, sir." Chane pulled up a chair and sat down.

"I hear you aren't all that impressed with the thought of inheriting ninety million dollars."

Chane scowled. "Sir, I—"

"It's just so much paper at this point, isn't it? Well, I've had a lot of time to think about this thing, and I've decided you're right. Ninety million dollars is too big to imagine and too abstract to sink your teeth into." Number One raised his hand and waved at his attendant, "So I've arranged a demonstration for you." The attendant walked to a connecting door and opened it. Halbertson stepped into the room, struggling with a big, red, sturdy wheelbarrow, its foot-high contents covered by a white cloth. He wheeled it forward and stopped before Chane.

"Take the cloth off," his grandfather ordered him.

Slowly, Chane reached over and lifted the cloth. Lamplight gleamed off a stack of gold bars. Chane counted them. Four bars high, six bars wide. Twenty-four gold bars. His heart skipped a beat and then settled into a heavier rhythm.

"Lift one of them," his grandfather ordered.

It was even heavier than he'd expected. It was cool and smooth in his hand. He caressed the solid gold bar, and a shiver went down his spine.

"You know how much money that one gold bar is worth?"

"No, sir."

"You're damned right you don't. Its worth changes every day, depending on the goddamned market, but I'll tell you one thing, whether it's worth between a hundred or seven hundred dollars an ounce, it's still the standard for every currency on the face of this earth. And don't you forget it. You have enough of that, and you'll never go without anything money can buy."

Chane frowned, wondering where this was leading. The gold felt good in his hands, better than anything he'd ever felt. It seemed to have a life of its own. His arm was getting tired of holding the weight, but he couldn't bring himself to put it down.

"So," his grandfather breathed, "you're starting to get a little respect for it, aren't you?"

"I never had disrespect—"

"Hogwash!" his grandfather rasped, interrupting. "You've never thought about it one way or another. So don't lie to me. You've had everything in life you've ever wanted, and it's made you lazy. You didn't have to work like a dog to scrape together that first little pile of money the way I did." He held up his hand to stop any further comment. "That whole stack is yours, if you give me your word."

"On what?" Chane asked.

"That you'll build that railroad and keep Laurey and Van Vleet from getting a dime of my money."

"Van Vleet?" Chane said weakly. "If you mean..." He groped for Jennifer's father's name.

"The old man's dead, but his daughter isn't, is she?"

"What has she to do with this?"

"You know damned good and well her father killed your cousin."

"Annabelle starved to death..."

"My ass! She died because that bastard seduced her and held her up to public ridicule!" his grandfather stormed.

Chane could have argued that starvation is a willful act, but he remained silent rather than taking the chance of precipitating another stroke or a heart attack.

"I know what you're thinking," his grandfather said, his tone hard and grating. "Van Vleet's dead, and to some that would end it. But I don't want any grandson of mine marrying anyone—and I mean anyone—with the name Van Vleet."

"How did you know?"

"I pay to know the things that are important to me," he said, cutting Chane off. "I may be numb in half of my body, but my brain still works. And I won't have one dime of my money going to support a Van Vleet, especially one who flaunts her body in public for money."

Chane put the gold brick down and stood up. "No thanks."

"What the hell do you mean, no thanks?" his grandfather roared. "This is over a million dollars in gold! Do you think there's a woman on this earth who's worth that?"

Chane didn't want to upset his grandfather, but he had no choice. "I choose my friends," he said carefully, quietly. "I'll choose my wife. I'm not willing to sell you either one of those rights."

"You just met her! How the hell can you be so sure she's wife material?"

"I don't know that she is, but I'm not willing to sell away my right to find out for myself."

"Damnation, boy! I'm trying to save you! The Van Vleets are nothing but trouble. They aren't like us! They're libertines! Do you want to be the laughingstock of New York? What the hell is the matter with you?"

"She's different."

"Do you really think there's a million dollars' worth of difference between any two women?"

He'd never thought about it that way. "It's the principle," he said finally.

"All right. I'm willing to gamble if you are. I'm willing to bet that if I give you the money, you'll be too smart to marry her. I'm not opposed to your having an affair with her. Might even make me happy if everyone in New York knows about it."

"What if I marry her?"

"I'd have you committed to an institution, if I could." Number One stopped. Chane was his only hope of getting that railroad built, the only one he trusted to do it and do it right. And there was no need to antagonize the boy. He had his own way of seeing to it that things didn't work out between them—Jason Fletcher, who was not above killing the Van Vleet whelp if it came down to it.

"If you're stupid enough to marry her, then I guess that's your problem. Take the gold. Maybe having that much gold will make you grow up, where nothing else could."

"What's the catch?"

"No catch. Just build my railroad and save it from Laurey. It's all yours."

"Even if I marry Jennifer Van Vleet?"

That galled the elder Kincaid, but knowing he'd already made arrangements to keep it from happening, he swallowed his bile and nodded. "Even if you're that stupid."

Jennifer didn't see Chane all day. But at five o'clock she received a message that she had a telephone call from her attorney. Bellini excused them for the day, and she rushed to dress and make the call before her attorney left his office. He was probably calling to give her the date for the estate sale, the date when all their possessions would go on the auctioneer's block.

Her heart pounding sickly, Jennifer went through the confusing ritual of waiting for the operator, asking for the attorney, and waiting while the call was put through. At last she heard a male voice on the other end of the receiver and asked for Mr. Berringer.

"Speaking."

"Mr. Berringer, it's Jennifer Van Vleet."

"Oh, well, young lady," he said, his voice changing to a tone that sounded very near a sneer. "I have some news for you about your parents' estate."

Jennifer closed her eyes, praying it wasn't going to be too soon.

"Yes?"

"You've heard it already, haven't you?"

"No, no. I meant that as a question."

"I'm sure you did." Something in his tone chilled Jennifer's blood. She had never particularly liked Berringer, nor he her, but usually he was more respectful. Perhaps as the estate diminished and she was being forced closer to penury, his true feelings were surfacing.

It was not uncommon for people to snub her or look down on her, but usually they were consistent. Berringer seemed to have moved very quickly from treating her with bare civility to being openly disrespectful.

"And what is your news?" she said grimly.

"All of the debts owed by the estate were paid today."

"Paid? By whom?"

"An anonymous donor."

"Anonymous? Does that mean you have no idea who?"

"No, it does not mean that at all," he said with obvious arrogance. "I didn't say I didn't know or that everyone else will not know."

"Well, if you know, please tell me at once."

"The contact person works for Chantry Kincaid the Third."

"Chantry Kincaid the Third," Jennifer repeated, stunned. "Why would he do that?"

"I was hoping you might tell me that."

"I have no idea."

"You do know the man?"

"Yes, but…I have no idea why he did it."

After a brief exchange in which she realized that Mr. Berringer didn't believe her, she finally hung up the telephone. The desk clerk motioned toward her, and a bellman carried a note over. Reluctantly, she took the note and read it. It was from Sammy, her agent. It was odd to receive two telephone calls in one day. Weeks went by without her ever receiving one. Puzzled, she rang the operator again and waited. Finally, she heard Sammy's voice on the other end.

"Hello."

"Sammy, it's Jennifer."

"Jennifer Van Vleet?" he asked loudly and jovially. "The toast of seven continents?"

Jennifer realized that he must have good news for her. Perhaps he'd gotten word from the ballet company in London. They had been waiting for months to hear about the appointment that could make her career, the appointment of the new prima ballerina. "Did you hear from London?" she asked.

"London? No, no. But you are one very lucky lady, my dear. We've just finished negotiating your new contract, and I can safely say that you are going to be the best-paid ballerina in New York."

"What do you mean?"

"I mean you're a star now, my dear, a big star."

"What do you mean?" she repeated. "How did this happen?"

"I mean you're now making almost ten times what you were making."

"Ten times!" Jennifer couldn't believe it.

"Well, aren't you happy?" Sammy cried.

"Where did this increase come from?" she asked suspiciously.

"You know Peter sold your contract to the new owner of the Bellini Company. Steve Hammond negotiated this for the Bricewood. You lucked out, my dear. Hammond seemed to have no idea what pitiful salaries ballerinas receive."

"And who is this Hammond person?"

"The acting representative for Chantry Kincaid the Third, naturally," Sammy replied.

"Naturally," Jennifer said, boiling with anger.

Kincaid! Jennifer put down the receiver and walked away. She had told him about her financial problems, and he had taken care of them. He probably thought she could be bought like the rest of his women. How dare he? Furious, she stalked to Kincaid's office and jerked open the door. Startled, Steve Hammond looked up from the tablet he'd been scribbling on.

"Where is Mr. Kincaid?"

"He left with a couple of attorneys a few minutes ago."

"When will he be back?"

"He's got three meetings this evening. I'm not sure."

"Would you leave him a note and ask him to call me at home?"

"Certainly."

At eight-thirty the doorbell rang. Jennifer heard it and wiped her eyes. Chane hadn't called, and her fury had dissolved into tears of shame and frustration. The tears had relieved her anger and let her realize she shared in the blame. She shouldn't have told him about her financial problems. He had undoubtedly assumed that since she'd told him, he was supposed to pay her debts and give her a huge raise. And the next logical progression was that he now owned her.

Well, maybe he did. Her sense of fairness told her that if she'd brought it up, she'd been asking for whatever she got. He'd only done the expected thing. A woman tells you her financial problems, it is natural to assume that she's naming her price. Why hadn't she realized this last night?

Downstairs, she heard Malcomb's voice and then Kincaid's. Trembling, Jennifer leaped off the bed and ran to her mirror. Her face was a mess. Her eyes were red and swollen, her skin blotchy.

She heard footsteps coming up the stairs. She picked up a comb and made a pass at her hair. Malcomb coughed at the open door. "Mademoiselle."

"Yes, Malcomb?"

"Mr. Kincaid is here to see you."

Her impulse was to tell him to tell Kincaid to go to hell, but she realized she had to see him one last time. "I'll be down in a moment."

Jennifer willed her hands to stop shaking. She dabbed powder on her cheeks, but that only made her eyes look worse. Finally, she washed her face in the basin, dried it, and tossed down the towel. It didn't matter if he knew she'd been crying. After tonight, she'd never see him again.

Kincaid paced the entry hall. When she started down, he stopped and looked up at her, but she refused to glance in his direction until she was at the bottom of the stairs.

He grinned as if his conscience were entirely clear. "Hello, princess." When she didn't respond, his face sobered. "What's wrong?"

"I take full responsibility for this latest debacle. However, it just proves to me—as if I needed any proof—that we are not in the least compatible."

A frown pulled his brows down. "What happened?"

"You paid off my debts and gave me an enormous raise, didn't you?"

Chane was certain he had told Steve to maintain his anonymity. "What if I did?" he asked cautiously.

"I can't accept either."

"Why not?"

Her pale face flushed with bright pink color. "Because I do have some morals. I'm not a strumpet who can be bought for a few dollars." The frustration on her lovely face tugged at his heart, and he realized suddenly that he had misjudged her, and in so doing he had shamed her. That knowledge stung him deeply.

"I didn't mean…Oh, God, I never dreamed that you would be hurt by it. I just wanted to make things easier for you."

She recalled the tone of Berringer's voice. Tears welled up and she began to cry. Chane stepped forward. She covered her face with shaking hands. "Here, let me," he crooned, pulling her close to him.

"No." Jennifer stepped back. "Don't touch me."

"Jennie—"

"I mean it."

"Is there any way you can forgive me?"

"No."

"I meant no insult."

Her lips trembled. "Do you have any idea how awful it is to be suddenly poor? To be held up to ridicule for the simple shame of having your parents die a terrible public death?"

"I didn't realize—"

"Well, that is nothing compared to the shame of having a rich man pay your debts, and having your attorney sneer at you as if he knows exactly what you did to precipitate such a generous act of charity." She wiped ineffectually at the tears that flooded her eyes. "I don't blame you," she said. "I shouldn't have told you my problems. I didn't think."

He realized suddenly how young she was, how sheltered she had been by her family and her work. The hot sting of shame washed through him, and he felt sick. She hadn't been negotiating with him last night, she'd only been unburdening herself. "I deserve any castigation you want to heap on me," he said quietly. "But don't send me away."

"I have to. Don't you see? We've done everything wrong. If I'm not burning down theaters, you're turning over carriages. You've ruined my reputation, such as it was, and any association with me will ruin you. We are not meant for each other. We're disastrous to each other. Don't you see?"

"No. I don't see. I love you, Jennie. Let me take care of you."

"Don't be nice to me," she said, dabbing at her eyes.

"Jennie, money means nothing to me. I just use it to solve problems—"

"Stop it!"

"I'm telling you the truth. I won't even notice the money spent today on your behalf. Except that it pleases me to be able to relieve you of worries. Please let me do that. We can't live our lives to please our enemies. What kind of life would be left for us under those conditions?"

Confusion and misery fought for supremacy on her lovely face. "Please," Chane repeated. "I love you. I want to marry you. I don't care what anyone in the world thinks about either one of us." He didn't tell her he had turned down a million dollars when he thought it would stand between them.

Slowly, he reached out and pulled her into his arms. She sobbed and collapsed against him, trembling violently. Chane was overwhelmed with love for her. She was so tender, so sweet and so unreasonable. In that moment, he would have died for her.

"Marry me," he whispered. "Let me take care of you."

She hiccuped, then laughed. "I'm such a mess."

"You're a beautiful mess," he said, kissing her eyes, her cheeks, and finally her mouth, which was cold and wet with tears. He kissed her until she warmed, sighed, and relaxed in his arms. Finally, he released her. "Where's your coat?"

"I can't go anywhere."

"We won't go out in public."

He took her to his apartment at the Bricewood. She knew he was going to make love to her, and even knowing it, she couldn't stop herself from getting out of the carriage and walking to the elevator.

"Are you hungry?" he asked as he closed the door behind her.

"No."

Again a fire was burning in the fireplace. "Who keeps this fire burning?"

"My housekeeper."

"Why don't I ever see her?"

Chane grinned. "She's careful to stay out of sight when I entertain."

"Oh."

He led her to the fire, took her coat off, and snuggled with her on the sofa. Resting in Chane's arms, gazing into the fire, slowly getting warm, all worked to relax her. Jennifer closed her eyes for only a second, then opened them to see that Chane was asleep and the fire had burned down. The room felt cold. Shivering, she tried to stand up to put another log on the fire. "What?" he asked, pulling her back into his arms.

"We must have fallen asleep," she said, smoothing the hair off his forehead. He looked so sweet when he was sleeping. Peter must have been wrong about him. This man couldn't have killed anyone.

"Why are you looking at me like that?" he asked.

"I don't know."

He stood and pulled her up into his arms. "I don't think this relationship will survive one more bungle on my part. It's time I put you to bed, before I freeze you to death."

He lifted her and carried her to his bed. He kissed her for a long time, then stood her carefully on the carpet while he turned down the covers. He unbuttoned her gown, took off her shoes, and then tucked her in.

"Aren't you going to sleep with me?"

"No. I don't think I can risk that again."

"What?"

"Be so near you and not make love to you."

"Well, could you do it if you did make love to me?"

Chane shook his head. "I'm not willing to bungle one more thing between us."

"Maybe we won't bungle it."

"With my luck, I would."

He leaned down and kissed her forehead as if she were six years old, then turned and walked out of the room.

Jennifer closed her eyes and tried to go back to sleep. The image of Chane sleeping, his handsome face so smooth and clean and innocent, tormented her. He had made love to many women in his life, and she had only made love to Frederick. Chane could be with someone who knew how to handle herself among men—like Latitia Laurey.

With his looks, money, position, and personality, Chane could have any woman he wanted. Jennifer bet that he was the most eligible bachelor in New York, surely one of the most eligible. And she was treating him like dirt. He could have any woman he wanted, and for some reason he had chosen her. She should be honored, but she didn't even know how to act with him.

Certainly, Latitia Laurey would not be sleeping alone in Chane's bed while he shivered on the sofa. She carefully slid out of bed and pulled off the top two blankets. Quietly, she walked across the room and opened the door. Chane was still on the sofa, but he had added logs to the fire. She tiptoed across the room and stopped beside him.

"Are you asleep?" she whispered.

One eye opened. "Almost."

"I brought you some blankets."

"Thanks, but I was keeping warm—" He stopped, unwilling to tell her that all he needed to keep warm were thoughts of her sleeping in his bed.

"Well, you'll need these before morning. Don't you have another bedroom up here?"

"I have several, but they aren't close."

"Oh. Mind if I lie down with you?"

Chane frowned. He had been only moments away from slipping into her bed. His willpower was at its lowest ebb. "Can't you sleep?" he asked.

"I got lonely."

But if she was the one in need, how could he turn her away? Reluctantly, he opened his arms and welcomed her onto the sofa beside him. She lay down and snuggled against him. Determined to behave himself, he pressed his cheek against hers and prayed for strength.

"You feel tense," she said softly.

"Do I?" he asked, feeling as taut as a steel rope strung between two stanchions. "I'm okay."

They lay in silence for a moment. "Chane..."

"Yes."

"Tell me about some of the women you've made love to."

In horror, he opened his eyes. "Is this a trap?"

"No. I'm just curious."

"Well, be curious about something else."

"Why?"

"Well, there haven't been all that many."

"Tell me about one of them, then."

"Do I look insane? Is there a sign on me somewhere that says this man has not even a particle of good sense?"

"No, I'm just curious," she said defensively.

"I won't ask about your lovers if you won't ask about mine."

"I'd be happy to tell you everything," she said ingenuously.

"Forget it. I'm not man enough to handle that sort of information."

"Well, maybe if I start, it'll be easier for you."

Chane clapped his hand over her mouth. "It's your bed-time, Jennie. If you don't get some sleep, you won't be able to dance."

Disappointed, she allowed him to hustle her back to bed. Again he kissed her on the forehead, tucked the covers around her, and left the room.

She closed her eyes and wondered why he wouldn't tell her about his lovers. He seemed terrified. Maybe he thought she'd be angry. That was probably it. She searched her mind and was happy to find that she didn't care what he had done before he met her. She imagined Chane lying atop Latitia Laurey, and she was both titillated and angered. She stewed for a moment and finally threw back the covers.

Chane's eyes were closed. "Are you asleep?" she whispered.

"What is it this time?"

"Are you mad at me?"

"No."

"Then why can't I lie with you? It's lonely in there."

Inwardly, Chane groaned. He had sworn to protect her, even from himself—but he was hanging by his fingernails. Well, he would just have to forget his own problem and try to deal with hers. He motioned her down and cuddled her close. "Better?" he asked.

"Much better," she said, snuggling against him. "Have you made love to Latitia Laurey?"

Chane drew his head back and scowled at her. "Who?"

"Latitia Laurey. Don't pretend you don't know her. So, what is she like in bed?"

Chane didn't know whether to lie and say he didn't know or tell the truth and be driven out into the cold by an enraged woman.

"Go to sleep, Jennie."

Instead, she stood up and slipped out of her camisole and pantalets.

"Jennie, my God," Chane protested, stunned by the sight of her naked body between him and the fire.

"It's getting hot in here," she said, lying down beside him again. "Why don't you take your clothes off?"

"No thanks."

Jennifer decided he was the stubbornest man she had ever known. Or the densest. She reached up, pulled his head down and kissed him. He ended the kiss. "Don't do that."

"Why not?"

"Dammit, I'm trying to behave myself here."

"Why?"

"I promised."

"That was for last night."

Chane groaned. "Jennie, I want things to be right between us. I want to do one thing right."

"Let it be something else," she said, pulling his head down and kissing him again. For a second she thought he was going to explode or break free of her, but he groaned and pulled her hard against him.

When the kiss ended, he whispered, "You'll be sorry."

"Hush," she said, squirming against him. Waves of intense feeling had driven her out here, and now they were operating her body as if she had no control whatsoever. She found his mouth again, and this time she was the aggressor. It felt good to hear the rasp of his breathing, feel the swell of his heaviness against her belly.

She moved his hand to her breast, and shortly his lips followed. Once started, he knew exactly what to do. His touch drove her wild, and him, too, if her perceptions could be trusted. He seemed as lost as she, as unable to stop himself as she. But he advanced slowly—so slowly that she was almost crying out for him to do more. His hands touched her tentatively and then with a sureness and magnetism that took her breath away. Wherever he touched her, she felt pulled in that direction, as if all of her attention were straining toward him.

Finally, he uncovered himself and slipped between her legs. Panting, she tried to move away, even though every nerve in her body screamed out for him to enter her. Chane's hands pinned her hips and his mouth covered hers. She tried to squirm away, but his leg wedged itself between her legs and he pressed into her.

She cried out, "No."

"Yes," he said softly, covering her mouth with his. He kissed her long and deeply, then pulled back and started the motion that brought with it ecstasy and agony. Wonderful sensations were washing through her.

She held tight to him and returned his kisses until it was over, and then they lay together, their bodies slick with sweat. Panting, he stroked her back and thighs. She could have lain like that all night. Chane inhaled deeply. "Are you cold? Do you need a blanket?"

"No, I'm fine. Well, at least this time nothing caught fire, got muddy, or turned over. And," she said, "neither one of us is hurt."

Chane started to laugh. She joined him. They laughed until they were both weak. Then he gathered her into his arms and carried her to his bed. He held her close for the rest of the night.

The next morning Jennie woke to find him gone. All her doubts about herself and about him resurfaced. She dressed and left the apartment without seeing anyone. At the elevator, she pressed the button, heard it ringing below, and moments later the elevator arrived, with Chane in it.

At the sight of her, he smiled. He was wearing a white shirt, a black frock coat, and matching trousers. Crisp and businesslike, he'd never looked more handsome. As the uniformed operator closed the iron gates, Chane guided Jennie back toward his apartment. "I was hoping I'd get back before you woke up. I brought breakfast," he said, lifting a sack and filling the hallway with bakery smells. He unlocked the door and swept her inside. At the table, he unpacked a bottle of milk and fresh jelly-topped rolls. "I don't know what you eat for breakfast."

"This is fine."

"Doesn't seem fine. What's wrong?"

"Nothing," she said, but she looked everywhere except into his eyes.

"I'm over here," he said, lifting her chin. "Jennie, look at me."

"What?"

"Even when you hide from me—don't shake your head, you know what you're doing—you are incredibly lovely." She looked tense and miserable, and he knew they had a serious problem. "We need to talk, Jennie. I want you to come with me on my ship."

"I can't."

"I want you to see the city from the prow of my ship. I want to hold you in my arms in the darkness and feel the spray on my face."

"We open with a new ballet in two weeks."

"To hell with the opening."

Jennifer groaned. "No," she whispered.

"You think the boss will be angry with you?" he teased, leaning down and kissing her. The magic was stronger than before, tingling his nerves and relaxing muscles that seemed to get tense when he went too long without seeing her. He kissed her again and felt her relaxing, too.

Jennifer closed her eyes and gave in to the magic of kissing him. His warm lips were like a soothing balm, and she forgot everything but him.

"Oh, Jennie," he sighed. "You have no idea what you do to me."

Jennifer closed her eyes to escape Chane's penetrating gaze, which confused her even more than Peter's claims against him. She didn't know whom to trust anymore. Peter said one thing, Chane said another. Peter wanted one thing from her, Chane another. Peter was her brother, but Chane was the man who caused her heart to pound and her body to tremble. She didn't trust him, but for some reason, she couldn't break away from him.

"No," she whispered. *God help me, but no.*

CHAPTER NINE

Jennifer was two hours late for practice. When she walked in from the wings and tried to slip into line unnoticed, every head in the theater turned toward her. She had the awful feeling that everyone there knew she had been in bed with a man.

Bellini hung his wand on the side of his stool and continued talking as if she had not just made an extremely tardy appearance. Jennifer flushed with gratitude and realized again why she loved the man. He was very forgiving of human frailty. He demanded the supreme sacrifice physically, but he rarely commented on anyone's personal problems, even when they spilled over into practice or performance.

The girls around her wore the oddest practice clothes. "I always wear my best practice clothes," Jennifer had told her mother. "Whatever is best, that's what I wear." But now, like Jennifer, her troupe mates had lost their best practice clothes in the fire and were dipping into their inventory of castoffs. It was customary to put together odd bits and pieces of clothing and to dress in a half dozen layers. As warm-up progressed, the layers came off one at a time. During breaks, the layers went back on. The day was spent taking off and putting on clothes. But the Bricewood, with its modern steam heating, was not the drafty Bellini. So by the afternoon, everyone had stripped down to bare essentials.

Frederick stopped beside Jennifer. "Did you give Kincaid his money's worth last night?"

"Excuse me?"

"You heard me," he said, smirking.

"What are you talking about?"

"Jennifer, it's me, Frederick. Anytime you get more money than I do, it's not for dancing."

"How did you know about that?"

"This is a small town, love. Everyone knows everything. You didn't think you could sell out without our all finding out about it, did you?" He laughed and walked away. Jennifer's face flushed with heat. She wanted to run after him and hit him as hard as she could, but she didn't. That would only add fuel to the fire.

Peter arrived a few minutes after five, just as the troupe was breaking for dinner.

Simone Marcelline looked up, saw Peter Van Vleet, and slipped around the corner of the dressing room so he wouldn't see her yet. Without thinking, she slipped off her tunic, removed her chemise, and replaced the tunic. In the mirror, her round breasts and dark nipples were clearly visible. She pinned madly at her hair until it resembled the picture of careless art—wispy and soft around her face. She grabbed a makeup pallet and touched rouge to her cheeks and lips, charcoal to her underlids and overlids.

Please God. Don't let him hate me.

She expelled a breath, rolled her eyes in resignation, and walked back into the theater. Peter stood twenty feet away, talking to Jennifer. He looked up, saw her, and his tawny eyebrows crowded downward into one of the most magnificent scowls Simone had ever seen. His piercing blue eyes almost stopped her heart.

She took hold of the practice barre and began her stretches.

Peter did not want to watch Simone, but his eyes kept straying back to her willowy form. With one leg resting on the barre, Simone lowered her head, grasped her ankle with both hands, and pressed her body close to her leg. Her body looked so flexible, and moved so effortlessly that an ache started low in Peter's body.

Jennifer followed his gaze. "Simone is sweet. I can't imagine why you keep punishing her."

"I'm not punishing her," he growled.

"Of course you are. You've always punished her."

"If you mean—"

"You hated every woman who ever slept with Reginald, but especially Simone. I think you're in love with her."

Peter scoffed.

"It's true."

"Why do you always defend them?"

"Do I?" Jennifer asked, surprised.

"Ever since I can remember, you've been defending the women he brought home. What the hell is a home supposed to be for? Certainly not for entertaining strumpets."

Jennifer flinched, wondering what Peter would think about her night with Chane. It was no use nagging him about Simone. He would think what he pleased. Suddenly, she was overcome with the impulse to tell him about Chane.

"Peter, I need to tell you...I'm seeing Mr. Kincaid."

"Well, that's great, Jenn. I knew you'd come around."

"I'm not spying on him, Peter, I'm..."

Jenn was talking again, but Peter's attention was on Simone, who bent low and turned her face to the side. Eyes closed, counting her beats or whatever a ballerina did while she waited for her muscles to accept each new position, she looked to him like an angel.

It was hard to realize, looking at such innocence, that Simone had been his father's mistress. The thought of his own father making love to the girl caused an odd tightening in his throat and loins. She looked no more than eighteen or twenty. Was it possible she had been seduced at fourteen? The thought made him angry at Reginald. What fourteen-year-old girl could withstand the determined advances of a grown man? Especially a charming, experienced, wealthy man who lavished gifts and attention on her?

Jenn paused, and Peter said, "Uh-huh." That seemed to satisfy her. She continued on her subject, and Peter let his mind stray back to Simone. In spite of her beauty, the girl looked starved for attention. He remembered the first time she came to the Van Vleet house. She had been so timid, she'd almost been afraid to sit on the furniture, and Vivian had smiled her sardonic smile behind the girl's back.

Peter had felt his ears burn for her. He'd wanted Simone to do something surprisingly sophisticated, to show his parents up, but of course she hadn't. Simone had been no better than he at holding her own in their glittering conversations. Though she had still had to try, to justify her position at the table, or in the bed.

"Well?" Jenn demanded.

Peter tried to remember her last words. He replayed the last sentence from memory by repeating it to himself, hoping to comprehend it so Jenn didn't realize he'd been lost in thoughts of Simone. *He's invited me to go sailing with him sometime.*

"Good, Jenn. Sounds like you're making progress. Do what you have to do. Just be careful, huh?"

Jennifer took a deep breath and rubbed her sweaty hands against her tights. The biggest hurdle was over—she'd told Peter she was seeing Kincaid. Now, at least she wouldn't be sneaking around.

• • •

Monday, a month and a few days after the fire, Jennifer awoke with the awful feeling that she'd forgotten something. At noon one of the ballerinas mentioned that her monthly had started during practice and she'd ruined one of her best practice outfits. Jennifer realized what she'd forgotten. She hadn't started her monthlies yet. Panic seized her.

It was December third. The building had burned the end of October. She hadn't had a monthly since the fire. She sagged onto her chair before her mirror and put her head into her hands.

Part of her wanted very much to see Chane's reaction, to see the fierceness and possessiveness she knew would flush his handsome face at the news that she was carrying his child. But once she told him, things would get out of control. As long as she was the only one who knew, she still had control. Her head spun with fear and confusion. She needed to talk to someone.

Christopher. She could talk to Christopher Chambard. He had practically raised her. He'd been her mother's closest friend, and whenever the Van Vleets swept out of town on one of their jaunts, Christopher was always there to pick up the pieces. Over the years, Jennifer had turned to him time and again for advice and explanations of grown-ups' puzzling behavior. Christopher would know how to sort out her present welter of emotions and make sense of it.

She told Bellini that she would not be in until after lunch the next day, and she told Chane that she needed to go home to see her brother. For the first time that week she slept in her own bed. The next morning, she dressed carefully in white and ordered a carriage to take her to Christopher's apartment near the old Bellini Theatre, in a brownstone that reminded her of Paris.

As she sat back and the carriage began to roll, she glanced at the house across the street and saw a man step quickly behind a tree as if trying to escape detection. She caught only a glimpse of the man, but something about him disturbed her. A chill ran down her spine.

She was sure it meant nothing, but her body sent her different signals. She was relieved when the carriage pulled around the corner and safety out of sight.

Jason Fletcher watched Jennifer Van Vleet skim down the stairs to street level and step into a waiting carriage. She was wearing a long white coat and a white hat with a long feather. She looked like a princess, and he liked that.

He watched her carriage roll out of sight. He was beginning to get used to these city types. He'd been in town a while now, and though it was colder than he liked, he was enjoying himself. He'd bought himself some fancy duds, and had been introduced into some private clubs where he'd won a lot of money in poker games. With the money old man Kincaid and Latitia were paying him, plus the money from the gambling and the last bank job, he'd be set for the winter, even if he hit a losing streak at cards.

He knew he could have killed Jennifer Van Vleet any number of times in the last few weeks. She was careless of her safety to the point of being stupid. She traveled alone with just a driver. She took long walks by herself. She was an easy target. And Latitia was anxious for him to get rid of Miss Van Vleet and set Kincaid free.

But an odd thing was happening to him. The more he followed Jennifer, the less anxious he was to move in on her. Sometimes, just following her, he felt a satisfying tingle in his body that reached all the way up to his head. That was worth a lot. Lately, he got no feeling at all killing a girl. It pleasured him thinking about Jennifer and what he'd do to her when he finally made his move. It made him think of the first girl he'd killed. Maybe he'd been rushing it with the others.

He was lucky this time, being paid to follow a girl he would have followed for free. He had a special weakness for slim, blond women. So he wouldn't lose track of how many he had killed, he kept a small vial of blood from each girl. He'd had well over a dozen vials several years ago. But they'd all been broken in a tornado that had swept through Dallas one night. That damned twister had picked up his trunk and smashed it against a wall of the room he'd been staying in. He'd seen that as a sign that he wasn't supposed to keep count. But he figured he'd killed a girl at least every two months since he was eighteen.

The first time had been an accident, sort of. He'd trapped this girl and gotten so excited by her slim young body and her shiny blond hair that he'd raped her, and once he'd done that, he knew he couldn't let her go. She'd just run home and tell her menfolk, and they'd come back and kill him, or try to. He figured he could take out most of them, because he'd be waiting for 'em.

But then he thought, why bother? Why kill five or six men when he'd just have to kill one woman? And knowing he was going to kill her gave him a lot more freedom to do what he liked. So he'd taken his time and tied her up and used a special knife he'd taken from a mean Indian. He reckoned the Indian had stolen it, because it wasn't the sort of thing an Indian could make. It was a hollow-bladed knife, crafted of the best quality steel by someone who knew what they wanted—the same thing he himself wanted.

The point was like a needle, and the rest of the knife was like a slim, sharp funnel. When he stuck it in the girl's side, just over the liver, she bled like a stuck pig. He had blindfolded her so she couldn't see what was happening, and once the initial sting was over, she had no idea that her blood was flowing out in a continuous stream and draining off the end of the knife into a bucket.

He'd climbed on top of her and kept doing it to her until long after she'd died. Then he drank some of her blood, and gave the rest to the hogs. He wrapped her in sacking and buried her behind the barn. Her menfolk scoured the countryside for her, and never did find hide nor hair.

He'd had two meetings a week with Halbertson, and one with the old man. Jason knew the old man was scared spitless that his grandson was going to marry the girl. Jason liked to just sit there and watch the old man squirm, trying to get up the nerve to ask him to kill her.

He had an odd ability to read old men's minds. Sometimes young men, too. But they didn't interest him. The slim blondes did. They heated up his blood so bad that he felt certain they must enjoy dying for him. They screamed and cried and begged, but he knew that was just an act to excite him so he'd do it to them. His mother had taught him about women. He knew that you couldn't believe anything they said.

At the memory of his mother, a cold chill threatened to ruin the warm glow he'd gotten from seeing Jennifer for those few seconds. He walked to the cabriolet he'd rented. He'd see where she was going. Just the thought of not knowing whether he would do it today made him feel good again.

Steve walked into Chane's office. "I met with Wentworth of Amalgamated Steel."

"How'd he take it?"

Steve sat down, pulled out a cigarette, lit it, took one long pull off it, and stubbed it out in the ashtray. "He was surprised as hell. When I told him we'd buy rails from him if they were up to our standards, he almost fell out of his chair. Apparently he's worked with Number One before. He didn't expect any standards."

"Am I paying you too much?" Chane asked. "That's the hundredth time I've seen you take one drag on a cigarette and put it out."

"You're not paying me nearly what I'm worth. I quit smoking."

An explosive laugh escaped before Chane could stop it. "You quit?"

"Yeah. Now when I want a cigarette, I light it, but I just take one puff."

"Sounds like I'm paying you too much." Chane shook his head. "I'm heading for a meeting with Roudenko and Beaver Targle right now. If their bodies are at all warm, I'm going to hire them to build my grandfather's railroad. Then you and I won't have to worry about it anymore. It'll be their problem."

Steve took out another cigarette and fondled it. "If God had meant us to roll at high speed on train tracks, we'd have been born with wheels," he said, realizing his fear was irrational. A man had to die of something, but he just couldn't tolerate the thought of it being in a train wreck. His fear shamed him, but not enough to pretend it didn't.

"Unfortunately," Chane said grimly, "trains and railroads are built by men, and even God can't keep men from screwing up just about anything they do." He had faith in man's ability to build anything he set his mind to build, but the way the government funded railroads encouraged sloppy construction and rewarded greed and graft.

"My grandfather is no exception. Few men in positions of power can resist the opportunity to rake off millions of dollars while building railroads so unsafe they slaughter several thousand unsuspecting passengers each year. If Wentworth delivers, we'll still make money, but we'll build a safe railroad in the process," Chane said.

"A first, I'd say."

Chane grinned. "As long as I don't have to leave New York."

"Hallelujah."

"By the way, have you seen Jennie?"

"Not today."

"I wonder where she could be?" It wasn't like her to stay away from the theater. She practiced every day. But this morning he'd gone looking for her, and Bellini had said she'd taken the morning off. As soon as he could break away from his morning appointments, he'd track her down and be sure she was okay.

The phone rang and Chane picked it up. "Mr. Kincaid." His secretary's voice came clearly over the line. "A Mr. Beaver Targle and a Mr. Louis Roudenko are here to see you."

Chane greeted the two men and motioned them to chairs across from his desk.

Roudenko was small, dark-skinned, and tight-lipped. Targle was a big, sunburned man with hands like hams. They seated themselves and waited.

"You've quite a bit of experience working on railroads, haven't you?" Chane said.

"Yes, sir," Roudenko replied, his words curt.

"You were with the…?"

"The Union Pacific mostly."

"And then…"

"The Southern Pacific for a time, but not too long…" Roudenko looked like giving that information pained him. Chane knew Roudenko hadn't been able to get construction boss work for a while. He'd been hurt two years before and lost his nerve. Working in the switchyard, he'd tried to show one of his men how to place a link pin between two boxcars, and the engineer had backed the train up and pinned him, almost crushing his chest. He'd been lucky. Only six broken ribs.

Chane didn't hold that against him. Any man could lose his nerve after an accident like that. He just didn't want a man who hadn't gotten it back yet in charge of his crews.

Chane asked questions for fifteen minutes. Roudenko answered grudgingly at first, then finally eased up and answered more frankly.

Chane grilled Beaver Targle as well. After an hour, he still wasn't satisfied, but feared it was them or no one. And they were more experienced with railroad building than he'd expected to find on such short notice. In spite of his misgivings, he hired them.

Roudenko would stay in New York to finish pulling together the thousand loose ends that still needed to come together. Beaver Targle would board a train for La Junta, Colorado, immediately. He would be the advance man, hiring locals, setting up the sawmill, cutting trees, finding a quarry site and beginning the quarrying that would provide ballast for the roadbed.

When they left, Chane breathed a sigh of relief that he wouldn't have to go to Colorado. He'd be free to court Jennie.

CHAPTER TEN

"Oh, Christopher, I am so ashamed. I would not have believed myself capable of it," Jennifer said.

Chris Chambard's fine gray eyes danced and twinkled. His dry, papery chuckle followed Jennifer to the window. "Oh, *chérie*, you have the fire and passion of a Venus, of an Aphrodite."

"Chris, I am *enceinte*!" Somehow, saying it in French was not so damning. She shook her head, amazed at her own stupidity. She had taken the precautions recommended by her fellow ballerinas. As if they were the most promiscuous women on earth, girls backstage spoke of new precautions daily. In reality, they probably had no energy left for anything besides collapsing alone into their beds. Perhaps they had never tested the precautions they swore by. Perhaps they had lied about their lovers. Perhaps she was the only one in the ballet company to ever take a lover. The rest merely pretended.

"I could kill myself, except I hate the sight of blood, and poison terrifies me," she said miserably. "I could jump off the Brooklyn Bridge, but heights scare me, too. What if I just broke every bone in my body and survived?"

Christopher laughed. "You said yourself Kincaid wants you to come to him. He probably wants to marry you. Have you told him?"

"No, not yet."

"Your mother was a ballerina. She managed quite nicely, but of course she didn't remain one."

"Mother was never a *serious* ballerina. She wanted to marry. I do not."

"So what will you do?"

"Peter believes Kincaid killed our parents."

Christopher Chambard squinted his eyes at the vision before him. Though she probably had not ridden, Jennifer wore a white velvet riding habit and a white fur hat with a jaunty white egret plume. The cut of the lush, white velvet showed off her slender curves to excellent advantage.

In an age when good health was positively vulgar, and young women went so far as to drink vinegar to attain the fashionable *souffrante* look, Jennifer Van Vleet glowed with health. Christopher had a proprietary pride in her appearance as well as her accomplishments.

"If I had to guess, I would say that your parents killed your parents. Perhaps your father took one too many mistresses, and finally enraged Vivian so much that she shot him. Then she panicked at what she'd done and shot herself."

"Mother might kill Father, but she would not kill herself." Jennifer paced the length of Christopher's studio, which was reminiscent of fashionable salons of the Rue de l'Université and the Faubourg St. Honoré. Compared to the American fashion for geegaws and frills, Christopher's apartment was austere and filled with light. It was a great barn of a place—a renovated schoolhouse remodeled on the outside to resemble the fashionable brownstones on either side. The town house managed, after years of Christopher Chambard's influence, to look as cosmopolitan as he.

"Drawing room society," as Christopher called the members of the *beau monde* who flocked there when he gave one of his rare soirees, imitated his style and truly believed they were glimpsing customs and fashions of Paris. Christopher enjoyed the fact that they rushed home to imitate a caricature of an imitation. He designed only for function, to let in light and keep out his musty demons. He had not seen Paris in thirty years. The ocean terrified him.

"Not on purpose, perhaps, *chérie*," Christopher said, patting the pillow beside him. "If Kincaid somehow precipitated their deaths, then that is a fact to be dealt with, but it is my belief that men and women have to be responsible for their own predicaments. No one else."

"I never should have let him…" Her eyes filled with tears.

"*Chérie*, what proof do you have that Kincaid caused your parents' deaths?"

"None."

Christopher shook his head and raised both hands in an elaborate shrug. Jennifer flashed him an exasperated look. "Peter's friend, Derek, thinks Chane tricked Vivian into his bed and used her to gain information to ruin Father."

Christopher shook his head. "If Reginald thought Vivian had slept with Kincaid and gotten them into a financial mess, he would have simply ordered her to go sleep with him again and get them out of the mess. Your father was no fool. Even facing bankruptcy, he was not a man to think of his own death as a solution for anything. Undoubtedly there have been other men who have thought of it—his death, that is—but not Reginald. A drink perhaps, another woman undoubtedly, but not death. Only a fool chooses death as a solution. I am an old man. I know."

Jennifer inhaled deeply. She, Christopher, Peter, and Derek had not believed the police department's theory of suicide and murder. Everyone else believed it—or pretended to.

Christopher picked up his cup and sipped at the tea he had heavily sugared and creamed. "Even if they died by Reginald's hand, how can you blame Kincaid? Many men have business reverses. Few kill themselves or their wives because of them."

"Perhaps Vivian did have an affair with Kincaid," Jennifer said. "You know how Mama was. She could be so gullible…"

Christopher laughed. "Make up your mind what you resent most. That you might be *enceinte*? Or that Kincaid may have slept with your mother?"

Wiping her eyes, Jennifer laughed. "How many men could I have this conversation with?"

"I have seen Kincaid at a number of functions. He would have no trouble getting me into bed," he said matter-of-factly.

Christopher Chambard pursed his lips and sighed at the memory of Chane Kincaid. Christopher was sixty-nine years old and had long ago come to terms with his homosexuality. It had not been easy. He had suffered horribly until he accepted himself and ignored those friends and relations who would not or could not accept him as he was.

Fortunately, the Van Vleets and their close friends were comfortable with any manner of sexuality. Jennifer had grown up in a household whose amorality would boggle most modern-day Victorian minds. Reginald's lovely, exotic little actresses, opera stars, and ballerinas had enlivened many a cold evening with their entertainments. Vivian had been just as free to choose and enjoy the many handsome young men in their circle.

"I don't think Chane had anything to do with their deaths," Jennifer said. "I've told Peter that…" She sighed. "I saw what happened to Alicia. How could I have fallen into the same trap? I must be insane!" Alicia had been her understudy. She now had four sons, and she hadn't danced in years.

Jennifer felt overwhelmed by fear. A lump formed in her throat. Tears welled up and blinded her.

"*Chérie*." Christopher stood up and walked to Jennifer's side. He took her slender, trembling body into his arms. Her shoulders shook with her ragged sobs.

"I'm not psychic, but I think you see this pregnancy as a limitation. Every limitation is also an opportunity. The one never comes without the other."

As a young man, Christopher had spent a year in India meditating under the direction of an Indian holy man. Christopher had appeared on several occasions to have psychic powers, but he did not flaunt them. He didn't need to. His solutions to problems were so different from other people's, they knew immediately he was not one of them. Jennifer considered herself odd because she generally understood him.

"It's the end of my life. I'm destroyed," she whispered. A small, hysterical laugh caught in her throat. Christopher took her by the hand, led her to the sofa and tugged her down beside him.

"The man does not exist who can destroy you—not for more than a moment. You are the phoenix—you will rise from the ashes of this experiment unsoiled, unless you choose otherwise." Christopher raised a hand to stop her protest. "You will never allow any journey, no matter into what darkness, to dim your fine spirit. Hear me, Jennifer Van Vleet. I know this about you," he finished sternly.

Jennifer looked down at her hands. "Christopher, I feel like everything I ever believed about myself is suspect. With Kincaid—" She swallowed and looked away. "—I'm not myself. I tried to avoid getting involved with him, but when I see him, I feel so alive. So much better than I've ever felt in my life. I even see better. I can close my eyes and smell the scent of his skin…" Jennifer stopped, her cheeks flushed.

Christopher reached over and patted her hand. The look that had fleetingly changed her expressive face spoke volumes to him. She was in love. And it had emerged suddenly, full-blown and awesome, before she knew how to deal with it.

"How could everything else work so much better and my judgment so much worse?" she wailed.

"Perhaps he had nothing to do with your parents' deaths."

"I know he didn't." Jennifer sighed. She would have to tell Chane. She had already fallen in love with the idea of having his baby. Ever since Kincaid had made love to her, she had been doomed. "How will I tell Peter?"

Christopher raised his eyebrows in mock horror. "This is Peter's business? Does Peter tell you about the young women with whom he sleeps?"

"Of course not."

Christopher shrugged as if he had made his point.

Jennifer leaned her head on Christopher's shoulder. She took a ragged breath and forced herself to look at him. "I'm afraid to trust him. What if he doesn't really love me?"

"That would be unfortunate, though I can't imagine it. Even I am almost in love with you."

Jennifer laughed and wiped a tear from her cheek. "I know he likes me. He has wonderful eyes. The warmest, wisest, kindest eyes I've ever seen..."

"Ahhh, young love..."

"And something happened to me. I can't explain it, but the moment he took my hand, I felt like a flower opened within me. It was uncanny."

Christopher smiled. "The gift. You have the same gift your grandmother had. She recognized her husband the first time she met him. She described the feeling in almost the same way, only she said it was like the strings of a harp quivering inside her..."

"Ohhh." An anguished moan escaped Jennifer's lips. Goose bumps rose up on her arms; pale, silky hairs stood on end.

"Ahhh. It was the same for you, *mon ange.*"

Eyes brimming with sudden tears met his gaze.

"What am I going to do, Christopher?"

Christopher raised both eyebrows and quirked his thin mouth into a sardonic slit. "You're worried now about losing your options. Real freedom comes from making your own choices from your own deepest feelings. Decide what you want most."

"I want what I've always wanted. I'm a dancer." She straightened her spine. "I won't see Kincaid again."

Christopher shook his head at the speed with which she had leapt to the wrong conclusion. "Do you expect to go blind before you reach the hotel? Don't let your fear make you blind to the surrender that may have already taken place in you," he said softly.

She didn't know what he meant, but a hysterical laugh burst from her lips. She covered her face with her hands. "I've already gone stupid. I might as well go blind."

After his appointment, Chane searched the hotel for Jennie, to no avail. At the practice room he learned that she still hadn't shown up for the rehearsal, either. Puzzled as to what she was doing, he went back to his office and tried to work.

Steve poked his head into the office. "How was the meeting?"

"Great, great. Just fine," Chane said, distracted.

"Good. Well, I have some good news and some not-so-good news."

"Sure. What's up?" Chane asked, glad to be interrupted from wondering where Jennie was and what she was doing.

"Well, I found out we got the loan guarantees from Washington."

"Excellent. Now what's your second bit of news?"

"Captain Kirkland sent a message in by another ship," Steve said, dropping into the chair across from Chane. "He's afraid the harbor is going to freeze over. He wants permission to take the *Golden Treasure* to Norfolk harbor."

The *Golden Treasure* was Chane's personal pleasure yacht. Kirkland loved the ship and would do anything to protect it. "Tell him to go ahead." Chane stopped. "No, wait. Hold him there until I find Jennie. Maybe she'd like to take a short trip."

Chane finally found Jennie in the exercise room. "I've been looking all over for you," he said.

"I visited a friend."

"I need to talk to you."

"Bellini would be furious if I left ten minutes after arriving," she said tensely. He reached out to massage her shoulder, but she stepped smoothly away.

"What's wrong?"

"Nothing," she said quickly.

Chane quirked his eyebrows at her. She didn't return the signal. Her face stayed carefully neutral. She was like a beautiful rosebud closed tight against him.

"So," he said, expelling a heavy breath. "We have a problem. When are you going to tell me what I've done?"

Jennifer's heart pounded so hard she felt sick from it. On the ride back to the hotel, she had decided to get rid of the baby and go to Europe, where she could study with one of the greatest teachers on the continent, Eduardo Valentini. She didn't want to have to face Chane, because she feared her courage would fail her. But he hadn't done anything wrong, and he deserved a decent good-bye. And a decent explanation.

"I can see you at five-thirty, after rehearsal," she said reluctantly.

"You'll be hungry. I'll have dinner waiting."

Jennifer did not trust herself to eat. The thought of food made her queasy. "I'm not hungry."

"It's not five-thirty yet."

She walked back to her dressing room. Chane watched her with a feeling of doom. His heart seemed to swell, turn cold, and sit like a rock on his stomach. Something had happened. Something terrible. She was going to tell him that she felt nothing for him, perhaps never had.

The energy drained from his body and sweat broke out on his forehead. His heart was pounding.

He stopped in Steve's office. The clock on the wall gave the time as three-thirty.

Steve looked up from the newspaper spread on his desk. "Did you see this story?" he asked.

"Which one?"

"About the train that jumped its tracks near Brooklyn. Derek Wharton called it an act of God."

"Must have been one of the Commodore's trains."

Steve whistled. "If *you'd* designed it, it would have been the crime of the century."

"When penny newspapers like the *Manhattan Times Record* want to expand their readership, they slander someone. It must be God's turn."

Chane had no energy to worry about Derek Wharton. He had two hours to wait. The clock's hands did not appear to be moving.

Simone looked up from the ice skaters on the lake in Central Park, and her heart almost stopped. On horseback, Peter Van Vleet had paused at the beginning of the riding trail at the park's entry. In a brown tweed riding coat with jodhpurs, and with the sunlight shining on his wheat-colored hair, he looked immaculate, untouchable.

Appearing not to see her sitting forlornly on the park bench, Peter turned to scan the other side of the park. His cameo-sharp features were ruggedly handsome. She imagined him taking her by the hair, pulling her onto his horse, and riding away with her. Her heart raced at the thought.

"What's wrong?" Bettina, a friend from the dance company, asked, turning to follow Simone's gaze.

Simone grabbed Bettina's arm. "Don't look. It's him."

"Him?"

"Jennifer's brother!"

Bettina smiled as if she had never fallen foolishly in love, and Simone could have strangled her with her bare hands.

Derek Wharton waved at Peter, and Peter raised his chin in acknowledgment and urged his horse toward Derek. As he rode beneath leafless trees, shadow and sunlight played on his features. To Simone, everything about him seemed perfect and deliciously manly.

She wanted to wave to him to let him know she lived in the same world as he, but she did nothing. Peter walked his horse within fifteen feet away, apparently without seeing her.

The sound of his rich, husky voice as he said something unintelligible to Derek triggered an old memory in her. She remembered lying in bed in Toulon, listening to Peter and Jennifer laughing and talking on the other side of the wall. His voice then had been a great deal like his father's, except huskier.

Peter looked just like his father, but he was more idealistic and purposeful. Reginald had been devoted to enjoying life. Peter was more earnest and serious. In school he had been an honor student. She knew, because she had made it her business to learn everything she could about him. At St. Cyr, a cavalry school catering to the *crème de la crème* of society, he had been among the best of the best.

That evening in Toulon, she had lain in bed listening in a dreamy state to his deep voice on the other side of the wall. Its manly charm had seeped into her very bones, until he said, "How long is she going to be with us?" The bitterness in his voice made her feel hot with shame.

"Shhh," Jennie had whispered. "She might hear you."

Simone had heard Peter's footsteps as he walked across the floor and stood next to the wall that separated her bedroom from the sun porch where they were lounging. "Well, we wouldn't want her to hear, would we? Pretty little Simone must be protected from the raw truth that not everyone in this family approves of Reggie's little whore."

"Why don't you call him Papa, like he wants you to do?" Jennie had asked.

Then she must have pulled Peter away from the separating wall. When he spoke again, it came from a different part of the room. "Reggie and Simone don't care that we lie in bed and listen to them making love. Why should I care whether she hears that I resent it?"

Simone had refused to let Reginald make love to her in that house again. He'd had to take her to hotels after that, but the damage had been done. She knew Peter would never forget what he'd heard. Or forgive her for her part in it.

Jennifer had apologized to Simone and assured her it was nothing personal, but of course Simone knew better. It was extremely personal, and Peter was entitled to hate her.

"They're back," Bettina whispered, poking Simone in the ribs.

To Simone's amazement, Peter stopped his horse a few feet from their bench, dismounted, and removed his hat. His sky blue eyes fairly sparkled as they looked at her. Derek stayed on his horse and seemed deep in thought.

Peter's gaze stopped on Bettina, who wriggled into her most seductive pose. "Yes?"

"I saw you in *Can-Can*, did I not?" Peter asked.

Bettina smiled and nodded. "Why, yes, I suppose so."

"I just wanted to tell you how much I enjoyed your performance. You were ravishing," he said.

"Was I as good as your sister?" Bettina asked.

Peter looked surprised. "You know who I am?"

Bettina laughed softly. "Please, Mr. Van Vleet," she said archly. "A handsome man is not invisible in the theater."

Peter laughed. He glanced at Simone, who prayed her mouth wasn't hanging open like a dog's. He looked so sophisticated and worldly, and he smelled of horses and tweed, an expensive, unreachable combination for a girl with her past. His slight Harvard accent reminded her that he was worlds above her and always would be. He turned and mounted his horse, which was almost as beautiful as he.

Simone struggled to hold back tears. Up close Peter was contradictory and devastating. He seemed to exude self-confidence, as if he had never been hurt by life. As if he never expected to be hurt by life. And yet, she knew he'd been badly hurt when he was expelled from Harvard and when his parents died. She had sensed his anger and pain when he stood on the other side of the wall, speaking for her benefit.

Simone's heart beat so hard she felt rattled by it. Peter probably had never seen Bettina perform in anything at all. He had made that up to torture her, because he knew she wanted him. He had known all that summer, too. He had bathed nude in the backyard pool. Oh, he'd been circumspect, with his well-placed towel and his bathrobe, but he had lain in full view of her room.

It had been like a pact between them. Simone wore her sexiest gowns, and Peter flaunted his perfect, golden body. He swam naked in the pool every day, and Simone watched. At night she swam naked in the pool and prayed he watched.

At last, mounted on his horse again, Peter acknowledged her. His gaze locked with hers, and she felt faint. "Miss Simone," he said, with studied formality.

She nodded mutely.

He touched his hat. The brim put his eyes into shadow, drawing attention to his seductive mouth. Her lips ached to touch it again. She could not believe he had actually kissed her the night of the fire. She felt faint.

"Good day, ladies," Peter said softly, kicking his horse's sides with his boots. She watched his lithe back until her view was obstructed by trees and the sound of hooves on the dirt path slowly diminished.

Bettina's pouty bottom lip pulled down at the corners into a sneer. "He's handsome, but he can't be too much, hanging around with a garden slug like the wart."

Derek Wharton had dated a number of ballerinas. Women usually ended their relationships with him by throwing things at him. Later they sneered whenever his name came up.

"Peter is different."

"Sure. They're all different," Bettina said bitterly. She picked up a stick, tossed it away, and glanced at the pendant watch hanging around her neck. "Our time's up."

Simone felt sick. She wanted Peter to like her, to love her, and he wouldn't. He would sooner die than love her.

Chane interrupted Steve. "I don't care what you've heard about his financial problems. If Peter Van Vleet wants credit to gamble, give it to him."

Steve frowned. "What if—"

"He's Jennie's brother. Give him whatever he wants. If he breaks the bank, we'll still build a railroad from La Junta to Timpas." Timpas was about ten miles from La Junta. "He's a kid. He'll gamble a little, lose a little money, and not be able to pay me back. So what have I lost? Unless he steals the chips, we're out nothing. It's all smoke."

"I hope he doesn't gamble as recklessly as he rides a horse."

"Steve, I know you're only trying to protect me, but I don't want to be protected from Jennie's brother. Her problems are my problems."

"As long as you remember that her brother hangs around with Derek Wharton—"

"They probably went to school together." Tom Wilcox, Chane's security chief, had given him a complete report on Peter Van Vleet. He had no history as a compulsive gambler, and in fact he had gone to school with Derek Wharton.

"That could be, but Wharton sold his soul to the Commodore a long time ago. Laurey owns that kid. That gives him the right to use Wharton and all his contacts. And the Commodore doesn't miss many tricks."

"I'll keep it in mind. Anything *else* happen I need to know about?" Chane asked.

"Latitia Laurey came by to see you."

Chane frowned.

"She said she'd be back."

The telephone rang. "Damn." He picked it up and spoke into the mouthpiece. "Yes."

"You sound so businesslike," a woman's voice said.

About mid-sentence he recognized it as Latitia's, and he was disappointed it wasn't Jennie.

"Chane, it's Latitia."

"Hello. What can I do for you?"

"Not a very good job of keeping the disappointment out of your voice. I'm in the lobby. Would you rather come out, or shall I come in?"

Chane had been dreading this confrontation. He'd put her off for the first two weeks, then she'd gone out of town for three weeks, and now it was time to face her. His first impulse was to have her come to his office, but he rejected that. Perhaps she would be intimidated by an audience. "I'll come out."

In the lobby, he found her engaged in conversation with an elderly gentleman. Her slim black patent slipper tapped nervously on the marble slab circling the water fountain in the center of the lobby. At sight of him, she excused herself and strolled forward, her face breaking into a smile.

Latitia had beautiful bone structure, a full mouth, and sultry brown "bedroom eyes." Her luscious body was encased in a flawlessly tailored red satin gown, and her auburn hair was arranged in a cascade of curls that complemented her dusky rose complexion.

"You look wonderful," she said, her dark eyes intent on his. She leaned close to him and sighed. "You smell wonderful, too. I'm not sure I can wait until the Van Vleet girl is through with you."

Damn her, Chane thought. Latitia always managed to kindle a fire in his loins. "What are you doing out in such bad weather?" he asked, hoping to sidetrack her from the topic she seemed most interested in. It had been snowing all day. The temperature was still dropping.

She took his arm and steered him toward the Burgundy Room. "Relax. Your little ballerina is working. She works for hours and hours. With her stamina, she must be wonderful in bed…"

Chane scowled, but kept quiet.

Latitia laughed at his disapproval. "She's a Van Vleet, darling. She's *accustomed* to being talked about."

The muscle in his jaw began to twitch. "Jennie is not like her parents," he said coldly.

Latitia laughed. "My my. It *is* love." Latitia went up on tiptoe as if she were going to kiss his cheek.

Chane stepped back. "Behave yourself. We're in public here."

"Behave myself?" she asked bitterly, flushing. "I *did* behave myself, and look where it got me. My man took up with another woman."

"So, where are you going from here?" he asked, hoping to remind her of other business.

Latitia giggled. "Don't look so frustrated, darling, I'll go when I've had my say."

"Which is?"

"You come from a very traditional family, Chane. Your mother is the only woman I know who has been faithful to her husband. You aren't going to be happy with a woman who doesn't know the meaning of fidelity."

Chane clamped his jaws. A gentleman could not do anything more; according to his father, anyway.

Latitia's eyes narrowed in spiteful anger. "Like it or not, it's true. Reginald bedded every woman in New York except the hopelessly ugly. Cocksman *extraordinaire*. And Vivian was his female counterpart. I understand Peter is following in their footsteps. He was expelled from Harvard for being caught with a girl in his bedroom after lights out.

"Of course, that probably means that Jennifer inherited their insatiable penchant for pleasuring herself. She had to have learned something from watching her father's *petite mademoiselles* parade through the house."

"Get to the point," he said grimly, wondering how he had ever thought Latitia attractive.

"I can see you don't want to hear this now," she said bitterly. "The new love affair is too grand. You're in rut for her, and who could blame you? Attracted as you are by low types. Well, play it out, at least until she shows her true colors, but be warned. I will not wait forever."

"Thanks for the warning," he said.

Latitia pulled her coat around her. "No need to see me out. I'm meeting some—oh, here he is now," she said, smiling at Frederick Van Buren. "Ta ta, darling."

Latitia took Frederick's arm. She enjoyed the feeling of physical power that emanated from him almost as much as the look of chagrin on Chane's face as she turned away. Let him stew. As soon as he'd stopped returning her calls, she had started doing some snooping of her own. She'd discovered that Jennifer Van Vleet was the reason for his lapses. A few more contacts revealed that Jennifer had had a brief affair with Frederick last year. Latitia decided that since Chane seemed determined to have an affair with Jennifer, she might as well back off until he got it out of his system. When Chane tired of that anemic little bird, he would be back. In the meantime, just in case, she would find out as much as she could about Frederick and Jennifer's romance.

Frederick took her to his apartment, which was little more than a place to eat and sleep. They talked for an hour about his career. Latitia knew exactly what he was hoping for from her, and she led him on. He had a reputation among her married friends as a man who knew his way around a woman. He held no fear for her, though. She knew her way around a man. She'd learned from her mother, who was one of the most successful of her time. Latitia had become curious about her parents and their relationship. By age ten she had become an accomplished sleuth, spying on them night and day. The moment that changed her life came after an afternoon of bickering between them. Latitia followed them upstairs and hid in her secret place, pressing her ear against the wall of their bedroom.

Her father continued to bicker at her mother. Suddenly, clear and strong, she heard her mother say, "Conrad, take your pants down."

Her father was silent for a moment. "You think that will solve this problem?"

Her mother gave a low, confident laugh. "It's solved all the others. Why not this one?"

Latitia heard the sound of clothes rustling and then she heard moans. Her father was a contented man the rest of that day. At barely ten years old, she realized that sex was the most powerful tool in the world. And once she had made that discovery, she spent all of her spare time figuring out how to use it. Unlike her friends, who were terrified of the very subject, she immersed herself in it. By the time she was twelve, she had seduced the handyman into building her a better spying place. She watched her mother's every move and noticed what worked and what didn't. Then she seduced the butler into becoming her ally. Shortly, she had a secret network of men who would do anything she asked. Sex was power, and she was the master, not the victim, as most of her friends appeared to be. She learned how to avoid pregnancy, how to lead any man anywhere, how to get what she wanted, and how to deliver anything a man wanted—for a price. It was never money. Always power.

Frederick glowed with the attention she was giving him. He was almost too easy a conquest. He would have sold his soul for a powerful sponsor who would assure him of star treatment at a fine ballet company.

"So," she asked, leaning forward to fondle his cheek, "how big shall we have them make the star on your door?"

"Big!" he said, grinning.

"This big?" she asked, reaching down to feel his manhood. Under her groping hand it swelled to twice its former size.

"Bigger," he said, his voice showing both surprise and passion.

She fondled him again. "This big?" she asked as it continued to swell.

"Yes…yes."

Latitia laughed. The ambitious young dancer had forgotten what they were talking about. His hand came up to squeeze her breast. His breath was coming faster now. She allowed him to roll her off the sofa and onto the floor, kissing her passionately the whole time.

She ended the kiss and whispered, "You have a beautiful body. I want you naked."

Swelling with pride, he helped her stand. She pressed him close and kissed him deeply. A satisfying jolt of energy passed between them. They tore off their clothes, kissing and whispering nonsense all the way to the bedroom. Frederick was passionate and strong. He made love to her four times before he rolled off her, mumbled something, and fell into a deep sleep.

This was what she had been waiting for. Latitia lifted his arm and slid away from him. She washed quietly over the washbowl and dressed herself with Frederick snoring softly on the bed behind her. Then she methodically searched his bedroom. She rummaged through the chest of drawers and then the armoire, looking for anything Jennifer might have left behind.

In a book hidden in the bottom drawer of the armoire she found a packet tied in brown paper. She untied the string and lifted out photographs. The room was too dimly lit. She walked into the parlor and turned up the lamp. The photographs were of Jennifer Van Vleet and Frederick Van Buren naked.

Latitia knew from her cousin Derek that one of the first things men did with the new, faster cameras was to capture naked women on film. It was all the rage. Photographs of naked women were highly prized. She knew because she had found Derek's photographs and teased him about them. He said most of the women photographed were professional models or prostitutes, but apparently a few so-called good women were letting themselves be talked into posing as well.

"Thank you, God," Latitia whispered, slipping the photographs into her purse. Then she walked back into the bedroom, leaned down and kissed Frederick lightly on the cheek, and let herself out the front door.

Five-thirty. Chane stood up and walked carefully around his desk. He checked his reflection in the mirror. He looked like she'd already told him the bad news. Steve joined him. In the lobby, a young man nodded at him, but Chane was lost in his own thoughts and didn't respond. As the attendant closed the elevator door, Chane saw Steve grimace.

"What was that?" Chane asked.

"The man you just cut?"

"I didn't cut him. I just didn't react in time."

"That was Jennie's brother, and I don't think he made that fine a distinction. I was watching his face after he passed you."

"Damn. Stop the elevator," Chane directed.

Edwin, the operator, reached for the lever to stop the lift, but the braid on his sleeve caught on one of the exposed gears. By the time he untangled his sleeve, the lift had risen to the second floor.

Chane ordered Edwin to return to the main floor, but by then Jennifer's brother was nowhere in sight.

"Damn!" Chane muttered under his breath.

CHAPTER ELEVEN

Bellini watched Jennifer Van Vleet, and a smile started at his toes and filled his entire body with energy. She had lied to him. Only a week ago Jennifer said she did not have the maturity to dance the role of Juliet in the Shakespearean ballet, yet today she danced as if she knew that Juliet embodied eternal woman, hopelessly in love in spite of everything. The enmity of the Montagues and Capulets meant nothing to her.

The Juliet before him bespoke a creative maturity he found amazing in one as young as Jennifer Van Vleet. He had known other dancers who found this level of identification with the heroine only at the end of their careers.

He remembered it was only rehearsal, and prayed she could re-create this mood during the show tonight. Other dancers looked askance at him, waited for him to call for a break. He ignored them. As Jennifer danced, Juliet's tragedy was clearly revealed to him and, he felt sure, anyone else watching.

When he could ignore a mistake by Simone no longer, he rapped his cane on the floor and showed her how she was supposed to execute her entry, then worked with Bettina, who had a tendency to get lazy.

Bellini stepped back and nodded to Jennifer, and she resumed her role as effortlessly as before. She breezed through the surprise and excitement of the first ball, the ecstasy of the first tryst with Romeo, the beauty and chasteness of the marriage ceremony, even the conquest of fear at the deathbed.

No matter how many times he had to stop the rehearsal and restart it because some minor dancer had forgotten her place, or leaped forward when she should have leaped backward, Jennifer's rendition of Juliet remained clearly drawn, beautifully understated, and thoroughly alive. Bellini could barely contain his excitement.

Never had he let a rehearsal play through from beginning to end, but he could not help himself with this one. He let things pass, just to continue watching Jennifer's complete absorption in her role. Dancers looked at him questioningly from time to time, but most were as caught up in Jennifer's portrayal of Juliet as he.

Chane watched from the wings. He had wanted to wait in his office or upstairs, but he couldn't. So he had finally given in and come down to watch the rehearsal. At least he'd know what time the ballet company broke for dinner. If he were upstairs...

Simone Marcelline, arms over her head, danced her way off stage *en pointe*. Taking a deep breath, she walked over to Chane. "Jennifer is possessed, *non?*"

"What's happening?"

One of the stage hands tossed Simone a towel. She wiped her hot face. "Who knows? Bellini is mad, a lunatic. He has almost killed all of us. Perhaps Jennifer has caught his madness. She dances like one possessed. Perhaps we will have to have her exorcised by the priests. But she is so beautiful."

"Aren't you supposed to be out there?" His own gaze went back to the spectacle of Jennifer, about to take the poison over the body of Romeo. Her portrayal quickened his heart and made his chest ache. He reminded himself that this was only a story, and that Jennifer was not about to die. But his chest had been aching ever since he had talked to her earlier.

Simone's voice brought him back to reality. "But of course, it is only rehearsal. No one will know or care. Not with Jennifer dancing in this fashion. The rest of us are only window dressing."

Chane glanced at Simone and was surprised to see her eyes shining with tears, her forehead puckered with the effort not to cry.

He had thought Jennifer was dancing brilliantly. Simone's reaction, mirrored on the faces of others who watched from the wings, confirmed it.

Jennifer pantomimed raising the goblet filled with poison to her lips. Chane held his breath while she drank it and slipped into the posture of death. An unexpected vise clamped around his heart. This was only a ballet, and yet his throat ached as if both Juliet and Jennifer had died. Beside him, Simone sobbed once and dissolved into tears and audible crying.

"Jesus!" Chane muttered. He'd never realized that ballet could be such an emotional experience. Bellini stood up from his seat in the fifth row and applauded. The opera company joined him. Chane clapped loudly, needing the release it offered.

Jennifer rose, bowed low, and tried to walk from the stage. The male dancer who had played Romeo rushed after her, caught her hand, and led her back to center stage.

"This is only rehearsal," Jennifer protested.

The young man shook his head. "Perhaps for you." He held her hand and presented her to the imaginary audience as if they were in their seats, stamping for an encore. Jennifer laughed, shook her head at the absurdity of it, and slipped her fingers out of the young man's hand. The other dancers, many wiping away tears, crowded around her. Bellini rapped his cane.

"Show time at eight."

Chane stepped forward to block Jennie's path. "You must eat something after that incredible performance. I had Mrs. Lillian prepare a light supper. We can eat in my suite."

Jennifer felt her legs buckling under her, but Chane's need to be with her exceeded her need to evade him. She nodded.

He followed her to her dressing room, helped her into her dressing gown, and led her through the back way to his private elevator. He didn't try to talk to her. He knew something had changed, and he wasn't ready to hear what it was.

The table before the fireplace had been set with gold table service. Light from the fire added a golden glow to the crystal goblets and warmed the bone china plates. Serving dishes gleamed on a mahogany and brass rolling cart beside the table.

Jennifer took in the elegance and abundance, and her stomach lurched. She would not be able to eat, but she allowed Chane to seat her.

His warm hand lingered on her shoulder. He had probably meant only to brush her bare skin in passing, but his hand quivered as if it could not bring itself to break contact. Jennifer closed her eyes. An ache spread out from her heart and encompassed her entire body. While she had danced, she'd forgotten everything except the world of Romeo and Juliet. Remembering Chane and the way she had chosen to solve her problem, she felt darkness filling her body and mind.

"Please, Jennie. Tell me what's wrong," he said softly.

"What?" The question was not unexpected, but Jennifer's mind refused to comprehend it. She turned and her elbow hit the crystal goblet, knocking it over, spilling the wine.

"Oh, no!" She reached for her napkin to dab at the reddish liquid soaking into the rich, dark blue lace of the tablecloth.

"Leave it," he commanded, taking the napkin from her, then taking her hands and lifting her to her feet. "We need to talk."

His face told her he knew she had made a decision. His eyes had lost their sparkle. An ache spread into her, then oddly turned to joy, knowing that he suffered, too. Part of her seemed to come alive.

"You've got something to tell me," he said.

She wanted to escape so she would not have to say the words that would drive a permanent wedge between them, but she knew she was trapped. Before tonight, before Bellini's standing ovation, she had still entertained the idea of telling Chane she would marry him, bear his children, and love him forever. But she had seen proof of her talent in Bellini's face. It produced a joy in her that delivered a death blow to her other hopes and dreams. She was a true prima ballerina.

The talent she had honed and struggled to attain had finally evolved into something that even she could ascertain. She would have an opportunity few other ballerinas ever hoped to have. She had felt it inside her tonight. She had prayed for this gift for too long to turn her back on it now.

And yet she could not remember what she had decided to say to Chane, who obviously loved her. His dread of hearing the words that would doom their love was almost audible.

"It's over, then?" he whispered.

Jennifer nodded.

"What happened?"

Her mind made no picture of what had happened. She could not remember why she was ending their love affair, or if she had been in love at all.

Chane pulled her close and held her. Her body reacted as a dry sponge reacts to water, soaking up his warmth and vitality. Tears slipped down her cheeks. "Oh, Jennie, love," he whispered. "Tell me what I did. If you would just tell me…"

She could control herself no longer. A sob shook her body. He enfolded her more tightly. "Jennie, for God's sake, tell me what's wrong."

Her hand closed around a small lump in her pocket. Tears welled up in her eyes.

Last night Bettina had given her the address of an herbologist only three houses from the grocery store where the Van Vleet cook shopped. Early this morning on her way to the Bricewood she had stopped at the woman's house. She now had a small wad of cotton root bark and instructions for boiling a tablespoon of the bark in a quart of water.

"Only take one swallow at a time. And no more than a cup a day. Else it might kill you," the old woman had said. Bettina swore by it.

"I'm dying." Where did those words come from?

Chane held her away from him and searched her face. "You're what?" His hands bit into her shoulders. "What? Tell me."

A knock sounded on the door.

Chane looked as though he was going to ignore it.

"You'd better answer it," she said.

"Tell me," he urged.

The knock came louder, more insistent. The loud knocking and Chane's intensity befuddled her so thoroughly she couldn't think. She blurted out the truth. "I'm expecting."

Relief showed clearly on his face. "Thank God! I thought you really were dying." A warm light rekindled in his green eyes. He pulled her back into his arms. Jennifer tried to figure out why she had handled this so badly, but her heart was pounding.

The knock sounded again, louder still.

Chane lowered her feet to the floor, steadied her as if she had not been landing on her feet for years, and touched her cheek with his right hand.

"I love you, Jennie. I know you think this is a terrible problem, and, momentarily, I'll grant you it is, but it will be a joy and a blessing long after it stops being a problem."

His hand dropped from her cheek to press lightly over her belly. "Tell your mother not to worry, little one."

He was the boldest, oddest man she had ever known. Not even her father, who was notoriously odd, had ever talked to an unborn baby and acted as if it could hear.

Chane stalked to the door and opened it. Steve looked grim. Chane stepped out into the hall.

"I'm sorry to bother you," Steve said. "But I need to talk to you about something right away."

"Can't it wait until tomorrow?" Chane asked.

"No," Steve said, clearing his throat nervously. "Meet me in the office."

Chane sighed. "All right. But give me ten minutes with Jennie first." Steve nodded and left.

Chane returned to the room. His hands encircled her waist as he turned her to face him. "We have to talk, Jennie…"

"There's nothing to talk about. I shouldn't have told you. I don't know why I did."

"You *should* have told me. You did the right thing. Tonight, after your performance, we'll talk," he said firmly, looking into her eyes. "Tomorrow's your day off. I have to be in Washington, D.C., by noon the day after tomorrow. I'm going to sail there. You'll come along so we can talk this out." Chane knew he couldn't afford to let her make this decision alone. With any time away from him, she might do it, too.

Without waiting for her to reply, he turned her and pulled her into his arms. He raised her face, and fresh tears slipped down her cheeks. He kissed them off. "Poor baby. Poor, poor baby," he crooned. The more he repeated it, the harder she cried. He held her until the rigidity left her tense body and her tears stopped.

He hated to leave her, but Steve had sounded terribly upset—and he never cried wolf. Even so, relinquishing Jennie was the hardest thing he'd ever done.

"I wish I didn't have to go, but Steve's waiting for me. Eat something."

Jennifer sniffed. For the first time in days she felt hungry. Chane knelt beside the table, pulled her down into her chair, and lifted a warm roll to her lips. It smelled yeasty and buttery. He nudged it against her lips until she took a bite. Her stomach growled.

"Eat and rest. I'll be back as soon as I can. If I don't see you before the performance, I'll see you after."

"What about you?"

"I'm not hungry."

When Chane left, Jennifer ate a little of everything on the serving table. She fell asleep in front of the fire, woke with a start, and searched the room for a clock. Seven-twenty. She barely had time to get made up for her performance.

In his office Steve told Chane the bad news. "Peter Van Vleet lost twenty thousand dollars playing roulette."

"Dollars or his marker?"

"His marker. What do you want us to do?"

"Ignore it. If he volunteers to pay it, fine. If he doesn't, fine."

Steve sat back. "That's what I thought you'd say."

"Steve, I'm going to marry Jennie."

Steve nodded. "Does she know?"

"Not yet, but she will."

By the time Jennifer reached the grand ballroom where the ballet company waited, she knew she had been wrong to tell Chane she was expecting, and even more wrong to agree to discuss it with him. She couldn't undo either, but she wouldn't go to Washington with him. She would tell him she had changed her mind.

Halfway through *Romeo and Juliet*, Jennifer glanced into the fourth wings and saw Chane slip into place beside one of the stage hands waiting to make the last prop change.

She finished the ballet with a pounding heart, and the audience surged to its feet. Curtsying, she held Frederick's hand and smiled at the tapestry of enthusiastic faces.

Taking her reverences, alternately bowing low and stepping toward the side of the stage, Jennifer finally reached the wings, accepted the towel Jim Farmer held out to her, and blotted sweat from her face. The applause became more thunderous. When it reached a crescendo, she swung the towel at Farmer and stepped back onto the stage to take another bow. She smiled, blew kisses, bowed deeply, then stepped behind the curtains.

"Juliet! Juliet! Juliet!" The crowd chanted and clapped with wild abandon and jubilation. Each time Jennifer stepped on stage to take another bow, Simone, smiling from the opposite wings, raised another finger. Ushers walked briskly down the aisles toward the stage, carrying enormous bouquets of roses, which they laid at Jennifer's feet. After the tenth curtain call, another ballerina joined Simone to add her fingers to the count. No one in the company had ever gotten more than ten curtain calls.

Jason showed his pass to the old man at the side entry. The man scowled at the pass and then looked at Jason's eyes very sharply for a minute. Jason held his bouquet of roses up a little higher and smiled right into the old man's eyes. Finally, the man nodded and let Jason pass. A flush of self-confidence warmed him. Smiles were a sight more useful than most people realized. He'd found if he smiled at a girl enough and said nice things to her, most girls would let him do just about anything, even tie them up. And once he got a girl tied up, he could take his time killing her as slow as he wanted.

From the stage, music filled the air. He could imagine the girls all on stage, looking pretty in their getups. He passed the big, communal dressing room, then found the first private room.

He pushed the door aside and peered in. The room was small. There was a rack holding a few costumes. And a mirror encircled with those newfangled electric lights dominated the wall opposite the door.

Jason heard footsteps and slipped into the room. The footsteps kept coming. He glanced around, saw the closet, and slipped into it just as the footsteps crossed the threshold.

At last, after the fifteenth curtain call, Jennifer stepped backstage, and the clapping subsided.

She felt grateful the show was over. Her cheeks ached from smiling. At the thought of facing Chane Kincaid and telling him her decision, her legs had grown weak. She'd brushed past smiling stage hands, accepted hugs from a bevy of misty-eyed ballerinas, smiled at Bellini's beaming face, and held Simone while Simone sobbed and whispered wild praise. Even Bettina, who never cried, looked deeply affected.

At last Jennifer escaped. The others seemed too keyed up to follow. They stayed behind, chattering among themselves. She avoided the fourth wings, where Chane waited, and ran toward her dressing room. She would not go with Chane. She knew what she had to do, but when she was with him she seemed to forget.

He mesmerized her with his deep, melodious, slightly British voice, and her mind forgot its own business and became caught up in his business. She could not tell if he tricked her or if her own mind did the trick. Perhaps her mind only appeared to work on her behalf. Then when Chane came near her, she still expected it to take care of business, but it did what her body, longing for him, wanted to do. It was too complicated for her to figure out. She decided the safest plan was simply to avoid him.

In the corridor, Jennie slowed down. Now that the tension of dancing had started to drain out of her, she felt the fatigue all the way to her bones. She would hurry home, have Augustine draw a warm bath, drink a glass of milk, and then sleep for ten hours.

She stepped inside her private dressing room, closed the door, and leaned against it. She had evaded Chane. Tears of sadness or exhaustion ran down her cheeks.

"You were even better than in rehearsal."

At the sound of Chane's smoky voice, Jennie froze in the doorway. Before she could think or move, his arms enveloped her and she was pulled into his familiar warmth. His mouth kissed the tears off her face. Her mind twitched as if it wanted to struggle against him, but her body refused. His warm lips claimed hers, and Jennie felt her arms lift and twine around his neck. Her hands already resented the jacket he wore because she couldn't feel the long, smooth muscles of his back.

Part of her still knew this was insanity, but another part promised she would just take these few kisses before telling him. Just as soon as her body stopped trembling with need.

He kissed her long and slow—fiercely and scaldingly—and she knew nothing except how his mouth tasted, how his skin smelled, and how her body ached to press itself closer to his.

Chane kissed her until he knew she wouldn't fight with him anymore, then lifted her into his arms and carried her out the private side door to his waiting carriage.

"Where are you—"

"Hush," he whispered. She tried to sit up, but he pulled her back into his arms and kissed her until someone tapped lightly on the door. Jennifer opened her eyes to see Augustine climbing into a second carriage with a bag, and looked askance at Chane.

He squeezed Jennifer's hand and brushed the hair off her face. "I took the liberty of having Augustine pack an overnight bag for you."

"I can't stay overnight with you."

"Not alone, you can't, but Augustine is coming with us."

He answered every protest with a kiss.

A dory waited at the harbor. Chane bundled them in furs. Snow fell steadily, but the ocean was strangely calm and quiet. She found herself sitting in a small boat being rowed out to Kincaid's yacht. The boat slipped through water effortlessly.

Temperatures had been below freezing for five days. The moisture in the air felt like ice.

In a surprisingly short time, the dory gently bumped up against a long, low-slung yacht, its masts and yardarms weighted with half a foot of snow.

A man in gold braid came forward to meet them.

"Evening, Captain. When will we get under way?" Chane asked, steadying Jennifer with a warm hand.

"The tide's going out now, but as you can see, we're becalmed. Strangest weather I've ever seen. If the wind comes up, we'll be in D.C. by early morning. If not…"

Men helped them out of the dory and onto the deck of the yacht. Chane arranged for Augustine's comfort, then carried Jennifer to a beautifully decorated suite of rooms.

Although Chane had brought Augustine along as chaperone, he put her in another room, so she wouldn't bother them if they wanted to make love. It was hypocrisy, but to come without a chaperone would have been insanity. Reputations were lost over technicalities, while people did exactly as they wanted. Jennifer's parents had lived quite happily among such craziness, but it made her head spin to try to remember all of the rules.

Chane led her to the bed that dominated one side of the small room and unwrapped her. Then he was kissing her again, urgently and hungrily, as if he would never let her go.

Jennifer floated in warm silence, the silence broken only by the soft sounds of their kisses and the lapping of the water against the ship's hull. Her body pressed blindly against his, her heart beat with his, her senses ignored everything except the warm, manly fragrance that was purely his. No man in the history of the world had ever smelled or tasted quite like this man.

Chane made love to her, and the world was reduced to flesh on flesh and the blood roaring in her ears, pounding through her, burning into her until she was only female to his male, softness to his hardness.

Afterward, he rolled over and pulled her on top of him. His hands stroked her back and buttocks. "Jennie, love, what you do to me," he whispered, and brushed damp hair off her face. He kissed her eyes, her cheeks, her throat, and then her eyes again, kissing away tears she didn't remember crying.

"Jennie, love, you've cast a spell over me. Are witches blond? I always imagined they'd have long, black, stringy hair, not shimmering strands of silver and the face of an angel."

They made love again, this time without urgency. Then, at last, they were able to talk—quietly, still enmeshed, still clinging together deliciously, naturally. Nothing mattered except each other.

Jennifer found it curious how a decision could get lost in her head while she did all kinds of things that flew in the face of the decision. She had made her decision carefully. Now it had no more weight than a balloon.

"I watched you tonight, dancing," Chane said. "You're so damned good it made me hurt all over. You had that crowd right here." He kissed the palm of her hand. "I didn't really think a ballerina could do so much with a story I know so well. You were wonderful."

The minute he reminded her she was a ballerina, the balloon popped. Now she had to tell him her decision, but it didn't feel like hers anymore. It felt like something her mother thought up.

"You almost gave me a heart attack with that costume you wore tonight. Those leggings looked like skintight gloves with a short skirt that didn't hide a damned thing."

"It reached all the way to my knees."

"Haven't you ever heard of corsets or stays? Dammit, Jennie, you're going to drive some man into a frenzy."

Jennie laughed. "I thought I already had."

"I mean someone else," he growled.

Despite her decision, which might or might not be hers, she still loved it when his voice became gruff and possessive and his big, warm hands caressed her, as if gentling a skittish mare. She remembered her decision, but it didn't seem like anything that needed to be acted on right away. Tomorrow would be soon enough.

"Does this mean you might fire me?" she asked hopefully.

Chane kissed her cheek and nibbled from just below her eye to her throat. "Fire you? Didn't you read the contract you signed?" His voice teased her.

"I trusted Sam to—"

Chane chuckled. "Never trust an agent. Didn't your attorney ever warn you about men like me?"

Vaguely, she realized that her mind had tricked her in this way before, but she couldn't seem to stop herself. She loved playing these games with him.

"I know you would never take advantage of me," she whispered, using her most innocent voice.

Chane chuckled and rolled her over to pin her beneath him. "Of course not. The contract was written by one of the best attorneys in New York. Besides, a smart woman like you will have no problem satisfying my simple needs." His hands bit into the softness of her shoulders, slipped down to cup her breasts. Jennifer moaned softly.

"Ever heard of white slavery?" He leaned down and bit at her nipples. His fingers dug into her hipbones. "I mean, before you signed that agreement?" he asked, his tone ominous. A fever started where she didn't think it could again so soon.

"Don't worry, love," Chane said gruffly, his hands rough and possessive on her sweat-slippery flesh. "I'll only use you for my own personal needs, unless—" He scowled down at her. "—unless you think that would be too dull for you…"

"What if I refuse?"

"Then I'd have to punish you," he said, his voice intimate and husky.

"Punish me?" she whispered, dazed by the very real feeling of submissiveness that had overwhelmed her.

"Of course, someone has to do it." Now his tone was innocent, accommodating.

"But why me?"

"Because you are very beautiful and very tempting. You don't think I would waste my time otherwise, do you? I have standards."

"But I haven't done anything to deserve punishment," she protested, her voice strangely breathless. Somehow her body had tricked her into getting caught up in the game. Her heart pounded as if it truly believed Kincaid was capable of doing terrible, wonderful things to her against her will.

His hands moved to her hips, tightened there, pressed her against him. "It's only a matter of time before you do something."

"Like what?"

"Oh, like arouse my baser needs. You could do that. In spite of my iron control."

"Iron control?" She snickered.

"Or you might insult me," he said ominously. His fingers bit into her hipbones again and found a sensitive place that made her laugh and cry out. He shook her gently. "You see how naughty and impulsive you are?"

"How could I be held responsible for your becoming aroused?"

"Who else? I'm an innocent victim."

"You're impossible, that's what you are."

"It's all right for a man to be impossible."

In mock despair, Jennifer covered her forehead with her arm.

Chane kissed her exposed breast. "I come from a long line of impossible men. Kincaid men are descended from a savage breed of ravishing Moors who spent all their time charging around the English countryside and carrying off fair-haired Saxon wenches. That's why Englishwomen are so lovely. We only spared the prettiest ones."

"Will ye be killing me then, sire?"

Chane's hand caught the hair at the back of her neck and pulled until her throat arched back. Heat flushed into her loins and wrung a moan of pure need and surprise from her lips. Chane's eyes burned into hers and his hand tightened in her hair, increasing the response that had devastated her. Slowly, as if satisfied that he had her attention and that she knew inescapably he was not teasing now, and maybe had not been teasing at all, he lowered his head and pressed his lips against the pulse that punched against her throat. "You will die a thousand deaths, my sweet wench, just as I will," he whispered.

His other hand touched her, spread her, levered himself into a position to claim her. His warm smoothness impaled her, and she pulled his mouth down to hers.

Jennifer woke slowly. Her eyes opened but she couldn't focus. She blinked. Still out of focus. She struggled into a sitting position. That was a mistake. Cold bit into her skin despite the squat, blackened stove in the middle of the small cabin.

Jennifer shivered and pulled the covers over her head. She remembered instantly where she was, but something felt wrong. The ship didn't rock. Every ship she had ever been on rocked with a recognizable sway and creaked with the sounds of the ocean against the hull. Two round portholes, fastened against the cold, were frosted over. She could see nothing except diffuse whiteness.

Outside, the wind, which had been still last night, howled loudly against the ship, but the ship did not appear to rock. Perhaps it had run aground and been abandoned.

Alarmed, Jennifer struggled out of bed. The floor felt like ice against her bare feet. Someone had laid her clothes out for her. The water in the basin was still warm. Close to the fire the room felt warm enough to allow her to slip out of her nightgown. She washed quickly, dressed herself, struggled into her coat, opened the door and stepped outside.

The howling wind caught the door and almost pulled it out of her hands. Swirling snow blinded her. She wrestled the door closed and turned to see an unbelievable sight—the ship caught like a fly on flypaper in the middle of New York harbor, which had frozen solid, trapping Chane's yacht and a half dozen other ships. Snow fell thickly, softening every outline.

Sailors in yellow slickers stood at the rails and looked at the city, several hundred yards away, blanketed with more snow than Jennifer had ever seen in New York.

Chane saw her instantly. Hanging onto the ropes strung across the ship, he inched his way across the icy deck to her side.

"What happened?" she yelled over the wind's howling.

"We were becalmed for several hours last night, long enough for the ocean to freeze around us. Then the snow came, then the storm."

Jennifer had never seen such a thing. Part of her did not believe it possible. "So, what do we do?"

Chane grinned. "We relax. We're trapped here."

"Are you a warlock?" she asked suddenly.

Chane laughed.

"Well," she said, laughing, "you have to admit that you seem to get more help from the elements than any man I've ever known. Theaters burn down. Ships freeze in the ocean. Almost anything is likely if it serves your purpose."

His healthy skin had been reddened by the icy winds, and his green eyes twinkled with good spirits. He smiled at her with such love, joy, and warmth that she almost wept. Then the cold seeped into her bones and she shivered.

"Seen enough?" he asked.

Jennifer nodded. Kincaid opened the door to their cabin, scooped her inside, and closed the door. "How am I going to get back to town?" she asked.

"It'll go one of two ways. Either the ice will break up quickly and we can sail into the inner harbor, or it'll get thick enough to walk on."

"That could take days."

"This happened in Boston harbor fifty years or so ago. The captain was just telling me about it. Ships were stuck for weeks."

"I can't be stuck for weeks."

Chane looked up at the ceiling. "You hear that, God?" His voice was stern and threatening. Jennifer laughed in spite of herself. Chane was doing it again. Acting as though even God might listen to his nonsense. She was accustomed to witty, outrageous men. Her mother had surrounded herself with them. But she had never met a man like Chane Kincaid. His sense of humor was different. She had not yet figured it out, or him. He was always surprising her.

"Don't be cross with me," he said gently. "I know you're upset, and with good reason."

"I'm not cross."

"Of course not. Your face only looks like a thundercloud."

"I have to get back into town."

"Everyone is entitled to a honeymoon. We can let the captain marry us here, and we'll honeymoon until the ice either thaws or thickens."

"I never said I would marry you..."

"You're carrying my baby. You can't marry anyone else." Gently, he pulled her close and kissed her. The warmth and taste of his mouth awakened a hunger in her that had nothing to do with physical desire. It had happened one other time, when she had held a tiny baby and smelled its sweet, powdery smell, and something deep inside her jolted awake.

"Don't kiss me like that," she said, burying her face against his soft woolen coat. Snowflakes had melted, leaving it slightly wet.

"How do you want me to kiss you?" Chane lifted her chin and looked at her as if her answer were the most important thing in the world. Jennifer tried to hang onto her decision, but even as she spoke she could feel it slipping away.

"My father asked our attorney, Mr. Berringer, to file a legal suit against you three months before he died. He claimed you cheated him out of millions of dollars. My brother thinks you bankrupted my father and caused him to kill my mother and himself." Jennifer couldn't believe she had blurted that out after so long. It seemed a betrayal of Peter.

"I never even met your father."

"According to the *Manhattan Times Record*—"

"We might as well get comfortable." Chane led her to the bed and sat her down on the edge of it. "This is going to take a while," he said, resigned. "My grandfather bought the St. Paul and Pacific Railroad from your father for four million dollars. Then he realized he'd bought himself a problem. He called me in and said if I could untangle the mess he'd bought, he'd give me a half interest in it. I spent eighteen months trying to keep the railroad running while I settled with everyone from the Knights of Labor to the suppliers. My hair almost turned gray. You see this silver at my temples? After I'd placated hundreds of people, a few senators and congressmen, the entire labor force of six cities along the route, and their labor unions, I had to take on your father."

"You didn't cheat him?"

"No." It was Chane's opinion that Reginald Van Vleet had cheated his grandfather by selling him railroad bonds representing a legal snarl, not a working railroad as implied in the purchase agreement, but he was not cruel enough to tell that to a dead man's daughter.

Jennifer digested that for a moment. "I'm confused. Why is my parents' attorney still probating the estate as a bankruptcy? Even though you paid our debts, we have no money to maintain the household. He's letting us live there as a courtesy until they finish the inventory."

"Ward Berringer is not a man of impeccable reputation. I wouldn't believe everything he said," Chane warned.

"My father must have trusted him."

Chane grinned. "You believe everything you're told, don't you?"

"Usually."

"You're going to be fun." He grinned. His eyes sparkled with challenge.

"Well, because you're worried," he said, "I'll have Tom Wilcox look into it. If your father died bankrupt, it was for some other reason. My grandfather paid four million dollars for that railroad. He didn't get it as a gift." He watched her for a moment. "We'll be married as soon as the captain can arrange it."

"I'm a ballerina." She groaned. "I can't marry."

"You're about to be a mother. You can't not marry."

"It isn't fair!" she snapped. "I've studied for twelve years and I'm just now beginning to reap the rewards for all my hard work. I might have starred in London. Now I'll miss my chance." Tears of anger welled up and spilled down her cheeks. She wiped furiously at them as if they were one more sign that her body was out of control. The angrier she became, the more she cried. Finally, she gave up and buried her face in her hands and just cried.

Chane had never realized before what pregnancy meant to a woman. Seeing Jennifer struggle with it brought the hardship home to him. She was a gifted artist about to be put out of business by her body engaging itself without her permission in the act of creating life. Many professions could be carried on without the body's help. He could still design buildings from a wheelchair if he had to. But Jennifer could not dance with a big belly.

He felt such tenderness for her suddenly. He had wanted her so desperately that he'd blithely given her his seed, as if it would be a blessing to her as well as to him. He might have ruined her. At the very least he had taken a beautiful, talented, spirited ballerina and used her like a broodmare. She could as easily die in childbirth as bring forth a healthy baby.

This realization chilled him. If he could, he would undo what he had done and set her free. His shame was so intense he couldn't speak or move.

Her shoulders shook with her weeping. Finally, her tears slowed. His own burden lifted enough that he could pull her into his arms and comfort her. "Jennie, love, please don't cry. Don't take it out on yourself. Take it out on me. I deserve it."

Like a little girl too stunned to understand, she rubbed her eyes and looked at him. "What?"

"I didn't realize what I was doing to you. God, Jennie, I'm so sorry. I can't tell you how sorry I am. I didn't mean to..."

Amazed, Jennifer looked up at him. His eyes were filled with misery. He gathered her into his arms. "I don't deserve you, Jennie. I'll never deserve you, but I promise you, if you marry me, I'll always take care of you and our baby. I'll do anything."

Jennifer sniffed. "Always?"

"I swear it on my grandmother's grave."

Her mind had resisted thinking about marriage as a solution to her problem. It resisted the whole idea of a baby, but if she didn't marry him, she would have to take the cotton-root-bark tea.

In her mind she saw a tiny duplicate of Chane curled in her womb. If she drank the tea, it would die. Her stomach knotted in revulsion. She wouldn't be able to do it. She probably wouldn't be strong enough to have a baby outside of wedlock, either.

"If I ever find out that you had anything to do with my parents' deaths, I will kill you," she said, sniffing back tears.

"If I ever find out that you married me for my money, I'll kill you," he said, grinning.

"I'm not joking."

"I know. But I'm not worried. I had nothing to do with it."

Jennifer sniffed. "I guess I will marry you."

Chane held her away from him. "What?"

"I guess I will..."

"Marry me?"

"I guess..."

With a sinking heart he realized that she did not love him with the same passion and intensity as he loved her, but he felt certain he could inspire whatever feelings in her he wanted once she had made a commitment to him. "You won't be sorry, Jennie. I promise you."

"It isn't fair, though."

"Life is not supposed to be fair, love. Otherwise we'd all be rich and male, and the species would die after one generation."

"I'm scared, Chane."

"I know, sweet, I know, but I promise you I will take care of you."

"What if you don't? What if you forget that you ever loved me?" She sniffed and gave one of those soft, shuddering breaths children take when crying themselves to sleep.

Tenderness overwhelmed him. "I won't. I can't. You're like a part of me. I'll always, always, always love you."

"I wish I didn't feel so scared."

"There's nothing to be afraid of. I'll protect you." He lifted her chin and kissed her until she relaxed in his arms.

"You won't forget?" she asked softly. He had never seen her so sweet or so vulnerable.

"I won't forget," he said gently.

"Okay, then." She looked like a person headed to the guillotine, not the wedding chapel.

"You won't be sorry, love."

Jennifer felt almost certain she was making a mistake, but felt it was a necessary one. She was miserable without Chane, and probably would be equally miserable married to him and raising his children instead of dancing. But her body had made the choice when it accepted his seed and let it grow.

There was only one thing that made marrying him seem to make sense, besides the baby. And it was a phrase she had heard long ago, which was used in a primitive culture that had no word for the term "love." Their nearest equivalent was "beautiful of the heart." Even the sight of Chane's craggy, angular face caused a feeling in her that could only be described as beautiful of the heart.

They were married at noon. The wind howled outside the captain's cabin, almost drowning out the words of the ceremony. Augustine cried, and Jennifer could barely speak the words. The captain kept clearing his throat. Chane looked so solemn and so handsome it almost hurt to look at him. When it was over, he bent down and kissed her tenderly.

Jennifer hugged Augustine, who wept discreetly into her handkerchief.

"I wish your brother could have been here, ma'am. He would be so…" Augustine's voice trailed into silence.

With a start of remembrance, Jennifer finished the sentence for her: *so…furious.* Oh, God, what had she done? Marrying her brother's worst enemy. And without even telling him…

CHAPTER TWELVE

The next morning Jennifer Van Vleet did not show up at practice. Bellini asked several of the girls about her, but no one seemed to know where she might be. He went to Kincaid's office to ask him, but he was not there.

That evening Simone went to Jennifer's house, knocked at the door, and waited in miserable silence. Her coat was not heavy enough for the icy wind that whipped her skirts and bit into her legs, and more importantly, she was terrified of the reception she would get from Peter.

At last the door opened. A tall, sterile-looking old man in severe black garb peered out at her. He seemed to resent having to open the door but was trying to hide that from her. Finally, he stepped back and motioned her inside. She complied, and he slammed the door against the storm. "What may I do for you?" he asked.

Simone appreciated that he had trusted her enough to let her in without first knowing her business. She doubted he remembered her. She had not been to the house in years.

"Is…is Jennifer here?"

"Mistress Jennifer is away."

"Is…Mr. Van Vleet here?"

"Who may I say is calling?"

"Simone…Marcelline." She hated giving him her name, because Peter probably would not see her if he knew it was her.

He nodded and started slowly up the stairs. Above the golden, intricately carved sideboard a portrait of Vivian Van Vleet, seated on a low Louis XV stool, looked blithely down on Simone. The entry hall was bigger than her entire flat. A fireplace crackled. Simone walked to the fire and held her hands toward the heat.

Footsteps sounded softly. Simone's heart raced. She turned and saw Peter pause at the bottom of the steps and then walk across the thick carpet to her side.

He looked as if he had just come home. His hair gleamed as if it were wet, his coat, which might have been hastily pulled on, looked damp as well.

"Is it still snowing?" he asked.

"Yes."

Her body felt hot, then cold, then hot again. All he had to do was speak to her and a fever started that seemed to wipe out her common sense. She had no reason to love Peter Van Vleet, but she did. His cool, incredibly blue eyes looked at her as if waiting for her to speak. His sensuous bottom lip had a small, almost imperceptible flat place, as if someone had touched it when he was very young and left an impression there. She tried to remember how his lips had felt, if she had felt the flat place when he kissed her, but her heart pounded so hard she could remember nothing.

Her body felt that something momentous was about to happen. Simone knew she would not be equal to it, just as she knew she was not really a dancer, the way Jennifer was.

"I was worried about Jennifer..." she said. Her voice sounded odd and small, as though about to betray her great agitation.

Peter held his hands toward the fire. His wrists were strong and manly. Even in wintertime his fine skin held its healthy color. He didn't look at Simone. "She went to Washington D.C. I expect her back—"

"We *expected* her, too—" Simone realized she had interrupted him, and embarrassment caused her voice to dwindle into silence.

"—this morning, actually, but she didn't come," he continued, his voice husky and rich. "She should have wired—" he said, realizing he had interrupted her and stopping abruptly.

"—yesterday. She missed the performance last—" she stopped just as abruptly.

"The weather has been beastly. Her boat may have washed ashore somewhere—"

"Bellini had to substitute—" Words kept jerking out of her mouth, interrupting him. Simone stopped speaking. She was incoherent. She was not making sense. He would think her an imbecile for coming here on such a weak pretense.

Peter had stopped speaking also. The silence stretched out. Finally, Simone said, "I guess I had best be going."

"It's cold out there. Would you like some hot tea?"

Part of her wanted to stay with him however she could, even when he offered things out of obligation. But part of her still had pride.

"No thank you. I must be going. I just wanted to be sure Jennifer was all right."

"I'm sure she is. She took Mamitchka. Augustine would never let anything happen to Jenn. She would let me know if they had a problem of some sort. I trust her."

"Well, thank you for letting me warm myself."

"Have you a ride back to the Bricewood?"

Simone searched his eyes. He had the most wonderful eyes she had ever looked into. They took her breath away. She wished she could say no, but she had asked the cab driver to wait for her. "I'm fine, thank you."

Peter walked her to the door, opened it for her, took her arm and helped her down the icy steps, across the sidewalk, and into the cab. Simone imagined she could feel the warmth of his strong hands through her thick coat. She felt giddy by the time she turned to face him. Again his fine blue eyes looked directly into hers.

"Thank you…"

"I'll tell Jenn you stopped by."

"Thank you."

The cabriolet started with a jerk and a loud crack as ice formed between the wheel and the street broke free. Simone waved. Peter turned and walked carefully up the steps, which had iced over again since their morning salting. His broad shoulders tapered into a lean waist and he carried himself like a young lord. Simone especially loved the way his head balanced on his sturdy neck, the angle of his strong chin…

The cab turned the corner. The Van Vleet house was now out of sight. Simone leaned back and covered her face with her hands. He had been nice to her! He had treated her like any decent person who had called on his sister. Her heart raced and pounded. Perhaps he *didn't* hate her.

Cautiously, Chane opened one eye. Jennie had come out of the small toilet adjoining their stateroom and had sat down in the rocking chair beside the potbellied stove in the middle of the cabin. She glanced over at him, and Chane simulated the deep breathing of sleep.

Thus assured of her privacy, Jennie leaned back in the chair and smiled. She rocked a few times, lifted her nightgown, and put her hands on her flat little belly. "You're lucky to have such a smart father," she said to the baby. "I didn't realize you were a baby yet. I hope I didn't frighten you. I wouldn't hurt you for anything in the world. It was just that I didn't know you were there yet."

She rocked a moment. "Maybe I just didn't realize it was time to stop being selfish. Ballerinas are a selfish lot. We think our aching backs and our aching toes are the center of the universe. It's a way of life. Maybe you'll grow up to be a ballerina. Then you'll understand. Or maybe you'll be a horseman like your uncle Peter. Or maybe a robber baron like your father."

Sighing, she rocked and stroked her belly. On the bed, Chane stretched, opened his eyes, and sat up.

Smiling, Jennifer patted her stomach. "I was just apologizing to our baby."

"You're going to make a beautiful mother."

"I'm probably going to be very bad at it."

"I have no doubts about your abilities in any area," he assured her.

A knock came at the door.

"That's my water!"

Jennie put on her dressing robe and opened the door to Augustine, who led a contingent of curious men into the cabin with a tub and buckets of steaming water.

They poured the water and left, and then to Chane's pleasure and amazement, Jennifer moved the screen aside as if it were nothing more than a nuisance. In plain sight, she stripped off her robe and nightgown and walked back to the steaming tub.

Chane sat up in bed to watch her. She stepped into the tub, sat down, and came right back up. "Hot!"

She stepped out of the tub, bent over, and picked up a bar of soap. Standing on towels next to the tub, she worked the washcloth into a fine lather and ran it over her legs, arms, and torso. Lamplight turned her skin golden. Soap bubbles blurred the sleek outlines of her body. Completely unselfconscious, she bent over to rinse her cloth. He'd never seen a finer line of thigh and buttocks.

She rinsed every part of her body with care, then tried the water again. This time she got in up to her waist before the heat drove her to stand up, panting. "It's still too hot."

Her slim waist and belly reminded him of a lithe, wiry kitten. "Take your time."

She sat down on the towels and trimmed her toenails and fingernails. He'd never enjoyed any sight more. He felt immensely privileged to watch her in such intimacy. To his regret, the water finally cooled and she eased herself into it.

"Want me to scrub your back?"

"That would be lovely."

Chane tossed the sheet aside and walked across the room to the tub. Jennifer smiled at the sight of him. He was well-made, in all areas. He had a strong, masculine body, covered with just the right amount of hair.

Chane knelt beside the tub and stuck his arm in the water to feel around for the washcloth. He ran his hand over her entire body before he found it. Jennifer had to put the soap into his hand. "You've missed it three times."

"How clumsy of me."

He scrubbed her back, her breasts, her shoulders, then turned her over and washed her hips and thighs and between her legs. "I've done all this," she protested.

"I just want to make sure you're clean."

His voice sounded thick.

"Oh, do you?" she teased.

"I don't allow dirty girls in bed with me. My wife wouldn't like it." Jennifer pinched him. Chane cleared his throat. "Actually, she'd probably like a break. She might be happy for any outside help she could get."

Jennifer pinched him harder this time.

"Owww!"

"Your wife might be the jealous sort," she said.

"Actually," he said, grinning, "I just wanted to feel your silky skin in the water."

"Maybe I'd like to feel your skin, too." To his delight, she took his hands and guided him into the water, which immediately began to spill out onto the floor.

"We're making a mess." Chane pulled her to her feet. Jennie knew it was too soon to make love again, but the feel of him so swollen and heavy against her belly made her breath come faster. Fortunately, he just held her close. She pressed her cheek against his chest and listened to the pounding of his heart. After a while she realized she didn't care if it was too soon. She slipped her hand down to squeeze him.

"Let's go back to bed," she whispered.

"No, he's all right."

"Liar!" She leaned back and smiled at him.

"That's no way to talk to your lord and master."

She loved the antic gleam in his eye when he teased her. She loved everything lately, ever since she had relaxed about when she would get back to the city.

"We're crazy, aren't we?" she asked, smiling into his eyes.

"I don't know about you," he said, "but I'm crazy in love."

Six days later Chane came back to the cabin with a long face.

"I hate to tell you this, princess, but the ice is probably thick enough to walk across."

"Is it dangerous?" Jennifer asked, glancing out the porthole. Few clouds dotted the bright blue sky, and the sun was so bright on the ice and snow, it almost blinded Jennifer.

Chane leaned close to her and lowered his voice to a whisper. "No more dangerous for you than going back to bed with me."

"Who cares if I fall through and have to swim back?" she teased. "The important thing," she whispered, pulling him close, "is to get out of bed with this maniac." Jennifer laughed and leaned close to his ear to whisper into it. "I know what the devil is now. It's a New York robber baron with nothing to do except make love to his new wife."

Reluctantly, Chane fetched Augustine to pack Jennifer's bag. When they were ready for the return trip, Chane led them outside. At the railing, Jennifer gazed across the frozen bay, covered with snow that sparkled in the bright sunlight.

"It's beautiful," she sighed.

"Not as beautiful as you," he whispered in her ear, guiding her hand to the rope ladder she was to climb down. He held her waist while she swung around to get into position. Wind whipped her hat, held down by a large scarf tied under her chin. Her weight on the rope caused it to bang against the side of the ship, almost knocking her feet off the rope.

"Ohhh!" she cried out.

"Wait," Chane said, pulling her back up onto the ship. "I'll climb down and steady the rope so it doesn't beat you to death against the ship."

That worked better. The climb down was hard on her hands, though. The rope was icy and burned through her thin gloves. At the bottom, Chane's hands caught her by the waist and lifted her down. She tapped her foot on the ice. It felt sturdy enough.

She glanced at her husband. It seemed strange to call him that. A week ago she had been single, and now she was married and expecting a baby. It amazed her how things could change so quickly.

Chane held the rope ladder so Augustine could climb down. A sailor lowered their bags on a rope. Chane untied them and hefted them for weight. Augustine tried to take her own bag so Chane wouldn't have to carry it, but he shook his head. Augustine looked at Jennifer as if expecting her to overrule Kincaid.

"You don't expect me to argue with him, do you?" Jennifer asked, smiling at Augustine, who seemed to genuinely like Chane.

"Follow me," he said, striding ahead of them. "Stay back at least ten feet. If we hit a thin place, there's no sense both of us going into that pneumonia water."

"You're a lot heavier than I am."

Out of the lee of the ship, the wind howled around them. Chane teased Jennifer, and they laughed halfway across the ice. At midpoint, when the ship behind them looked as small as a toy trapped in the ice, a stab of fear swept through her, filling her with unnamed dread. Her steps slowed. Chane turned around.

"Getting tired? We can stop."

Jennifer frowned and remained where she was. Chane put down the bags and walked back to take her into his arms. Augustine pretended to study the city's profile.

"Are you cold?" he asked softly.

"I'm scared."

"Of what?"

"I don't know."

He lifted her chin and looked deeply into her eyes. "I'll take care of you, princess. Always."

"But what if you stop loving me?"

"As long as I have breath in this body, I'll love you," he said quietly.

Something lightened in her. She reached up on tiptoe and kissed him. When the kiss ended, she sighed. "I'm okay now."

Chane strode back to the bags. They trudged over the snow-packed ice until they reached the wharf, where a crowd had gathered to watch them. People pointed and smiled. It was an event in New York—people walking from ships to the shore.

Men dropped a rope. Chane passed their luggage up, then turned to lift Jennifer up in his arms. With one arm holding the rope and the other her, he rappeled up the slippery bank. People cheered. He set her down gingerly and said to no one in particular, "My bride and I had to get back to town."

People smiled warmly. Jennifer felt she might be blushing. Her skin felt hot, but perhaps it was only the icy wind that burned her cheeks. Chane carried Augustine up the bank and hailed a cabriolet.

"Where to?" he asked Jennifer.

"To my house. I want to tell my brother before he hears it from someone else."

"Good idea."

The Van Vleet town house was surrounded by trees encased in ice from their trunks to the tips of their limbs. Fat, silvery icicles gleamed against the reddish-brown brick building and the blue sky. The sun shone brightly, but the wind was so cold nothing melted.

Peter was not home, but Malcomb beamed at the sight of Jennifer. "Good to see you safe, mademoiselle. Mr. Van Vleet went to a friend's country home—a weekend of riding, I believe."

Augustine volunteered to leave the Van Vleet town house and move to the Bricewood, but Jennifer took her aside and asked her to wait until she could discuss it with Peter.

"Mamitchka, please don't tell him I've married. I think it best I break the news myself."

"Yes, mademoiselle—madame!" she corrected herself.

"Call me the minute Peter returns," Jennifer said.

At the Bricewood, Steve was waiting with a list of emergencies needing special attention. Chane escorted Jennifer upstairs. Mrs. Lillian took one look at Chane's face and smiled.

"I'd like you to meet my wife," Chane said, grinning.

Mrs. Lillian hugged Jennifer and then Chane. "Your mother will be so happy." Then to Jennifer, "You see, they'd just about given up on him marrying. They'll be so pleased," she said, smiling brightly.

Mrs. Lillian had been a member of the Kincaid household since before Chane was born. She'd come from Sweden as a fourteen-year-old *au pair* girl to work for Number One, and had stayed to become the governess to two generations of Kincaid children. When Chane's parents began traveling extensively to keep track of their many investments, she came to live with Chane. She had cornflower blue eyes, pale skin that blushed easily, beautiful Swedish bone structure, and thick, silver-white hair. She was almost seventy, but vibrant good health made her look ten years younger.

Chane kissed Jennifer on the cheek. "I'll be back as soon as I can."

"Please don't tell anyone else that we're married. I want to tell Peter first. I feel terrible that I didn't tell him *before*..."

"I have to tell Steve, but he won't tell anyone. Don't worry your sweet head. If it seems appropriate, we can forget we were married onboard ship. I could probably be talked into marrying you again, in front of God *and* your brother. You might like a more formal wedding, anyway."

"Once I tell Peter, you can tell anyone you like."

Chane smiled at Mrs. Lillian. "Arrange a party for that, would you? We're going to have to do something formal to keep everyone from being furious they weren't invited."

Mrs. Lillian beamed. "Two weeks or so away?"

Chane looked askance at Jennie. "Okay," she said.

"I haven't entertained in a long time anyway."

Mrs. Lillian nodded. "Good. I'll get right to work on it. A party is just the thing to announce wonderful news."

Chane kissed Jennie and left her to unpack while he went downstairs to tackle the problems that had piled up during his absence. Mrs. Lillian emptied drawers for Jennifer's things.

While Jennifer filled the drawers with undergarments and ballet practice clothes Augustine had hastily packed, Mrs. Lillian had another armoire moved into the room for Jennifer's gowns. Chane's bedroom was spacious, with high ceilings. A fire in the fireplace on the north wall radiated enough heat to warm the entire room, except near the windows, where even heavy drapes were not enough to keep out the cold.

"Which side of the bed does Chane sleep on?" Jennifer asked.

"Next to the window."

Jennifer slipped her nightgown under the pillow on her side of the bed. When she traveled, she did that. It always seemed more like home if she could reach under the pillow, even if she'd never seen it before, and find her nightgown there.

Augustine would deliver the rest of Jennifer's things to the Bricewood over the next week. Jennifer had asked her to wait until after she had talked to Peter. She couldn't imagine anything worse than Peter's coming home from a pleasant weekend to find his sister completely moved out and married to a man he considered an enemy.

They had only been home an hour when the doorbell rang. Chane was sitting at his desk in the library, going over correspondence that had accumulated while he'd been gone. Jennifer read a book in a chair before the fire. Mrs. Lillian walked into the room with a frown on her face. "It's Miss Laurey," she said quietly.

Chane considered telling Mrs. L. to get rid of her, but that would be the cowardly way out. He owed Latitia an explanation.

"I'll be right there." He walked over to where Jennie sat and leaned down to kiss her lightly on the lips. "I'll be right back."

Latitia waited impatiently in the entry hall. At the sight of Chane, she stopped tapping her foot on the marble floor.

"What brings you out in such bad weather?" he asked.

"Where have you been?" she demanded, ignoring his questions. "I've been waiting and waiting to hear from you."

"We were trapped on the frozen bay."

"We?"

"My wife and I."

"You married that slut?" she asked incredulously. "After all I told you?"

"Careful, Latitia, you are talking about my wife."

Latitia shook her head bitterly. "Then I'm too late. I came to tell you that I just learned that she's working with Derek Wharton and her brother to ruin you."

"I don't believe it."

"Then you're a fool," she said, her eyes flashing with sudden rage. Before he could respond, she turned abruptly and left. Chane waited for a moment, then returned to the library.

"That didn't take long."

"No. Once I told her we were married, she lost interest in me." Jennifer sensed there might be more, but he seemed unwilling to share it if there was.

Halfway through dinner Steve appeared unexpectedly. "Sorry to interrupt," he said apologetically to Jennifer.

"Won't you join us?" she asked.

"No thank you, ma'am." Then, turning to Chane, "Remember that bridge we built across the Raritan River in Jersey?"

"Yes."

"We got a telegram saying it's about to collapse."

Chane put down his fork. "That's not possible."

"They've closed the bridge, but they want you to come right away."

Chane stood up and dropped his napkin on the table. This was every engineer's nightmare. He couldn't imagine how that bridge could fail. It was light and efficient. He would have bet that bridge would last a hundred years.

"Wire them and tell them I'm on my way."

Steve left, and Chane strode into the bedroom and began packing an overnight bag.

"Do you have to go?" Jennifer asked.

"In ancient Rome, if a man built a public structure that failed, they tried him. Depending on the damage caused by the failure, they could hang him or make him pay for the replacement or put him in prison. Fortunately, we're not in Rome, but I feel the responsibility anyway."

"Is there anything I can do to help?" she asked.

"Other than mourn my loss? No."

Jennifer's heart felt like it had gained three pounds. "Aren't engineers allowed to make mistakes?"

"No," he said grimly, "they're not."

Jennifer took over and packed his clothes while he packed drafting tools, paper, and supplies. Too soon, he was ready to go. At the door, he pulled her into his arms and hugged her.

"Take care of yourself and my son."

"Please be careful."

"You're the one who needs to be careful. You're doing the important work," he teased.

"Maybe this was all a trick so you can get out of the house and meet your mistress."

"There are many things I can tease about, but that isn't one of them. I will never cheat on you, Jennie. And I hope to God you never cheat on me."

The teasing light had died out of his eyes. They were deadly serious. Her own smile felt like an embarrassment. She stifled it. "Understood," she said, straightening her shoulders and clicking her heels. She saluted smartly.

Chane knew she was trying to make it easy for him to leave, but it wasn't. He had the feeling that he shouldn't leave her. That he should either take her with him or stay. That he would regret leaving her. But it was going to be a hard trip through bad weather, and she'd be safer here.

A knock sounded on the door, and Chane pulled her into his arms for one last hug. "I love you, Mrs. Chantry Kincaid the Third."

Another knock sounded. "Come in," he called.

Mrs. Lillian opened the door and peeked in. "The carriage is waiting."

Chane leaned down for one last kiss. "Take care of our son," he whispered. "I'll be back as soon as I can."

CHAPTER THIRTEEN

Peter tossed his bag onto the bed and Augustine stepped forward to unpack it.

"Is Jenn home?"

"No, monsieur. She is at the Bricewood."

He glanced at the clock. He'd forgotten she had a performance tonight. She wouldn't be home until ten.

"She wanted me to call her as soon as you arrived home," Augustine said.

"Well, it's not possible now."

Augustine frowned. She had been given instructions by her mistress. "You'll stay home tonight, then?"

"Yes."

Augustine trudged down the stairs to where the dreaded telephone sat on the library table. She would leave a message so madame would know her brother was waiting for her.

Just as her hand touched the hated instrument, the bell inside it let out a rough shriek. She jumped. "Oh, *mon Dieu*!" The instrument shrilled again. With shaking hand she picked up the receiver. "Van Vleet residence," she stammered.

"Is Peter Van Vleet there?" a male voice asked.

"One moment please."

"Is that for me?" Peter called down the stairs.

"*Oui*, monsieur."

Peter took the stairs two at a time, smiling at the consternation on Augustine's face. He took the receiver from her visibly shaking hand.

"Hello."

"Mr. Van Vleet, this is Mr. Noonan at the Bricewood." The voice was gruff and forced, as if he found speaking on a telephone uncomfortable.

Peter wondered if something had happened to Jennifer.

"I'm calling about the money you owe Mr. Kincaid."

"What money?"

"You've had your fun, Mr. Van Vleet. Now Mr. Kincaid would like his twenty thousand dollars…tonight."

"I don't know what you're talking about."

The man sighed audibly into the telephone. "Gamblers lie, too, do they? Well, it doesn't surprise me."

Peter struggled to control his temper. "There must be some mistake, Mr. Noonan. I do not gamble. I especially do not gamble in any establishment owned by Mr. Kincaid."

Peter slammed the receiver down and counted to fifteen, which was usually enough to be sure the operator had disconnected the previous call. Then he picked it up again and asked the operator to get him the Bricewood.

The telephone rang. A woman's voice answered on the other end. "Hello?"

"Is Mr. Kincaid there?"

"No, I'm sorry, Mr. Kincaid has gone out of town. We don't expect him back until tomorrow night."

Peter put down the earpiece. He would have to wait until tomorrow night to confront Kincaid with his mistake. In the meantime he would find Derek Wharton. If Derek had run up gambling debts in his name, he'd beat the stuffings out of him. Peter grabbed his coat and hat. "I'll be back later."

"But monsieur!" Augustine protested. "Your sister—"

The slamming of the back door told her she was wasting her breath.

Jennifer paid the cabriolet driver and rushed up the steps to the door. Augustine met her in the entry hall.

"Mamitchka, is Peter home?"

"No, madame. I gave him your message, and he even said he would stay here until you returned, but then a man called, and it seemed to upset him."

"Do you know who it was?"

"He didn't say, madame."

"I'll stay here tonight and catch Peter before he goes to work tomorrow."

Jennifer slept fitfully that night and woke with a start. At first she expected to find Chane beside her, then she remembered that he was on his way to or already in New Jersey.

A fire crackled in the hearth. She slipped out of bed and put on her robe. Peter was not in his room. She hurried down the stairs. Augustine was in the kitchen, talking to the cook. They both looked up.

"*Bon matin*, madame," they said in unison, the cook's heavier voice mingling with Augustine's soprano.

"Have you seen Peter?"

"No, madame. He didn't come home last night. I kept an ear peeled for him, too," Augustine said.

The clock in the entryway bonged seven times. She had slept later than she'd thought. She would barely be able to get back to the Bricewood in time for practice.

"When he comes home, ask him to wait for me tonight. I'll be back after the performance. I need to talk to him."

"Yes, madame."

Jennifer couldn't believe her bad luck. The simple task of telling Peter that she had married Kincaid seemed to be turning into a nightmare. Well, she would just have to come back again tonight. She shouldn't worry so much. He wanted only her happiness, of that she was sure. It bothered her that he hadn't come home, though. It wasn't like him.

By five o'clock Peter was exhausted. The brokerage house had experienced more than its usual pandemonium today, with men buying and selling frantically as the prices of steel and cotton dropped faster than they should have. Rumors flew all day that an English company had bought Bethlehem Steel.

Peter picked up energy as he neared the front door. He would try the newspaper where Derek worked. If he didn't find him there, he'd give up for tonight. After working all day without sleeping last night, finding Derek seemed less important than getting some rest.

At the newspaper office the clerk told Peter that Derek was on vacation. "Gone out of town, I heard."

At home, Augustine took his coat. "You look tired, monsieur."

"Exhausted, Augustine. I'm going to take a nap until dinner. Will you wake me?"

"Your sister asked me to tell you she needs to talk with you. She wants you to wait here for her. She'll come as soon as she can get away from the performance."

"I want to talk to her, too. Be sure she wakes me when she comes home."

Peter lay down on his bed and closed his eyes. He must have passed out. He felt Augustine shaking him, heard her telling him dinner was ready, but he only shoved her hand away from his shoulder and turned over to shut her out. He felt her cover him with a quilt and was grateful for the warmth.

He woke later with the sense that he had slept through the evening and night and was late for work. Groggily, he sat on the side of the bed. The lamp was turned low. It flickered and threatened to gutter. The room was cold, and the north wind howled around the dark windows.

He couldn't figure out what had awakened him. Then it came again. A knocking at the front door. Muscles in his legs twitched. He felt too tired to move quickly enough to reach it in time. The front door opened. He heard a murmur of feminine voices, but the wind howling under the eaves blotted out the words. Peter stood and walked to the door.

He pushed through the doorway and took the stairs two at a time. He could hear Augustine answering a question, then he recognized the other voice as belonging to Simone. Slowing, he ran his hands through his hair and glanced at the mirror in the entryway, but on the fly as he was, it was impossible to tell if he looked as bad as he felt.

Simone looked up and saw him. Augustine turned. "Oh, monsieur, I thought you were sleeping."

"Thank you, Augustine. I was."

Augustine walked quickly back toward the kitchen, her heels clicking on the hardwood entry.

Simone's coat looked thin, too thin for this kind of weather. He remembered Jenn telling him that some of the young women in the dance company lived from hand to mouth. He felt sure Simone must be one of them. "Would you like to come to the fire and warm yourself?"

A look of surprise flitted across her pretty face. "Yes, thank you." She stepped toward the fire in the entryway. Peter took her by the elbow and guided her into the library. "This is warmer and not so drafty. Would you like hot tea?" he asked.

Simone unbuttoned her coat. Under the influence of his intent blue eyes, she felt her hands trembling. The lamplight softened the healthy teak of his skin and cast a shadow under his sensuous bottom lip. Her fingers tingled with the need to touch his lean cheek.

Peter helped her out of her coat and laid it over the back of a chair. "Why are you being nice to me?"

He shrugged. Simone flushed, and her big, dark eyes flinched away from meeting his. Her bottom lip started to tremble. She sucked it into her mouth as if she could hide it from him. Her breasts looked round and plump beneath the simple wool gown. It was not the fine, soft wool Jenn wore, but more like the wool in army blankets. Her slim white hands, so elegant and expressive, picked at the tiny white collar of her dark gown.

"You seem different." Her nervous gaze connected with his. She had beautiful eyes. Her thick, dark hair was pulled back in a bun the way Jenn wore hers when dancing.

"Did the ballet let out early?"

"No…no…I…uhm…didn't feel up to it tonight."

The silence lengthened. She looked away, finally stood up and walked away from the fire. Nervously, she clasped her hands behind her, unclasped them, then clasped them again. Her hands trembled visibly.

He walked over to stand behind her. "Why don't you just tell me what you're up to," he said.

Simone's heart almost stopped. His deep voice sent chills down her spine. She felt faint from his nearness. She realized that he hadn't rung for the tea he had invited her to have. That must mean he wanted her to leave.

"Thank you for letting me get warm…"

She willed her legs to walk to the door, but they ignored her. Peter stood behind her. She felt the harsh heat of his lithe body. His hands clamped on her shoulders. A shaft of heat started in her belly and speared downward to that nervous place between her legs. "I asked you a question," he said, his voice gruff.

Simone could not remember his question. Dumbly, she shook her head. His hands tightened on her shoulders. Slowly, he turned her. His blue eyes had narrowed into slits. A pulse pounded in her throat.

"Why don't you just tell me everything," he said. He'd changed somehow. The polite young man had been replaced by an angry man. The sharp light in his eyes caused blood to race through Simone in waves. She felt faint. His strong fingers bit into the soft flesh of her arms. A lump swelled darkly in her throat.

"Now," he growled.

"I can't," she whispered around the lump.

"Oh, yes you can," he said grimly.

"Oh, God…"

"Tell me," he said, giving her a little shake for emphasis. He knew she knew Derek Wharton, and he felt certain she knew something about the phony gambling debt. "Tell me," he gritted.

Simone groaned. She might as well tell him. Nothing could be worse. "I fell in love with you that summer," she said, her voice breaking at the end. "I wanted you to notice me. That's why I swam naked in the pool…"

He scowled at her, and her voice faded away. Shame flushed into Simone like a wave of smothering heat. She jerked away from him. She wanted to flee, but her feet felt rooted to the spot.

Tears added the final touch to her shame. She wiped angrily at her eyes, rummaged in her reticule, but found no handkerchief. Peter reached into his coat pocket, pulled out a clean kerchief and put it into her hand, a smile twitching at his lips. Simone dabbed at her eyes, shoved the kerchief back into his hand, then turned to flee. She wanted to die, to shrivel up and disappear out of sight. He was laughing at her.

She picked up her coat and ran toward the entry hall and the front door. At the door to the library, Peter caught her and turned her to face him. She fought him for a moment, but lost energy.

He pulled her close against him. The warmth and richness of his body almost caused her to swoon. "I'm not laughing at you," he said, his husky voice low, insistent.

"I don't need your sympathy…"

"You won't get it, either."

Her arm seemed to come up of its own accord. He grabbed it and put it behind her, pulling her harder against him with one hand and taking her coat and tossing it on the floor with the other. "You won't be needing that."

A small tingling current moved from his hard body into hers, making it impossible for her to think or move away. One of his warm hands released her wrist and moved up to her face. "Was that why you kept tormenting me, because you wanted me?"

Simone wanted to die. He *was* laughing at her. His warm hand stroked her face. He lowered his head and pressed his smooth, warm lips to hers. Slowly they insinuated themselves into her mouth and opened it to his ravaging tongue. She felt certain no greater thrill or pain was possible. To be kissed in this savage way by a man she loved and could never have.

At last he lifted his head. "I must have wanted you from the first moment I saw you…standing in the hallway with your pitiful little carpetbag."

A rush of blood through her brain almost blinded her. "All those times we tormented one another," he whispered, and lowered his head to kiss her again. Simone didn't know if he was making fun of her or not, but now she didn't care. His kisses caused such a burning in her, such need.

He kissed her until they were both panting, until his slitted blue eyes blazed with passion.

"I thought you hated me," she whispered.

"I hated the way I felt, knowing you were sleeping with my father—"

A knock at the door interrupted.

Peter steadied Simone and stepped away from her. "Come in," he yelled.

Malcomb opened the door. "Will you be needing anything, sir?"

"No, Malcomb. You may be excused for the night."

"Thank you, sir."

"Is Augustine in bed?"

"Yes, sir. Would you like me to send her?"

"No, thank you. Sleep well."

Malcomb nodded his thanks and closed the door.

"Would you like some tea?" Peter asked.

Simone shook her head. "No. Only you," she whispered.

Peter suppressed a groan. He wanted Simone, but he had learned his lesson about making love to young women. He'd been expelled from Harvard because a young woman climbed in his window and slipped into his bed the night of a surprise bed check. It might not have been terminal to his education except the young woman was the dean's daughter.

Simone misunderstood his silence. Flushing, she turned away, bumping into a table and almost knocking down a lamp. "Oh! Sorry! I'm so clumsy. I really must be going. I forgot I have practice early tomorrow!"

She grabbed her coat and ran for the front door. Peter cursed and pounded after her, caught her as she fumbled with the inside locks.

"Simone! Dammit. You're skittish as a colt."

He forced her face around. Tears streamed down her cheeks. She trembled under his hand like a rabbit. A flame started deep within him and would not be extinguished.

"Simone…"

She tried to force her chin down. He caught her hair and forced her head back, then captured her wet, salty lips and kissed her until her lips warmed and opened beneath his and the flickering flame within him roared into an inferno. He picked her up and carried her up the stairs.

Simone didn't remember his undressing her. His body was more beautiful than any she had ever seen. His shoulders were wide, his hips slim. As he leaned over her, his blond hair fell over his eyes, and he brushed it away. Everything about Peter was purposeful. Some men were hopelessly clumsy at undressing a woman. Peter had somehow undressed both of them without her knowing. He kissed her neck—warm, nibbling kisses—and she burned with the need to surrender everything to him.

And that was the way he took her, as if he wanted everything. She'd never felt more taken in her life. She felt branded by him. Changed. His slightest touch caused such a fierce hunger in her; his lovemaking was wild and selfish the first time, slower and more satisfying the second. He had fire and passion and blinding beauty. She didn't want him to let her go…ever.

But unfortunately, she still had to earn a living. Reality could not be pushed aside indefinitely. The clock struck nine o'clock. "Ohhhh. I have to go," she groaned.

"I'll take you home."

"No. I can easily get a cabriolet."

That was true. The cab drivers combed Fifth Avenue from dawn to dark.

They dressed, and Peter went down to stop a cab.

"Will you call me?" she asked after he kissed her good night and helped her up into the cabriolet. His warm lips made her impervious to the cold wind.

"Yes, of course," he said, touching her cheek.

At the corner she leaned out and waved. Peter waved back and walked up the stairs to the front door. His body felt tired, but good. He'd leave a note on Jenn's pillow to be sure she woke him when she came in.

He closed the front door and climbed the stairs to his room. Just as he reached the top stair, the door chimes rang. Simone must have forgotten something. He took the stairs two at a time and swung the door open. Three huge men stood on the front porch.

"'Bout time you came home, boy."

Peter recognized the voice as that of the man who'd called him about the gambling debt.

"We don't appreciate your hiding out for the last couple of days," Noonan growled, stepping forward to block the door so Peter couldn't close it. "Kincaid wants his twenty thousand dollars, and he wants it now." The two men stepped close to Peter. One smelled like fish, the other like manure—a sailor and a farmer. He felt dwarfed by their size.

"I've never set foot in Kincaid's gambling casino."

"You hear that, boys? I told you he was innocent."

The sailor grinned, put his shoulder against the door and shoved his way into the entry hall.

"Hold on!" Peter yelled.

The farmer stepped around Noonan, grabbed Peter's arms and held him. The sailor knelt and held his legs. Noonan raised his fist and sent it crashing into Peter's face. Light exploded in his head. He staggered backward, vaguely aware of the men cursing as they struggled to hold on to him. He tried to get free, but they couldn't be dislodged. The blows kept coming, and Peter stopped fighting. Noonan rained blows on his face and middle. Blood poured down Peter's face, blinding him.

He realized with surprise that Noonan seemed bent on killing him. He knew he should try to save his life, but it was too late now. The men holding him were too strong. Pain came in continuous waves, punctuated by crashing blows from Noonan's meaty fists. At last, one of the blows knocked him unconscious.

The next sound Peter heard was of someone screaming. He ached, but it was nothing like the pain he'd felt earlier. He tried to open his eyes, but they didn't seem to work. The woman screaming sounded like Augustine. He wanted to comfort her, to tell her not to worry, but his mouth didn't seem to work either. Blackness came again.

Jennifer rang the doorbell and waited. Wind whipped and howled in the skeletal trees overhead. The moon shone down, illuminating a wide band of the snow banked on both sides of the road in front of the Van Vleet town house.

It was taking Augustine forever to get to the door. Jennifer glanced again at the strange buggy parked at the curb, but she didn't recognize it.

At last the door opened. Augustine gave a little cry of surprise and joy at the sight of her. "Oh, thank God you've come, madame. *Mon Dieu*, the young master's hurt bad."

"Peter?"

"*Oui.*"

"What happened?"

"Three men…" Tears filled her eyes. "They were animals! They dumped the young master on the floor of the entryway and left him there, like a dog."

"Oh, Lord! Is he…?"

"Dr. Hamilton is with him. I don't know…"

Jennifer ran forward and stopped in the library doorway. Peter lay on the floor before the fire. "We thought it best to bring him to the fire...I'm so sorry, madame."

Jennifer ran forward and knelt beside Peter. Blood had soaked into his white shirt, turning it dark brown. His face was swollen, his nose obviously broken. His beautiful nose...

"Who did this?"

Peter didn't move or respond.

"Peter, can you hear me? Who did this to you?"

Jennifer touched his hand. It felt cold. Fear cramped her stomach. She doubled over. "He's not..."

Dr. Hamilton shook his head. "He fades in and out."

Jennifer carefully touched Peter's undamaged hand. Dr. Hamilton opened Peter's shirt and exposed ribs that were black and blue. He touched one of the bruises, and Peter winced.

"Peter, it's me, Jennifer. Can you hear me?"

His hand moved under hers. He squeezed her fingers.

"Who did this to you?"

"Kin...caid."

"He's delirious. It wasn't Chane. He's gone."

Peter's eyelashes flickered, but his eyes were so swollen and blackened they didn't open. "His men..." Peter whispered, his voice little more than a hoarse croak.

"No. No. I don't believe it."

"It was...Noonan."

Nausea overwhelmed Jennifer. She didn't believe it, but Peter did.

She and Augustine stayed by his side all that night. Jennifer felt feverish with the need to confront Chane with her questions. She willed him to return, to confirm what she knew—that he would never hurt her brother.

Toward morning Peter opened his eyes and seemed to know her. She gave him warm broth and held his hand and told him how much she loved him. He mumbled something.

Jennifer leaned down. "What?"

"I need to see Jenn, to tell her."

Augustine shook her head. "He doesn't even know you're here, madame."

"I need to warn her," he whispered.

Jennifer kissed Peter's forehead. "I'm here, Peter."

"Tell her to stay away from Kincaid—"

"Hush! Rest now, love." Peter slipped back into sleep. Jennifer handed the washcloth to Augustine. "Take care of him," she whispered. "I'll be back soon."

"If I need you..."

"I'll be at the Bricewood." Chane should be back today. She would see him at once. He would explain.

CHAPTER FOURTEEN

Jennifer waited all morning in Chane's office. Twelve noon came, and still Chane hadn't arrived. She asked Chane's secretary to call her as soon as Mr. Kincaid returned. She knew he could explain. She just wished he would hurry back and do it.

Reluctantly, she walked back to the Grand Ballroom to watch the beginning of rehearsal. She sat next to Bellini in the fifth row.

"How's your brother?"

"Badly beaten."

"Do you know who did it?"

Jennifer felt sick. "No, not yet."

Watching as a spectator made her feel jumpy, as if the energy she usually used dancing had pooled inside her and turned to nerves.

At three o'clock one of the hotel employees came in and whispered to Bellini, who stood up and rapped his baton on the wood trim of the upholstered seat in front of him.

"No performance tonight," his voice boomed. "Blizzard coming. If what they say is correct, it's going to be a bad one. We'll resume when weather permits."

Grinning dancers looked at one another in amazement. They saw it as a chance to play hookey, to stay home and wallow in all the excesses dancers rarely had time for. They headed toward the dressing rooms, talking excitedly.

"Best get home before you get stuck here," Bellini growled.

Jennifer didn't know what to do. Peter needed her, but it was imperative that she see Chane, who might be within minutes of arriving. Unless he was trapped somewhere by the weather.

She walked past Steve Hammond's office. He stopped what he was doing when he caught sight of her and waited respectfully for her to speak.

"Have you heard from Chane?" she asked.

"The telegraph wires are down," he replied. "The last we heard, the blizzard had closed everything. You'll be safe in the hotel. I wouldn't try to leave here, though."

"Thanks," she said forlornly.

She walked toward the lobby. Frederick stood by the doors, waiting. Seeing her, he walked over. "Do you have a ride? Or are you staying here?"

"I don't know. I want to go home…"

"I'll take you."

Something about his solicitousness made Jennifer uncomfortable. "I live in the other direction," she said stiffly.

"This is no time to be huffy. You won't get another cabriolet in this weather."

As they headed toward the exit together, Frederick waved at Latitia Laurey. Jennifer scowled, wondering uneasily what Latitia was doing at the Bricewood again. It unnerved her slightly to realize that Frederick knew the woman. Frederick flushed. He would probably prefer she not know he was being courted by a rich and powerful woman. Frederick was not above succeeding however he could, but he always wanted everyone to think it was because of his great skill as a dancer. He tightened his grip on her arm, and she decided that her need to check on Peter outweighed her concern about Latitia, Frederick, and everything else except Chane. And he would not return today, anyway.

Through the arched doors leading out of the Bricewood, snow fell continuously. Frederick helped her into the small, covered cab. The driver's coat and hat were covered with an inch of snow. He shouted at them, "You are my last passengers of the day."

The wind howled so loudly and the snow swirled so thickly they seemed lost as soon as they emerged from the sheltering overhang. Snow swirled against the canvas window cover on her side. Jennifer tried to peer through the ragged, wind-driven flakes, and hoped the driver knew his way.

Wind rocked the cabriolet. She could hear the sounds of the horse's hooves slipping occasionally on the icy street. At one point the driver stopped, jumped down, climbed the streetpost, and wiped snow off the sign. "Third Avenue! I thought we'd past that long ago," he yelled as he clambered back on board.

Only two blocks to go. Frederick lived on East Twelfth and First Avenue, just a few blocks from the old Bellini Theatre. Even wrapped in her heaviest coat and bundled in blankets, Jennifer felt the icy coldness of the wind. They passed few buggies and almost no pedestrians. Apparently, the rest of the town had already stopped trying to travel.

At last they reached Frederick's apartment. The driver jumped down and helped Frederick clamber out of the cab over the curbside snowdrift. Then he held his hand out to Jennifer.

"I think there's been a misunderstanding. I'm not getting out here. I live at Thirty-second Street and Fifth Avenue."

He shook his head. "I may have misunderstood, but now that I see how long it's taken, I'm not going back uptown again tonight."

"I must get home."

"Sorry. It looks like I just can't make it."

"But I have to get home."

"I only live six blocks from here, and I ain't going another foot more'n I have to. Five more minutes and my horse'll freeze to death."

Frederick cupped his hands to be heard above the roaring of the wind. "Come in. You can stay with me."

"I have to get home."

"Not in this weather!"

The driver looked cold and tired and sorrowful as he said, "You'll have to be getting out, miss. My old horse don't do well in the cold."

Reluctantly, Jennifer climbed down. Frederick took her hand, and the two of them made their careful way across the icy sidewalk through blowing snow. Frederick unlocked the front door of the building.

The entry hall was dimly lit. His apartment was dark and cold. Frederick lit a fire in the fireplace. Jennifer filled the teakettle and lit the kindling in the iron stove in the kitchen. He had a typical dancer's apartment—a place to sleep. A cold-water flat, it lacked many of the amenities.

Frederick added wood to the fire and they huddled before it, shivering.

"Do you have anything to cook?"

He laughed. "They'll find our bodies here when the ice melts. I can see the headline now. 'Lovers starve to death in spite of everything Frederick Van Buren could do.'"

"We're not lovers."

"Well, we damned sure used to be."

"We're not anymore."

"Because you sold out."

"Sold out?"

"You bought that bastard's line, hook and sinker," he said bitterly.

"I fell in love."

"With his money."

"My family has always had money. I didn't need to marry it," she said angrily.

"Not anymore, from what I heard," he said smugly. "Your parents died penniless. And I'm not saying you'd deliberately marry for money. But you're young and naive enough to be influenced by his money and power. You just haven't seen yet what a blackguard he is."

"Money alone does not make a blackguard."

"No, we have to factor in his lying, cheating, and stealing, don't we?"

"You're just jealous because you're almost twenty-nine years old and you haven't made anything of yourself."

"My, how you've changed," he crowed. "You used to think that being a dancer *was* something."

Jennifer flushed. "I still do, but—" She stopped before she admitted she didn't think him that great a dancer.

Frederick must have read her mind. Anger flashed in his dark eyes. "He's a lying, cheating blackguard, and he's taking you for a ride. He'll throw you over the same way he did Latitia just as soon as the next pretty face comes along. He'll never marry you."

"He already did," Jennifer blurted.

"I don't believe it."

"Well, it's true."

"If a man of his stature had married, it would have been all over the papers."

"We married on shipboard. No one knows. I'm keeping it a secret until I've had time to tell Peter. And you'd better not say a word, if you value what's left of our friendship."

"Oh, so it's a friendship now, is it?"

Jennifer ignored him and walked into the kitchen. "You have the most barren pantry I've ever seen." She opened every cupboard. They were all empty. Frederick went upstairs to borrow groceries from his neighbor. He returned with six potatoes, an onion with its top sprouted, a quart of milk, a pat of butter, and a loaf of stale bread.

Jennifer peeled the potatoes, then cut them up with the onion for potato soup and set them to boil. It was the only thing she knew how to make by herself. Frederick sat at the table and fretted about his mistakes in rehearsal.

Listening to his griping, Jennifer slowly relaxed. She had known Frederick for years. He might be less than a gentleman, but she was comfortable with him. Being trapped by the snow gave their adventure the air of an out-of-town performance. Jennifer worried about Peter and Chane, but she realized there was nothing she could do. The blizzard had taken control of her life. Somehow, they would all survive, and Chane would be able to explain.

Frederick found a bottle of red wine. "We're stranded here," he said happily. "Might as well enjoy ourselves."

Jennifer refused the wine. They sat before the fire on Frederick's thin rug. He questioned her about Peter, and she told him everything she knew about the beating.

"Kincaid did it," Frederick said firmly.

"No, he didn't."

"What if he did?"

"He didn't. And I don't appreciate your saying he might have."

Frederick rolled his eyes. "Sorry."

By seven o'clock the soup was done. Jennifer seasoned it with a little butter, salt, and pepper. Frederick sliced the stale bread, and she toasted it in an iron skillet with the last of the butter.

It made a fine dinner. The soup was hot and filling. The toast was crisp and buttery. They ate ravenously. Outside, the wind roared and rattled the windows; inside, it was warm and cozy. A full stomach made Jennifer relaxed and sleepy even though it was still early. She hadn't slept at all last night, except for a few minutes on the way to the hotel.

She curled up on the sofa and left the bed for Frederick. "Are you going to sleep there?" he asked. "You don't have to. I'll behave myself."

Jennifer's disbelief must have telegraphed itself to him. He scowled and turned away. "I hate that bastard."

"Why are you acting jealous now? You were happy to be rid of me."

"I was not!"

"Yes, you were. You didn't once ask me to reconsider."

Frederick flushed. "I was too mad."

"Liar! Besides, you were already having an affair with your secret admirer!"

"She confused the issue, I admit that, but I always loved you..."

"Oh, spare me!"

"What do you know about it? You're not exactly Miss Virginity."

"How can you even mention your seduction of me. Especially after those awful lies and all that finagling on your part!"

Shamefaced, Frederick subsided.

Two days and nights passed in this fashion, and still the storm did not let up. Frederick continued to pout about her not loving him anymore; he seemed to be growing more and more maudlin about their past relationship. As she made her bed the second night, he grumbled sourly. "There was a time you would have slept with me."

"We don't want you walking those 'hallowed halls' again, though, do we?" she snapped.

"Jennifer, please don't be mean to me. I love you."

She knew that he loved himself more, but she kept quiet. Without warning he glanced over at her with such bitterness that it stunned her. "I hate Kincaid. You know good and well he had Peter beaten. It's common practice in this town to whale the tar out of men who welch on their gambling debts."

"Peter doesn't gamble."

"Maybe Peter doesn't *admit* he gambles."

"He doesn't gamble. I know for a fact. If anything, it was probably that Derek Wharton he hangs out with. Derek is a known gambler, and a cheat, and a liar. He probably gambled under Peter's name."

"What a fool you are," Frederick said bitterly, shaking his head. "Everyone in town knows that Kincaid employs thugs for the very purpose of beating deadbeats."

"He isn't like that."

"Look, I wasn't supposed to tell you this, but I got it on very good authority…" He paused, pressed his lips together as if he still might not tell her, and then sighed. "But I think I better." He glanced up at her, as if gauging her readiness to hear this news. "Look, I know Kincaid ordered your brother beaten. I was trying to tell you without telling you. But I know it was not accidental or done by anyone else. Kincaid ordered it because he knows Peter is plotting against him. He may not have wanted him beaten so close to death's door, but he wanted him hurt bad enough so that he would get the message."

Jennifer's heart felt like a lead weight. "How do you know that?" she asked. If Chane could do that, he was a monster.

Frederick frowned, and she knew he was trying to decide what lie to tell her. "A woman," he finally said.

"A woman you are sleeping with?"

"You threw me over. What the hell was I supposed to do?" he asked bitterly.

Jennifer closed her eyes and shook her head in weariness. She didn't care if he had six women. But she knew it would only hurt him if she admitted it. "It's okay," she said.

He stared glumly into the fire, looking thoroughly miserable. "I love you, Jennifer. I'll always love you." Without warning he started to cry, his face twisting with grief. "How could you be so blind and loyal to that bastard? Now you've married him, and he'll take you away, and you'll have babies until your body is as fat as a sausage and your ankles are swollen and falling over your shoes like those old Italian women in the market. You're a ballerina, Jennifer, a butterfly. Other women can have babies, but you...you...God! You're a dancer. Now...now you'll never dance again." His anger and grief overcame him and he doubled forward, crying like a furious three-year-old. And once started, he couldn't seem to stop crying.

Filled with revulsion at the picture he had painted of her future, and filled with sudden tenderness for him, because he cared so much, she reached over and stroked his shoulder. Blindly, he pulled her into his arms. Crooning words of comfort, she held him, and he cried more softly now.

Frederick had always been intense. Before, they had been intense together, about their dancing. Now, he was hurt and furious that she had given it all up to do something he could never understand.

Still holding her, he slowly lay back onto the rug. As she stroked Frederick's head, a sinking feeling started in her belly. Frederick was right. She had no business marrying anyone. But the baby inside her had trapped her. And with a man like Kincaid, there'd be other babies. A long string of them until she died or wished she'd died. She started to cry, too. She realized she had betrayed Peter and herself. The one she should have betrayed was Chane.

Frederick felt the resistance go out of her. "Hey," he said softly, smoothing the hair back from her beautiful face. Tears cascaded down her cheeks. She wouldn't open her eyes. "Hey," he crooned, kissing her eyes, her cheeks, her lips. Slowly, without breathing, he pushed her skirts and pantalets aside and slid his hand up her thigh. Still she didn't resist. He covered her mouth with his and kissed her for a long, slow time.

Part of Jennifer wanted to stop him, but part of her didn't. The grief at Chane's betrayal was too paralyzing. She couldn't seem to move. Frederick nudged her thighs open, and still she couldn't move. Part of her screamed at the violation, but part of her wanted to hurt Chane, to call him there so he could watch.

She let Frederick enter her, and it was like a small death, a suicide. But it felt appropriate. She wanted to die and kill Chane in the same breath. She wanted to punish herself for ever falling in love with him, and him for being the rat he was.

Jennifer felt caught in a dream—knowing it was a dream, but unable to stop it. Her face was stained with tears—every part of her cold and mean and grief-stricken. She felt no arousal at Frederick's touch, but no guilt, either. It just seemed to be what she had to do to punish herself.

Chane paced the length of the parlor, stopped abruptly, and walked to the window. Outside his Pullman coach the ceaseless wind drove gusts of heavy snow against the windows.

At last he was on his way home. He'd found the proof he needed to clear himself of negligence charges in regard to the shaky bridge. Someone had removed a number of iron bolts in strategic places. It had taken two days to fix the bridge, mostly because they couldn't find the right-sized bolts. But now it was done, and he was on his way home to Jennie.

Unexpectedly, the train slowed and stopped. The engineer struggled through three-foot drifts to his Pullman coach. Chane met him on the observation deck. "What happened?" he asked.

"A tree across the tracks. I'm afraid we're stuck here until the railroad sends out a crew…"

"One tree?"

"Aye, but it's a big one!"

It was big. Covered with snow, it looked like a circus tent.

"Do we have an ax on board?" Chane asked.

The engineer looked at him as if he were crazy. Chane laughed. He might be. But he couldn't imagine sitting in the comfort of his private car while Jennie waited and worried at home.

Reluctantly, the engineer found the ax they kept on board for just such occasions. Chane picked the likeliest place to start chopping and raised the ax. At least he would not have to worry about having nothing to do tonight.

Jennie woke with a start. The lamp still burned on the table. Frederick's head was still pressed to her breast.

At the remembrance of last night, bile boiled upward from her stomach. She clasped her hand over her mouth and scrambled to free herself from Frederick's entangling limbs. She ran to the lavatory, where she doubled forward and vomited. She emptied her stomach, but the queasiness remained. She made tea and forced herself to drink some of it.

Outside, the blizzard continued to rage, and inside, Frederick continued to sleep. Jennifer felt sick at heart. Her marriage was over. And she had no idea how Peter was. Outside, the wind howled so loud it drowned out everything else. Her head hurt and even her skin seemed to ache. She realized she must have the influenza as well.

"I can't rightly believe you cleared that tree off'n these tracks."

Chane straightened and rubbed his back. He could barely credit himself with it, either, but he had chopped the tree in half at center track. With any luck at all, the train would be able to push its way through.

While Chane worked, the engineer and fireman had cleaned off the snow plow on the front of the locomotive.

"Let's see if it works!" Chane yelled. He picked up the ax and climbed into the cab of the locomotive.

The engineer eased the throttle forward. The train strained hard against the two halves of the tree trunk, but they didn't move.

"Back it up. Get some momentum."

The engineer looked at Chane like he might be daft, but he reversed the Johnson bar. They chugged backward slowly for a quarter of a mile. "Okay. Let's try it again," Chane said.

"How fast?"

"We just want enough momentum to push the two halves of the trunk aside."

The locomotive chugged forward at fifteen miles an hour. It hit the two stumps, shoved them aside, and kept going. One half rolled away and the other plunged into the culvert at the side of the roadbed. They were free.

The rest of the trip passed with agonizing slowness. The train had to push so much snow off the tracks, it barely covered ten miles an hour. It was going to be a long trip home.

Chane opened the apartment door with his key. He was three days late. He walked quietly, not wanting to wake Jennie, at least not with noise. At the thought of her lying only a few short steps away from him, his body forgot how tired it was. He had missed her every moment. His mind seemed distorted with missing her. He couldn't believe he'd been gone only four days. It seemed a lifetime since he'd been with her.

The fire had burned low in the fireplace. He stopped and added two logs. Jennie might want to come out here. He didn't want it to be too cold for her. She was too thin to stand the cold.

He crossed the parlor, strode down the darkened hall, and stopped at the door to his and Jennie's bedroom. Carefully, he turned the knob and opened it. Aided by the dim light from the window, he crossed the floor and stopped. His gaze searched the shadows, but no form darkened the smooth, unruffled bedcovers. She wasn't there.

Disappointment struck hard. He and his engineer had finally met one of the road clearance crews, and Chane had commandeered them to help him get through. They had risked life and limb to clear the track. He could have killed a good crew and himself as well. Fortunately, they'd made it, though there were men on track clearance who would likely never forget him. The ride across town from the train station had been even worse. It had taken four hours to make the twenty-minute trip from the station.

Jennie must have gone home. He couldn't think why, unless, like him, she'd gone there for something and gotten trapped, as he had. He would just have to go find her.

He headed for the door and stopped. She might not appreciate his waking her at this hour of the morning. And being a new bride, she might not feel comfortable having him climbing into her bed in her brother's house.

Women were funny about that. His own mother had been. He'd heard his father complain of her squeamishness a number of times. Sleeping in a strange bed always stirred the animal in his father and the prude in his mother. As a boy, he'd heard them arguing when they thought he was asleep.

In deference to Jennie, and to his driver who'd just about now be getting to his own bed, he'd better just get some sleep and go for her in the morning.

He undressed and climbed into bed, and despite his worry about Jennie, sleep came.

Chane woke with the sun streaming in the window. The room was cold, but his body felt impervious to it. He crossed the room and pushed back the heavy draperies. It was a clear, bright, beautiful day; the blizzard was finally over. Traffic was already building as carriages and buggies slogged through the heavy drifts. They'd soon beat it down to size. Nothing could withstand New York traffic for long. He'd slept too late. Mrs. Lillian must have let him sleep. He couldn't imagine her not knowing he was home. It must be eight o'clock. He never slept that late, but he'd been tired. He pulled on his pants and stalked into the library to use the telephone. At least he could speak to Jennie. He lifted the earpiece and waited for the operator's voice to come on. Nothing happened. He realized the lines must still be down.

He dressed quickly and hurried downstairs to order a carriage. The hotel was usually bustling with people by this time. Today, the lobby was almost empty.

His carriage finally came. He gave the driver the address and climbed inside. It was slow going. They were stopped time after time by traffic jams caused by snowdrifts piled over fallen trees, overturned carriages, and in one instance, by the wall of a brick building that had collapsed from the weight of too much snow on the roof. At the fourth traffic jam, Chane worked with a crew that uncovered the body of an old man caught out in the blizzard. He was as brittle as an icicle. When Chane lifted the old man's legs to put him in the work crew's buckboard, ice crackled as if the ankles would break off in Chane's hands.

What should have been a half-hour trip took five hours. Finally, clammy and sweaty from working on a half-dozen road clearance crews, Chane arrived in front of Jennifer's house. He leaped out, bounded up the stairs, and banged the door knocker.

After a lengthy wait, Augustine opened the front door. "Is Jennie here?"

Augustine seemed to recoil visibly at the sight of him. "No." Even her voice sounded withdrawn, surprised. She barely resembled the woman who had sniffed through their wedding ceremony only a few short days ago.

"Do you know where she is?"

"No. You're not welcome here," she said, trying to shove the door shut in his face.

"I'm married to Jennifer, and I'm not leaving until I see for myself that she isn't here."

"Haven't you done enough?" Augustine said, grunting as she tried again to slam the door.

Chane pushed the door open and stepped inside. "Which room is hers?" he demanded.

"You aren't welcome here," Augustine said again, fear making her voice quiver.

His mind seemed to ignore her statement, even though part of him acknowledged hearing it. "I need to find her. She isn't at the Bricewood."

Augustine gasped in alarm. "We haven't seen her in days."

"How long ago?"

"Since before the storm."

The woman might be lying to him. He stepped around her and took the stairs two at a time. Four doors opened onto the upper hallway. He opened the one closest to him. The room was darkened by pulled drapes, but he could see a man standing over the bed.

Startled, the man turned, dropping a pillow and pulling a knife. A bandanna hid the bottom half of his face. He flashed the knife at Chane and yelled, "Get back or I'll cut yer gizzard out."

Chane stepped away from the doorway, and the man edged past him and ran down the stairs. Chane heard Augustine scream and then footsteps pounding through the house, heading toward the back. Alarm for Jennie's safety overrode all other concerns. He stepped over to the bed, afraid he'd see Jennie dead there.

To his relief, the still figure was that of her brother. Realizing he may have just seen the man who killed him, Chane grabbed Peter's wrist and groped for a pulse.

Jennifer opened her eyes cautiously. For the first time in days her head was not pounding. The influenza that had held her in its grip seemed to be passing at last. Perhaps today she would have the energy to go home and see Peter.

Through the limp draperies straggling down on either side of Frederick's parlor window, sun shone with painful brightness. She shoved the draperies aside. Traffic appeared to be moving for the first time in days. She hadn't seen Peter since the night of his beating. The pressure to get back to him was a worrisome thing, though the flu had blunted most concerns except for her own survival.

Frederick had gone out, hopefully to buy groceries. She hadn't eaten in days and felt weak and tired. She washed in the basin near the kitchen stove for warmth, then walked into the bedroom to get her clothes so she could dress in front of the fire.

A knock sounded on the front door. Jennifer opened it to find Simone there, tears streaming down her cheeks.

"Simone…" The look in Simone's eyes caused a cold place to form around Jennifer's heart. "What is it?"

Simone shook her head. Tears flooded down her cheeks. "We just got word at the theater. I came at once. It's Peter. He's…dead."

Chane rushed back to the Bricewood and turned it inside out looking for Jennie. He found one employee who thought he had seen her stepping into a cabriolet the afternoon the blizzard started, but no one had any idea where she was going or if she had gotten there.

Tom Wilcox turned up another employee, a bellman, who thought he saw her getting into a cab with one of the dancers—a young man. Tom Wilcox sent his men out to interview cabbies.

By four o'clock Chane had exhausted every lead. He and Steve sat in Chane's office and tried to think where she could possibly be. Mrs. Lillian confirmed that Jennie had been missing since before the blizzard started, but she thought Jennie had returned home and been caught there by the storm. She had tried to call Jennie, but the lines had already been pulled down by the storm.

At four-thirty Chane's secretary stepped into his office. "Excuse me, Mr. Kincaid."

"Yes?"

"There's a young man here to see you."

Chane glanced quickly at Steve, then followed his secretary out into the hall. A thin young man in a cheap wool hat and coat stood beside George's desk.

"Are you Mr. Kincaid?"

"I am."

He handed Chane a large brown envelope. Chane fished a bill out of his pocket and held it out to the young man.

"Thank you kindly, sir," the sallow-faced youth said, grabbing the bill. Then he backed away a few steps, turned, and broke into a run. Chane strode back to his office, picked up his letter opener, ripped the end of the envelope and pulled out a note and two photographs.

At first they were upside down and his eyes didn't focus the patterns into recognizable shapes. Then, slowly, he turned them and recognized what he was looking at. It was a traditional pose; Frederick Van Buren was seated and Jennie was standing complacently behind him. It could have been any formal photograph, except that Jennie was naked, and so was Van Buren.

Chane's mind became oddly analytical. He had seen a number of photographs of naked women—it was one of the first uses to which the camera had been put—capturing on film what should not be shared with anyone except the men who loved them.

But then his mind veered back into the personal again. He recalled an image of Jennie rocking in the rocking chair on the ship, holding her flat little belly and talking to their unborn child. Were these photos a hint of an ongoing affair with Van Buren? How could the woman who had been cherishing her unborn child go from that to another man's bed? A wave of nausea swept upward from his stomach. He steeled himself to keep from vomiting, concentrated on the ticktock of the clock on the wall opposite his desk, forced himself to count the seconds until the urge to spew up his lunch passed.

He decided this must be a trick. Jennie couldn't have betrayed him with her dance partner. These might be old photographs. She never claimed to be a virgin. And she was young and high-spirited. Perhaps these had been taken long ago.

Chane realized Steve was still standing behind him. He must have seen at least a glimpse of the photographs, since he was looking carefully at his shoes. Chane could not imagine sharing this information with anyone, not even Steve. But he'd need to tell someone, and he could trust Steve.

Who could possibly have sent these photographs, and what did they hope to gain? Was Jennie being held prisoner somewhere? He realized one sheet felt different from the others. It was a note. He slipped it on top of the pictures.

Jennifer Van Vleet is waiting for you at 358 First Avenue.

Kincaid, his mind corrected. Jennifer Kincaid.

He shoved the photographs back into the envelope. "I'm going out," he said shakily.

Steve Hammond was appalled by the sudden change in Chane. His friend's healthy color had receded, leaving him gray. "I'll go with you."

Steve looked determined, and Chane had no energy to argue. He might need Steve's help. "All right."

Simone insisted on staying awhile with Jennifer. But Jennifer was so grief-stricken, all she wanted was to be alone. Simone took her own grief with her back out into the frozen city.

Jennifer lay down in the front room where she'd slept these past few days. Tears flowed freely, but they brought no relief from the crushing grief that gripped her. Peter's face filled her mind. The longer she cried, the more enraged she felt.

She lost track of time. A knocking sound startled her. It sounded like the front door again.

"Who is it?"

"Jennie, it's Chane. Open the door."

At the sound of his voice, her heart leaped into a wild, erratic rhythm.

"Jennie!" Even through the door, his voice commanded her. The sound became confused with the memory of their wedding. "Do you promise to love, honor, and cherish this woman until death do you part?" Her mind seemed to work oddly now, to spurt out thoughts in disjoined little bits and pieces.

"Jennie!"

Jennifer glanced at the clock on the dresser. Five-thirty. And already dark outside. A few days ago she would have thrown open the door and rushed into his arms. Now she walked to the chest of drawers where Frederick kept his revolver, took it out, fumbled with the cylinder until she was sure it was fully loaded, then put it into her skirt pocket.

Chane pounded on the door.

Every nerve in her body jerked. The pounding came again—*bam, bam, bam.*

Rage flushed through her with such heat she felt dizzy. Her fingers tightened on the cool, smooth metal of the revolver. She gripped it with one hand and turned the doorknob with the other. The door swung wide.

Chane loomed at her in the shadowy hallway. His suit was wet and rumpled. He looked as though he'd slogged through mud in it. His face was haggard and unshaven.

At the sight of her, Chane's eyes glittered with unaccustomed hardness. Oddly impersonal, his gaze jarred her, and she realized that he probably had killed her brother.

Chane had managed to hold himself together this long because he knew that the second he saw Jennie, he'd know how things stood between them. And he was right. Looking into her eyes, he knew, and hope died in him. But part of him continued to function, to record information. She looked ill, pale and gaunt. And she'd been crying.

Despite the sure knowledge that she'd betrayed him, for one moment he wanted to reach out and pull her into his arms. He'd wanted her so badly these last few days that he could hardly bear to give her up just because he knew he had to. He wanted to hold her and bury his face against the silky sweetness of her hair and skin one last time. But of course he wouldn't. Part of him knew better and felt ashamed.

Jennifer recoiled as he shook a brown envelope at her. "Take it. I want you to see..." Fire kindled in Chane's eyes as he reached into the envelope and pulled out a picture. He shoved it toward her, demanding that she look at it.

Jennifer recognized it immediately as one of the photographs Frederick's sister had taken last year. She had burned most of them before Frederick could stop her. Stronger and more determined, he had saved the others from her wrath. She had demanded *he* burn them, but he'd talked her into letting him keep them. Now, with Peter dead at her husband's order, they were irrelevant.

"These are old photographs," she said dully.

"Did you let Frederick make love to you?" Chane asked, his voice deadly quiet.

Jennie's gaze wavered and dropped. Grief filled Chane. He felt sick with so much grief and pain.

Jennie reached into her pocket and pulled out the gun, which she pointed at him. "You killed my brother," she whispered raggedly.

Chane looked down at the gun, but its meaning did not register in his mind. The pain of her betrayal was dull and sickening. It rose within him like a tide of filthy water. He felt suffocated by it. He'd been a fool to marry a woman who'd do this to him. A fool.

She hadn't fired the gun yet, but a wound opened in him and throbbed with intense grief. This was worse than if she had died, because she was still here, needing to be dealt with. He had to talk to her, to arrange things between them, to acquit himself in a manner that wouldn't add any more shame to what he'd done—falling in love with a woman who felt nothing for him, a woman who had betrayed his trust as if it were of no consequence. Latitia's words lashed him. He'd been warned, and still he'd let it happen.

"How many ways can you kill a man, princess?"

His husky, pain-filled voice reached down inside Jennifer. He was trying to confuse her. The only important thing she needed to remember was that Peter was dead, and Chane had caused it. Her finger tightened on the trigger. A wave of dizziness almost overwhelmed her.

The gun was aimed at his head. Chane looked into the muzzle and sighed. "Your hand is shaking. You might miss such a small target." He reached out and lowered the pistol until it pointed at his broad chest.

The gun felt too heavy. Jennifer could barely hold it.

"Here," he said, tapping the center of his chest. "At this range, one bullet is all you'll need."

Jennifer's finger squeezed on the trigger, and she felt it waver between holding its position and giving in to the pressure. In one second he would be dead. Her mind stripped away his dirty shirt. Once again she saw his broad, naked chest covered with crisp black hairs curling around flat nipples, furring the lean taper of his rib cage, swirling around his belly button.

If she pulled the trigger the way his sea green eyes dared her to, he would never use that tall, lean, clean-muscled body to lure another woman to her doom. One tug of her finger on the trigger and she would avenge her mother, her father, and her brother. Just a little more pressure...

Her consciousness closed down to a pinpoint of light at the end of a shadowy tunnel. She flung the gun away from her, sagged against the wall, and covered her face with her hands, crying raggedly. She'd had too much of death already today.

"What's the matter, Jennie? No guts?" His rich, husky voice taunted her.

Jennie turned on him. "You dare mock me? After what you've done?"

"You'll understand if I have Steve take care of you instead of doing it personally, won't you?"

"Of course," she spat bitterly. "You certainly wouldn't handle these nasty little details yourself."

For one second Jennifer was tempted to make Chane shoot her himself. But not even her rage and grief could stand up to the glacial scorn she could see in his eyes.

In the dark hallway, Steve wondered what was taking so long, when a distraught Chane emerged from the apartment.

"Take her wherever she wants to go. Give her whatever she needs. I don't ever want to see her again."

Steve frowned. "Are you sure?"

The look in Chane's eyes stopped Steve. It was a look of such bitterness and determination that he flinched.

"I'm going to walk back to the hotel," Chane said.

"Take the carriage. I can get a cab."

"I *want* to walk."

Chane strode through the snowdrifts blindly. Near Washington Square Park he became aware that someone was calling his name. He came out of himself enough to stop and look around.

"Mr. Kincaid!"

Chane finally located the person yelling at him. Derek Wharton, reporter for one of the yellow rags, stood beside Edgar Noonan, a man Chane disliked almost as much as Derek. Noonan turned furtively away, as if he didn't want to be seen. But Derek strode toward Chane, a cocky smile on his pale face.

"Hey, Kincaid, I just heard that one of *your* bridges collapsed in Jersey. What do you have to say for yourself?"

For a moment Chane listened in silence, but the image he'd seen earlier, of Wharton and Noonan together, suddenly made sense to him. Noonan had been a saboteur during the Civil War. He had the engineering knowledge to disable a bridge. And he'd been known to do odd jobs for the Commodore.

Wharton and Noonan! Was it possible that Wharton, who was a known gambler, had run up gambling debts in Peter's name? Had Noonan beaten Peter? Were these the enemies Jennie had alluded to?

Wharton stepped closer and poised his pencil over his tablet. "Tell me, Kincaid, how do you feel now that the tables have turned?"

A red veil fell between Chane and the world. With his left hand Chane grabbed Derek Wharton by the coat lapels; with his right, he hit him. Wharton's fear only increased Chane's rage. Once started, he couldn't seem to stop himself. He just kept hitting him because it felt so satisfying.

He probably would have killed him, but Edgar Noonan ran over and tried to drag him off the limp reporter. Chane turned on Noonan, just as happy to hit him as Wharton.

The thought came to him that Noonan might have been the man in the red bandanna in Peter's room. Noonan was big and meaty and he fought well, but even he was no match for Chane. Soon Noonan collapsed and fell back, but Chane kept hitting him until someone pinned his arms behind him.

Chane fought with all his strength, but the man yelled for reinforcements. Finally, panting and cursing, Chane recognized his coachman, Patrick Kelly, as one of the men holding him. Slowly, all the fight drained out of him.

"He knows us," Patrick said. The pressure on Chane's arms was released. He struggled into a standing position.

"I told you I'm going to walk back to the hotel," Chane said.

"I'm beggin' yer pardon, sir, but ye're a bloody mess. Ye've a cut over that eye that needs tending…"

CHAPTER FIFTEEN

Jennifer felt sick. Chane was gone. He had motioned Steve aside, spoken to him in low tones for several minutes, then left without another glance at her.

Jennifer knew she could probably reach the gun, but her limbs felt too heavy. The weight of losing both Peter and Chane at the same time was too much to bear. Let him kill her.

"May I take you somewhere?" he asked.

"Do it here." She had no energy to go anywhere.

"Very well." Steve cleared his throat. "Mr. Kincaid has asked me to handle all the details of the divorce. He has, ummm…asked me to provide for your needs. He has an estate north of here, White Acres…if you'd like to go there for your confinement."

Jennifer's mind dumbly repeated the words, *divorce, confinement.* Apparently he didn't have to kill her. He'd killed her brother and her will to live, but she was no threat to him. Steve's voice droned on. Jennifer forced herself to try and hear his words.

"Mr. Kincaid has canceled your brother's gambling debts. He will provide monthly support for you and your brother, so you may continue to live in the house on Fifth Avenue, he will…"

Steve apparently did not know Peter had died from the beating Chane's thugs had administered. It didn't help, except it was good to know Peter wasn't supposed to have died. At least Chane had not meant to hurt her in this terrible way.

Jennifer doubled forward, the pain within unbearable. It was a surprise to her as well. Part of her mind worried about the image she presented to Steve Hammond, a stranger who no longer liked her, who saw her as an unfaithful wife. Another part marveled at the way she could just fold forward and cry as if she had no control at all.

"Mrs. Kincaid—" Steve stopped. Jennifer cried silently. Her slim shoulders shook with the intensity of her crying; it seemed to act on him in a curious way. Steve could not continue. A swirl of his own vague, painful memories crowded to the surface of his mind, as if summoned there by the sight of her crying.

He waited in confusion and frustration. Finally, when he was sweating as if he had run a mile or more, she looked up. Her eyes were red and swollen. "Mr. Kincaid doesn't need to be so generous. My brother is dead," she whispered.

Steve frowned. "No, your brother is alive. Chane interrupted what was apparently an attempt to kill him."

Jennifer uncovered her face and looked at Steve.

"What?"

"Chane saw your brother alive this morning. He's been badly beaten, but he appears to be recovering."

"Simone said Peter was dead…" Hope sprang alive in her. "Will you take me home?" Jennifer asked, wiping her eyes.

"Do you have a coat? It's cold outside."

Steve found it in the entryway closet. In the carriage, he sat across from her. They didn't talk. Jennifer had no need for words, and Steve could think of nothing except Chane's pain and grief. Chane had looked like hell. Steve had never seen him so smitten with a woman as he had been with Jennifer Van Vleet. His loss was proportionately large. Steve was glad women didn't seem to take to him. It had probably saved him a lot of grief.

The carriage rolled steadily through the darkness. Most of the obstacles had been cleared away by earlier traffic. At the Van Vleet town house, Steve helped Jennifer down. As he started to escort her, she tore away from him and ran up the stairs. She banged the door knocker again and again. At last a gray-haired woman let Jennifer inside. Steve returned to the carriage to wait. In a moment his eyes closed in exhaustion and he dozed.

Augustine was appalled at how ill Jennifer looked. But she was forced to answer a torrent of questions. She told Jennifer the whole story about the man who had somehow sneaked into Peter's room and had been holding a pillow over his face when Kincaid walked in on him. The man had escaped on foot.

Jennifer realized she'd been horribly wrong. It was Chane who had saved Peter. When she fully understood what that meant, her gratitude was intense, but so was her grief. She'd been wrong to believe the lies Frederick had told her. Tears burned her throat and eyes. She had made a foolish, foolish mistake. Her marriage was over, and there was nothing she could do about it now.

She checked Peter's room. He was sleeping soundly, and she didn't want to wake him. Standing by his bed, she gazed down at him and wept as she gave silent thanks that he'd survived.

When the tears passed, she straightened herself and rejoined Steve in the carriage. "You were right," she said stiffly. "My brother is alive and recovering." Her color and spirit had returned. "Will you take me to the Bricewood?"

Steve considered her question. Chane had directed him to take care of Jennifer. In his opinion that probably meant doing whatever she needed so she could reestablish her life without him. But it certainly didn't mean bringing her back to him.

"Excuse me, ma'am, but Mr. Kincaid doesn't want to see you again, right away anyway. If you don't mind—"

"I do mind."

She looked like a woman he wouldn't want to cross. Startled, Steve rapped on the carriage and told the driver to take them to the Bricewood. They rode in silence for a while.

An icy chill seeped through the windows of the carriage. Steve picked up a wool blanket from the seat and spread it over Jennifer's lap. Snow had begun to fall again. The sun, so bright and welcome this morning, hid behind angry storm clouds. Wind gusted against the carriage, rocking it. Steve wished Chane had asked someone else to chaperone his soon-to-be ex-wife.

At the Bricewood, Steve helped her out and took her arm. A look of panic crossed her beautiful face.

"I can't stay here," she whispered.

Steve was glad she at least understood reality. "I know that, but we'd never make it back to your house in this weather." As he spoke, one of the hotel employees yelled and pointed. Steve followed his pointing finger. One of the great old sycamores lining lower Fifth Avenue slowly toppled across the road, blocking traffic.

Carriages tried to circumvent the fallen tree by driving into the Bricewood's covered entryway. Within seconds, the entry was clogged with carriages topped by drivers screaming, "Out of my way! I was here first!"

Steve took Jennifer's elbow. "You'll be safe here. This storm might not last long," he said, more as a prayer for himself.

• • •

Chane sat up on the side of the bed. Mrs. Lillian tapped lightly on his door, walked in and stopped, apparently not surprised to see him there. "I know you said you didn't want to be disturbed, but Jennie's here and she says she has to see you. She has something important to tell you."

A thousand-pound weight pressed against his chest. "Send her away."

"I tried," Mrs. Lillian said, "but she won't leave."

He struggled to bring his energy up. When he had mustered all he could, he stood up, put on his coat, and walked to the back door. He trudged down the stairs and out of the hotel. The icy wind stung his face, and he raised his coat collar. He didn't know where he was going, but he couldn't risk any more encounters with Jennie.

Arctic blasts of wind whipped around him. He felt too tired to force himself forward, but he was unwilling to go back. He walked south. He could have walked north, but it seemed easier to put the wind at his back.

"He left, dear. I'm sorry." Mrs. Lillian's eyes were filled with love, compassion, and finality.

Jennifer realized it was over. He really wouldn't see her again. Despair almost swamped her.

She walked to the elevator and took it down to the Grand Ballroom. She would see Simone, find out why she had carried a lie to her. She sat down in the fifth row beside Bellini, watching dancers rehearse on an almost empty stage. Apparently, a few had stayed at the Bricewood for the duration of the storm.

Bellini glanced over at her. "How's your brother?"

"Alive and getting better."

"Good. Good."

On stage, Simone and Frederick rehearsed the second half of the peasant scene from *Giselle*. He executed the *développé sauté* flawlessly.

The *pas de deux* ended and Jennifer strode toward the stairway to confront the pair of them. She found Simone first. Her face was pinched with grief. Her eyes had the haunted look of a woman for whom the world had ended.

"My brother is alive," she said, watching Simone's reactions carefully. At the news, Simone burst into tears. There was no mistaking her joy and relief. She looked like a woman who had been given a second chance to live.

"Thank God," she breathed. "Are you sure?" she asked, sniffing back tears of joy.

"Yes, I just left him. He has been badly beaten, but he is recovering." She told Simone the story Augustine had told her about someone trying to smother him, and Chane interrupting just in time.

Simone raised a shaky hand to her eyes. "Oh, thank God," she repeated again, tears flooding her eyes. She stepped into Jennifer's arms and held her tight.

"Who told you he was dead?"

"A messenger came with a note. I didn't see him."

"I wonder if the messenger was sent to coincide with his being murdered? Whoever sent that messenger may have hired the would-be killer." Out of the corner of her eye Jennifer saw Frederick trying to slip past unnoticed. She let go of Simone, caught Frederick by the arm, and whirled him around.

"You gave him those pictures! How could you?"

"What pictures?"

"You know what pictures! The ones of us!"

"I gave them to no one!"

"Chane had them!"

"Well I didn't give them to him. I swear to you!"

"Liar! I'll never, ever forgive you for that!" Jennifer said through gritted teeth. "I hope you rot in hell, Frederick Van Buren."

"Jennifer, dammit! Kincaid is a bastard! I tried to warn you about—" A terrible thought flashed across his mind. "Jennifer, wait...Latitia—"

"I don't ever want to hear that woman's name again."

Frederick caught Jennifer's arms and shook her.

"Dammit, Jennifer, we belong together, just like that pair of robber barons. They deserve each other."

"I hate your guts, Frederick! I hate you!"

His look beseeched her, but she turned and ran from the stage. Her life was over. And it didn't really matter whether it was bad luck, carelessness, or deliberation that had ended it.

Jennifer took the elevator to the room Mrs. Lillian had set aside for her. She tried to call Peter to tell him she'd gotten trapped at the Bricewood, but apparently the telephone lines were down again, or still.

She found a blanket and draped it over her shoulders so she could stand at the window watching the raging storm. Chane was out there somewhere. She thought of him and her heart ached.

New York was still and silent. Not a vehicle rolled through the white-blanketed streets. Not a man nor a woman was to be seen on the sidewalks. Except for the howling wind and the blowing snow, nothing moved.

She prayed that Chane was inside, warm and safe and asleep.

The next morning, to pass the time, Jennifer joined the troupe and worked out at the barre for two hours. During the break, Simone whispered that Bellini had fired Frederick.

"Do you know why?" Jennifer asked.

"Not really. I think it...I heard a rumor that it was a suggestion by the management of the hotel." She shrugged, embarrassed. "But I don't know."

Jennifer didn't know how she felt about that. She could certainly understand why Chane wouldn't want Frederick around. But to destroy his career?

The break ended and Bellini ordered them into the center of the room. "We'll start with your first solo, Jennifer."

She was only ten beats into it when Bellini rapped his cane on the barre. "Listen to the music! You are two beats behind where you're supposed to be."

"Two beats?" Jennifer couldn't believe it. Usually her timing was her most reliable asset. She started again, saw Bellini shaking his head, and stopped. "Now what?"

"Feel the music, Jennifer!"

"I do feel it."

"Then why are you now three beats behind, and you've only just begun?"

She tried six more times, and failed. Finally, with tears in her eyes, she walked back to center stage, determined that she would do it this time or die.

Bellini walked over to her, took her hand, and started her at the right time. Seconds later he rapped his cane on the barre again.

"Now what?" she asked, perplexed.

"I just don't know how you could get so far off the beat in only a few seconds."

He was glaring at her as if she were doing it on purpose. Jennifer's chin started to tremble. Tears burned behind her eyes. Bellini shook his head in chagrin. "Take a break. We'll try again later."

Jennifer intended to spend Christmas alone in her room, but Mrs. Lillian invited her to Christmas dinner. It was a glum affair, subdued by Chane's continued absence.

Without knowing how she knew it, she realized that the longer Chane stayed away, the slimmer were her chances of reaching him once he came back.

"Hello," Steve said into the telephone mouthpiece. There was no answer. He waited a second. "Hello."

Chane had to force himself to speak. "Steve...Chane here. I, uh... just wanted to see how things are going."

"Business has been slow, what with the blizzard and all." He paused. "And Jennie's still here at the Bricewood. She got stuck when the last blizzard blew in."

"Thanks," he said. "I'll call again before I return."

"When will you be coming back? Where are you? Mrs. Lillian's been worried about you."

Without responding, Chane hung up and sagged back into his chair. In spite of everything, part of him ached to be with Jennifer. Another part of him knew better, but it felt too damaged to ever function again. The rest of him would have to drag that part of him around forever. It would serve to remind him that he had no business falling in love. Colette had certainly given him reason never to love again, but he hadn't learned that lesson.

Shame filled him, triggering the memory of an event he had all but forgotten. When he was seventeen and serving with the Texas Rangers, his friend Charlie had been captured and killed by the Comanches. They'd scalped him and cut off his testicles.

Chane had helped dig the hole to bury him, but even that hadn't worked off his anger. When he finished digging, he hurled the shovel away from him, barely missing one of the other Rangers.

His captain took Chane aside. Pulling off his hat and dragging his arm across his perspiring brow, the captain said, "Charlie was your friend. You didn't want him to die. But he and his maker had other ideas. You kin either keep on being mad or you kin make a good stagger at life like the rest of us."

"I don't know how to do that," Chane had admitted, wiping tears out of his eyes.

"Jes plow to the end of the row. Ya gotta accept what ya cain't change. I have a rule for myself. Anything my dog trees, I'll eat. Simple as that."

He had treed Jennie. Now he would get over her.

Chane willed himself to accept the prospect of life without her. It helped to pretend Jennie had died. He willed himself so sternly and so persistently that within five days he could sit up straight and eat a meal. When he had eaten three meals in a row and slept most of a night, he decided he was ready to go back and make a good stagger at life.

On Wednesday, a week after the blizzard that had brought New York to its knees had ended, Chane returned to the Bricewood.

Jennifer heard the news of Chane's return from a young waiter rolling a dinner cart into Chane's suite down the hall from hers. He was back. Her heart pounded, and her body seemed tense as a buggy spring, but she felt paralyzed. Before, she'd wanted to rush to see him, and now she couldn't bear to face the hatred she would see in his eyes.

That afternoon, Steve Hammond called on her, looking uncomfortable. His eyes avoided hers. "I, uh…brought an agreement… outlining the things we talked about earlier."

"We already have an agreement."

"This is a little more comprehensive, and it's written." Steve knew the fallacy in verbal agreements between men and women. He was not a complete innocent.

Jennifer read it in silence. Chane was proposing to pay her a thousand dollars a month if she would stay away from him. He was willing to settle a hundred thousand dollars on the child at birth to assure its care. He would change his will to make her child his heir. He would settle other sums on the child when it reached certain ages.

"It seems all right to you?" Steve asked nervously. "We can negotiate the amounts. He wants to be fair. Whatever you say…"

"It seems fine." Holding the agreement in both hands, she tore it cleanly in half lengthwise.

Steve had worked for hours on that document. He couldn't believe she would just tear it up like that. Staring at her beautiful, relentless face, he realized that women had a lot more violence in them than he had thought.

She let the long strips flutter into the wastebasket beside the mahogany desk and lifted her gaze to Steve's.

"As difficult as you will undoubtedly find this to accept, I am refusing his generous offer. I will not sell him his freedom or my right to his name." Rage was apparent in every word. "He is my husband. He married me for better or for worse, and I intend to hold him to that."

She walked to the door, opened it for him, and watched with satisfaction as Steve walked through it and quickly away.

For the first time in days she wanted something specific and attainable. She wanted to talk to Chris Chambard.

CHAPTER SIXTEEN

"Jennifer! *Mon ange!* Come in. Come in. *Mon dieu,* what has possessed you to stand on my doorstep with slush up to your knees?"

Christopher Chambard didn't wait for her reply. He pulled her into the room, slammed the door, and guided her shivering body toward his fireplace.

"That is a long story," she replied grimly. She had walked away from the Bricewood expecting to find a cabriolet, but every vehicle passing her had been filled. So she'd had to walk all the way to Chris's house, on Park Avenue in the forties, an area of fine old homes that formed the core of an exclusive residential district.

Her feet were wet and cold, and her back ached. Her coat had barely helped. After a short time of walking through snow, the bottom of her skirts and petticoats had become sodden and filthy up to her knees.

"We need to get you out of those wet things," Chris said, ringing for Newgate, his butler.

Newgate smiled warmly at Jennie and led her into Christopher's bedroom, where a fire crackled in the hearth. Newgate brought one of Christopher's bathrobes, waited outside the door until she had changed, then took her dirty clothes.

Jennifer walked back to the library to rejoin Christopher. Newgate brought a tray with hot cocoa and tiny sandwiches. Jennifer sipped the warm, chocolaty milk and sighed. At last she warmed up enough to stop trembling.

"*Mon ange...*" Christopher prompted.

Jennifer told him what had happened between her and Chane. Christopher listened, his fine gray eyes telegraphing his compassion and support.

"So where do you go from here?"

"To see Peter. I have been so worried about him. But he probably thinks I've forgotten him. I only managed to visit him once, and he was asleep..."

"Peter knows you love him. How could he not? You have been dotty about that young man since he was an infant."

Jennifer smiled at the truth of his words. "Men forget. They're more likely to ask, 'What have you done for me recently?'"

Christopher laughed. "Ah, women are getting smarter." After a moment he asked, "What about Kincaid?"

"He hates me now. It's over."

"Who ended it?"

"He did, of course."

"Ahhhh," Christopher said, shrugging his dismissal. "An affair of the heart is not over until the woman says it's over."

"I might wish that were so, but I know better."

Christopher smiled and shook his head.

"Christopher, what are you saying?"

"That you are abdicating your responsibility," he replied simply and emphatically.

"Abdicating! With any other man perhaps, but not with Chane Kincaid—" Her voice broke on his name. A rush of hot, intense feeling pressed like a wedge against her throat. She could not continue.

"Jennifer, we are trapped in these human bodies. We have no choice. We can fight our battles with people we love and know well or we can keep training new people to fight with."

Jennifer laughed, brushing aside quick, hot tears. A gleam of love and compassion lighted Christopher's eyes. She looked frantically away. She could handle anything except tenderness. "Don't be sweet to me."

"I should be mean to you?" he asked gently.

"Yes, please."

"Sorry, *mon ange*, but I could never do that. You are like a son to me."

Jennifer laughed. To Christopher that was the ultimate compliment. Tears streamed down her cheeks. She reached up and brushed them aside.

"Stay here tonight. It is almost dark. I will not have you traveling these streets alone."

"I need to see Peter."

"Call him. The telephone lines seem to be up, at least in some parts of the city."

Jennifer asked the operator for the Van Vleet town house and waited. Augustine came on the line, sounding wan and unsure of herself.

"Augustine, it's Jennifer. Is Peter there?"

"No, madame." Her tone brightened at the sound of a beloved voice. "He went back to work today. I don't expect him until later."

"Tell him I called, will you? I'm going to spend the night with Christopher."

"That old man! Pah!"

Jennifer laughed. "I'll tell him you said hello."

Augustine snorted her disgust.

"Tell Peter I need to talk to him…I'll call him later. If he comes home early enough for us to talk, perhaps I'll have him send the carriage for me…"

"Are you well? We've been worried."

Jennifer reassured Augustine and ended the conversation. Christopher guided her gently into the guest bedroom where Newgate had started a fire. "Lie down until dinner, *mon ange*. You look exhausted."

Jennifer did not remember falling asleep. She woke suddenly, as if something had startled her, but heard nothing. A lamp burned on the bureau. The room was too hot. She had thrown her covers off. She felt sweaty and sticky, and her back ached terribly. She struggled into a sitting position and looked around her, trying to remember where she was.

Christopher's house. She had spent many nights in his house as she was growing up. He always left a lamp burning for her. Her stomach growled, and she smiled at the thought of him letting her sleep through dinner.

Another familiar pressure reminded her she needed to pee. She slipped off the high, feather mattress and squatted to look under the bed for the chamber pot. She saw it and stood up, rubbing her aching back with her free hand.

Her borrowed nightshirt felt wet. In the dim light from the fireplace, it looked black. Puzzled, she touched the darkness and recognized it as blood.

She pulled the covers back. Another dark spot soiled the indentation where her hips had lain.

A terrible thought crossed her mind. Had she miscarried? What was she to do about it? She'd heard all the usual horror stories about miscarriages, but she'd never heard anyone say that anything made a difference. A doctor probably wouldn't help. She knew nothing about having babies, but she felt certain that the minute blood appeared, it meant the baby was dead.

Confused and chilled, Jennifer took off the wet nightshirt and picked up the towels Newgate had brought for her earlier. She put one over the blood, climbed back into bed from the other side, folded the other towel under her hips, and covered herself to stop her shivering. She felt badly that she'd ruined Christopher's fine feather mattress ticking. She would have it replaced for him.

Jennifer was devastated about the baby. She had promised she would take care of it, but somehow she hadn't. It had probably already died. She wanted Chane. She needed him. She hoped this was a bad dream. She wanted to wake up in the morning to find the bed clean and dry, and her baby safe inside her. She felt feverish. Chane should be here with her. He had said he would take care of her, and she needed him now.

Then she remembered how Chane had looked. *How many ways can you kill a man, princess?*

She had killed him and the baby. Grief filled her. And then hopelessness. She had failed him and her baby. Chane had been right to banish her from his life. She made too many mistakes. Her whole body felt as though it were crying. She pulled the covers over her head and closed her eyes.

She woke to see Newgate's concerned brown eyes peering into her face. He had sad, asking eyes that reminded her of a terrier Peter had brought home once. She had the urge to reach up and pat his head, but her arm didn't respond to the signal. He seemed to need something from her she was unable to do. He kept calling her name. Her eyes closed.

She woke again. This time a man she'd never seen before was frowning down at her. "Mrs. Kincaid...I'm Dr. Antonovich. I need to examine you." He had a Russian accent and kind eyes.

He probed her belly with his fingers, asked questions about her last monthly, looked at the blood in the bed, and sighed. "You seem to have miscarried. Based on your last menses, you couldn't have been more than six or eight weeks along."

Sadness welled up from some deep place in her. It was so spontaneous and hot that she could not control it. Tears filled her eyes and ran down her temples into her hair. She wanted Chane. She rolled over and covered her face with her hands.

Part of her cried and part didn't. It felt odd to cry over a baby she didn't know, would never know. Part of her wondered at her sincerity, but not the part that was crying. With the loss, she had finally realized that the baby had been real.

Embarrassed, the doctor cleared his throat, walked to the door, and opened it. Christopher must have been pacing in the hall outside. The footsteps stopped.

The doctor spoke in hushed tones. "She's miscarried. Appears to be fine, though."

"She will recover?" Poor Christopher. He was like a mother to her. His voice was tight with worry.

"She needs rest. Lots of it."

"*Oh, la la,*" Christopher breathed.

"Keep her in bed a week. She's lost a good deal of blood. Send Newgate to my office. I'll have the nurse make up some pads for her."

For days Jennifer was glad to be in bed. She had no desire to talk to anyone, not even Peter. The thought of lifting the telephone filled her with despair.

The doctor came again on the fourth day. She endured his checkup stoically, then sat up and pulled her gown around her.

"When can I go back to work?"

"What kind of work do you do?"

"I'm a ballerina."

"Oh, not for a week or so. Wait until the bleeding stops completely."

"Isn't this bleeding more like my monthlies?"

"I suppose," he admitted weakly. He didn't appear to enjoy discussing these intimate matters with a woman.

"I'm not hemorrhaging, am I?"

"No, no, it's not that sort of bleeding."

"Then I can go back to work as soon as I feel like it?"

The morning of the sixth day dawned bright and clear. The sky looked misty toward the ocean, but crystal clear inland. Mid-morning, Jennifer walked down the long curving stairs for the first time since her miscarriage.

The warm kitchen smelled of bacon and yeasty, fresh-baked rolls. Newgate was an excellent chef who could have worked for prestigious giants of industry, but he'd chosen not to. His only regret was that Christopher Chambard was too light an eater. Christopher failed to eat the enormous quantities most of the wealthy consumed, but Newgate appeared happy in spite of it. Christopher entertained the *crème de la crème* of the artistic community.

They breakfasted before the fireplace in the kitchen. Few French aristocrats ate in the kitchen, even in a fine, cozy kitchen such as this one, but Christopher was old enough, and rich enough, to ignore any convention that displeased him.

"How are you feeling, *ma petite*?"

"Like I've honeymooned with a legion of praetorians."

"Are you trying to excite me?"

Jennifer smiled. "Make you jealous, maybe."

"Too bad you're a woman. You would make a charming companion for this old man." She was a delightful-looking female creature. Her creamy white skin, enormous violet-blue eyes, and silver-streaked ash-blond hair set her apart from other women. Even without her sleek young goddess's form, she could stop traffic at Times Square.

"You've had days, Christopher," she said. "What did you find out?" She knew him well enough to know that he had immediately begun contacting his powerful friends.

"I hate to spoil your breakfast."

"I'm not that fragile, even now," she said, taking a big bite of a biscuit between mouthsful of Newgate's delicately herbed omelette. The coffee was rich and black, and she had laced it liberally with sugar and heavy cream. "Tell me, Christopher."

He held the crystal butter dish in place for her while she stabbed at the pale yellow mound. Then he pursed his thin lips. "I could not find out much, but even that was helpful. By piecing together the scraps, I came to the conclusion that your husband's enemies are out to destroy you. Latitia Laurey is busily telling her friends that Chane Kincaid has already thrown you over and is in love with her. They are having a party to announce their new and very public alliance, which may include business as well."

Jennifer's smile faded into sadness.

"The party will be on Saturday night," he continued, "for a few close friends and wealthy investors who might be willing to invest in Kincaid's railroad venture."

"But in reality," she said, putting down her fork, "it's to announce that his marriage to me was a short-lived mistake and that he has now come to his senses." Jennifer felt as if she'd been kicked in the stomach. A knot formed there, threatening to push her breakfast back up. She knew Chane had every right to survive this. She didn't blame him, but it hurt that he had turned to Latitia so soon.

"What are you going to do, *mon ange*?"

Jennifer shook her head. "Nothing. It's over. I'll do as the doctor says until I can dance again—"

"You'll just give up?" he demanded, interrupting.

"Chane won't see me. He won't even talk to me."

Christopher gave a very Gallic shrug. "Kincaid lives in his head. When a man lives in his head, it has a tendency to get out of order without his realizing it. Like," Christopher waved his hand, groping for words to explain, "my cluttered desk. For a long time I am comfortable with the clutter, then one day I realize I no longer know where my most important papers are."

"Is that why I didn't realize how much I cared for Chane until it was too late?"

"You live in your body. When a dancer lives in her body, as you do, it has little accidents without her noticing. One day you look down and see a bruise."

"I can't believe Chane would give a party now. He was too wounded to even consider such a thing." She sat a moment in silence. "Oh no!"

"What?" Christopher asked, frowning.

"This was supposed to be *our* party...to announce our marriage to his friends. I remember when he told Mrs. Lillian to send out the invitations..."

Christopher waited.

"It was our party," she repeated. "You told me that an affair of the heart isn't over until the woman says it's over. Do you think that's really true?" she asked, fixing him with a piercing stare.

"Of course."

"Then I'm going."

"Is that wise?" he asked, putting down his fork. "I mean, your condition. You're still weak."

"Christopher, I've babied myself and wallowed in misery for days, but I feel fine now," she said dismissively. "A little blood may unnerve a man, but I'm a woman."

Upstairs, Jennifer chose a blue gown Newton had had delivered from her house only yesterday. She arranged her hair and dressed with great care.

When she was finished, she stopped before the mirror and gazed at her reflection. Something had changed in her. Hope had returned. As soon as she'd realized that Chane hadn't planned the party to accommodate Latitia, she'd begun to feel more hopeful. Perhaps Christopher was right. Perhaps women did decide matters of the heart. At any rate, she was going to test it.

• • •

Christopher's carriage delivered Jennifer to the steps of the Bricewood. Faces turned and mouths dropped open. The usual heavy buzz of numerous conversations stopped. She realized that everyone in the hotel must know what had happened. She didn't know who would have told them, but with Derek, Latitia, Frederick, and Simone privy to her business, it could have been anyone.

In the pindrop silence, except for the click of her heels, Jennifer swept through the lobby. She found Steve Hammond in his first-floor office next to Chane's empty one. Steve almost knocked his swivel chair over backward as he rose hastily to his feet.

"Good afternoon," she said, smiling.

Steve's mouth dropped open. Jennifer stood before him in a lovely blue gown and bonnet, her beautiful eyes gleaming with determination, her pale face lit with a transcendent glow. To his amazement, she reached over gently and nudged his chin up with a warm hand, smiling into his eyes as if she were accustomed to men's mouths dropping open at the sight of her, and as if she had every right to be here, as if she owned the place, or would in a matter of minutes.

"How have you been, Steve?"

Steve considered her coming here such a serious blunder on her part that his mind went numb. Her smile set off every alarm in his body. "Uh…fine, yourself?"

"Couldn't be better," Jennifer said. "How is Mrs. Lillian?"

"Uh…fine, fine."

"And Chane?" she asked sweetly. "How is my husband?"

Steve's eyebrows shot up, and he forced them down before she did it for him. Her eyes smiled with innocent sweetness. Her face glowed.

"Uh…fine, fine." Steve felt foolish. He had said fine so many times, he felt out of control. "How…may I help you?" he asked.

"How sweet of you to ask," Jennifer purred. "As a matter of fact, Steve, there is one tiny little thing you can do for me."

"Would you care to sit down?" He waved a nervous hand at the wing chair across from his desk.

"Why, thank you. I'd like that very much." She still smiled that terrifying, honeyed smile. Beads of moisture broke on his brow.

"Would you like something to drink? Tea?"

"I had a lovely lunch with a dear friend. Are you comfortable, Steve? You look…odd." Her dulcet tone was solicitous, unnerving. Her only wish seemed to be to make him comfortable, but the more insistent she became, the more distressed he felt.

"Oh, no, no. I'm fine." Steve heard himself saying that damned word again and loosened his ascot. Heat flushed into his face. He felt like a schoolboy.

"Steve," she said, smiling happily, as if about to confide a wonderful secret. "I need to do some shopping this afternoon. As you know, I'm temporarily short of funds. I was wondering if you might give me a letter of credit..."

"I'm sure you know I cannot authorize expenditures without Mr. Kincaid's approval."

Smiling, Jennifer leaned forward and pushed the telephone toward him. "Of course," she said, leaning back in her chair. "Call him."

His forehead burned. Steve reached for his handkerchief. Embarrassment almost overwhelmed him. He couldn't see himself calling Chane with her sitting there smiling at him. He also couldn't see himself asking her to leave the room while he called her husband.

Jennifer lifted a pendant watch and glanced at the timepiece, then back at Steve. He cleared his throat, reached for the telephone, and cranked the handle. The operator came on the line. "Ring Mr. Kincaid, please."

Steve tried to organize his mind, but Chane's voice on the other end of the line startled him so, he almost dropped the telephone.

"Hi, uh, Mr. Kincaid, uh..." Steve said, feeling doomed. Chane would know already that something was amiss. Steve never called him Mr. Kincaid. Steve tugged at his ascot again. Jennifer's chin lifted and her lovely eyes narrowed on him. Steve's mind stopped working. "Mrs. Kincaid is here, in my office..." he blurted.

"Mother?"

"No, umm...your wife."

Silence stretched out between them. Finally, Chane asked, "What does she want?"

"A letter of credit."

"Give her whatever she wants."

"Up to?"

"Whatever she wants. And then get rid of her."

"Well," Jennifer asked. "What did he say?"

Steve hesitated. His own experience with women precluded him from telling her. She might go buy herself a ballet company or a hotel when all she'd wanted was a new hat. Chane had money, but there was no sense giving any more of it than necessary to Jennifer. And with the railroad venture, they needed to spend every dime wisely. But Chane was a man of his word, and fairly helpless before Jennie. In the process of marrying her, he had pledged to provide for her. Steve knew her indiscretion would not invalidate Chane's promise, at least not in his eyes. "He said I should go along and pay for your purchases."

"How sweet of him," Jennifer said, playing the role she'd decided upon before she realized how difficult it was going to be. "So utterly like him."

Steve nodded his agreement.

Jennifer rose gracefully from her chair. "Shall we go?"

Steve rose with her and stiffly held out his arm for her. He was so polite and proper—and nervous. Jennifer felt sorry for him.

Steve was struggling with two equally strong emotions—loyalty to Chane and a desire to help her in any way he could. With her before him, glowing with an inner fervor and vitality that he had never seen in another woman, he realized he wanted Chane to forgive her. In spite of all the evidence to the contrary, he wanted them back together.

But he was smart enough to know that that was not about to happen. Chane had been burned before. "No one gets two shots at me," Chane had once said grimly. "One per customer." That would be especially true for Jennie.

Jennifer frowned. "He was with a woman when you called him, wasn't he?"

"What?" Steve asked, startled.

"He was with Latitia Laurey, wasn't he?"

Steve licked suddenly dry lips. He had no idea who Chane had been with, but the look of fury on Jennifer's face numbed his usually quick mind.

Chane put the telephone down and sagged back in his chair. Just as he did, Latitia tapped lightly on his study door and stepped into the room.

"I hope I'm not interrupting," she said softly. Her voice was low and dark.

Latitia ran two of her father's companies and did a very credible job of it. She was respected for her business acumen and her ability to get things done. In a man's world, those were not small accomplishments.

But here, in his house, she became softer and more feminine, and he couldn't tell if it was an act or something that just came over her when she was around him. His ego liked to think that his masculinity dominated her so completely that she just automatically became submissive around him, but he was enough of a skeptic to doubt that.

She'd stopped by with the excuse that she wanted to help Mrs. Lillian with the party arrangements, but he knew that she wanted to continue their relationship where it had ended when he met Jennie. Part of him wanted to comply, but he felt too sick at heart. Fortunately, she hadn't pressed it.

He had forgotten about the party until yesterday. Mrs. Lillian had suddenly remembered that she'd sent out the invitations while he was in New Jersey, and, with all the subsequent excitement, she'd forgotten to cancel them. The party that was supposed to announce his marriage to Jennie would now be used to pay back his social obligations and court investors for his grandfather's railroad.

Latitia was watching him closely. He realized that she wanted him to make some sort of admission that he'd been wrong to marry Jennie, and he wasn't going to do that. At least not in words. She also wanted him to get a divorce and marry her, and he wasn't about to do that, either.

Despair rose up in him as he realized that somehow he had to get away from both Jennie and Latitia. Their needs were squeezing the life out of him. He felt suffocated. He had felt like this when he was five and his seven-year-old sister, Nell, had died of scarlet fever. He'd spent the next year thinking he saw her or heard her. Every time he did, he ached inside. After a time he grew tired and irritable from it. If he'd been a crier, he would have stayed in bed and cried, but in his father's household no male child cried or stayed in bed.

He hadn't talked to anyone about it, so no one had told him the feelings he'd felt then were grief, but now he knew. It hurt so bad, he wanted to double forward.

"God, you look awful, darling," she said softly, reaching out to touch his cheek.

"You're too young and pretty to act like my mother."

"Oh, am I?" She made a small, dark sound and stepped close to him, sliding her arms up around his neck. She pressed her breasts against his chest and her hips against his. In spite of the numbness around his heart, his body remembered what to do. A pulse started in his loins, and it felt good. She lifted her lips to be kissed.

Chane hesitated. Technically, he was still married to Jennie. Something hardened in him. Like hell he was. He put his arms around Latitia and pulled her close. "What are you doing here?" he asked softly.

Latitia gazed up at him with dark, solemn eyes. She wasn't like other women. "Here?" she asked, emphasizing the question by pressing her pubic bone against him.

It felt good to be treated like a man. He'd been treated like a fool long enough. The expression in her eyes was entirely wicked. Most women smiled too much. Latitia did not. That was one of the things he liked about her. She almost never smiled. She was like a man in that way, probably because she had been raised by her grandfather.

"I know you're technically still married to that woman, but we've never been one to stand on technicalities," she said, kissing the left corner of his mouth, then the right. Her breath was hot, her lips smooth and warm. Slowly she moved to the center of his mouth, and her tongue flicked out. A spear of heat plunged to his loins, and he was instantly grateful to her. At least he still had this.

"Excuse me," a familiar voice said.

Chane's head jerked up. Jennie stood in the doorway, hands on hips, eyes blazing.

"If you do not leave this instant, I will throw you out that window," Jennie said through gritted teeth.

Latitia released Chane and faced Jennie. "Please try," she said, her low-pitched voice tight with challenge. She smiled suddenly, and Chane realized that it was the wickedest smile he had ever seen.

Jennie started forward, and Chane grabbed Latitia by the arm and walked her toward the other door. "She's leaving."

"No, I'm not. I'll tear her to pieces," Latitia said, trying to jerk free of him.

"Not here," Chane gritted.

Furious, but unwilling to alienate him, Latitia allowed herself to be escorted to the back door.

Chane closed the door and then turned back to Jennie, who looked furious enough to tear him apart as well. "What are you doing here?" he demanded. "You have no rights here, Jennie. Our marriage, or whatever that was, is over."

The fight suddenly went out of her. Confusion washed over her lovely face. "I don't know," she said, turning suddenly. "I don't know. I guess I thought that you might have actually loved me, but...obviously I was wrong."

"You betrayed me," Chane rasped, grabbing her arm and glaring into her eyes.

Jennie returned his look for a second, stared down at his hand on her arm, and waited. Furious himself, Chane let go of her arm, and she stalked out the door. Shaken, Chane walked to the nearest chair and slumped into it. He fully intended to survive this, but every contact with Jennie left him feeling gutted. Somehow he had to get away from her.

Suddenly, the solution came to him. He would go to Colorado and oversee the building of the railroad himself. That would solve all his problems with both women, and make his grandfather happy as well.

Jennifer rode the elevator down one floor and asked the attendant to let her out. She walked around a corner to a window seat and sat down. She was sick and furious and ready to kill, but she forced herself to breathe evenly. When her hands stopped shaking, she stood up and rang for the elevator.

Steve Hammond was still in his office. He looked at her oddly, as if he wanted very much to ask her what had happened, but she ignored the look.

Steve guided her through the lobby and toward Chane's carriage, which had been brought around front. He settled her into the luxurious seat, and she forced herself back into the part she'd decided to play.

Steve stole a look at Jennifer Van Vleet. Her cheeks were unnaturally pink, almost as rich as the maroon velvet on the seats.

"Have you done this before, Steve?"

"Well, never for his wife." He tugged at his ascot, which felt suddenly tight. "Where do you want to go?"

She had never been a shopper. She generally ignored the need for clothes until she was on the verge of being disreputable. "The Ladies' Mile."

Steve wanted to groan. This could take all afternoon. The Ladies' Mile was a stretch of shops that seemed to go on forever. He directed the driver and settled back in his seat. The carriage rolled forward.

The Boutique de la Mode was next door to Tiffany's Jewelry and Notions, on Union Square, where Fifth Avenue met Broadway at Fourteenth Street. Owner-couturier Gabrielle d'Orsay provided exquisite copies of the latest Worth originals and Paris designs—gowns featured on the pages of *Journal des Demoiselles* and the envy of housewives all over the United States and its territories. Madame d'Orsay, a slender, chic, middle-aged Parisienne, catered to the wealthy.

In the shop, the thick, watermelon-red carpet beautifully set off the veined marble columns and walls. Matching red draperies screened the dressing rooms from the luxurious viewing salon.

Steve introduced her. "Madame d'Orsay, I would like to present Mrs. Chantry Kincaid the Third. She wishes to make certain purchases, today and perhaps in the future."

"But of course, madame! I am honored, madame, honored that you would consider my humble establishment."

The name Kincaid registered in Madame d'Orsay with a shock. She barely heard the beautiful Mrs. Kincaid's smiling response. *Oh, la, la!* A dress hung in plain sight near the back of the store that Mrs. Kincaid must not see. Latitia Laurey had charged it on Mr. Kincaid's account only yesterday, and the tag was clearly visible. Perfectly pressed, it was awaiting delivery this afternoon.

To Jennifer, Madame d'Orsay looked a little frantic. Jennifer followed her to the left side of the spacious shop.

"Please be seated, madame, m'sieu," Madame d'Orsay murmured. "I will have my models show you the most suitable gowns."

Jennifer smiled. Madame d'Orsay seemed beside herself with nervousness. "That will not be necessary. I know what I like. I can simply pick a few and try them on myself."

Madame d'Orsay looked horrified. Jennifer swept past her toward a purple gown that had caught her attention near the back of the shop. Madame d'Orsay followed closely behind her.

"Come. Let me show you—"

"What about this one?"

Madame d'Orsay felt faint. The very one she did not wish Mrs. Kincaid to see. She reached out and covered the tag. "This one is not for sale."

"A pity. It's quite the most beautiful one in the shop."

"I have many beautiful gowns, madame…"

"But that one is *my* color—"

"I beg to differ with madame. With your glorious hair, this silver-white gown by Worth will be sensational!"

Madame d'Orsay pressed the gown on Jennifer. Disappointed, Jennie held the silver-and-white creation up to her and walked to the mirror. It did pick up the silver glints in her hair, but it made her look too pale. She handed the gown to Madame d'Orsay and walked back to the purple one. Lifting the hanger off the rack, she carried the dress to the mirror. Immediately, her skin glowed and her eyes picked up the rich purple color.

Jennifer fumbled for the tag to see who would be wearing her gown. Madame d'Orsay rushed forward. "Madame, please allow me—"

THE LADY AND THE ROBBER BARON

Jennifer finally found the tag and read it. Chantry Kincaid, III!

Madame d'Orsay made a small strangled sound, but Jennifer smiled brightly.

"Please wrap it. My husband was probably going to surprise me with it as an anniversary present." Her smile dared the poor, distraught woman to disagree.

"But madame, I cannot—"

"Such a pity to spoil his surprise, but surely it's not your fault. The gods themselves must have brought me to this particular shop this afternoon, no?" Jennifer asked.

Madame d'Orsay turned her pleading gaze on Steve.

Steve shrugged. "I'm sure Mr. Kincaid would not want his bride of less than two weeks to be unhappy," he said significantly.

Madame d'Orsay's eyes rolled back in her head. Latitia Laurey would be furious with her. She took the gown with trembling fingers and gave it to her assistant to wrap in tissue. Jennifer picked one other gown, two crinolines, three chemises, a pair of slippers, and two hats. Enough to revive Madame d'Orsay's spirits.

Steve staggered under the load. He piled the boxes on top of the carriage and followed her into the next shop. Jennifer chose an ermine jacket and a matching fur cloche—the latest fashion from Russia, with the fur worn on the outside.

"I'll take them," she said, turning to admire herself in the mirror. She looked flushed and triumphant in white, and Steve knew in that moment that Jennifer Kincaid had come to reclaim her husband. If he could have, he would have warned her against the futility of it, but he knew better than to get between them.

Steve loaded the two new boxes onto the carriage and followed her into Tiffany's. Charles Lewis Tiffany strode over to greet Jennifer. He looked his usual stiff and dour self.

"I don't believe I've had the pleasure," he said, looking down his nose at Jennifer.

Steve cleared his throat. "Mr. Tiffany, I'd like you to meet Mrs. Chantry Kincaid the Third."

Jennifer smiled her gratitude at Steve. Tiffany blinked, and Steve could almost feel all of the man's resistance dissolve. What had survived her dazzling smile had been vanquished by the Kincaid name, which, thanks to Number One, ranked with Vanderbilt, Rockefeller, and Morgan.

Tiffany brought out a tray of his finest European crown jewels. Steve could have kicked himself. Ensuring that Jennifer was treated with respect might have just caused the one thing he'd come along to prevent. Jennifer reached at once for an amethyst pendant on a diamond-studded chain. It was stunning. Its tear-shaped purple stone nestled between Jennifer's breasts would be more than Chane could bear if he saw it, and Steve was sure that was her intent.

"Steve, it's terribly expensive. Maybe I shouldn't."

"The necklace belonged to the Crown Princess of Holland," Tiffany said. "Ten thousand," he added reverently.

Steve understood New York politics too well to blink at the price. If he did, Tiffany might just mention to an associate that Kincaid must have money problems. A rumor like that could finish Chane. Loans would no longer be available. The railroad would be doomed.

Jennifer frowned, but Steve grinned as nonchalantly as possible. "I'm sure Mr. Kincaid would want you to have it."

Jennifer searched Steve's eyes, then turned back to Tiffany and nodded. "That will be fine."

Outside the shop, Steve said, "I'm curious. Are you going to a party?"

"Of course," she said, smiling that sweet, dreadful smile again. "Chane's and Latitia's party."

Steve shook his head in wonder and admiration. It was disloyal to grin, but he couldn't help himself.

"What time should I be there?"

"Drinks at seven. Dinner at eight."

What she planned made her heart pound. "How many people?"

"A small, cozy affair for twenty friends and business associates." Steve hesitated. "You know he never expected to see you again. Latitia is an old friend."

"Oh, yes," she said with a terrible brightness. "I know."

Steve wisely dropped the subject.

CHAPTER SEVENTEEN

Chane stopped in the doorway to Steve's office. Steve looked up, a guilty flush darkening his cheeks.

"How did the afternoon go?" Chane asked.

"Expensive."

That explained Steve's guilt. And Jennie's strategy. If she wanted to destroy him, that would be one way to go about it—if she didn't know about the gold his grandfather had given him.

"How expensive?"

"Eleven thousand," Steve said miserably.

Chane frowned. "She wanted her own ballet company?"

"An amethyst-and-diamond pendant—she fell in love with it before she learned it was a crown jewel."

Steve looked as if he blamed himself. Chane shook his head. "Forget it. We've got bigger problems than that." He waved a telegram at Steve. "Remember Roudenko, the man I just hired? He tried to make a deal with Jim Hardy. Offered to let Jim overcharge the Texas and Pacific for steel rails if Jim would kick back part of the overcharge to him."

Steve groaned. That was the worst possible news. He felt moments away from being stuffed into a train and sent hurtling toward Colorado. "What do we do now?"

"While you were out with Jennie, I fired Roudenko and decided to build the railroad myself."

Steve groaned again.

The sun burst through the clouds and shone on the glistening snow. Carriages with sledge runners carved wide, deep ruts through the white powder. Jennifer stepped out of the carriage and walked toward the Bricewood. It felt good to walk.

At the bakery, the smells of fresh-baked bread drew her in. "'Morning, ma'am."

"I'll take this," she said, pointing to a roll covered with cinnamon and glaze. Jennifer paid and started to leave.

"Ma'am," the girl called after her.

Jennifer stopped. "Yes?"

"Well, it may be nothing, but—" She paused. "—I just thought you ought to know. I think a man is following you."

"Me? What makes you think that?"

"I've seen him watching you almost every day."

"Do you recognize him?"

"No, he's a stranger. And he keeps his hat real low and the bottom part of his face covered by his topcoat, like he's real cold, you know. But I think it's just so we won't get a look at his face."

"What does he look like?"

"A tall man, kinda slim. I've never seen much more of him than that."

The description was vague, but it evoked an odd feeling in Jennifer. She remembered the man she'd seen near her house, and a chill raced down her neck.

Saturday night, Steve stationed himself left of the arch leading into the dining room. From here he could watch the front door for Jennifer's arrival, if she came. The other guests were scattered around Chane's parlor in companionable groups.

The room glowed with the soft light of imported gas chandeliers, faceted lead crystal drops sparkling like thousands of tiny diamonds. Beyond the arch the dining table gleamed with golden candelabra, gold-trimmed bone china, and Mrs. Lillian's thinnest crystal.

At precisely seven-thirty the doorbell rang. Mrs. Lillian opened it for Jennifer and her escort, a small, trim gentleman with a classic French profile—a sharp beak of a nose, slanting brow, and balding head. The man removed her coat and passed it to Mrs. Lillian.

No one else seemed to have seen Jennifer's entry. Chane stood with his back to the door. Latitia smiled prettily at powerful banker, Andrew Thaxter, president of Chase National Bank. Then she glanced up and saw Jennifer, wearing the purple gown she'd ordered for this very party. She let out a cry audible all the way to where Steve stood, and started forward.

• • •

Christopher heard the warning sound and turned to pat Jennifer's cold hand. "You are stunning, *chérie*. If girls had looked like you when I was a young man…who knows?"

From across the room Chane turned slowly. Jennifer knew the exact second he saw her. His eyes narrowed and his lips thinned into a threatening slit.

"Thank you, Christopher. Excuse me, won't you?"

Heart pounding, Jennifer glided forward to greet Latitia Laurey and her reluctant husband, who could not possibly avoid her in front of his guests.

She had taken great pains with her hair and gown, but she saw no glint of appreciation in Chane's cold, green eyes as he watched her cross the room. Out of the corner of her eye Jennifer saw Steve step forward and intercept Latitia.

Scowling formidably, Chane strode forward and stopped Jennifer in the middle of the enormous room. Conversations died as people turned to watch them. Jennifer had known better than to expect real warmth in his eyes, real welcome in his smile. The achingly familiar hollows on either side of his mouth filled with shadows as he forced a smile for the benefit of those watching. But it was a sardonic curling of lips, without warmth or welcome. His eyes watched her with measuring calculation.

"Well, if it isn't my beautiful wife," he said, his voice so low that it couldn't be heard by listening ears, but cool enough to let her know he didn't mean it.

"Chane, darling," she gushed, loud enough for others to hear. "It's so good to be back."

Latitia shook off Steve's grip and followed them into the middle of the room. "Where did you get that gown?"

"Oh," Jennifer said, smiling coolly. "Do you like it? My husband bought it. I was so surprised to discover it," she said, deftly reminding Latitia that she had erred in charging it to Chane.

Andrew Thaxter, smiling warmly, walked over and joined them. Latitia controlled herself with an effort.

"Well, well, Chane!" Thaxter said, slapping Chane on the back. "What have we here?"

"Andrew," Chane said, his voice ringing with barely controlled fury, "I'd like you to meet my…wife, Jennifer Van Vleet…Kincaid."

Thaxter smiled warmly at Jennifer, took her hand, and kissed it. "You don't remember me, Mrs. Kincaid, but I was one of the men who pulled your carriage through the streets of New York after your debut at the Bellini."

Jennifer smiled in spite of herself. That had been one of the happiest days of her life. She had dreaded her New York debut, because she thought New Yorkers would be too jaded to accept another European-trained ballerina. They had amazed her in a great many ways—serenading her hotel, pulling her carriage to the theater, and piling the stage high with roses.

"It is about time you finally unveiled your bride, Chane. But now I can see why you've tried to keep her from us. She is even more exquisite than before.

"We do get to kiss the bride, don't we?" Thaxter asked, pulling her forward and pressing warm lips against her cheek.

Every man and woman in the room queued up to meet her. After his initial shock, Chane stayed by her side and introduced her. Jennifer was complimented in the most glowing terms by men and women alike.

To all outward appearances, Chane played the adoring husband. His manner was correct, even to the degree of warmth with which he smiled at her, as long as they were being observed, but after the last introduction, he steered her forcefully into a quiet corner. Alone with her, he dropped his pleasant mask.

"What do you hope to gain by this charade, Jennie?" he asked, his husky voice grim.

Jennifer set her champagne glass down on the sideboard next to her. "Smile, darling, Mrs. Teasdale is watching you."

Chane turned her so his back was to the assemblage. "I don't give a damn what they think of me, and you know it. But I had hoped to spare us both a public display of our dirty laundry."

Jennie's skin was as smooth and flawless as carnation petals in the golden glow of the chandeliers. Her lovely mouth reflected the rosy hue of her gown. Even her eyes had taken on a rich purple cast. Every line and curve, even the delicate yet heady fragrance of her Gillyflower perfume, called out to his senses. Part of him wanted to pick her up and toss her out the seventh-floor window. Another part of him felt alive for the first time in weeks.

"I've no pride, Jennie. I'm willing to beg you to leave and never come back, if that's what it takes…"

She lifted her chin as if daring him to kiss her. A flash of pure hellcat flickered in her eyes. "It didn't take you long to find a replacement."

"Latitia is an old friend."

"Then she won't mind if I kiss my husband."

Without taking her gaze from his, she stepped close to him. One hand touched his face and the other rested on his jacket. He knew he should move away, but her touch burned into his chest and paralyzed him.

Jennifer felt his helplessness and pain all the way to her toes. She might have stopped, spared him and herself, except her only hope was to take control, however she could get it. If she had been powerful before, she must still have some of that power. If she didn't use it, she would regret it the rest of her life.

Deliberately, her hands slid up behind his neck, felt the familiar stubble of hairs there, slid around until they rested lightly on either side of his face, cupping it. And once she had touched him, the ache and the need were there, fierce and hot within her.

Chane would have given anything in the world if he could feel nothing, but his heart and body, probably even his soul, quaked before this woman. She touched him, and her hands seemed to control him, even the rate and rhythm of his heartbeat.

"I could break every bone in your body," he whispered hoarsely.

"Then do it," she replied, gazing intently into his eyes.

Chane cursed himself for his weakness, but he just stood there, outwardly tall, powerful, and sturdy, and let her do what she wanted with him. He felt as if his whole awareness was focused on her. She seemed to be supporting his entire weight with two cool, trembling hands on his face. Her warm, satiny mouth touched his tentatively, and the shock neutralized any energy he might have used against her.

Supported by her hands on his face and her mouth, moving over his, he felt incapable of anything except the response he couldn't control. Part of him wanted to fling her away from him. But the part that controlled movement was mesmerized by her tongue tip darting with diabolical skill, destroying him totally and effortlessly. His hand fell away from her arm.

Finally, she relinquished his lips and opened her eyes. He wanted to say something to deny what she had done to him, but words did not come.

"I had to talk to you," she said. She reached for her glass, but her fingers trembled, so she hid her hands behind her.

"We have nothing to say to one another." The steely look in his eyes told her he was back in control. And determined to stay that way.

"I was tricked into going to Frederick's. I had no choice. Frederick made it seem as if the driver would take me home during the snowstorm, but the driver wouldn't."

Chane shook his head in disgust and turned away.

"It's true," she said, stopping him before he could walk away from her. She felt certain that if he did, it would all be over. "Frederick might have planned this, or maybe someone gave him the idea."

"Who would do that?"

"Your enemies."

"I don't have any enemies. Except you."

"I was never your enemy. I admit my brother tried to enlist my help, but I refused. Who told you that I was working against you?" Chane shrugged, but she sensed the truth. "It was Latitia, wasn't it?"

"What if it was?"

"Perhaps *she* is your enemy."

"I told you, I don't have enemies."

"What if it was Latitia who sent you those old photographs? And what if it was Latitia who set up the whole thing?" Jennie demanded. But when Chane's face turned ashen, she knew she'd gone too far. Her voice quivering, she said, "Chane, I need to talk to you about something."

"About what?" he asked, his color slowly returning.

"I...had a miscarriage. I lost...the baby." Her voice broke, and unshed tears sheened her eyes. Defiant and embarrassed, she looked away as if trying to keep him from seeing her reaction, but he had already seen it.

"I'm sorry, Jennie," he said gently, meaning it.

Mrs. Lillian rang a tiny crystal dinner bell. "Dinner is served," she announced to the assemblage.

"Do you want me to leave?" Jennifer asked, her voice barely more than a whisper.

"I assume you're going to do what you came here for, whatever that may be," he said bitterly.

Jennifer took heart. He had wanted to say yes, but he couldn't bring himself to do it. Another man might have denounced her in front of a roomful of friends, but he hadn't done that, either. She felt weak from all the things that could have gone wrong, and still might.

Andrew Thaxter walked over and held out his arm to her hopefully. "Your guests await you, Mrs. Kincaid."

He walked her to the queen's end of the table, deposited her with a flourish, and took the seat on her right, place cards be damned.

Christopher took the seat on her left. Chane guided Mrs. Thaxter to his end of the table. Edmée and Nathan Brantley, Chane's friends whom Jennifer had met at the German Winter Garden, were seated near her.

Conversation and wine flowed freely. At the center of the table Randolph Harrington turned to Latitia. "What a nice surprise this must have been for you. Your friend arriving out of the blue like this."

Latitia was unable to reply. Harrington finally turned to the lady on his left. The serving maids seemed to hover around Latitia, refilling her glass at every sip, offering her service in a dozen irritating ways while gay conversations were going on all around her. Meanwhile, Jennifer was reigning like a queen, and Chane didn't look at Latitia once. She felt worse than she'd ever felt in her life. Jennifer was wearing *her* gown, but Chane fairly vibrated with awareness of Jennifer. Everyone had forgotten that Latitia Laurey existed. Except Christopher Chambard, who knew too much about her. She did not expect him to share any of his information, but the careful way he kept track of her rattled Latitia, made her feel sick and trapped.

Tears crowded her eyes and had to be blinked back a dozen times. Finally, unable to stand it any longer, Latitia stood to leave before she humiliated herself completely by crying in public.

Halfway to the door a hand on her arm stopped her. Latitia tried to shake it off, but it was Jennifer. Her eyes narrowed with rage, she rasped, "What are you doing in our home?"

"You betrayed your husband. It's not your home anymore," Latitia said coolly, as if she were astonished that Jennifer had had the nerve to come back. "And, you stole my gown."

"How dare you to slither in here and try to take my husband while our wedding vows are still echoing through the halls."

Latitia felt such a surge of hatred that it was all she could do to keep from springing on Jennifer. But Chane had done nothing to throw out this bitch who had made a fool of him and of herself. And until he did, she would be shamelessly out of line in the eyes of society. If she wanted to hold her head up in this town again, the first move had to come from him.

Frustration was so strong in Latitia that she almost could not bear it. Abruptly, to keep herself from doing the wrong thing, she turned away from Jennifer.

A maid balancing an enormous silver platter of honey-roasted Muscovy ducks in a sea of Madeira and currant sauce tried to sidestep Latitia. But she was not quick enough. The platter tipped, and the ducks and sauce slid forward, hovered in midair for one horrible moment, like an oncoming tidal wave, then poured into Latitia's décolletage and crawled slowly and messily down the length of her stylish red satin gown.

Latitia screamed with rage and slapped at the ducks in sticky sauce as if they were still alive and attacking her. When the silver tray hit the carpet, just missing her toes, she let out one final, piercing scream and flung herself out of the room.

Jennifer turned away in amazement. Mouths hung open the length of the table.

"Whatever happened?" Mrs. Harris asked.

"I saw it, but I have no idea!" Mrs. Teasdale gasped.

"Good grief!"

Jennifer's gaze flew to Chane's face. For one heartstopping moment he reminded her of a marauding barbarian. Andrew Thaxter, who seemed determined to protect her, stood up and walked around the table. He took her elbow and guided her back to her chair. "The Wellfleet oysters are excellent, my dear. May I call you Jennifer?"

"Please do."

Table conversations resumed. Silver tinkled against china. The look in Thaxter's twinkling eyes told her he understood more than had been explained to him, and he took great pains to keep Jennifer involved in answering his questions.

Maids rushed in and cleaned the duck from the plush mahogany-colored carpet.

At last dinner ended. Jennifer realized anew the difficulty of what she was attempting. At any moment Chane could denounce her and send her out of the room in humiliation. Her nerves felt raw.

Andrew Thaxter turned her over to his wife, who seemed as kind as he. Thaxter pulled Chane aside. The women strolled into the parlor.

"Beautiful young woman. As fine a young woman as I've ever seen," Thaxter said, watching Chane closely.

"Thank you, sir."

"I would hate to see her unhappy."

Chane felt sure his shirt collar was about to suffocate him. He pulled at his cravat. "Glad you could come tonight, sir."

"I've been a friend of your father's for many years. Fortunately, I know that a Kincaid's word is his bond. Kincaid men take their wedding vows seriously. I'm sure you will do everything within your power to keep her happy."

"All women are not wives, sir."

Thaxter ignored that cryptic remark. "I noticed you leaving *that bank* yesterday as I was coming back from an appointment. Did everything go the way you wanted it to?"

Chane sighed. New York was worse than a small town. The bank Thaxter referred to as "that bank" was the First National. "No, but I can't fault Smithson. I think I shocked him."

"How much did you ask for?"

"Four million."

"Well, maybe the First National isn't good for it." His eyes twinkled with mischief. "Maybe I should start a rumor to that effect."

Chane laughed. New York was a town where a man could start a rumor in the morning, hear it and not recognize it at lunch, and act on it in the afternoon as if he had just received vital information.

Thaxter grew more serious. "Can you pay it back?"

"I believe so. As you may have heard, I'm going to oversee the building of my grandfather's railroad. We need operating capital before we can hope to sell bonds."

"To extend the Texas and Pacific to California?"

"From La Junta into New Mexico along the Santa Fe Trail first, then on to California."

"Ahhh. Yes, I had heard you were going to take that over for Number One. How is his health?"

"His doctor says he's hanging by a thread. But he doesn't seem to be deteriorating."

"He's a tough old bird. And how are your folks?"

Apparently, his mother had told no one about her health problem. Chane would not be the one to reveal it. "Supposedly on vacation, but I suspect my father is starting a new business enterprise in the Mediterranean. I doubt he knows how to take a vacation."

"You're not going to spend all the four million at one time, are you?" Thaxter asked, eyeing him shrewdly.

"No, sir."

"We can cover your needs as they arise?"

"Yes, sir."

"Good. Come by tomorrow so we can take care of the paperwork."

Chane's eyebrows rose. He'd sweated blood with Smithson and gotten nowhere. "Just like that?"

Thaxter shrugged. "You have excellent taste in wives. Jennifer is delightful. If you don't repay the loan, she's mine."

Chane took the amused glint in Thaxter's eyes to mean he was teasing about taking Jennifer. "You're serious about the loan?"

"About both." He sighed heavily. "Unfortunately, you probably won't have an opportunity to find out. I fully expect you to repay the loan *and* keep your wife happy."

Thaxter held out his hand. Chane took it. Andrew Thaxter was one of the most honorable men he knew, and a keen judge of character. Somehow Jennifer had fooled him.

An hour later he caught Jennifer by the arm and guided her into an alcove. "What do you want here?"

"I want my husband back."

"Why?"

"You promised to love, honor, and protect me."

"And you promised to be faithful."

"I made a mistake."

"As I did." He glared into her challenging eyes for a moment and saw she wasn't going to back down. "All right. You've won a questionable place for yourself—if you want it. I wouldn't."

His eyes burned into her. Her heart pounded hard. She searched his face. He was telling her that she could stay, but it would never be the same again.

"I still want to stay," she whispered.

"What about what I want?" His tone was harsh.

"I'm hoping you will relent."

"I can't love a woman who could do to me what you did."

"It was an accident…"

"I've never accidentally made love to anyone myself. You want to explain to me how that happens?" he demanded bitterly. The deep hollows in his cheeks above the jawline made her heart ache with the need to touch him.

"Give me a chance," she pleaded.

"I thought you were staying, no matter what I want."

"Is there any way you could *let* me stay?"

"You mean give you my blessing?"

"Yes…Please?" she whispered.

Chane felt dizzy with pain. His heart felt as though it would stop under the weight of what she was asking. "I promise you nothing."

"I accept your promise."

At midnight Mrs. Lillian closed the door on the last departing couple and walked to the telephone to call for a cleanup crew.

Jennifer looked at Chane. "Good night."

"Why are you doing this?" he asked.

"I'm your wife."

"Right," he said dryly, his voice husky and grim. "What happened to your need to be a full-time ballerina?"

Jennie's face crumpled with misery. "I can't dance anymore. I still want to dance, but my body won't cooperate."

"So you have to make peace with me in order to dance?"

"It seems so."

She leaned against the wall to steady herself. Suddenly, she looked pale and shaky. Chane realized she couldn't have lost the baby all that long ago. He scowled and shook his head. "You're exhausted. Get some rest."

"I don't know where…"

Seeing the look of confusion on Jennie's face, Chane turned to Mrs. Lillian. "Put her in the extra bedroom."

Jennifer was surprised that he was going to allow her to stay in the same apartment as he. She had expected him to suggest the adjoining suite. She'd been all set to resist it, but it hadn't been necessary. Perhaps he was just trying to keep up appearances, since it seemed to be necessary for his investors. But whatever the reason, she was glad.

"Excuse me, sir."

Peter looked up from the book he was reading. Malcomb stood in his doorway. "A…Miss Bettina here to see you." Peter scowled and laid the book on the bed beside him. "Tell her I'll be down in a moment."

Before Malcomb could turn to deliver his message, Bettina slipped around him and stepped into Peter's room.

"Thank you, Malcomb," she said firmly. She returned Malcomb's scowl and closed the door in his surprised face.

Peter put his book down, coiled forward and stood up.

"He's a bit stiff, don't you think?" she demanded.

"He's good at his job."

Bettina threw off her coat and let it drop on his carpet. Her slim young body was encased in a white blouse and black skirt. Her blond hair, slightly darker than Jenn's, was pulled back from her pretty face and tied in a bun. She reached back, undid the bun, shook her hair out, walked right up to him, and put her arms around his neck. "I've always wanted to see what a young swell's bedroom looks like."

"Would you like some tea? I think Malcomb could be persuaded to serve…"

Bettina giggled. "I want a kiss for starters, then I have something to tell you."

Peter laughed. "You're too shy for me."

Bettina patted his cheek and stood on tiptoe to kiss him. Her tongue slipped into his mouth and sucked his tongue between her teeth. She bit him just hard enough to cause a heated stirring in his loins, then leaned back, laughing. "Not bad," she said, "for a man caught by surprise." She squirmed her hips against him and led him over to the bed. "Now let's see what you can do with a little warning."

"Why are you doing this?" he asked.

"You've seen me making eyes at you at least a dozen times over the last two years."

"Lots of girls make eyes. Not many of them come into my bedroom and try to lay me down on my own bed."

Bettina giggled and squirmed against him again. "Well, I might've never done anything about this hankering I have after you, but I got some information you need. Thought I'd just do us both a favor and bring it on over."

"And just what do you know that's so important?"

"Well, I'm glad I finally got your attention."

She kissed him again. Then she tugged until he lay down on top of her. "I like to feel a man on top of me."

"I'm not going to make love to you here."

"You feel real good on top of me. That old man'll be asleep in a matter of minutes."

Peter rolled off her. She giggled and rolled over on top of Peter. He felt foolish with a young woman sitting on his hips, grinding herself into him. The fever she awakened in him was eating away at his good sense. Another few minutes and he wouldn't remember his own name if he didn't do something.

Bettina kissed him. "Too bad you're so uncooperative. I'll just have to keep my news to myself."

"Tell me!"

"Oh, no."

She reached up and unbuttoned her blouse. She wore no shift or chemise underneath. Her white breasts jiggled with her squirming. She had the pinkest nipples he'd ever seen—the color of strawberries. His mouth filled with saliva. Beads of sweat broke on his forehead. He swallowed with difficulty.

"Give me a hint," he said, his voice thick with desire.

"It's about your sister and Kincaid."

Something else in Peter hardened. He took her by the wrists and forced her over onto her back. "Tell me."

Bettina searched his face. Everything about him had changed. Before, he had looked boyish and uncertain. Now he looked like a man—determined and ruthless. She felt herself getting wet between the legs.

"You're hurting my hand," she whimpered. Peter loosened his hold on it, and she slipped it down between their bodies and caressed him through his trousers. She strained upward to kiss him, caught his bottom lip between her teeth, and bit hard into it.

"Owww," he growled, pinning her down and taking her.

Afterward, Peter lay there cursing himself. If Kincaid's men were waiting outside for him again the way they had after Simone's visit, he deserved whatever they did to him.

Somehow they had both gotten naked. Bettina lifted her bottom up in the air and waggled it at him. He slapped it hard enough to leave a red handprint.

"Go get us some food," he said.

"What do you want?" she asked, smiling lazily, as if the evening wasn't over yet.

"Bring everything." All of his appetites seemed to be working suddenly.

Bettina scampered cheerfully off the bed, grabbed his robe out of the armoire as if she'd been there a dozen times before, and did as she was told. She came back with a tray piled with cheese, wine, chicken, apples, and pie. He hoped Malcomb was asleep. The sight of her, with the robe gaping to reveal one plump, jiggling, strawberry-tipped breast, would have finished Peter's reputation and sent Malcolm to bed with a problem of his own.

They ate in the middle of the bed. Her mouth full of apple, Bettina finally decided to talk.

"Did you know your sister came back from her honeymoon the other day?"

"What do you mean, honeymoon? She went to Washington."

"What kind of brother are you anyway?" She giggled, took another bite of the apple, and continued. "What a surprise that was! Her marriage to Kincaid."

Peter felt as if all the blood in his head had drained away.

JOYCE BRANDON

"Peter, you're not listening to me."

He arranged his face into a listening mask and tried to ignore the hard ache in his chest. He couldn't believe Jenn had married Kincaid without even telling him. He felt as if his vitals had been ripped out.

"Your sister came back like one of the furies. I'm glad I'm not Latitia Laurey."

"What? Why?"

"Your sister may look like such a lady that butter wouldn't melt in her mouth, but she can sure fight for what she wants. Can you imagine? They're barely married two weeks, and he moves another woman into what was supposed to be their love nest."

Bettina wiggled in anticipation, watching him with her enormous, baby-doll eyes as if he would be able to explain his sister's actions. Pretending his sister was no concern of his, he shrugged and plumped the pillow at his back. To distract Bettina, he reached over and caressed the firm underswell of her breast and saw the nipple blossom and harden.

"Peter, stop that. I won't be able to concentrate." She squirmed her bottom into the bed like a chicken settling into its nest. "Your sister came back in the middle of a big, ritzy party Kincaid and Latitia were giving. One of the serving girls told me about it. Well, not exactly, she heard it from one of the girls who was there, though. Anyway, your sister threw Miss High-and-Mighty Latitia Laurey out of that party, bag and baggage. Can you imagine? In front of all Latitia's hoity-toity friends! Jennifer even had enough spunk to dump a bowl of soup down the front of Latitia's dress. She ran out of there screaming like a banshee. I bet that was a real cat fight," she said with obvious satisfaction.

Peter closed his eyes. The thought of his sister lowering herself to the level of a street-fighting, hair-pulling harridan for a man like Kincaid nauseated him. He leaped off the bed. "Time to go, little one."

"What? I thought we'd—"

"You thought wrong." Peter helped her into her clothes and hustled her down the stairs. He opened the front door and thanked God for Malcomb, who had called for the carriage that waited in front of the door. Peter hustled Bettina down the steps and into the carriage.

"Where do you live?"

She gave him the address, and he shouted it to the driver whose face and head were covered against the icy wind that whipped the skeletal limbs of the trees.

The carriage pulled away, and Peter raced back inside to the telephone. He rang the Bricewood and asked for Mrs. Kincaid. Within moments he heard Jenn's voice.

"Hello?"

Peter closed his eyes and replaced the earpiece back into the cradle.

Jason had no idea where the address he'd been given was, but it didn't matter. He had no intention of taking Jennifer Van Vleet anywhere except to his own flat.

He barely felt the cold that the team of horses so clearly resented. What he'd been waiting for had finally happened to him today. Following Jennifer had finally triggered that thing in him that he both loved and hated. Lust had grown so strong that he had to act. His whole body was on fire with it. So he had waited in front of her house all day, and finally she had arrived. He'd heard her ask the driver to wait, and as soon as she was inside, he'd approached the cabriolet, overcome the driver, and taken charge of the carriage.

Now, he stopped the carriage, got down stiffly, and opened the door.

"This isn't the place. Why'd you stop?" the woman asked, her face a pale oval in the dim light of a street lantern. Disappointment surged in Jason. She was the wrong woman. He cursed, and at first couldn't think what to do, but as he looked at her staring back at him in sudden fright, he realized that she, too, was slim and blond and pretty. His disappointment was sharp, but lasted only a moment. He could think of this one as extra. After he killed her, he would still have Jennifer.

Jason pulled his rope out of his back pocket. "Just need to secure something here."

He stepped into the carriage, grabbed her hands, and began to tie them together. She fought like a tigress, but she was no match for his strength. He tied her hand and foot, and then pulled her head up by her hair.

"You wait for me here," he said softly, wiping her tears with his free hand. Her skin was soft, and he felt it all the way to his loins, which ached damnably. He wanted to take her now, but he was not that big a fool, even in the shape he was in. And, if he wanted it to be good, he had to do everything in exactly the right order.

He drove to his apartment, secured the team, slung her over his shoulder, and carried her inside. He had rented a brownstone with this in mind. His flat was on the corner, so he had only one neighbor who could see his front entrance from a window, and that apartment was rented by a young couple who had better things to do at night than watch the neighbors' houses.

He stopped in the parlor to light a lantern, then carried her to his room and tossed her on his bed. She lay still while he rummaged through his carpetbag for his equipment. He found the small satchel and carefully opened it. His special knife gleamed softly in the lantern light. He was careful, so the woman didn't see it. He turned away so she couldn't watch him, and he pressed the knife to his throbbing member, holding back the groan that shuddered through him. Finally, he put the knife aside; he wasn't ready for it yet, but when he was hot like this, he needed to feel it and see it, since it was going to bring him the relief he needed.

Reassured that relief was in sight, he rummaged through his bag until he found a handkerchief. He walked back to the girl and held the lantern close to her face. She was still crying, and that made it hard to tell, but she did appear to have blue eyes. A jolt of heat caused him to tremble inside. Blue eyes were important. Blue eyes were necessary. They all had blue eyes. He swallowed and tried to remember to breathe through his nose. He hated mouth-breathing, because it made his mouth so dry, but sometimes he just couldn't help himself. He got so excited.

Her eyes reflected terror, and he couldn't think why she'd be so scared. She had no idea what was about to happen to her. He pried her lips aside and looked at her teeth. "You got some pretty teeth there, missy. If you scream, I'll break every tooth in your head," he said softly. "You wouldn't want me to do that, would you?"

She shook her head. He used the handkerchief to cover her eyes. Then he got out the rest of his equipment. He set up the tubes and bags and connected the special hollow-tipped knife to the drainage tube. He checked all his connections to be sure there was no leakage. When he was certain that everything was in readiness, he undressed himself and the girl. She cried and begged and whined, but he ignored her.

He made up a solution of soapy water and made her drink it. She threw up in the bucket until her stomach was empty. He carried the bucket to the back porch and poured the contents into the hole he'd dug earlier. He covered it over and walked back to the bedroom.

The ritual of doing everything in the same order and in the same way increased his excitement to where his blood felt like it was boiling. Sweat poured off him. The girl shivered with cold, but he had no idea why. He was on fire and should have provided enough heat for both of them.

Next, he tied her hands to the headboard, and her feet more loosely to the footboard of the bed. Then he carefully chose a place on her neck and inserted the knifepoint.

Peter was up and dressed by seven o'clock the next morning. He asked Malcomb to have the carriage brought around. He put on his coat and went outside to wait for it. He found a man sprawled behind one of the enormous concrete balustrades that framed the steps leading up to the door.

Peter knelt beside the man. "Hey, Robert, this is no place to sleep." He shook his shoulder. Slowly the man turned and rolled over.

"What happened?" he asked.

"I don't know."

The man frowned. "Someone hit me." An alarmed look came over the man's face. "Where's my cab?"

"There's no cab around here."

"Someone stole my cab," he said, struggling to his feet.

Peter took the cabbie inside to use the telephone. A policeman came out to make a report, and Peter gave the cabbie a ride to his home, which was far across town. Then he went downtown to talk to an army recruiting officer. Within minutes he had purchased himself the rank of captain in the United States Cavalry.

He signed the necessary papers, then invited the heavyset man, Sergeant O'Leery, to go with him for a drink to celebrate. When they were served and finally alone, Peter leaned toward him.

"Sergeant, I was wondering...I suppose with so much paperwork—" He paused. "—do enlistment papers ever get...misplaced?"

O'Leery took another sip of the excellent whiskey Peter had ordered for him and a grin spread across his solidly Irish features. "Well, lad. Accidents happen, to the best of us."

"I realize it's hard to keep track of so much paper. It'd be a shame if something happened to *my* enlistment papers...for a month or so." Peter reached into his pocket and pulled out fifty dollars.

A scowl of disapproval darkened O'Leery's red face. "You did a young lass wrong?"

"She did me wrong."

O'Leery fingered the fifty-dollar bill, a month's wages for him. "A month at the most," he growled.

Peter shrugged. "She'll give up if she can't find me right away."

O'Leery took the fifty and slipped it into his pocket. "If she keeps looking for you, though…"

Peter shrugged. "Then she deserves to find me."

Jennie stepped out of the elevator and paused. Chane looked up from where he sat with the hotel manager, saw her, and stopped speaking. She had meant to walk casually past with a nod of acknowledgment, but she stopped in front of him. His forest-dark eyes watched her warily. The brick wall was still solidly in place, but she knew he was still in there somewhere, and she had the feeling he could be reached, if she had the courage to keep trying.

The manager made an excuse and walked quickly away.

"Going for a walk?" he asked. His voice started a lonely ache in her throat.

"My doctor recommended it."

"Probably just the thing…"

"Only around the block actually…"

Chane forced himself to look away from her lovely face. She was still, in spite of everything she'd done to him, incredibly pleasing to look at. She had the most beautiful skin—as flawless and as pure as a baby's—and the softest eyes.

"When can you dance again?"

"Who knows? The doctor said a week or so, but with my rhythm off so badly…"

She wore a simple high-necked rose gown that emphasized the creamy whiteness of her skin and hinted at the small round breasts beneath the soft cashmere. Breasts that he knew felt as satiny as carnation petals. His hands ached to reach up and touch them.

"Do you ever take walks?" she asked.

"Not on purpose."

"Maybe you could pretend it's research."

His defenses failed him. "All right." He wasn't getting anything done anyway. He was so useless, Steve had practically thrown him out of the office.

"Will you help me put this on?"

Hames, the bell captain, flush-faced and resplendent in gold-and-white livery and gold tricorn, rushed forward. "May I be of assistance, Mr. Kincaid?"

"No, thank you, Hames. I think I can help her into her coat by myself." Chane felt foolish, letting a young man's eagerness make him cranky and short.

Hames's face fell in disappointment. He stepped back and turned away. Every eye in the lobby had been on Jennie ever since she had stepped out of the elevator. He remembered what Mrs. Lillian had said. "She has charisma. I've seen women more beautiful, but none more riveting."

Chane held her coat while she slipped her arms into it.

Instead of crossing to the park, they walked south on Fifth Avenue for several blocks. The sidewalks were crowded with people passing from shop to shop, some pushing perambulators with sleeping or crying infants inside, others just out for a walk in the afternoon sunshine.

Lower Fifth Avenue was known as Millionaires' Row. It was lined on either side with looming chateaux and elegant brownstones. They were filled to overflowing with the trappings of opulence—outrageously expensive imported European sculpture and paintings, rare tapestries, and delicate antiques.

As they entered the orderly precincts of Washington Square Park, Jennifer glanced over her shoulder. Was that someone just slipping behind a tree? A shiver of fear ran icily up her spine.

"Are you cold?" Chane asked. "Shall we go back?"

"No, no, I'm fine," she said, grasping his arm a little tighter. "Let's go on."

They walked across the park in silence. Jennifer was so glad to be near him, she didn't want to risk saying the wrong thing and causing him to turn back. But as they crossed West Fourth, she couldn't help looking behind her again.

Chane stopped and watched her. "Whatever's the matter with you? What are you looking for?" he asked sharply.

Jennifer looked up at him and hesitated. She wasn't sure she should tell him. "I think someone is following me."

Chane sighed as if horribly burdened suddenly. "It isn't going to work, Jennie."

"What isn't?"

"Inventing some danger."

"I'm not making this—"

"I don't want to hear any more of your lies."

"I've never lied to you!"

"Jesus," he growled, frustrated beyond thinking. "Well, maybe you should have. If you're so damned trustworthy, why did you do it, Jennie?"

She looked away. "I thought you had betrayed me by having Peter beaten. And, I don't know how it happened. I thought I could trust him."

Chane expelled a frustrated breath. "You trusted a man who took you to his apartment? Why in God's name do you think a man takes a woman to his apartment?"

She hated it when he spoke to her in that tone, as if she'd planned the whole thing just so she could climb into bed with Frederick. Wordlessly, she stalked away.

Chane strode angrily after her, caught her by the arm, and turned her forcibly, his face twisted by frustration. "A woman has to know how to take care of herself if she's going to retain her veto rights. If you go to a man's apartment, you've forfeited that right."

"I had no choice! There was a blizzard. The driver wouldn't take me farther. His horse was freezing to death!"

Tears brimmed over and ran down her cheeks. "And...and then Frederick told me that your men had beaten my brother and left him for dead."

"Not my men. And not by any order of mine. I don't have people beaten," he said grimly.

"They worked for you. They beat him up."

"Well, hell, I don't own them. They do what they want after hours. Maybe your brother pissed them off. I find it hard to believe that a young man with such poor judgment only has me for an enemy."

Chane turned her back in the direction they'd been walking.

"Poor judgment! How dare you make derogatory remarks about my brother, who is half dead because of you!"

Frustrated, Chane turned her back toward the hotel. He never should have gotten this close to her, much less married her, but he'd been besotted by her. Fortunately, that was over now, and he was thinking clearly again. His enlightenment had come too late to save him, but not too late to serve as a warning. Next time he'd listen to his grandfather.

CHAPTER EIGHTEEN

Simone looked up at the enormous Van Vleet town house on Fifth Avenue and Thirty-second Street and shivered. Icy wind whipped around her, swirling her skirts and chilling her legs. She was wracked by indecision. It was too late to be calling on anyone, especially Peter, but she couldn't help herself. She hadn't seen him since he'd been hurt. She knew she shouldn't have come here again, especially since he hadn't tried to contact her since the night they'd made love, but she couldn't seem to stop herself.

Before she could turn and flee, she reached out and banged the door knocker against the metal plate on the heavy mahogany door.

She waited a full minute, counting. Just as she was ready to leave, Malcomb, his stiff white collar askew as if he'd hastily put it back on, opened the door and peered out.

"Is Mr. Van Vleet here?"

Malcomb motioned her into the vestibule. "Come in, come in. The wind…" He slammed the door and grimaced at the loudness of it. "You may wish to warm yourself by the fire."

He led her into the library, where a wood fire was burning with a slight hissing sound. The heat felt good, but a little harsh to her cold hands.

"I'll see if the young master is in," he said, backing out of the room. After what seemed an eternity, Malcomb returned. "Mr. Van Vleet will be down in a moment."

Peter considered asking Malcomb to tell Simone that he wasn't in, but he realized he wanted to see her before he left. He found her huddled before the fire, looking thoroughly miserable and cold.

"I heard you were fired," he said, walking across the room to stop beside her.

Simone looked startled. "Who told you that?"

"Just a rumor, I guess—"

"Bellini yelled at me, but he didn't fire me. Perhaps you heard that I'm going to be fired. That's more likely. Bellini has never truly believed I give my best to ballet. And in truth, I don't. I'll never be the dancer your sister is. None of the troupe will be, but..." Her voice failed under the accusing look in his eyes. She waited, but he didn't speak.

"I heard you were beaten," she said, staring at his face. Before he had been beautiful. Now his nose looked broader, more aggressive. He had a red scar beneath his right eye. Bruises tinged his face various shades of green, lilac, and yellow. A red scar ran from his temple into his blond hair.

She ached to take him into her arms and soothe him, but the look on his wary face made that a faint hope at best.

Peter jingled the coins in his pocket. "I've half a mind to back you against the wall and wring the truth out of you."

Simone blinked, not believing what she was hearing.

"There you were, pretending to moan in pleasure," he continued, his voice grim, "but all the while you were waiting for Kincaid's men to arrive and beat me senseless."

"No! I swear to you. You don't think that I—"

"Don't I?" he growled.

"*Mon Dieu.*" She stopped, too distraught to continue. "I had no idea..."

His eyes remained level and unconvinced. The sensuous curve of his lips thinned.

"I love you, Peter," she whispered desperately. "I had no idea...I swear to you...on my mother's Bible."

Peter expelled a heavy breath. "You don't have to lie to me anymore."

"Please...I can't believe you think that I would...that I could...I waited and waited for you. I hoped you would come to see me."

Peter realized the incongruity of what he was doing, expecting more of her than his own sister. Simone may have been taken in and used by Kincaid, too. "I joined the cavalry," he said, to change the subject.

"Oh, Peter, *chéri*..." She started to cry. Still crying, she reached up gently and touched his face. "Oh, your poor face, your poor broken face...It was so beautiful," she said mournfully.

Peter grimaced. "Maybe Kincaid did me a favor. I like this better."

Her lips trembled and tears streamed down her pale cheeks. "Those men who did this, they came right after I left, didn't they? Oh, Peter, I swear to you…I didn't know."

"It doesn't matter."

Simone turned away from him and sobbed brokenly. Her back looked so slender, so delicate. He reached out and pulled her into his arms. "It's all right."

"No, it isn't. It never will be. I love you. More than anything. More than life…I will die if you leave me."

"Hush, people don't die of love."

"Why are you leaving?"

"I'm not cut out for this life." What he couldn't tell her was that he wanted to live among rough men and simple peasant girls, girls who would blush and giggle when you looked at them. No more modern young actresses and dancers who tracked a man into his own bedroom.

But Simone felt so thin against him, so bird-boned and fragile, that a flood of compassion rose in him. She cried so hard, as if she had lost something of such value, that sweat broke out on his forehead. Her arms around his neck were slim and wiry, the arms of a child.

"You'll die there. I know you will."

"Hush," he whispered. He expected the cavalry to be challenging— the army was at war with the Sioux. But even so, he expected to survive it.

Simone sobbed louder.

"Hush, Simone…"

She pressed her wet mouth to his neck. A shudder rippled through her entire body, which created an answering response in his body. He lifted her chin and kissed her, and the passion he felt in her evoked an urgency in him. She surged against him, and he gathered her into his arms and kissed her hungrily, unable to stop himself.

"I love you, Peter," she whispered raggedly, between kisses.

He liked the way she said his name. It sounded like Petair, with the accent on the *tair*. He didn't know anything about love, but he did know he didn't want her to cry anymore.

"I'll die if you leave me."

He knew she wouldn't die, but he also realized she was different from Bettina, from all the girls he'd met in New York. Simone was moved by need and love, not manipulation. She had been injured as much by his parents as he had. To take her away from this place and these people might save her, might redeem something in her and in himself. They could start a new life in new circumstances.

"I don't suppose you'd want to come to North Dakota."

"Oh, Peter! Thank you, thank you, thank you…"

Jennifer found Chane in his office. He looked up, and his straight black eyebrows lowered.

She cringed inwardly. It hurt to see the hardness creep into his eyes every time he was forced to deal with her. She was staying at the hotel, in the same suite with him, but not the same bedroom.

"I'm sorry to bother you, but I want to go home and see my brother. I just wanted to let you know where I'd be. I'll take a cabriolet."

Chane stood up across the desk from her. "I don't want you riding in cabs. You could damage my reputation that way."

"What if I take your carriage just before you need it?"

Chane grimaced. "I have more than one."

Augustine met Jennifer at the front door, her thin face pinched. "Ahh, madame."

"Oh, Augustine, I've missed you. Is Peter home from work yet?"

Augustine glanced quickly at Malcomb, who had stepped into the other end of the hall.

"Monsieur Peter isn't here, madame. He won't be coming back, I think."

"What do you mean?"

"He has left."

"Left?"

"I tried to call you, but—" Augustine glanced angrily at the telephone. "—I couldn't reach you."

"Where did he go?"

"I don't know. He said to tell you good-bye."

"That's all? Just like that. Tell Jenn good-bye?" she asked incredulously. Augustine nodded. "He said, tell Mrs. Kincaid good-bye."

"Oh, God." Jennifer bowed her head. Peter must have heard she'd married Chane.

Jennifer arrived back at the hotel after dinner. Mrs. Lillian opened the door for her, and she strode directly into Chane's den unannounced. He glanced up from the newspaper he was reading and scowled.

"I went to see my brother today," she said.

"I trust he is fully recovered," Chane said politely.

"He's gone," she whispered, sitting down in the chair next to him before the fire.

"Gone where?"

"I don't know." Her bottom lip trembled and one tear slid down her pale cheek. A flame of compassion tried to ignite in him, but he pinched it out by sheer force of will.

"I didn't have a chance to tell him I had married you, but he found out somehow. And he...he..." She turned away to keep him from seeing her cry, but sobs shook her shoulders.

"Someone has to know where he's gone," he said impatiently. "I'll put Tom Wilcox to work on it right away. Tom can find anyone."

"Thank you," she said, her voice shaky. With her face wet with tears and twisted with anguish, she looked ten years old.

She left. Chane picked up his newspaper and began to read again. A few moments later Mrs. Lillian walked to the door of the den. "It's for you."

"I didn't hear the telephone ring. Who is it?"

"Tom Wilcox."

"What does he want?"

"He doesn't want anything. I called him. You told Jennie you would be calling him..."

"I'm glad someone believed her story," he growled.

"You didn't?"

"Of course not."

Mrs. Lillian looked irritated with him. To placate her, he took the telephone. "Tom? I want you to run a routine investigation..."

The week passed in a daze for Jennifer. She grieved for Peter as if he had died. Anything was possible. He could join the Foreign Legion or volunteer for some deadly mission. He was truly capable of anything. She explained this to Tom Wilcox, who listened patiently and assured her that he and his men were questioning the list of Peter's friends, acquaintances, and business associates she'd given them and were checking out every possibility.

She tried to work, but she had no heart for it. Bellini finally sent her to her dressing room to rest. Even he did not have the heart to yell at her anymore. She could still do her barre work, but she was so forgetful she found herself staring off into space when she was supposed to be doing pliés. She could barely endure two hours a day at the barre. Rehearsals bored her. They seemed to go on for hours. Her rhythm was so bad, she didn't even try to perform.

Bettina and Simone hadn't shown up for rehearsal this morning. It wasn't like either of them, but especially Bettina, who was her understudy. She knew Jennifer was not ready to dance performances. Jennifer fully expected them to appear at any moment, but the morning passed and no one heard from either of them.

Chane opened the door and leaned outside the carriage to see why they'd stopped.

"Sure and the whole intersection's blocked," Patrick said. "It's a horrid accident, it is. Would you be wantin' me to drive around this mess?"

"No, Patrick. Maybe we can help. Stay here unless someone needs you." Chane climbed down and walked toward a policeman standing next to a rope that blocked the street.

"Afternoon," he said amiably. "What's going on?"

"Been terrible happenings here," the policeman said, shaking his head. He lowered his voice and glanced around to be sure none of his superiors was watching him. "A young woman was murdered."

"Murdered? How?"

The policeman shook his head in consternation. "Well, I'm not at liberty to say, sir, but I can tell you we've hit on bad times when a thing like this can happen. The coroner said he's never seen the likes of it."

"Where did they find the body?"

"In those bushes over there."

Chane decided to leave. He was not one to gawk at accidents or disaster scenes. He walked back to the carriage to tell his driver to back up or turn around. As he approached, two men stopped within ten feet of him and he heard one of them say, "Bricewood." Frowning, he approached the men.

"Excuse me."

Irritated, the men glanced at him.

Chane shrugged in apology. "Sorry, but I heard the name of my hotel mentioned."

"And who might you be?"

"Kincaid. Chantry Kincaid the Third."

The men looked at one another. "What are you doing here?" one of them asked Chane.

"My driver stopped because the road is blocked, and I got out to see what was wrong. The Bricewood Hotel is just around that corner."

The men withdrew to confer for a moment, then walked back to Chane. "A woman's been killed and her body dumped here. We found this in her hand. Do you know why she might have it?"

The detective held out a tiny cloth purse with the words BRICEWOOD EAST lettered on it. Chane hefted it, wondering what was inside. "It's the container housekeeping uses to put favors in for our hotel guests. Generally they put chocolates in these and leave them on guests' pillows. Anyone could have one."

"Any chance she might work for you?"

"No idea."

"Would you be willing to take a look at the body? She's got no other identification. There's a good chance we won't be able to identify her anytime soon, unless we get real lucky."

Reluctantly, Chane allowed himself to be led to the spot where a blanket covered a small mound. "You ready?"

"Just her face," Chane cautioned.

The detective nodded.

"Okay. I'm ready."

The detective peeled the blanket back. The woman was obviously young and frozen solid. She was white as the sheet that covered her. And her eyes were matted with what looked like frozen tears. The sight caused Chane's stomach to wrench. "God. What happened to her?"

"We don't know yet. But the coroner says it looks like she's got no blood in her body. Never seen anyone so white."

Chane searched his memory. "You know," he finally said, "she looks like one of the dancers in the ballet company that I've recently hired for my theater."

The detectives looked at each other and then at him. "Can you find someone who might be able to give us a definite?"

"Is there a telephone near here?"

"No."

Chane drove back to the hotel and found Bellini. Together they drove to the morgue where the body should be by that time. They waited almost an hour, and Bellini identified the woman as Bettina, Jennifer's understudy. Chane took a very shaken Bellini back to his home and then drove to the Bricewood. He found Jennie in the long, mirrored exercise room. At the barre, graceful as a gazelle, she bent forward from the waist, pressing her cheek to her leg.

As he watched, she straightened. Her face was serene and appealing, solemn with dreamy self-absorption as she moved to the center of the gleaming hardwood floor and executed the positions her coach chanted like a human metronome. A man seated at the piano in the corner of the room played a Handel melody. Even in simple exercises her movements were fluid—she was the most articulate dancer he had ever watched.

She posed with arms gleaming whitely above her head, spun twice, and stopped abruptly in one of those movements that seemed impossible to complete as noiselessly as she did.

Even from a distance Chane knew the moment she saw him. She seemed to quiver and go completely still. Then she said something to the man playing the piano. He murmured something in return and scurried out the door. Chane's heart hammered a warning at him, but he walked forward in spite of it.

Jennifer couldn't believe Chane had actually come here to seek her out. Until this moment he had carefully and politely avoided her. Something seemed different about him. Even more different than his coming. He stopped an arm's length away.

"Bettina—" His voice, which was unusually hoarse, broke after the name. Searching his eyes, Jennifer tried to discern the source of his pain.

"Bettina…was killed."

"Bettina? How did it happen?"

Chane told her what he knew. Tears came slowly at first, then in a torrent as the realization hit her. She stepped forward, encircled his waist with her arms, pressed her cheek against his chest, and began to cry. Instinctively, he buried his face against her neck and held her shaking body. She cried with such vehemence she sounded ten years old.

After a time, he gave her shoulders a gentle shake. "Hey, hey," he whispered. "You're going to make yourself sick."

"Do they know who did it?"

"No, they don't," he said, his voice husky with pain.

"How did she die?" she whispered, leaning back to look into his eyes.

"I don't know." As if her questions had triggered something in him, he shuddered and stepped away from her. "I'm not sure," he said, dazed, lifting his hand to his forehead. "I don't know why I came here."

Chane knew that was an odd thing to say, even though it was true. If he'd been in his right mind, he wouldn't have come to Jennie with this or any other problem. Something inside him must have malfunctioned. His internal wiring must be as mechanical as that for a drawbridge. It was a sobering thought. He hadn't realized a switch in him could get thrown and he'd walk into the arms of a woman who had betrayed him.

Embarrassed, ignoring the beseeching look on her face, Chane cleared his throat and turned away from her. Jennifer sniffed back tears. "Maybe you knew I needed a friend," she called after him.

Chane walked away. It seemed kinder than to tell her she could no longer afford to consider him as a friend.

The next morning, Steve brought in a pile of newspapers and was reading them at his desk. Curious to find out everything the police knew about Bettina's death, Chane sat down across from him and opened the *Times*. The headline fairly screamed at him: MONSTER MURDERS BALLERINA.

The article was based on an interview with the coroner who did the autopsy. Chane skimmed over the repetitions about the horror of it all and gleaned that the only thing they knew for sure was that the murderer had somehow siphoned all of Bettina's blood out of her body and put most of it into her stomach. And he had pushed carpet tacks into her skin at one-inch intervals from her mid-thighs to the tops of her breasts. The purse found in Bettina's hand had contained carpet tacks. And about a half-pint of her total expected volume of blood was missing. The writer wondered if perhaps the maniac who had killed her had drunk her blood. Chane shook his head in disgust and consternation. Either the *Times* was becoming as bad as the tabloids, or this was truly the most gruesome murder he'd heard about in years.

Bettina's funeral was at St. Patrick's Cathedral. Jennifer was amazed at how well-attended it was. The main floor of the enormous chapel was almost filled to capacity. Apparently, everyone who had ever seen Bettina dance must have come to pay their last respects.

Chane rode to the church with Steve. Jennifer rode with Mrs. Lillian. Somehow they ended up in the same pew, but he didn't speak to her. The mass was in Latin. Jennifer managed to get through most of the service without crying, but at one point, as the music rose to a crescendo, the priest stepped up to the casket and slammed the lid shut, startling a loud sob from Jennifer and gasps from others. Mrs. Lillian pulled her into her arms and held her as she cried.

Later, somewhere near the conclusion of that interminable mass, Jennifer realized that Bettina's body was in the casket, but Bettina was not in the body. She didn't know where that thought came from, but it comforted her.

After the funeral, she and others from the ballet huddled in a warm place next to the church and talked in low tones. The girls were terrified because Simone had not been seen for two days. Jennifer had tried to call Peter, but he was still not home, either.

"Do you think the killer has Simone?" a girl asked.

"I think he's going to kill all of us," another girl said, shivering violently.

Bellini shushed them. "Don't get morbid. Simone could be anywhere. She'll probably be waiting for us when we get back."

Even so, Jennifer was frightened for Simone. And for herself. The man who had killed Bettina might be the same man who had been following her.

Chane did not appear for dinner that night. At nine o'clock Jennifer saw him briefly as he walked from the elevator to his bedroom. He nodded to her, which seemed an improvement. It was a curt nod of acknowledgment only, but it was proof she existed.

Two days later, unexpectedly, he appeared again at the practice room. She looked up to see him standing in the doorway, watching her.

"That looks like work, in spite of how easily you do it," he said, walking toward her, looking slightly embarrassed. His voice seeped into her pores and caused odd things to happen. Her legs felt suddenly weak, her lungs tight.

Jennifer picked up a towel and walked toward him, wiping her perspiring face. "What time is it?"

"Two o'clock."

"That late?"

Chane wanted to look away, but her hair was pulled up in a bun. Wisps of flaxen curls escaped to frame her face in softness. A light film of perspiration gleamed whitely on the smooth skin of her lovely neck. She caught his look and brushed at the strands, then wiped perspiration off her flushed cheeks and forehead. Her wide violet-blue eyes watched him intently. She had a way of going still, of waiting. He would give anything to be able to get this close to her and feel nothing.

"I have some—" He coughed to clear his throat. "—some bad news. I received a note from Nathan. He and Edmée want us to go out with them on Saturday. They've got their hearts set on us going to the opera with them."

"What are my options?" she asked softly.

Chane spread his hands. "I'm asking you. You could beg off, saying that it's too soon after the death of your friend."

Jennifer shook her head. "Nathan and Edmée are your friends. I've met them only twice, but I think of Edmée as a friend. I wouldn't want to hurt her feelings. But she'll know something is wrong between us."

"Not by any word of mine."

She believed him. He would never deliberately embarrass her. She had come to count on his generosity and gallantry. He was one of the few remaining gentlemen. Too stubborn, perhaps, but...

"I think we should go with them," she said, watching him closely.

Chane paled, and she knew his worst nightmare had just come true. He would have to spend at least one evening being nice to her.

On Saturday, Jennifer dressed carefully. She had never had what she thought of as real breasts. But now, probably because of her short pregnancy, they pushed a little too tightly against the shimmering fabric of her bodice. In desperation, she slipped out of that gown and chose another, looser gown with a high-waisted Empire style. It was made of the finest Lyon silk, and the mauve complimented her coloring and brought out the purple in her eyes.

Marianne Kelly, her lady's maid at the Bricewood, meticulously curled and pinned Jennifer's hair into a mass atop her head. After Marianne left, Jennifer continued to sit at her vanity, agitated by the thought of spending the evening with Chane. Their guests would be here any moment. She was not sure why she had wanted to do this. It would be impossible to play the happily married couple for Edmée, who would instantly see through anything so juvenile. Jennifer was sorry she'd pushed Chane into this evening, especially since it would probably be harder on her than him.

A knock sounded on her door.

"Yes?"

Chane opened the door and stepped into the room. In starched white shirt, black cravat, and black evening suit, he looked solemn, crisp, and heartbreakingly handsome. His gaze captured hers in the mirror and held it.

Seemingly embarrassed, he said, "I brought you something." He stepped forward and placed a necklace around her throat. The warmth of his hands and the cold of the necklace confused her senses. The icy gleam of diamonds made her look askance at him. He fastened the catch and stepped back.

"They were my grandmother's." They both stared at her reflection in the mirror. "Diamonds become you, Jennie." His voice sounded raspy, deeper than usual. "I thought it might confuse Edmée into believing our...lies. She will recognize these."

Jennifer feared she might cry. She hated crying at the thought of her husband, who no longer loved her, giving her a necklace she couldn't keep and hadn't even wanted two minutes ago. But now it had opened a wound in her that ached dully.

She leaped to her feet and walked to the floor-length mirror beside her armoire. "Does this gown look indecent to you? I must have gained weight. Christopher fed me hourly."

Chane had been avoiding looking at her. Now he couldn't resist. Her breasts had filled out. The gown was a little snug, but not unusually so. Her lovely cheeks were pale and devoid of their usual vibrance, but her eyes were intense and impossible to ignore. Just looking into them made his insides knot with longing.

Then bitterness flooded through him, tasting like gall in his mouth. He could not imagine how any woman as slight and delicately built could be so strong and resilient. Here he was, still devastated by her betrayal, and she had already recovered and gone back to work.

"You look fine," he said, turning away.

CHAPTER NINETEEN

Edmée hugged Jennifer and leaned back to smile into her eyes. "You've filled out a little. It looks wonderful on you." She turned to Nathan, who looked handsome in his black suit. "Doesn't she, Nathan? If I gained three ounces, I'd look like a sow."

Nathan shook his head and smiled at Chane. "She lies about everything. I don't know what to do with her."

They rode the elevator down, with Edmée chattering the whole time. It clunked to a halt on the ground floor, and Chane fastened Jennifer's coat against the cold wind and helped her into the carriage, sitting near her without quite touching her.

Seated across from them, Edmée appeared too engrossed in teasing her husband to notice anything amiss with the other couple. "Kiss me," she whispered to Nate.

"Behave yourself, you greedy wench, we're not alone in here," he said, glancing apologetically at Jennifer.

"Don't be silly, Nate. They're married. They don't care what we do." Edmée leaned close to him and parted her pretty lips for his kiss.

Nate leaned down and kissed his wife. When he withdrew, Edmée sighed expressively. "I love your kisses. And I love the opera, too."

"I think I'm getting a headache," Nate teased.

"You've never had a headache in your life. You're going to have an ache, though, if you're not careful," Edmée whispered teasingly.

Their playfulness only emphasized Chane's stony silence beside Jennifer. On impulse, Jennifer reached over, slipped her hand into his, and slanted a look up at him to see what he was going to do about it. Chane flashed her a look of warning, which clearly told her that she would answer for any liberties she took. Ignoring him and continuing to hold his warm hand with her cold one, Jennifer realized just how desperately she had needed his touch.

After a time, he reached up with his other hand and tugged at his cravat as if it had suddenly become too tight.

Too soon, the coach glided to a halt on the gaslit, tiled concourse of the Metropolitan Opera House. Chane retrieved his hand. Nathan straightened in his seat. Even Edmée tried to look more ladylike.

Their carriage rolled slowly now, one in a long line of sleek, elegant coaches creeping forward to deposit bejeweled ladies and top-hatted gentlemen at the foot of the impressive flight of steps leading up to the colonnaded doors of the Met.

This was a special gala performance, the first American presentation of *Carmen*, acclaimed the best of Bizet's operas.

The interior of the opera house was built in the traditional horseshoe fashion. The stage was wide and draped with heavy gold curtains. Flanking it on both sides were five levels of boxes that encircled the interior of the horseshoe. From the stage, Jennifer knew the five tiers of ornately carved and draped boxes looked like balconies on a tenement, except nothing in the diamond glitter and satin gleam of their occupants reminded one of poverty.

Their box, on the second level directly opposite the stage, sported a small bronze plaque with the word KINCAID engraved in Gothic script. He or someone in his family had acquired one of the choicest locations in the house.

Chane and Nate stood at the back of the box and talked about the railroad. Edmée wanted to introduce Jennifer to all her friends, but Jennifer declined, having no desire or energy for calling on anyone or for receiving callers. Edmée left without her, while Jennifer sat in grateful silence and gazed out at the stage and the floor below.

A familiar haze floated above the enormous chandelier hanging from the vaulted ceiling. The gallery was noisy and restless. Local dandies strutted up and down the lower aisles, preening like peacocks. Some posed with arms held stiffly behind them, their top hats shining. At last the symphony stopped tuning instruments and played a few chords. The people scurried toward their seats.

She envisioned the singers backstage applying the last touches of makeup, adjusting costumes, exchanging quips with one another, and waiting tensely for the lights to dim and the curtain to rise. A sudden wave of homesickness for the ballet rose up within her.

"Will you be going to Colorado yourself?" Nate asked Chane.

"Yes, the superintendent I hired didn't work out."

"When are you leaving?"

"A few days yet."

Jennifer felt as if a hand had closed around her heart and was squeezing. He was leaving. And without her.

In deep pain, she fought back the tears that burned in her throat. The orchestra played the first bars of Carmen's theme song. With a murmured apology, Edmée seated herself between Jennifer and Nate. The music of the overture wove a spell, and Jennifer gratefully let herself be drawn out of her own pain and into the safety of the drama unrolling before her.

"It's so authentically Spanish, isn't it?" Edmée whispered to Jennifer. "I was afraid, when I heard what they intended, that it would be merely Spain *à la française* again. The story is quite earthy and exciting. I love all the blood and passion. Too bad we can't smell it as well. And Don José, he is *magnifique*, eh?"

Edmée kept up a running commentary. "That Célestine Galli-Marié is a fancy little piece of fluff, isn't she?"

"Sings beautifully," Chane added.

The curtain dropped on the first act to rousing applause. "Georges Bizet has a hit at last! I knew he could do something really fine," Edmée said, applauding enthusiastically.

"I'll get the champagne," Nate said. Chane followed him out of the box and strode toward the bar.

Edmée turned and smiled. "So…" She paused and seemed to change her tack. "I've never been one to beat about the bush…Something is wrong between you and Chane, isn't it?"

Jennifer nodded.

"Would you like to tell me about it?"

"I guess so." Haltingly, she told Edmée what had happened. Edmée paled and gripped Jennifer's hand in sympathy as Jennifer poured out her story, stopping frequently to grope for words to describe what had happened. Jennifer was grateful for Edmée's loving support. She realized it could have gone another way, and she could have made Chane and his friends furious with her.

"So how is it between you now?" Edmée asked.

"Now…he hates me and is going off to the wilderness so he won't have to see me again."

"Don't let him."

"How can I stop him?"

"You are still his wife. Demand to go with him."

"What will that do for me?"

"It will keep you in his life. He is incredibly stubborn, and probably incredibly wounded by what has happened. You see, this is his second wound in the same place. There was another woman, several years ago, who did almost the same thing to him. He expelled her from his life with uncommon dispatch. So, it is doubly important that you do not give him a chance to do the same to you."

Edmée took Jennifer's hand. "Go with him wherever he goes. Or you will lose him."

"I used to think that was what I wanted. But now…oh, God, Edmée. I've made a terrible mess of things."

"Life is messy, my dear. Speaking of messes, would you like to go to the powder room?" she asked, patting at her hair.

They waited in the customary long line, and returned to the box to find Chane and Nathan sipping champagne. A bottle and two glasses sat on the small table at the back of the box.

Nate stood up to pour for the ladies. "We thought you'd been kidnapped by a band of wife snatchers."

Edmée laughed. "Paid by whom? You didn't bring that much cash with you."

"Touché," he said, handing each of them a glass. "Champagne for the two loveliest young bravas in the audience."

They drank a toast to friendship. Nathan started to make another, but Edmée interrupted. "Nate, did you bring my chocolates?"

"You didn't say anything about chocolates."

"Nate, you know I love chocolates at the opera." She turned to Jennifer. "He knows I have to have my chocolates. Please excuse us. We'll be right back."

Their departure left Jennifer facing Chane. The easy camaraderie she'd had with Edmée disappeared. Chane looked pale and tense. The same light that paled his cheeks also darkened his eyes, making them impenetrable, unreadable.

He was going away in a few days. That thought tormented her. Jennifer's hand trembled. Feeling suddenly self-conscious, she turned to put her glass down.

"Would you like to sit down?" His voice was polite, noncommittal.

"Yes, thank you." Her legs had begun to shake as well.

Seated, his broad shoulder brushed hers. All her awareness seemed to pool at that point. She felt her soul pressing against his shoulder.

"Are you enjoying yourself?" she asked.

"Yes," he lied. "Have you seen this before?"

"I danced a version of *Carmen* in Paris five years ago as an understudy to Arianna Monteverdi."

Chane rested his left hand on his knee. Jennifer longed to touch him. Black breeches hugged his strong legs. An inch of white cuff extended beyond the black cloth of his sleeve. Seeing the easy strength in his lean hands reminded her of the way they felt on her body. She glanced up at his profile, which looked completely unforgiving. Under her gaze he tugged at his cravat and pushed his chin out a little. She averted her gaze, turned slightly away from him.

House lights dimmed and the curtain rose. Edmée and Nathan swept back into the box.

"Chocolates, anyone?"

The curtain rose. Carmen's *verismo* style gripped the audience again, and Jennifer tried hard to get caught up in it. Near the end, the music reached a crescendo. Edmée shuddered beside Jennifer and gripped her hand. "Don't you love these earthy, savage arias?"

Jennifer squeezed Edmée's warm hand. Chane appeared unaffected by anything on stage or off. Jennifer felt light-headed from the effort to appear normal. At last the final curtain descended. Thunderous applause filled the theater. The prima donna and the tenor came forward to take their bows. A large bouquet was presented to Carmen, a red rose to Don José. The applause rose again. The other soloists joined the stars, and finally the entire cast. Again and again they all bowed. Even the conductor was called up for a bow. Disheveled and smiling, he motioned the symphony to stand.

At last it was time to leave. Jennifer hung back, so heartsick she could not stand it. Being so near Chane was more torture than she had realized possible. Now, the thought of going home to separate rooms, separate beds, was unbearable. She wondered when he was leaving.

Thankfully, Edmée entertained Chane and Nathan with a charming monologue about her emotions during the opera. Jennifer walked to the railing to watch the audience below slowly fill the two center aisles. Crumpled programs, empty chocolate boxes, and paper wrappers littered the floor. Tears flushed into her eyes. She swayed.

"Oh, God! She's falling!" Edmée screamed.

Jennifer tried to right herself. A rough hand grabbed her right arm and pulled her away from the railing.

Edmée gasped. Chane's eyes were furious as he searched her face. His hand gripped her arm painfully.

"Sorry. I felt faint." She tried to pull her arm out of his steely grip.

Tears could no longer be held back. They blurred her vision and spilled down her cheeks. Edmée stepped forward and whacked Chane with her fan. "Chane, for heaven's sake. Do your husbandly duty. She's crying. Can't you see?"

Chane scowled down at Jennie. Edmée tugged on his arm. "Hold her! What on earth is a husband good for if he doesn't hold his wife when she needs him!"

Reluctantly, Chane clamped his jaws and did as he was bid. His hand cupped her head and held her stiffly and dutifully to his chest. The heavy thud of his heart and the warmth of his strong, lean body overwhelmed Jennifer. She started to sob.

Edmée pulled Nathan out into the corridor and closed the curtains, leaving them alone in the box.

Jennifer couldn't stop crying. She didn't know if it was about Bettina's death, a delayed reaction to losing the baby, the tension of being out in public with a man who hated her, having to take the comfort he offered so begrudgingly or needing it so desperately. In the middle of it all, she wondered what he was thinking as he stoically endured her bout of crying.

Chane was beyond thinking. Jennie's shoulders shook and her hot tears soaked through to his skin and ignited a flame of compassion deep within him. Once, a long time ago, he had seen a man's leg being cut off. That same flame had ignited then—it had been almost unbearable. It was the same, now. He hated her, but he didn't want her in pain. Torn by conflicting needs, he held his wife's slender, trembling form, and felt her small, hard breasts press against his chest where his own heart pounded painfully hard. He was confused and angry and disgusted with himself.

"This isn't going to work," he said aloud.

"What?" she murmured.

"Nothing you can do will change how I feel."

"I know," she said, new tears welling in her eyes.

The familiar fragrance of her Gillyflower perfume filled his nostrils and made him dizzy. In spite of his resolve, he wiped her tears, lifted her damp face, and kissed her cold, wet lips.

Touching her had been a mistake. Holding her trembling body as if it were any ordinary body was something only a fool would attempt. But kissing her...kissing her wet mouth, feeling it open and draw in breath from him, open wider and cling, was crazier than anything he had ever done.

Jennie strained upward into his arms. Her silky hair brushed his face and her lips moved against his with a hunger to match his own. Part of him surrendered to that need, but another part of him flashed a picture of Jennie naked in Van Buren's arms.

Chane opened his eyes and firmly disengaged himself from his wife's clinging arms.

"Noooo," she whimpered softly.

"Yes."

His tone caused her to open her eyes, and what she saw told her that he was back in command.

"It's time to go," he growled.

Woodenly, she walked to the back of the box where her coat hung on a peg. He helped her into it, put on his own overcoat and top hat, and led her through the thinning crowd and out into the cold night air.

Icy gusts of wind whipped around her ankles. Chane gave her his arm and led her down the many steps, angling toward where his carriage inched forward in the long line of carriages filing past to pick up their occupants.

Nathan and Edmée were waiting at the curb. Edmée reached out and squeezed Jennifer's hand. Jennifer knew she wanted to ask how it had gone, but there was no opportunity to tell her, and she could probably guess from their expressions.

At last the carriage reached them. It was cold inside, but at least they didn't have to contend with the icy wind. Jennifer pulled the lap robe up around her and sank back in the plush seat.

Edmée seemed dreamy and distracted. Nathan put his arm around her and snuggled her close to him. She pulled his head close and whispered, "You have to talk to Chane."

"About what?"

"Shhh! About Jennifer."

"Why?"

"Later," she said, beginning to hum a strain from the opera.

The carriage finally pulled out of the slow-moving cavalcade and headed back toward the Bricewood. Snow swirled against the windowpanes.

The carriage hit a pothole in the pavement and sent Jennifer slamming into Chane. He caught her arm to steady her. His shadowy face, so close above hers, made her dizzy. She reached up and touched his lips, stroked the deep smile lines beside his mouth, and slipped around to caress the short, crisp hairs on his sturdy neck.

"Hold me," she whispered.

"This isn't going to get you anywhere," he warned her softly, but she kissed the side of his mouth, and he dragged in a ragged breath and put his arm around her. She snuggled close to him. They rode in silence until the carriage rolled to a stop under the shelter of the Bricewood's carriage entry.

She was in a transport of bliss that he had actually continued to hold her. He helped her out of the carriage, up the step to the tiled entry, and between the pine trees that sheltered the private elevator.

At the penthouse Edmée smiled dreamily at Jennifer and Chane and led Nathan toward the bedroom they shared.

Jennifer longed to take Chane's hand and lead him to the bedroom they had shared so briefly, but after Nate and Edmée disappeared into their room, Chane led her back out into the hall and to her own suite.

"Would you like to come in...for a moment?"

Chane's jaws clamped in consternation. "What I want is for this night never to have happened."

"We need to talk," she said, searching his face.

"It would be better if we didn't," he said grimly, "but maybe we need to say certain things one time, just to get them out in the open."

That had an ominous sound to it. He stepped inside and closed the door after him. A fire burned in her room, making it comfortable enough to take off her coat.

Chane kept his on. A signal he wouldn't be staying.

"I'm through, Jennie. What happened can't be fixed. But maybe I owe you something even if I can't forget or forgive what happened with Van Buren."

"You owe me nothing, but we have something special together. Tonight was no accident."

"Tonight was...proof of my stupidity." He expelled a frustrated breath. "Jennie," he began again, "I would *like* to excuse what you did with Van Buren, but I can't."

She gazed into the fire. Her profile was as beautiful as ever, but he could not stop now. "I won't say this to you again, but for your own good, remember it, because I mean it. Even if I believed that you didn't set out to betray me, which I don't, I wouldn't commit myself to a woman who could let that happen to her, even by accident."

Jennifer blinked back tears.

Chane cleared his throat. "For any number of reasons. It goes too deep in me, it's too basic to my nature. A betrayal of that magnitude can't be excused or ignored. Maybe by some men, but not by me." His voice had become harsh. "But I still care what happens to you."

No longer able to contain her tears, Jennifer put her head in her hands to hide her face from Chane.

Seeing her this way, chastened, humble, and yet still the beautiful, talented, and charming creature she was and would always be, even if she lived to be a hundred, he finally faced the full extent of his problem. From the moment he'd seen her, he had craved her presence, her happiness, and finally her love. Even when he'd tried to ignore her existence, he had found himself hanging on Steve's every word about her, rereading Tom Wilcox's dull reports just to see her name, daydreaming about her until he had almost lost his mind.

"Part of me," he said slowly, "the part I can't seem to control, even by an effort of will, still wants you. I can't reconcile that with how I feel about betrayal, but I also can't seem to change it. I've tried, but tonight... well, you can see for yourself how well I handled myself."

"What does that mean, exactly?"

"I guess it means that I need to come to some agreement that will allow us to normalize our relationship. We can't go on like this."

She bowed her head, seemed to struggle with herself for a moment, and then sighed. "I wish I hadn't betrayed you, but I did. I'm sorry. I'm so horribly sorry that I feel sick from my toes to my eyebrows, but that won't change what happened. So tell me how it has to be. Toss me out of your house. I'll stay out this time," she said quietly.

"Don't you understand anything I've said to you?" he asked fiercely. "If I *could* toss you out, you'd be out."

Jennifer turned away in confusion.

"Jennie...Jennie," he whispered, his voice ragged.

"What?"

"I don't trust you!"

"I didn't do anything so horrible. I didn't kill anyone. I didn't—"

"Stop it!"

"I love you," she cried. "I want to be your wife."

Chane shook his head. "Trust is more important than love. It's the basis of love, Jennie. Without trust there can be no love."

"You don't trust me, so it's over," she said softly.

The words tore his heart. "We have something," he said. "Maybe we don't have trust, and maybe I'm too damaged to ever love you again, but I still care."

"It's over," she said, shaking her head. Despair filled her eyes.

Chane knew the exact second she accepted the end of their marriage, and when she gave up, something in him changed sides. "Maybe," he said, "we could try again, but there would have to be conditions."

"Like what?"

"Like I won't sleep with you."

"Don't you want to?" she asked incredulously.

"I'm not an animal. I can't carry on a relationship with a woman I don't trust."

"You didn't know me well enough to trust me the night of the fire, and you almost made love to me then."

"It may have been premature, but I did trust you."

"Do your parents act like this?"

"My mother and father have been true to one another since the day they fell in love," he said firmly.

"How do you know that?"

"Don't use my parents to justify your sordid actions." He turned away as if he were going to leave.

Jennifer reached out and touched his shoulder. "I'm sorry. My own parents had a number of casual affairs. I never realized how unusual their behavior was."

Chane turned, frowning. "You knew they had affairs?"

"My mother told me. My father...once he even invited his paramour on holiday with us. She went with us to France for the season. She even became a friend of mine..."

Chane grunted in disgust.

Jennifer shrugged. "At times I have wished for a more perfect family, but not since my parents died. Either death has made them seem more perfect than they were, or it has made me more accepting."

Chane felt dazed with the glimpse he'd had of her life prior to meeting him. He had only himself to blame for falling in love with a woman as incomprehensible as Jennie. Latitia had warned him about her family. He should have listened.

"I made a mistake," she pleaded. "I didn't realize what was happening. But I give you my solemn promise I will never, ever allow myself to be tricked again...So, where do we go from here?" she asked.

"I'm going to Colorado. And you're going back to work. Maybe in a few months, when we meet again...who knows..."

"Does this include anything on your part?" she asked.

"Like what?"

"Like...fidelity."

"Infidelity has never been one of my problems, Jennie."

"What do you call your relationship with Latitia?"

"She is an old friend."

"What if I want to go with you?"

"I don't recommend it. It's going to be a long, miserable trek down the rails."

"Fortunately for you," she said grudgingly, "I'm still a ballerina."

Chane tried, but he couldn't hide his relief. He nodded his thanks and left.

Jennifer watched the door close behind him and felt the tiredness and despair wash through her. Until tonight she'd still had hope. Now she fully understood the depth of his stubbornness. He would not relent. He would put up with her, but she would never see the love she needed in his eyes again.

It was over. But he had agreed to let her share his life, as an unwanted piece of baggage. If she wanted that role. Somehow that concession hurt more than his wanting her completely out of his life.

Grief and loss overwhelmed her. She walked to the sofa, put her head down, and cried.

CHAPTER TWENTY

Rehearsal was not going well. She shouldn't have tried it today. At last Bellini called for a break. Jennifer grabbed a towel and walked toward her dressing room.

Nicole, her new understudy, fell into step beside her. "Would you rub my back right there?" she asked. "I have a charley horse in that muscle."

Nicole was slim, with a tiny waist that tapered into full hips and sturdy legs. Her mouth was wide beneath a short nose and dark brown eyes. No one would ever mistake Nicole for her, Jennifer thought, but it was nice to have an official understudy, as she still had no desire to dance.

Jennifer massaged the knotted muscle in Nicole's back until it relaxed. "There."

"Thanks. I'll do you now."

"I'm okay."

Nicole shrugged and followed Jennifer into her dressing room. Jennifer sat down at her dressing table and started taking pins out of her hair so she could repin it. Clumps of wet hair hung around her face. Her white stockings hung down the side of the dressing table, their tops held in place by a paperweight.

Nicole walked over to the closet. "Can I borrow your pink stockings?"

"They might be dirty, but help yourself."

Nicole shoved the closet door aside. Jennifer peered into the mirror. Her cheeks were flushed, her face shining with perspiration. She started to reach for a towel, but caught sight of a mirrored reflection of a pair of eyebrows above her costumes. Just then Nicole let out a full-bodied scream that would have impressed an opera diva. Jennifer whirled around, picking up the paperweight as she did. A large handkerchief covered the intruder's face to just below his eyes. Nicole hopped backward, screaming as loudly as she could. The man parted the costumes, charged through them and knocked Nicole aside as he ran for the door. Jennifer threw the paperweight, catching him on the left shoulder.

Nicole's screams brought a dozen dancers running toward Jennifer's room. "Stop him!" Jennifer yelled.

The man pulled a knife out of his boot and flashed it. Horrified girls gasped and backed away from him. He tore past them, reached the outside door and jerked it open. Pausing for a moment in the doorway, he turned and looked back at Jennifer. The look in his eyes sent a chill of fear down her spine. It seemed to say, "I'm not through with you yet."

The man got away clean, and everyone decided he'd been a love-starved fan just trying to get a glimpse of the prima ballerina. Everyone except Jennifer. Something about him terrified her. She tried to put it out of her mind, but couldn't.

Slowly, her nerves settled down. She heard the call to return to practice, and bent down to adjust her toe shoes. As she did, she saw something in the bottom of the closet. Curious, she walked over and picked it up. It was a tiny drawstring purse with BRICEWOOD EAST printed on it in white lettering. She opened the drawstring and saw carpet tacks. Fear jolted through her. The newspaper had said the man who killed Bettina had pushed carpet tacks into her skin.

She told Bellini she had to take some extra time, then went looking for Chane. She couldn't find him, and she panicked.

Steve explained exactly how it had happened, then ended with, "Jennifer thinks it was the man who's been following her." He paused for a second. "And the man who killed Bettina."

Chane sighed. "It isn't going to work," he said grimly. "She's making things up to get my sympathy. Don't you see it?"

Steve frowned. "What if she's not? After the man ran away, she found a small packet of carpet tacks."

Chane sighed. "Even that could have been staged. It would be easy to obtain one of those small purses from housekeeping...and as many carpet tacks as she wanted right here in the hotel." Steve frowned and narrowed his eyes at him. Chane sighed again. "All right. I better go see her."

"She's with Tom Wilcox and a couple of security men."

Chane found Jennie in Tom's office. She looked pale and shaken, her violet eyes solemn. Tom quickly summarized what had happened and then left them alone. Chane glanced at Jennie. "You look okay."

"Did Steve tell you who it was?"

Chane suppressed a smile. "He told me what you think."

"No one believes me," she said, puzzled.

Chane shrugged.

Jennie flashed him a look that damned him to hell, then she turned abruptly and stalked away. Tom Wilcox stepped back inside, closed the door and faced Chane. "I guess you'll want me to keep an around-the-clock watch over her. Even if the guy is just a lovesick fan, he might be dangerous."

"That won't be necessary."

"It won't?"

"No. She'll be fine." He started out the door. The memory of Bettina's white face stopped him. "All right," he said, turning back. "Put a guard on her, nothing too obvious. I don't think it's necessary, but better safe than sorry." He didn't explain that his wife was not trustworthy. No sense in saying anything to diminish her in his staff's eyes.

The next week passed in a blur. Jennifer avoided Chane. She threw herself into rehearsals, which were long and grinding.

Today's workout was grueling. Chane had fired Frederick, and Jennie was adjusting to a new dance partner. He was trying hard, and she sympathized with his struggle, but he lacked Frederick's power, talent, and determination.

She wiped her face, stepped back into position, and waited for Bellini to acknowledge her. Bellini tapped his wand.

The music started and Jennifer swept into the graceful movements of the solo they were rehearsing. One, two, three...one, two, three. Bellini was keeping beat with his wand, and it was growing louder and louder. Startled, Jennifer realized she was in the wrong position. Flushing with embarrassment, she stepped back.

Just as she did, a blur of something dropping very fast beside her caught her attention. It crashed within inches of her and a large hole opened in the floor, wood splintering and flying. Then the floor next to the hole gave way beneath her feet. Jennifer tried desperately to get the leverage to leap clear, but her feet had no stable place, and she slid toward the hole, unable to stop herself.

Her new dance partner tried to grab her, but his hand merely brushed hers. His face registered horror as she slid past him into the gaping hole in the stage floor.

Steve found Chane in the library on the first floor.

Chane looked up from the tablet on which he'd been making notes and waited for Steve to speak. Something in Steve's eyes made Chane put his pen down.

"What?"

"Jennie's been hurt."

Chane stood up. "How bad?"

"We don't know. Half a dozen weights went crashing down from the flies through the stage floor and took her down with them. They were getting a ladder to try to get her out. They called out to her, but she didn't answer. I was waiting there until we saw how bad it was, but I—"

Dread gripped Chane's heart with an icy hand. He crossed the room in two strides and broke into a run, with Steve following. Chane couldn't think of anything heavier than a half-dozen stage weights falling from thirty feet up. If they'd hit her, she'd be dead.

As Chane reached the Grand Ballroom, two men were lowering a ladder into the gaping hole in the stage floor. One stood up to test the floor near the hole.

"Stand back. I'll go down," Chane said, pushing through the crowd that had gathered on the stage.

"Wait a minute," Steve said. "They're coming with boards to reinforce the floor around the hole." Ordinarily, a stage this size would have had a door leading into the understage, but it had been so hastily constructed on such short notice to accommodate the ballet company that they'd cut corners.

At the sight of Chane, silence descended on the white-faced ballerinas clustered around the splintered wood.

"Is she alone down there?" Chane asked.

A young dancer stepped forward, his face twisted with misery. "I tried to catch her…"

Men arrived with four two-by-sixes and crisscrossed them over the opening to reinforce the floor. Gingerly, Chane stepped onto one of the two-by-sixes and walked across it to the ladder, which extended a good three feet above the shattered wood. He checked to be sure it wasn't resting on Jennie, swung over, tested the ladder with his weight, then started down.

At the bottom, Chane stepped over Jennie's body and knelt beside her. Light from above revealed she was lying beside the weights. Her back seemed arched too far and at a strange angle. Sweat beaded on his forehead.

He stepped off the ladder and knelt beside her. Her skin was still warm, but of course it would be. It had only been a matter of minutes.

"Jennie..."

He pressed his fingers against the artery in her neck. Her skin was damp, her hair wet and plastered against the side of her face. At first he felt nothing. His heart thundered in his chest. He moved his fingers and dug them in deeper. A tiny pulse felt like a brush moving under her skin, caressing his fingers briefly and receding, briefly and receding. Relief and exultation swelled up in him. His fingers were reluctant to let go of the reassuring feel of her pulse.

"She's alive!" he croaked. He felt so weak he had to sit down. "She's alive."

Overhead, ballerinas murmured and scuffed their feet. The sounds seemed amplified. Every movement echoed in the cavernous pit beneath the stage.

He was reluctant to move her. He might lift her only to discover that her neck was broken, or her back.

"Jennie..."

He leaned close to her. "Jennie."

Her eyelids fluttered.

"I'm going to carry you up a ladder. Can you move your legs, your head?"

Jennie pulled her legs toward her. "Ohhh! My foot."

He picked her up and waited for her to relax in his arms. She gritted her teeth, covered her face with her hands, shuddered once, and finally relaxed against him.

Slowly, carefully, he started up the ladder. She winced, but that was all. At last he reached the top. Steve was waiting and took Jennie as Chane maneuvered himself off the ladder and onto one of the cross beams.

"Her foot's broken," Dr. Campbell said, snapping his bag open.

"How badly?"

Campbell shook his head and pulled on his gray goatee. "She won't be dancing for a while. Maybe never."

"That's all? Just her foot?"

"I doubt she'll think it insignificant." He patted his goatee. "She'll have some nasty bruises as well."

Chane waited outside while Campbell set the foot and bandaged it. Jennie cried out once, and he could hear her panting to keep from doing it again. Sweat broke out on his forehead. Chane wanted to go in there and toss that doctor out a window, but he restrained himself with difficulty. When the doctor finally came out, made his report, and left, Chane wiped his face again, eased the door open, and walked into Jennie's bedroom.

At the sound of his shoes crossing the carpet, she opened her eyes. "Can you think of anything more worthless than a ballerina with a broken foot?" she asked, her eyes bleak.

The only thing that came to mind was himself without her. The thought that he was still so weak-minded sickened him. Thank God he was almost ready to leave for Colorado.

Chane got up earlier every day, but he seemed to be falling further behind. The day before he was supposed to leave, Tom Wilcox walked in at eight o'clock in the morning and handed him a telegram from Tom's contact in Denver.

LEGISLATURE PASSED LAW YESTERDAY REQUIRING THAT ANY RAILROAD THROUGH STATE HAS TO BE BUILT BY RESIDENTS OF COLORADO STOP.

"Damn!" Chane crumpled the telegram and tossed it into the trash. Over the past weeks, he had purchased tons of supplies—food and bedding for a couple thousand men, spikes, hammers, axes, carts, pulleys, dynamite, and hydraulic jackhammers, which might or might not work, since they'd just come on the market. All month he'd worked feverishly, overseeing the moving of this equipment from the warehouse to the train depot.

He wasn't about to give up now, just because some hick legislature had changed a law. He retrieved the wire, brought it to Steve's office, and tossed it on his desk. Steve looked up from the brief he was writing.

"Bad news," Chane said.

Steve read it and frowned. "Laurey isn't a resident, either," he said.

"But Gould is. He can front for both of them."

"So what now?"

"I need a favor."

Steve realized what Chane was going to ask him. The blood drained from his face. "No trains. I won't ride anymore trains."

"It's our only hope. If you don't go and break things loose, I might as well kiss all the money we've spent on this venture good-bye."

Steve groaned. He knew Chane had sunk almost a million dollars of his grandfather's money into the purchases to begin the railroad. Without the railroad, he'd be stuck with that stuff indefinitely.

Jennifer called home every day, but Peter still had not returned. This time Augustine answered the telephone. Her timorous voice on the end of the line made Jennifer homesick.

"Augustine? It's me, Jennifer."

"Madame!"

"Have you heard from Peter?"

"No, madame."

"Did I get any mail?"

"Oh, yes, madame. A letter from London."

Jennifer closed her eyes. It had come. She had waited all this time. "Could you send someone over with it?"

The messenger arrived an hour later. Jennifer tore the letter open and read it.

> Dear Miss Van Vleet,
>
>   As director of the Royal Ballet of London it is my extreme pleasure to tell you that we are most thrilled by the opportunity presented by your agent. We therefore invite you to come to London and dance the lead in any of a number of ballets upon which we can agree. We look forward to hearing from you as to your expected arrival date and will wait for your reply. We are most anxious to accommodate a ballerina of your range and power.
>
>   Respectfully yours,
>   Wollencott Edwards

Jennifer crumpled the letter and sank back against her pillows. She had waited all her life for this letter, and now it had come. Too late. She might never dance again. No one knew how a broken foot would mend, or if it would mend at all.

She turned over and stared at the pattern on the wallpaper, surprised that she felt no bitterness. None at Chane, and none about this terrible loss. A strange feeling of gratitude welled up from deep inside her. She was being punished exactly as she deserved.

A week went by with agonizing slowness. Chane's departure was delayed by one problem, then another. At first Jennifer had been resigned to letting him go without her. But slowly, as she lay in bed, struggling against the fairly constant pain and the ever-present boredom, she could feel her life coming into clearer focus.

One of the first things she realized was that she truly loved Chane. She had expected her love to die along with his, but it hadn't. The more he avoided her and tried to ignore her, the greater her hunger for his attention became.

Dr. Campbell came every day to check on her progress. During his Tuesday visit she learned that Chane was leaving the next day. After Campbell left, Jennie asked Mrs. Lillian to send one of the lady's maids in to help her change. Marianne Kelly washed her hair and dried it, then Jennifer changed into a prettier nightgown and rubbed a little color into her pale cheeks. When she looked as good as she felt she could, she asked Mrs. Lillian to send for Chane.

Then she hobbled into the big four-poster bed that, according to Mrs. L., had been brought over from England for Chane's great-grandmother. The bed was so big, and Jennie so slim, that she seemed to disappear into the folds of the feather mattress. She picked up her hand mirror and gazed into it. Her eyes were bigger and darker than she'd ever seen them. With her silvery blond hair framing her face in light and her features scrubbed clean, she looked twelve years old. Maybe that would soften Chane's hard heart, she thought. Her own ached dully. She had lost too much in the last year—her parents, her baby, her brother, her dancing, and now she was about to lose her husband, again.

Chane tapped lightly on the door.

"Come in."

He walked in and looked about the room as if he'd never seen it before. He looked everywhere except into her eyes. Finally, he cleared his throat and glanced at her. "So...how long does he expect you to be laid up?" he asked.

"Three or four months."

"Damned shame."

"You're going, aren't you?"

"Tomorrow, yes."

"Is Steve going?"

"He's gone." He told her briefly about the residency problem. "Steve will try to find a loophole that will allow us to build through Colorado. If not, we'll have to jump off from Topeka and build through the plains to the desert. It won't be pleasant, but it can be done."

"Please sit down," she said, motioning to one of the chairs. "I need to talk to you."

Chane carried an armchair from beside the fire, sat down and stretched his legs out in front of him, all without looking at her again.

"As you know," she began hesitantly, "I've had a lot of time to think lately."

Chane nodded.

"I realized that part of the reason I've worked so hard at being a ballerina is that it's kept me from having to deal with my difficult family. It also saved me from marriage, until recently. It's done everything I wanted it to do and more. Well, that's gone now, and it may never come back. Dr. Campbell says I may never dance again. I won't know for months."

Chane waited in silence. Jennie couldn't help but notice how his dark hair curled around his left ear, and how a shadow of beard darkened his cheeks.

"I know you don't want to hear this, but I've discovered I love you in a way I never thought I could love any man—totally and all-consumingly. I suppose it's…too late, but my feelings are real, and overwhelming to me."

"You *suppose* it's too late?" he asked incredulously, his voice low and thick with pain.

"I think I could earn your trust again."

"No," he said with finality. "It won't work." His profile looked grim and set against her. The brick wall he'd built between them was solidly in place. He thought himself safe behind it.

She refused to let that stop her. "I want to go with you."

"Building a railroad is not like going on tour with a ballet company."

Jennifer lifted her chin. "I'm your wife. I want to go with you."

"That's because you don't know how boring it is riding the rails behind a crew that only moves a few feet a day. You'll be better off in New York near a doctor."

"You loved me once. Maybe you can again."

"This is no picnic we're going on. It's either boring or dangerous," he continued, as if he hadn't heard her. "We'll be doing most of the work in the winter. It's bitter cold," he said, looking into her eyes for the first time. "It's a punishing sort of cold, and very little else to do but suffer through it."

The look in his eyes told her he was talking about the cold that now filled his heart. "I don't care," she whispered, a lump rising in her throat.

"You say that now."

"I promise you I will die before I complain."

"Jennie, it won't work—"

"I think my life is in danger." She ignored the disbelief in his eyes and plunged ahead. "First I was being followed. Then someone tried to kill me. You promised to take care of me. Was that just talk?" she asked bitterly.

Chane scowled, but she sensed weakening and plunged ahead.

"I'll need a doctor, though," she said.

Chane sighed as if his burdens were almost unbearable. "I'm taking Campbell anyway," he admitted grudgingly. "With three thousand men, accidents happen."

"I won't be any trouble. I promise."

"You won't be anything but trouble," he said grimly.

That hurt, but it didn't matter. If she didn't go, she had no chance at all. Even if she did go, she might have no chance, but she wouldn't know until she tried. And she loved him too much to give up now.

His teeth clamped together, and muscles bunched in his lean cheeks. "All right. But don't say I didn't warn you."

Chane left, and Jennifer telephoned Augustine.

"We miss you, madame."

"I miss you, too, Mamitchka." Jennifer paused. "I'm going away for a while. Can you pack all of my warmest clothes? I'll have a man pick them up. Will you call me and let me know when they'll be ready?"

"*Oui*, madame. May we ask where you will be going?"

"Colorado."

"Where is that?"

"It's out West."

"Oh, no."

Jennifer knew that Augustine had heard a great many bad things about life in the West. She was convinced it was inhabited by cold-blooded killers, thieves, and bloodthirsty Indians.

"I'll be fine. Don't worry about me. I'm going with a very large party. I'll be well-protected."

"Should we close the house, madame?"

"No, Peter may be back any day. And where would you go?"

"With you, madame."

"All of you?"

"*Oui.*"

Jennifer had to decline, knowing it would push Chane's patience to the breaking point. Next, she called her father's attorney, Ward Berringer, and told him that she was leaving.

"How long do you expect to be gone?" he asked.

"About six months, maybe more."

"Well, as you know, the estate is in probate, which limits what I can reasonably do for you, but since your...husband has taken care of the outstanding debts, I'm sure I can continue the payments to keep the house running and the servants paid during your absence."

"I still do not understand how my parents' estate could go from being worth millions of dollars during their lives to being worthless after their deaths," she said.

"As you know, there were some dealings with certain unscrupulous people..."

"You're implying it was Mr. Kincaid, aren't you?"

Berringer cleared his throat. "Your brother told me himself..." His words trailed off as if his feelings were hurt.

Jennifer didn't like the man, but she took pity on him and dropped that line of thinking. "It was not my intent to criticize, Mr. Berringer. I know you're doing the best you can."

Jennifer ended the conversation and put down the telephone. She had reassured everyone but herself.

CHAPTER TWENTY-ONE

January 1881

Chane's warning about the coldness of the journey turned out to be prophetic. He avoided her whenever possible, not touching her once on the almost six-day train trip. It was as though he'd turned to ice inside. The few times he looked at her, she had the feeling something vital had died in him. It hurt her in a way nothing else could have.

She knew part of it was because of his grandfather and some of the things he'd done—the crooked deals he'd arranged that Chane had dismantled. And part might be fear that he'd fail to save the railroad. It was odd to her that his problems didn't soften him, but rather, seemed to harden his heart, against her and everyone else. To her he was curt and businesslike, but not rude. He stayed to himself and seemed to be reverting to something more primitive. He seemed like a man with his back to the wall. He wanted nothing from her, except to be left alone.

It was long after sunset when they finally reached La Junta, Colorado, a small bustling town situated on the banks of the Arkansas River. The tiny town was to become the railhead and the northernmost station in Chane's budding railroad empire.

Their train was met by two men who worked for Chane. Jennifer noticed an instant change in her husband. Faced with strangers who worked for him, he had to at least be civil to her. He helped her down from the Pullman coach and then carried her overnight bag. She balanced on crutches on the dimly lit station platform as the men shook hands all around. Cold wind whipped Jennifer's skirts and bonnet.

"This is my wife," Chane said gruffly, nodding to the younger man. "Tom Tinkersley. Tom is in charge of security."

Tinkersley reminded Jennifer of Peter; he was blond and handsome, with an earnest light in his eyes. He wore two guns low on his lean hips. He seemed entirely comfortable with them and with himself.

"Tom has a contingent of Apache scouts and ex-soldiers guarding our railroad crews, supplies, and right-of-way."

"Nice to meet you," she said quietly.

"Mrs. Kincaid." Tinkersley's voice was deep and respectful, but a smile started in his eyes that told her he found her attractive. The scowl on Chane's face indicated he'd seen it as well.

"And this is Beaver Targle," Chane continued, gesturing to a big man with a pear-shaped body. "Beaver is in charge of the laborers who're going to build the railroad."

"I'm shore sorry, Mrs. Kincaid, about not having no proper carriage and all, but this here buckboard is the best I could do on short notice," Targle said, waving his arm at a horse-drawn vehicle near the station platform. His loud, booming voice carried a western twang.

Chane surprised Jennifer by picking her up and carrying her to the buckboard. He lifted her up onto the seat and climbed aboard himself. When the wind ballooned her skirts, Chane stuffed them back under the hem of her coat. Targle stowed her crutches in the wagon bed behind them and climbed up next to Jennie. Tom Tinkersley rode his horse alongside.

Jennifer moved closer to Chane. Gusty winds tore at her bonnet and sent shivers up her stockinged legs. Kerosene lamps on the station platform flickered as they rode away. Shadows moved and swayed with the wind. Smells of wood smoke and cooking beans filled the air.

Tinkersley rode close to them to speak to her. "It's too bad it's dark. In the daytime you can see the Rocky Mountains to the west and the Arkansas River to the north." His voice had a soft southern accent.

"Where are you from, Mr. Tinkersley?"

"Texas, ma'am."

This time Tinkersley caught Chane's scowl and he dropped back a ways. The buckboard lived up to its name, almost bucking her off twice. If she hadn't been wedged in between Targle and Chane, she probably would have gone flying into the wide, rutted road that ran between two rows of buildings outlined darkly against the enormous star-studded sky. Music from an out-of-tune piano wafted out from one of the buildings up ahead. Coarse laughter, an occasional yell, neighing horses, barking dogs, and a few night-singing birds added to the cacophony.

"Frightened?" Chane asked, his breath warm against her cheek.

It was practically the first thing he'd said to her since they left New York City. "You're asking a woman who has slipped into more towns in the middle of the night than a burglar if she's scared? Of course."

"It won't seem so bad tomorrow."

"You've been here before?"

"Only once. I was sent to bring back a prisoner."

"Did you?"

"Yeah."

His tone changed, hardened. She slanted a look up at his profile, dark against the skyline. "Something went wrong," she guessed.

"He tried to escape. I killed him."

"You couldn't have been very old."

"Nineteen."

Beaver Targle reined the team in front of a building where a hotel sign hung slightly askew. Except for a high false front, the hotel's exterior looked like a barn she'd seen on the outskirts of Paris.

Chane helped her down. The interior was dimly lit by two smoky kerosene lamps hanging from the ceiling. The counter was deserted. Targle yelled, "Hello, thar, anybody to home?" and banged his fist on the wooden counter.

Behind the counter a door opened and an old man stuck his head out. Over his shoulder, brooms, mops, and buckets filled what looked like a broom closet.

"Howdy, howdy," he said, stepping out and closing the door behind him. "What kin I do you fer?"

Targle introduced Kincaid, saying Chane's name proudly, obviously impressed by Chane's importance and his own by association. Jennifer suppressed a smile. Tinkersley saw it and winked at her.

Chane bent to sign the register. His broad shoulders stretched the fabric of his greatcoat. The dark hair on his neck was longer than usual. It curled over the top of his collar. Her fingers fairly itched to stroke it.

As Chane straightened he glanced at Tinkersley, and his gaze stayed a little too long. Then he looked at her, quirking his eyebrows as if to say, "I made my bed, I guess I can lie in it." Jennifer was torn. Part of her resented his worrying about every man they came across. Part of her ached for him.

"Follow me," the old man said, walking around the counter toward the stairs.

Jennifer adjusted her crutches and took a tentative step forward. Chane stopped her with a slight pressure on her arm. "You can't walk upstairs with those things."

"I've never tried. Maybe I can."

The pressure on her arm increased. His warm hand seemed to bleed off some of the pressure that had built up in her on the long trip here.

She turned, and without a word he lifted her into his arms and carried her up the stairs. He seemed to labor more than she'd expected.

His heart pounded so hard she could feel it against her shoulder. She looked up at him, but he didn't return her gaze.

At the top of the stairs Jennifer said, "I can walk from here."

"I'm strong enough for this short distance…"

"Even on crutches, I can keep up with him," she insisted, nodding toward the old man.

Chane lowered her feet to the hardwood floor.

The room wasn't as bad as she'd expected. It was large and clean. A potbellied stove in the corner radiated warmth. The old man tapped the stove with his walking cane.

"Better go light up some more stoves. You've taken all the warm rooms." With that he left them alone.

Jennifer sat down on the edge of the only bed. Her foot throbbed painfully.

Chane realized his mistake as soon as he saw the double bed beside the window. He couldn't believe he'd left the train, signed the register, and carried her up the stairs without realizing he would be sharing a bed with her. Part of him seemed to go to sleep at critical moments. He only woke once he'd gotten himself into trouble.

"I have to go see to my men. Don't wait up for me."

"Have you heard from Steve?"

Chane grinned for the first time in weeks. "He'll be here tomorrow morning. The Colorado legislature forgot to insert in their new law a clause repealing the old law that allowed incorporation without any of the fancy trimmings required by the new law. He immediately filed under the old law, and even managed to get one of the senators to introduce legislation to exempt railroads from taxation for six years. I think we're going to be fine."

He seemed to remember who he was talking to, turned abruptly, and walked out the door. Jennifer undressed and climbed into bed. She went to sleep wondering if he'd be back in time to sleep in the bed next to her.

"Pantaloons! Pantaloons? Who larnt you to call 'em pantaloons? Trying to git above me, air ye? Talkin' like quality folks! You ain't niver heard me call 'em anythin' but britches, nor you shan't neither. Thar, take that!"

Someone yelled, and two sets of footsteps took off running. Jennifer had listened to the lengthy tongue-lashing with her eyes closed. Now she opened them.

Sunshine streamed into the strange room. She sat up. The other side of the bed was empty and undisturbed. But the clothes Chane had worn yesterday hung over the back of the ladder-back chair beside the bureau. Her crutches leaned on the foot of the bed and her trunk squatted by the door. Someone had stoked the stove. The room felt comparatively warm. Shivering, Jennifer washed in a basin of cold water and dressed in a brown-and-white houndstooth cashmere gown. Hunger drove her downstairs. With her crutches in one hand, she held on to the banister and hopped down on her good foot. Marianne Kelly, who had come along as her lady's maid, was already there, talking to the man behind the counter, a different man from last night.

"'Morning, mum!" Marianne said, walking over to meet her. For the first time since they'd set out, Marianne's eyes sparkled with excitement.

"Are you hungry, Marianne?"

"No 'm, I ate. But Mr. Hammond and Mr. Kincaid are still in the dining room. Mr. Kincaid asked me to get some things at the store. Unless you need me…"

Jennifer dismissed the girl and limped into the dining room on her crutches. Four men in rough garb and big hats, engrossed in conversation, were facing away from her in the back corner of the room. Except for them, the room was empty. Marianne must have been wrong about Chane being here, Jennifer thought, choosing a table by the window so she could watch the street. She scanned the menu and chose the closest thing she could find to a normal breakfast.

"Coffee, miss?"

"Yes, please. I'll have the scrambled eggs and fried potatoes."

The four men she had noticed got up from their table.

The sound of Chane's voice made her look up. She barely recognized him in blue denim pants and a black frock coat. On his right hip a gun rested in a holster tied down with a leather thong. A tan felt hat hung by a chin strap behind his head. Only his craggy face resembled the New York millionaire who had swept her off her feet.

Jennie glanced from Chane to a man she finally recognized as Steve, then to Tom Tinkersley and Beaver Targle. Steve was dressed much like Chane, except the scarf tied at his throat was red. But even in the rough garb he still managed to look like an attorney.

"I'm glad you survived your train ride," she said.

"I may buy land here to keep from having to go back." They all laughed.

"You all look like desperadoes today."

Chane nodded to her. "It's more comfortable for what we've got to do."

"Even the gun?" she asked.

"I promise not to shoot myself, if that's what you're worried about," he said, smiling. Chane seemed different today, less distant somehow. Jennifer wondered if the smile was for Tom Tinkersley's benefit. Tom hadn't looked at anything except her since he'd seen her.

Targle laughed. "Wal now, ma'am, I expect I can relieve yore mind on that score at least. You don't have to worry about him hurtin' hisself with that gun. Yore husband, if you'll pardon me for braggin' on him, was one of the fastest guns in Texas when he was rangering. Bill Longley, one of the killingest gunslingers west of the Pecos—he had ten notches on his gun—went out of his way not to meet Mr. Kincaid not too many years ago. Longley was pards with Ben Thompson in Kansas just before the big shoot-out there—"

Chane leveled a narrow-eyed look of irritation at the suddenly talkative Targle.

"Beaver, why don't you show Steve to the livery stable. We're going to need some horses."

Steve and Targle walked out of the hotel. Tinkersley nodded respectfully to Jennifer and followed them out. He even walked like Peter. Slim of hip and broad of shoulder, from the back he could have passed for Peter.

Jennifer turned to face her husband. His eyes looked more piercing—tougher and more remote somehow—in the clear western light streaming in the dining room window. He looked blatantly masculine and virile in his rough western garb, able to withstand anything, especially her.

He suddenly looked like a man who could have said all those hateful things to her the night after the opera—a man who could resist her forever. Until this moment she had believed she could overcome his reservations about trust and make him love her again. Now she felt alienated, as if she'd never really known him at all.

"They're waiting for you," she said.

Tinkersley, Targle, and Steve stood outside in the bright, cold, sunlit street.

Chane looked angry. She had no idea why he should be, but flames seemed to dance in the depths of his eyes. "I may not be back until late," he growled.

Jennifer felt balanced on a high fence in a strong wind. On one side was safety and warmth and the possibility of forming a new, more stable relationship with her husband. On the other, she felt the icy breath of the gaping maw that threatened to open at any time. She realized that if she hoped to win Chane back, she'd walk this razor's edge every moment of every day.

"So?" It wasn't what she had wanted to say. It was all wrong. She expected him to turn on the heel of his scuffed boot and walk away, but he amazed her by pulling her so close to him she could feel the warmth and strength of him against her.

This was totally unlike him, and just as unacceptable, but the dining room was empty, and she knew no one was watching them except Tom Tinkersley.

"If you're going to pretend to be my wife, you'd better remember that I won't tolerate your flirting with one of my hired hands," he rasped, pulling her closer. He lifted her chin with a rough hand and searched her eyes.

"I know that," she whispered, suddenly furious.

"Do you?" he demanded, rage flickering in the depths of his eyes. His hand gave her no chance to look away. "I've put up with a lot from you, but even castoffs have their pride."

"I've done nothing wrong!"

"It takes less now," he warned.

"I swear to you—"

He must have forgotten why he mustn't kiss her. He bent his head, and the feel of his lips, warm and hurtful against hers, seemed to release something savage and ravenous in him, something stronger than his usually strong will.

Jennifer knew the kiss was strictly for show, but it devastated her. Her body, starved for any contact at all with him, however humiliating, responded wildly and hungrily to his touch. She reached up with both hands and grasped his face, biting his lip just hard enough to cause him to suck in a startled breath.

She thought he was going to push her away, but his hands bit into her back, swept her up against him, and his tongue pushed into her mouth, taking control.

Once before, Chane had showed her this side of him, this wildness and possessiveness. Just knowing he was still capable of it filled her with hope and exultant joy. He ended the kiss before she could do more. His hand forced her chin up, but her eyes remained stubbornly closed.

"Insecurity becomes you, Jennie." He turned her forcefully, set her down in her chair, and left.

Jennifer watched him walk away. Something trembled deep within her. Chane had changed. He no longer seemed a man so affected by her that he couldn't touch her. He had mastered touching and was moving on to taking.

Maybe she had finally seen the real Chane. A man who could kill a man he didn't want to kill. A man who could end a marriage he had wanted to last forever. A man who could kiss her in public to show Tom Tinkersley that he could.

A chill swept through Jennifer. She shivered and pulled her wrap closer around her shoulders. This was going to be harder than she'd expected.

Chane joined Steve, Tom, and Beaver on the sidewalk. He ignored Targle's foolish grin, Tinkersley's and Steve's silence, and asked the first question he could think of to get their minds back on business. "How wide is our right-of-way?"

"Four hundred feet," Steve replied, looking at him oddly. Steve knew he knew the answer to that question, but he would never embarrass Chane in public.

Before Chane could ask another question, a freckled boy ran up and stopped, winded. "Mr. Kincaid?" he asked, his gray eyes darting from Steve to Chane. Chane raised a hand.

"Telegram."

Chane reached into his pocket for a dime, flipped it to the boy, took the telegram and read it.

> CONGRESS GRANTED IDENTICAL CHARTER TO LAUREY AND GOULD STOP L&G BUILDING SOUTH FROM PUEBLO DOWN TAOS TRAIL TO NEW MEXICO STOP FIRST RAILROAD TO REACH NEW MEXICO WINS LAND GRANTS AND CHARTER STOP L&G BEGAN CONSTRUCTION TWO WEEKS AGO AND MAKING GOOD TIME STOP
> WILCOX

In silence Chane passed the telegram to Steve. According to the charter he'd thought he had before this telegram arrived, he would have had two years to build the first fifty miles, a year for each fifty after that. Now with Laurey and Gould building south on a parallel alignment to New Mexico, the land grants they'd counted on were in serious jeopardy.

If Laurey and Gould beat them, they would get the land grants, and his grandfather would get nothing, except the right to operate the railroad without government grants, and against stiff competition from Laurey, which made it too risky financially. With the land grants, Laurey and Gould would be able to cut prices and corner the most lucrative corporate customers.

"Damn," Steve growled, crumpling the telegram.

"Now that Number One has dumped enormous sums of money into the railroad, we learn he's been given a sieve to dip water with," Chane said.

"Raton Pass is about a hundred and ten miles from La Junta," Steve said. "But the Taos Trail is longer. Laurey and Gould had the advantage of surprise, until Tom Wilcox somehow found out what they were doing. They may be ahead of us, but not decisively so."

Chane nodded his agreement. "Bless Tom and his network of informants."

Steve passed the crumpled telegram to Targle, who reddened and waved it away. "Ain't never been much for book larnin'."

Tinkersley read it out loud.

"I guess we'd better go see to the Chinese," Chane said.

Targle stiffened. A stubborn, bulldog look tightened his lips into a slit. "I may not have got past the flyleaf of a primer, but I'm smart enough to know a mistake when I see one."

"Meaning?" Chane asked.

"I know you're the boss, Mr. Kincaid, but I've never been one to get a sore crotch from straddling the fence. Them chinks look a mite prissy-assed to me. Building a railroad is a job for real men. We don't need a thousand men to carry over the rough spots."

"I'll keep that in mind. If they don't pull their weight, you can rest assured I'll send 'em packing."

"Much obliged."

"How long do you think it'll take us to lay a hundred and ten miles of track?" Steve asked.

"Depends on too many things to estimate," Chane said. "Weather, how well the men hold up in the cold, how many trestles we have to build, and how far we have to transport timber and gravel."

"What are our chances of beating Laurey to Raton?"

"Not good."

About the same as the chances that the rest of his life would be bearable, Chane thought.

Chane rented horses for Steve and himself. Targle and Tinkersley had their own mounts. They stopped first at Beaver Targle's camp east of town. Some men were camped by the railhead; some had already moved into the railroad sleeping cars. They were playing cards, arguing, lolling on cots. According to Targle, fights had already blacked two men's eyes.

"We're going to have to restrict the sale of whiskey if you want this road built this year," Targle said.

"Then do it."

They found Kim Wong and his Chinese laborers camped south of town by the river. Smoke from their cook fires curled upward in the cold, still air. A thousand Chinese made more noise than a herd of buffalo. From a half mile away Chane heard singsong voices yelling and laughing.

Dank-mud river smells mingled with the odors of cooking fish, steeping tea, and mesquite smoke. The Chinese camp spread out along the riverbank for a half mile or more. As they approached, the Chinese fell silent, stopping what they were doing to watch.

Chane reined up at a campfire. Six pigtailed men in blue tunics squatted on their haunches around the fire, warming themselves. A man fishing at the river's edge looked around.

"I'm looking for Kim Wong, the agent."

One of the Chinese nodded vigorously and pointed to the south. Chane turned his horse in that direction. The man who had directed him let out a shrill cry, which was taken up by first one and then another.

Kim Wong walked out to meet them. He was taller and heavier than the average Chinese, and looked slightly Caucasian. He had heavy arched brows over shrewd eyes, a broad Oriental nose, and a full, smiling mouth. He wore the usual blue tunic, and his hair was shaved to mid-crown and the back half braided into a pigtail worn by all Chinese laborers. Chane had been told he spoke English and six Chinese dialects necessary to communicate with the men he'd recruited.

Kim Wong looked from man to man, trying to guess which one would be Kincaid. A tall man with piercing green eyes, very near his own age, stepped forward and offered his hand. He had expected Kincaid to be older.

Kim Wong took the broad hand and gripped it hard, the way Americans did.

Chane introduced his comrades and then said, "I see you found plenty of men to come."

"No ploblem getting men, Mista Kincaid. No ploblem," Kim Wong said, dropping automatically into pidgin English. He spoke fluent

English and had been educated at an English university in Hong Kong for three years, but he found it advisable to speak pidgin to white men. They looked even more suspiciously upon Chinese who didn't.

Recruiting men to come to America had been easy. Famine, border skirmishes with Russia, threats to China's coastline from Russian gunboats, the British opium trade, fights between supporters of the Manchu Dowager Empress and the rebels—the Red Turbans—all made this a good time to leave China.

Kim Wong had had his own reasons for leaving. A Red Turban himself, he had barely escaped execution. He'd jumped into a sampan and fled Canton while less fortunate members of his tong were being executed by loyalist soldiers. The streets had run with blood. He had seen fifty or more severed heads hoisted in a fish net and tied up at the city gates for all to see. He was lucky his head had not been among them. And grateful to Kincaid for this opportunity he would have scorned two years ago.

In China he would be castigated for building a railroad. The masses hated the iron monster. In 1876 the government had finally allowed a railroad to be built in his province. The people had been terrified. They felt certain the railroad would disturb the good joss of the land, anger the land gods, and disturb their honorable ancestors' graves. They had deliberately walked in front of the trains, believing that in death they would be transformed into powerful hostile spirits to combat the railroad and to protect their living relatives. The deaths had caused such an outcry, the government had had to buy the railroad and dump the locomotives into the river.

Fortunately for Kim Wong, those same men who had opposed the railroad in China were happy to build one for the "Melicans." It pleased the Chinese to retaliate against their enemies by disturbing the good joss of the Melicans' land and disrupting their ancestors' sleep.

Kim Wong bowed low.

"Between your crew and Targle's crew, we've got about twenty-five hundred men," Chane said. "We need to break 'em into crews and get 'em busy. We need men to grade the roadbed, cut timber, quarry gravel for ballast, operate the sawmill, build the trestles, blast cuts through the passes, level slopes, string telegraph lines between the camps, and lay rails."

Kim Wong nodded. "We do all that."

Targle snorted and shook his head. "Probably didn't understand a word you said."

"Understand velly good. We do all that and more. Even survey and build blidges."

"Reckon they can do just about anything for ten minutes or so, but can they do it from bust of day to good dark?" Targle growled.

Kim Wong nodded. "Chinaboys work hard. You see."

Chane spent a good hour arbitrating between Kim Wong and Beaver Targle. Beaver was fairly easy to manipulate. If Chane wanted him to take on a particular job, he introduced it as the most difficult. Kim Wong was a wily one. Smart and determined, he hid greater intelligence beneath the jolly, mindless façade that completely fooled Targle.

Finally, the tasks were evenly divided and responsibility assigned. Targle's crews would operate the quarry, transport the gravel and supplies to the bridge sites and work sites, grade the roadbed, lay the ballast and rails, and cut timber. Kim Wong's crew would carve the grade south, build the minor bridges over the tributary feeder streams, build boxcars and passenger cars, and operate the sawmill.

Targle grunted his satisfaction. "I expect they'll work a week and collapse."

Chane secretly bet that within a week they would be running small businesses in their spare time—selling cooked food, washing clothes, and operating gambling tables.

Kim Wong bowed and walked back to his campfire.

Targle shook his head in chagrin. "You're wasting your money paying them Chinaboys for men's work."

It struck Chane as odd that Targle would still be arguing with him about something that would become plain as soon as they started work. The Chinese had played an important role in building the Union Pacific Railroad in '69, and most of the U.S. railroads since then. They had a history of pulling their weight day in and day out without being pushed.

"If the Chinese don't work out, I'll deal with that when the time comes."

Targle acted like a man who knew it was time to stop but couldn't anyway. "I know how they're gonna do. They're gonna raise hell with morale. Not one man in a hundred will put up with them getting equal pay for carrying half a man's load. Did you see how little they was? Why, I could carry one under each arm."

Chane slapped him on the back. "We need a thousand head of horses, a couple hundred steers, and some mules and oxen. I imagine you've got that pretty well lined up."

"I've been buying for weeks, but we need hundreds more horses, oxen, mules, and cattle." Targle walked to his horse, mounted, and rode away at a canter, still shaking his head.

Steve expelled a frustrated breath. "Well, I'm glad we got that settled."

"I don't expect that to solve all the problems we're going to have between those two. If we're going to beat Laurey, we need to finish the line in less than three months," Chane said.

"I don't see how we can pay for that much rail in that short a time. It would take a miracle."

"Only one?" Chane grinned. "That shouldn't be any problem at all for a smart attorney like you. Look at the bright side. What we use in steel rails, we save in salaries."

Steve knew Chane was tense and edgy, boarded up like a town waiting for a tornado. He wondered if Jennie knew how bleak the prospects were for her happiness. But being who he was, if Chane decided to stay married, he would. But she might suffer for it.

To Steve's way of thinking, it was to Chane's advantage to stay with Jennifer. Having watched his own parents, he knew better than to expect a perfect marriage. But at least with Jennifer, Chane would be buffered against the kind of misery he'd suffered before.

For Jennie, the kiss in the hotel dining room was a revelation. She realized that Chane must be jealous of Tom Tinkersley. If that were true, then there must be a flicker of feeling for her left in him somewhere. She'd just have to bide her time.

Up in their room, she noticed an envelope on the bureau with her name scrawled in Chane's handwriting. She picked it up and ten bills fell out, fluttering to the floor. A note inside said, *Buy whatever you need. We'll be rolling down the tracks in a few days. You might not have an opportunity to shop for a while. Chane.* Jennifer counted $950.

Ignoring the looks of interest in her crutches and possibly her camel-wool coat, too elegant for the small town, she hobbled to the town's few stores. Soon her underarms were sore from the crutches. Since she couldn't carry anything but herself anyway, she went back to the hotel, made a list, and sent Marianne back to the stores.

Chane was gone all day. He came back to their hotel room about nine-thirty that evening, pleased and tired and dirty. He made no reference to the kiss. Nor did she.

"How long will we stay here at the hotel?"

"A couple more days," he said, sagging into the only upholstered chair in the room.

"Have you eaten?"

"I grabbed a bite with the men."

He was asleep in the chair before she reached their bed. She didn't wake him.

Chane needed to be everywhere at once. He rode to the quarry site, which was farther away than he'd wanted it. Then he rode to the place on the river he and Targle had chosen for the sawmill. One crew would cut timber west of La Junta, another would float it a short way down the river, and another would buck logs into the saws that would spew forth ties, bridge pilings, and lumber for trestle construction and railroad cars.

Axes rang in the forest. Men graded the roadbed. He rode ahead, following stake flags left by the surveyors who had started six weeks before his arrival. When he came to a gully or a small water bed that had to be spanned, he took his measurements, sat down and drew a rough design. Then he rode back, recruited a crew, and led them and wagonloads of supplies to the new trestle site. This way the trestle could be finished by the time the track reached it.

As the track-laying crews moved forward, another crew strung telegraph wire beside them.

Chane sent a telegram to Wilcox to find out when the Commodore and Gould had started building south. As a precaution, Chane sent one of Tom Tinkersley's Apache scouts to Pueblo to follow the Commodore's crew as they laid rail. They sent coded telegrams back so there wouldn't be any more security leaks.

Chane worked longer than anyone else. Since everyone knew he and Jennie were staying at the hotel, he felt obliged to keep up a charade so as not to invite undue speculation. Most nights when he came to bed, Jennie was asleep.

Tonight was no different. He knew he should sleep in the chair again, but his back ached, fairly crying out for a warm, comfortable bed.

In the dark he undressed down to his union suit, slipped into bed beside his sleeping wife, and waited for sleep. Unfortunately, either he wasn't tired enough or he was too tired. The sound of Jennie's soft breathing, the smell of her, so warm and heady beside him, oozed into his body. He lay there stiff and miserable, his body humming like a telegraph wire.

He turned his back to her. Jennie turned over and snuggled up with her breasts against his back and her knees nestled into the crook of his knees. The feel of her was so unexpected and so delicious, Chane could barely breathe. He knew he should just get up and walk to the train, but he couldn't bring himself to do it. The silky feel of her was so delicious, so warm and sweet and soft. It would be easier to cut his leg off than to move away from her.

He must have been crazy to bring her along, he thought. His body burned with a terrible, weakening fever, but he knew he couldn't make love to her. He had promised to take care of her, and he would keep his word if it killed him. But the less he took advantage of her, the better position he'd be in when he got to the point where he could break free of her. Chane had had second thoughts about Tom Tinkersley. Maybe he could use Tom to attract Jennie away from him. Jennie seemed to like Tom. And Tom obviously admired her. Chane had seen him smiling at her any number of times. Tinkersley didn't need to be marriage material. He just needed to serve as a bridge, from one situation to another. As soon as Jennie transferred her feelings to Tinkersley, she could let go of him.

His heart sank at the thought of it. But better that than the misery he'd feel the rest of his life if she stayed with him.

Jennifer woke to another cold, sunny day. Chane was already dressed.

"I didn't hear you come in."

"You were asleep."

"Are you angry?"

"No." He picked up his heavy coat.

"You look grumpy."

"I didn't get much sleep last night."

"Oh."

"I'm moving back to the train today. We're heading down the tracks. You can stay here. It'll be more comfortable for you."

"Did I do something wrong?" she asked, puzzled.

"No."

"Then why are you angry with me?"

"I'm not angry," he yelled, slamming down the coat.

Startled, Jennifer decided it might be best to ignore his outburst. "I want to come with you."

Chane looked like a man pushed beyond his limits. And she had no idea what had caused it.

With a visible effort he controlled himself. "Can you be packed in an hour?"

"Yes."

"Okay, then." He jammed his arms into his sleeves and stalked out. "I'll send a man for your luggage," he said over his shoulder.

A train waited for them on the siding. Chane lifted her out of the buckboard and carried her to his palace car. The locomotive chuffed loudly, sending black coal smoke high into the cold blue sky. They reached the work site within minutes. The train whistle blew a signal to the brakeman. Jennifer heard him on the roof, tightening down the brakes. Within seconds the train ground to a halt.

Beyond the laid track, men worked fifty abreast, leveling the roadbed. Ahead of them the Chinese cleared the right-of-way.

Jennifer marveled at the progress already made. They had laid at least two or three miles of track. The Pullman coach they'd taken from New York inched forward on new steel rails.

Beside the work site the Arkansas River was wide and slow, bordered on each side by a long slope of sagebrush. Hills lay dark in the distance. The sky was a perfect blue, with scattered white clouds near the horizon.

"I'm leaving now," Chane said. "I'll be working on a trestle about five miles ahead."

"I thought you'd stay here in the Pullman coach."

"Too much trouble to run back and forth every day."

"May I go with you?"

"No, men working in water don't wear too many clothes."

Jennie laughed. "In this weather?"

"We've got to span a creek," he said, as if that explained everything.

"I'm not trying to be difficult, but what if I want to ride over and see you sometime?"

"I don't advise it, but if you must, then see Tom Tinkersley. He'll take care of you while I'm gone."

Chane walked to the crew shack and found Tinkersley. "I brought my wife to the site today. She may want to take an occasional horseback ride. It'll be your job to keep her safe."

"My job?" Tinkersley's eyes narrowed suspiciously.

"Her safety will be your personal concern. Unless you can't handle it."

Tinkersley hooked his thumbs in his belt and fingered his silver buckle.

Chane realized he'd aroused Tinkersley's suspicions. "You're in charge of security. If you can't handle the job, just say so."

Tom scowled. "I can handle anything you can throw at me."

"Then I don't see why you're having such a hard time with this." Chane turned and stalked away before Tinkersley could respond.

Meals were a problem. Marianne was taking lessons from one of the male cooks assigned to the railroad crews, but he wasn't much help to her. She was prepared to measure in cups, spoons, and pinches, and they talked about twenty-pound bags of this and that.

Marianne settled it by just walking to the cook tent and bringing back enough food for herself and Jennifer.

One afternoon Steve stopped by to tell Jennifer he was going into town. "Marianne," Jennifer called out. "Would you like to ride into town with Steve?"

Marianne poked her head out of the kitchen. "Do we need something, ma'am?"

"A cookbook."

On the way back from town Marianne kept glancing from Steve Hammond's clean profile to the beauty of the setting sun. They reached the camp, and Steve turned toward the office car, a Pullman coach he shared with Rutherford, the bookkeeper.

"Sure is a pretty sunset, isn't it?" she said.

The sky was scarlet and purple with golden streaks. Steve glanced at the sky, then at her. He wasn't much interested in sunsets, but Marianne, with her clear Irish complexion and her rosebud lips, was looking prettier to him every day.

"I sure wish I could take a walk down by that river," she said, sighing wistfully.

"Why can't you?"

"Mrs. Kincaid told me not to go off by myself."

"Oh. Well, I guess I could take you."

"Would you?"

They walked along the small creek that emptied into the Arkansas. They couldn't stray too far because of the fear of Indians. Tinkersley said bands of hostile Utes and friendly Arapahoes occasionally passed this way. Steve couldn't tell the difference between them, so he preferred to avoid all Indians.

She turned toward him. "You're nice. You don't act like what I thought you would," she said.

"I don't?"

"No."

"How did you think I would act?"

"I don't know. Usually you look like a bundle of loose nerves."

"Maybe you have a settling effect on me."

"Sure, and I'm glad of that."

Steve considered himself a practical man. His parents had had a good marriage until his father died at sixty of a stroke. His mother had maintained their comfortable brownstone near Madison Square. After the funeral, she'd asked Steve if he'd like to move back in. He was home so seldom, he could see no reason not to. With a well-run home as a base, he had been content to stay single even though men his age were expected to marry. But he had long ago realized that he had no knack with women. The things he generally talked about—bond issues, law cases, and stock transfers—seemed of no interest to them.

And his job kept him too busy. Chane was a dynamo. If they weren't building luxury hotels or untangling railroad disasters, they were buying or selling steamship lines or silver mines. Only a month ago Chane had traded his brother Lance an interest in the Texas and Pacific for an interest in a silver mine. Now that trade seemed a better bargain for Chane than Lance.

"You don't talk much, do you?" Marianne asked.

"I do all I need to get my business done, which seems considerable." He liked the sound of her voice, though. She had a raspy, smoky sort of voice that stirred odd reactions in him.

She laughed. "Sure, and you don't look at a girl much either, do you?"

Steve could tell by the tone of her mocking voice that she wasn't serious, but he flushed and shoved his hands deeper into his pockets. "I was raised to treat a woman with respect—which, in my mother's opinion, was not to stare, not to speak ill of her, and not to swear in her presence."

"Most men look at every part of me but my face. At least you look right into my eyes, so I guess you're not so bad."

Steve tightened his jaw. He didn't want his mouth hanging open, in case it was trying to. This plain-speaking young woman was buxom and fairly brimming with good health.

"Do you know what folks do around here for fun?" she asked.

"I don't consider myself an expert on entertainment west of the Mississippi. But my cousin who used to live in Nevada said that folks do pretty much the same sorts of things, maybe pop some corn, play whist, or just sit on the porch talking, if they have a porch."

"Sure, now, and how does a young lady find out if there'll be a dance in town sometime soon?"

"I guess I don't know the answer to that."

"Well, find out. I might want you to take me to the dance—if there is one," she added, smiling up at him.

Steve made a point of taking Marianne for a walk almost every evening after that. She usually didn't have much to say; she just walked along and stole sideways glances at him. Finally one night when they were about to turn around and start back, she slipped into his arms and kissed him.

The kiss was soft and sweet at first, then her tongue surprised him by getting playful. When the kiss ended, he was breathing hard and wondering what to do next. Marianne answered that question for him by going up on tiptoe and kissing him again while guiding his hand to her breast. It was firm and round, and he could feel her heart pounding as hard as his own. The combination of her hot mouth on his and her body pressing tight against him made him dizzy. He ended the kiss with regret.

"You'd better be careful," he cautioned.

"And what will happen if I'm not?"

"I might forget to stop kissing you," he said huskily.

"And what would be happening then?" she asked archly.

"Mrs. Kelly's fine Irish daughter might find herself in a heap of trouble," he said, peering at her through the dimming light. The sun had gone down, and he was suddenly aware of how alone they were and how dark it was getting.

"And what if she's not the tiniest bit worried about all this trouble?"

Steve leaned down and kissed her again. Playfulness had turned to passion in her, too. Her mound jutted against his belly and caused a searing shaft of need to suffuse his whole body. Her mouth clung to his while her hands rubbed his chest and stomach. His hands cupped her breasts and moved lower to feel her soft stomach and see if he could touch her between her legs before she stopped him. He slipped his hand there and she groaned, but she didn't try to shove his hand away. She just ground herself against it as she kissed him.

Steve had very little experience with women, but he knew a clear signal when he felt one. He eased her down onto a grassy place on the riverbank and lifted her skirts. He entered her and hung on. She cried out and bucked wildly against him, almost jarring him loose until he grabbed her buttocks and took control, easing them into a smooth rhythm that quickly brought them both to that moment of frenzy they craved.

Marianne sobbed and panted and laughed. Slowly she settled down and grew quiet. Steve continued to hold her and kiss her face, amazed that she was such an excitable woman. He was flushed with gratitude to her and filled with relief that he had handled himself well enough that she didn't seem to notice his inexperience.

For several moments they lay together in companionable silence.

"Sure, and I suppose you'll be wanting to know about the other men," she said.

"No." Steve could not imagine wondering about that. What women did when they were away from him was something he'd rather not know about. The reality of making love to a woman was so different from hearing about other people that the two did not seem the same at all.

Marianne squirmed around, then sat up. "Well, there haven't been all that many. Unless you count heavy flirting. Do you count that?"

"No." Steve tried to think of some way to stop her, but she seemed determined to talk frankly and aimlessly about a subject no one else ever talked about at all.

"Sure, and that's probably best," she said. "I only had one husband, when I was fourteen. My brother, Tom, picked him for me. His name was Joseph, and I think he liked me, but he died in a railroad accident. He was a brakeman. And when the train he was riding hit the rear end of another train, he went flying off the top and landed on his head. Never knew what hit him. I never wanted to marry again…till maybe now…"

CHAPTER TWENTY-TWO

With Chane away at the trestle work site, Jennifer had a crisis to deal with almost every day. Men injured themselves. When the wound was bad, she'd get them to Dr. Campbell, but if he was already busy, she nursed them herself.

One of the horses fell on a wrangler and almost killed him. Then an ox stepped on a grader's foot and broke most of the bones in it. Jennifer discovered Chane had made no provisions for a hospital car, so she directed the Chinese carpenters to convert one of the flatcars into a rolling hospital by building walls with wide windows that opened easily.

She asked endless questions of Dr. Campbell, until she learned enough about the injured men's needs at least to keep them comfortable. It wasn't easy getting that information out of Campbell. Even though he was a doctor, he seemed to have no idea how to make another human being comfortable.

By the end of each day, her underarms were sore from swinging around on her crutches. Her injured foot was swollen and aching. And the next day was a repeat of the others. And the next. The men constantly seemed to find new ways to injure themselves.

It was just as well she had things to keep her busy. Chane stayed busy from dawn to dark. Most nights he stayed at the trestle site.

The train crew was being shadowed by a herd of sheep that Chane suspected were shepherded by one of Laurey's operatives. The man seemed to keep his herd within sight of them at all times.

Against Chane's implied orders, Jennifer rode out with Tom to meet the shepherd. He was an elderly Basque, obviously a real sheepherder, and spoke no English. He had merry, smiling eyes, though, and Jennifer could see he liked her.

"He's no threat," she told Chane.

Chane looked at Tom, who nodded his agreement.

"Glad to hear that."

It irritated Jennifer that he didn't even trust her judgment on a simple thing like that. She started to turn away, saw that his thumb was black and swollen, and stopped.

"What happened to your thumb?"

"I hit it with a hammer."

"Did you do anything for it?"

"Yes, ma'am," he said, mimicking Tinkersley's Texas accent. "As soon as I noticed, I stopped hitting it with the hammer."

"I mean besides that."

"That was all it needed. Soon as I stopped hitting it, it felt a lot better."

"Let me look at it."

"You've got enough men to worry about," he said, standing up and stalking out of the Pullman coach.

Sometimes sheep strayed into camp, and the old man came after them and stayed a few minutes to chat with Chane's Basque workmen. Chane had hired a dozen men from the Pyrenees. They lived lustily, worked hard, and all seemed to have the merry, smiling eyes of the old sheepherder Jennie liked. She decided the old man stayed nearby because he was lonely.

To keep limber, Jennifer practiced ballet stretches an hour a day. Her foot ached so much she couldn't manage more than that. Occasionally, accompanied by Tom Tinkersley, she rode one of Chane's blooded mares around the campsite and up the Santa Fe Trail.

At first Tinkersley was polite, reserved, and watchful—the perfect employee.

"Where is your family?" Jennifer asked.

"Texas."

"What part? Or is Texas just one small town?"

He grinned, and sunlight flashed off a gold filling in his canine tooth. "You could ride for a week and still be in Texas," he said proudly. "My folks live in a little town called Tinkersley. My father owns the place."

"Sounds like the perfect arrangement. Why'd you leave?"

"Because my father owns the place," he said, grinning ruefully. His skin was tanned to a smooth teak color. His eyes sparkled with humor, and she felt a small stirring when he smiled. She hoped it was because he reminded her so much of Peter.

"Do you have any brothers and sisters?" Jennifer continued, curious.

"Two of each."

"And what are they doing?"

"My father wants to be governor someday. My sisters and brothers are raising the next generation of voters right this minute."

Jennifer laughed. "And you are the laggard."

"Got that right. My father hates it, but at least he hasn't sent any Texas Rangers after me yet."

They rode together every day, and Tinkersley remained thoughtful and respectful, no matter how much they talked or how intimately. He was a man of depth and spirit. She knew why he'd had to leave his home and make his own mark. He could never be satisfied trudging along in his father's footsteps.

Jennifer quickly fell in love with Colorado. She adjusted to the altitude—and the cold nights, and she had not expected such beautiful days. The railroad followed the Purgatoire River, called the Picketwire by locals. The land they traveled was as flat as a tabletop for the most part, but because they followed the river, they had to span a number of creeks that emptied into it.

The second week, a man poured blasting powder into a hole, set the fuse, and waited two minutes for it to go off. When it didn't, he used a spoon to try to get it out of the hole and blew off three fingers and part of his hand. Jennifer helped Dr. Campbell cut away the unsavable parts of the hand.

Later, she overheard a man telling another man that Chane had told Beaver Targle that from now on Chane himself would handle the explosives. The men laughed. "Hell, I had a beautiful wife like that, you wouldn't catch me within a mile of a stick of dynamite. Kincaid must be crazy."

The other man nodded. "Works like it, don't he?"

The next time Chane came to visit, Jennifer confronted him. "I heard you're going to handle all the explosives from now on."

"That's right."

He didn't look like he wanted to discuss it, but Jennifer persisted. "Isn't that an odd thing to do? The most valuable man in the crew doing the most dangerous work?"

"All men are equal when it comes to dying."

"Well, they aren't all equally expendable when it comes to getting this railroad built. If something happens to you, they'll all be out of work, your grandfather will lose a great deal of money, and I'll..." Unable to finish that thought, her voice trailed off.

"Dynamite isn't magic, Jennie. It works a certain way, and if you respect the rules, it's no more dangerous than a bar of soap."

Chane couldn't be swayed. Early next morning he left for the trestle site. About noon the sound of a man cursing loudly and creatively brought her out onto the observation deck. A short, fat man in a black bowler hat drove up in what looked like a converted hearse. He whipped his team of splay-backed mules and yelled at them, but the mules held their ground. Finally, the man set the brake and climbed down. He walked around to the back and banged on the window.

"Might as well get down, girls. I think we're here."

The curtain on the back parted and three girls with brightly made-up faces peered out. One opened the glass door and stood on the step. "This ain't no place." She was plump and redheaded, and her low-necked blouse strained against her ample bosom.

"Well, it might not be New York City, but it is someplace," he corrected her.

"What the Sam Hill are we supposed to do here?"

"Earn your keep. What do you usually do?"

It was clear they had not noticed Jennifer on the observation deck.

"Among these railroaders?"

"They got money, don't they? They ain't exactly fighting off the women, are they?"

"I can smell 'em from here."

He sniffed the air. "Let Hessie Mae go first. She's got that sinus infection that keeps her from smelling anything."

"Y'all talkin' 'bout me?" A slim, blond, blue-eyed girl stepped out of the hearse and looked around.

Jennifer felt an instant kinship with the girl, whose eyes sparkled with determination and mischief.

"He was saying you should try your luck first, 'cause you've got that sinus infection."

Hessie Mae shook her head in chagrin. "I may not be able to smell much, but I got better sense than to take on a bunch of men who ain't had a bath since La Junta."

"Aw, they probably bathed a couple of times since then."

"You felt that water when we crossed the last creek. You couldn't get me into that water, and these men don't look determined enough to take a bath for no reason. Let 'em find out we're here first."

"Excuse me," Jennifer said.

Four sets of startled eyes turned her way.

The man took off his hat. His merry little eyes were half hidden by fat cheeks. "How do, ma'am."

"Are you looking for someone?"

Two of the girls giggled.

"Just thought we'd stop and offer our services," he said.

"I can easily see what services the young women could offer," Jennifer said, "but what can you do?"

The man flushed red as a persimmon. "Why, ma'am, I'm surprised you'd say such a thing to me. Why, I've taken care of these girls until they think of me as their father. I've protected them and nursed them and—"

"I see. How long do you intend to stay?"

One of the girls snickered. "As long as the money holds out, I reckon."

"Are you in charge here, ma'am?"

"I'm Mrs. Kincaid. My husband owns the company building the railroad."

The man bowed low, sweeping his top hat almost to the ground. "Bunker Hilton at your service, ma'am."

Jennifer hesitated. She wished Chane were here. She didn't feel at all sure of herself, but she had the strong conviction that she had to protect the men in Chane's employ. Anything less would be a betrayal of the women and children who had seen these men off. "I don't suppose we can keep you away, but I can insist that your women be checked by our doctor before they get anywhere near our men."

Bunker Hilton blinked. A look of outrage mottled his features. "Why, madame, I certainly cannot see subjecting these fine young ladies to the indignity of an examination by a stranger."

"Fine. Then I'll have my husband bring his shotgun and escort you on your way."

The girls looked at one another.

Bunker Hilton sputtered. Never in his life had he had such a blunt conversation with a woman who looked like a lady. Ladies did not acknowledge sporting women, much less ask them to submit to a medical examination. His usual penchant for easy conversation failed him completely.

A man carrying a sack of potatoes walked by on his way to the cook's car. "Ezra," Jennifer called out to him.

"Harumph," Hilton interrupted quickly. "That won't be necessary, madame. Where do we see this…doctor?"

Jennifer sent Ezra to fetch the doctor. Campbell trotted from the infirmary car, a surprised look on his face. She explained as delicately as she could what she wanted him to do. Campbell stifled the grin that threatened to break his composure and led the girls back to the infirmary. Bunker Hilton followed with the mules.

Jennifer didn't know if she'd done the right thing, but she knew that if she ran the girls off, they'd camp a half mile away and do whatever they wanted. It seemed best to control them, so every man in the company wouldn't disappear over there every night. They might freeze to death on their way back to the sleeping quarters.

Three days passed before she saw Chane again. He rode up to the Pullman coach and got down stiffly. She wondered if someone had told him about her handling of Bunker, but she couldn't tell by looking at him. She decided to wait until he'd eaten dinner and relaxed for a few minutes.

"I made dinner," she said, suddenly unsure of herself.

"I didn't know you could cook."

"Well, maybe I can't. Will you take a chance and eat with me?"

"I have a few things to do first."

"It's almost ready."

Chane came back alone. Jennifer had set the table. While he looked at a newspaper someone had brought from La Junta, she put the food into serving dishes.

"It's ready."

Chane moved to the table. "Looks...fine," he said.

He cut into the meat she had cooked. Blood ran into his plate. Without blinking, he cut off a bite of the meat, put it into his mouth, and started to chew. And kept chewing.

"Is something wrong?"

"No, nothing," he said around the wad of meat in his jaw. He chewed for a while and finally swallowed.

"It's not done, is it?"

"It's fine," he lied.

Jennifer felt miserable. No matter how hard she tried, she couldn't get anything cooked the right amount of time.

"I cooked it until it had blisters," she said.

"Blisters?"

"See?" She turned the meat over and showed him the underside.

"About how long?"

"At least twenty-five or thirty minutes."

"Well, Jennie. I think this is a roast. I don't know anything about cooking, but I remember my mother used to cook a roast for a few hours."

"Hours? I didn't start dinner until five-thirty."

Forlorn, Jennifer pushed the near-raw roast aside. In silence they ate over-boiled potatoes and soggy vegetables. Finally, she could stand it no longer. "I had a problem while you were gone."

"Oh?"

"I'm not sure I handled it right."

"Oh?"

"Well, a man and three young…women came into camp the other day."

Chane put down his fork and waited.

"I think they're…working women. So I asked Dr. Campbell to check them to be sure they don't have any unfortunate illnesses they could pass on to your men."

"Working women," he repeated, a smile creeping into his eyes and tugging at the corners of his mouth.

"You know. Sporting women."

"And did Dr. Campbell check them?"

"I believe he did."

"And did he give you a report?"

"He said they appeared to be in fine health."

Chane picked up his fork, stabbed a piece of boiled potato, and brought it to his lips. "Thank you, Jennie. You did well."

A sigh of relief escaped her. "You don't know how worried I was. I was afraid you'd say…"

He suppressed a smile. "What?"

She hesitated to tell the truth for fear he would agree with her. "That I didn't have any morals."

"I'd say protecting my men's health is a pretty moral thing to do."

"I was afraid maybe I should have run them off."

"They'd go about a quarter of a mile out of sight and set up camp. We wouldn't see them, but we'd probably lose about half our men. I prefer to keep a snake in sight, so I can see what he's doing."

Her thinking exactly! Chane had approved of her decision. She was so grateful she felt giddy. It felt like a red letter day.

• • •

January thirtieth was the Chinese New Year. All the Chinese workers celebrated with loud Chinese music, firecrackers, red paper flags, and special dishes they invited everyone to share.

The Chinese camped on one side of the tracks, the rest of the men on the other. Out of boredom, the other men, immigrants and Americans, walked to the Chinese encampment to watch the festivities. Chane and Jennie were honored guests of Kim Wong, who had prepared a special dinner for them. He explained this year was called *Sin-Se*, the Year of the Snake.

The weather was nicer than usual. Warm enough to sit in the sun with coats on instead of going into the sleeping and dining cars. Most of the Chinese preferred being outdoors unless the weather was brutal.

"Why don't your men eat beef?" Jennifer asked. She'd noticed they ate fish and chicken, but they refused the rations of beef Chane provided to the crews.

Kim Wong bowed low. "The men respect cattle and oxen as fellow workers. It would be most rude of them to eat their compatriots, would it not?"

"What happened to your pidgin English?"

Kim Wong looked perplexed. "So solly, Missy. What you say?"

"For a moment you didn't speak pidgin. You forgot, didn't you?"

Trapped, Kim Wong admitted that he had forgotten. On the way home, Chane mentioned it.

"That was pretty observant of you, noticing he'd slipped out of pidgin." A sharp light momentarily brightened his eyes. Pride?

"Was it?" she asked, surprised.

But he didn't follow it up.

Chane left without saying anything else to her. A few days later Jennifer rode past the Chinese encampment and saw them yelling, spitting, and shaking their fists at one another, apparently upset about something. The non-Chinese workers looking on seemed tickled. They cheered the Chinese on.

Seeing her, men stopped yelling and cheering and went back to work. Later she noticed that three rough-looking men had set up a makeshift blacksmith shop near the company smithy, who had been provided a workplace on a flatcar following the coal bin. The three beat and pounded metal into what looked like swords with long handles.

She stopped beside the man she recognized as Rooster Burnside. She knew him because Rooster couldn't sign his name to receive his weekly pay, so the bookkeeper asked Jennie to witness Rooster's X. A giant of a man, his broad face was shiny with sweat sheen, and his thick arms were bare.

"What are you making, Rooster?" she asked, stopping beside him.

Nicknamed for the unruly brush of red hair that stood up like a rooster's comb, Rooster scowled and looked at his partners. Bobo Boschke, a sturdy Polish immigrant, just looked blank, and Irish Jim Delany, small and wiry, remained his usual silent self.

Rooster was on his own. He tried a bluff. "Why, we ain't doin' nothin', ma'am."

"I can see you're making something. I'd like to know what it is."

"Uhhhmm." He looked trapped and angry, but he still got no help or encouragement from his comrades. "A spear, ma'am," he said, sighing heavily.

"Why are you making a spear?"

"To sell."

"To whom?"

"Who to?" he echoed, scowling ferociously. His words were still respectful, but his eyes sparkled with antagonism. He looked quickly around at Bobo and Jim, who watched him with a mixture of delight at his discomfort and fear that they'd be in for it next.

"To...them chinks."

"But why?"

"It's not my place to say, ma'am."

Jennifer could get no more out of him. Behind the shed she saw that they had a stockpile of close to a hundred spears, and from their work she guessed the pile was growing daily. They were odd weapons, but they looked deadly.

She went to Kim Wong and told him what had transpired. "What's going on, Mr. Wong?"

"Not good you ask."

"But I did ask. And you have no need of your pidgin English with me."

Kim Wong smiled. The expression on his face changed, softened. "Hard times in China now. A bad faction is running the government—the Manchurians. My people, the Red Turbans, are seen as rebels opposing the Manchu government and the Dowager Empress. They fight with the Cantons and the Hong Kongs."

"What are these Cantons and Hong Kongs?"

"Associations formed for protection and to make money. We call them tongs. The Red Turbans are determined to overthrow the government."

"But what has that to do with us?"

"Same here."

"You mean among these men there are Red Turbans, Cantons, and Hong Kongs?"

"Yes, Mrs. Kincaid. Same here."

"Well, can't you stop them?"

"No, the Red Turbans have been insulted. They demand an opportunity to save face."

"How were they insulted?"

"One of the loyalists—" He paused. "—not something a gentleman can discuss with a lady."

Jennifer could get nothing else out of Kim Wong. But she watched the activity with foreboding. After the workday ended, Rooster and his friends were busy all evening hammering out weapons. Jennifer knew if she ordered him to cease and desist, he'd probably quit, set up shop again out of her sight a few hundred feet away, and make five times as many weapons.

In frustration, she walked back to the Pullman coach she shared less and less with Chane.

One afternoon a week later, Marianne came running up the steps, panting and out of breath.

"What is it, Marianne?"

"I heard men talking…I think there's going to be a big fight tonight…after work," she gasped.

"The Chinese?"

"Yes, mum. The men were all laughing about it. They think it's going to be more fun than a cockfight."

Jennifer realized Chane couldn't make it back in time. She found Tom Tinkersley in the kitchen nursing a cup of coffee. "Tom, get some of your men and follow me," she said determinedly.

"What's going on?" he asked, grabbing his hat.

"I've got a job to do."

"Is this a job Mr. Kincaid would approve of?"

"We won't know until he comes back. By then it could be too late. Are you coming or not?"

At the blacksmith shop she directed Tom to have his men pick up all the weapons. By now the three men had a stack of spears two feet high and six feet wide.

Rooster Burnside, a scowl on his broad, shiny face, came running from where he'd been lifting rails and stepped between Tom and the pile of long-handled swords. "These are our spears," he bellowed. "We made 'em in our spare time."

Men stopped working on the railroad and walked back to see what was going on.

"I've decided to buy your weapons. Every one of them," Jennifer said flatly. "And in the future all weapons made within ten miles of this camp or with scrap metal owned by this railroad will be mine. That's a rule."

Rooster pushed up his sleeves as if he were about to wade into a fight. All semblance of politeness was gone from the big man's face. Now his eyes shot arrows of anger and resentment. A rumble of discontent started among men watching.

"Can she do that?" a man asked.

Tom Tinkersley stepped forward. "You heard her."

Rooster eyed Jennifer warily. "How much you willing to pay for these here spears?"

"The going price."

Rooster's eyes narrowed. "I could sell these for five dollars apiece."

"Sold." Jennifer said.

Rooster frowned, but he was too confused to know how to proceed. Tom motioned his men forward to pick up the spears. Onlookers grumbled about the fun they were going to miss, but they weren't inclined to take on an armed man of Tinkersley's reputation leading more armed men.

"Count the spears," Jennie ordered.

Burnside nodded and started in. The men dispersed, but Jennifer had the feeling this wasn't the last of it.

An hour later the three men came to Jennifer's Pullman coach and knocked on her door. She picked up her crutches, hobbled to the door, and opened it.

"There were one hundred and twenty-two spears," Rooster growled.

"I'll be right back." She hobbled to her desk, did the multiplication on a tablet, and took out the money Chane had given her in town. She counted out $610 and walked back to give it to Rooster.

He fingered the money for a second. "We can make lots more of them, at this price."

"Those spears were made out of materials you found here, so in truth they belong to my husband. If you decide to make anything else, please check with me first to be sure it's something I want to buy."

The men were so confused by her remarks they couldn't decide whether to give in or put up a fuss. Tom Tinkersley walked over. "Everything all right here, Mrs. Kincaid?"

She looked at the men. They looked down at their feet and shuffled off the observation deck. Tom walked up the steps and stood beside her, watching them walk away.

"They're likely to be soreheaded about this, you know."

"I won't have any warmongering among the men. Please lock my spears in one of the sheds, Tom."

Tom grinned broadly. "Yes, ma'am."

Two days later, after quitting time, Jennifer rode her horse up to the forward point, where the Chinese were clearing brush out of the right-of-way.

As she approached she heard yelling. Around a bend in the path, hundreds of Chinese had squared off to fight. Spears and swords gleamed dully in the sunlight.

Kim Wong was nowhere in sight. Since she hadn't planned to leave camp, she'd told Tom not to come with her.

The combatants hadn't seen her yet. Chinese men yelled and shook their fists and spit at one another across a space of less than twenty feet. The white men were cheering them on.

Men who had spears shook those and yelled at the top of their lungs in guttural grunts and honks.

One man shook his spear and ran forward as if he were going to stick it into someone. Jennifer kicked her horse into a run and rode in between the two factions.

At the sight of her, the men stepped back and fell silent.

"What's going on here?" she demanded.

Shamefaced, Kim Wong ran from behind one of the temporary construction shacks and came forward.

"Mr. Wong, what is going on here?"

"I'm sorry, Mrs. Kincaid. These men fight."

"I know that. Why? And where did they get those spears?"

"Some men already bought spears before you stopped men from selling them. They fight because of him," he said, pointing at a small Chinese man cowering beside the locomotive. "Cooky is a loyalist. These men are anti-Manchu. They want to toss him out."

"But why?"

"For saying something about a Red Turban's honorable father. They will not rest till he leave, but he won't go. So they have decided to fight until they kill him."

"Does he speak English?"

"Yes, he was cook to an Englishman in Hong Kong. He ran away to America to get rich."

Jennifer rode her horse over to the young man. "Why won't you leave?"

"Needed work when I came, missy."

"These men are going to kill you."

"Yes, missy."

"Come with me," she ordered.

The young man followed. When they were away from the clearing, she stopped her horse. "Were you really a cook?"

"Yes, missy."

"Would you come be my cook?"

He thought about that for a moment. Finally, he smiled. "Yes, missy."

"What's your name?"

He grinned. "No can pronounce, you. Call me Cooky."

"Okay, Cooky."

Jennifer expected his leaving to solve the problem between the warring factions, but it didn't. From Cooky she learned that the loyalists supported the Ch'ing Dynasty founded by the Manchus. The Red Turbans were determined to overthrow the Ch'ing Dynasty because it favored foreign interests at the expense of the Chinese, even allowing importation of opium, the bane of China. Cooky was a loyalist because his father had been one. He didn't approve of the policy regarding opium, but he would not change now. He missed his father too much.

Chane came back that night. Jennifer told him about the war and what she'd done to combat any further atrocities.

"You should have sent for me," he said, scowling.

"If I did that every time I have a little problem here, you wouldn't get anything done."

"A war between two outraged gangs of Chinese laborers is not a 'little problem.' They may look small, but Chinese men have no problem at all laying down their lives for their politics. I'll have a talk with them in the morning."

The next morning as the men shuffled from the dining cars, Chane climbed up on a flatcar. Kim Wong herded the Chinese around it. Jennifer watched from fifty feet away.

"I heard talk of your fighting among yourselves. I'm here to tell every one of you that if there's any more fighting, I'll deal with it harshly."

He paused to let Kim Wong translate. Wong talked a lot longer than Chane had. Finally, he paused and bowed to Chane.

"I don't want any bickering. You either get along with one another, or you'll all be on the next boat back to China. Any man who injures another man will be fired and sent home in disgrace. Any man who kills another man will be hanged."

Kim Wong translated again, this time with much arm waving. He ended with a curt nod and a deep bow from the waist toward Chane. The men muttered and scowled, but no one spoke up. Finally, Wong led his chastised, silent workers to the forward work site, where they began clearing the right-of-way.

Chane stalked to where the non-Chinese workers were picking up their shovels and hammers. He delivered a slightly different message to them.

"Any man caught instigating fights among the Chinese will be fired. If the fight results in serious injury or death, the man will be hanged. Are there any questions?"

Men muttered and shook their heads, but no one challenged the edict.

Chane headed back toward the office. Jennifer hobbled over to intercept him. "Can you do that? Hang a man without a trial?"

"I'll give 'em a trial. On a railroad construction gang, miles from civilization, there's no law but the boss's. If I don't provide direction and limits, they'll be doing what they want in no time. No one will be safe, especially you. Next time, don't wait so long to send for me."

"Yes, sir!" she said. She mimed clicking her heels.

Chane expelled a frustrated breath. "Sorry, Jennie. I realize you're doing the best you can. I know I shouldn't be leaving you alone so much, but there's just so much to do and so little time to do it."

Jennifer drew herself up the way she'd seen Peter do when training for the cavalry in France. "Forgiven, sir!"

Chane grinned. The rest of the day, no matter what she was doing, whenever she remembered how he'd looked grinning at her impertinence, she smiled.

They ate a delicious lunch together prepared by Cooky. She waited for Chane to notice how much better the food was, but he rode back to the trestle site without saying a word.

In frustration, she sought out Tom Tinkersley and asked him to take her for a ride. Tom's eyes narrowed at her, and she could see him calculating just how upset she was before he nodded. "I'll get the horses," he said, turning back to the men he'd been talking to. "You know what to do," he told them and walked toward the temporary remuda where the horses grazed.

They rode for several minutes in silence. Jennifer could feel his concern, and she was grateful that he didn't ask any questions. She didn't want to break down in front of him. "Could we ride faster?" she asked.

"You set the pace. I think I can keep up."

Jennifer kicked her horse into a run. The ground was level and fairly clear. She knew she was risking a fall, but it didn't matter. She leaned low on the horse's neck and slowly settled into the rhythm. It felt good to have the wind in her face and to feel free. She ran the horse until it was lathered, and then pulled it in. "That was glorious," she said, acknowledging Tom at last.

"Need to stop a minute," he said.

They reined their horses. They dismounted and Tom checked his horse's hooves. A rock had wedged itself into a crack in one of the front hooves. Tom took a knife and pried it out. "Doesn't that hurt?" she asked, leaning close to watch.

"The horse? Nah. It would hurt to leave it in, though." A pained expression clouded his features.

"What's wrong?" she asked.

"You're the prettiest thing I've ever seen. You have the face of an angel." His voice had dropped into huskiness. She knew he was falling in love with her. Part of her exulted in that knowledge, but another part of her was filled with guilt. She knew it was hopeless.

"That's very sweet of you to say."

"I'd give anything in the world…"

Something stirred in Jennifer. For just a moment she felt young and carefree and hopeful. A small voice told her that she didn't have much of a marriage. Her husband hated her, resented her, and wanted to be rid of her.

Tom's skin was moist from the ride, and it seemed to glow. His lips were smooth and slightly parted. Jennifer's fingers itched to reach out and touch them. Just once. Everything in her strained toward the comfort he could offer, but she was not ready to give up yet. She still had hope that Chane would relent. And as long as there was any hope at all…

She turned away before Tom could say anything more. "Time to get back," she said, realizing as she did that her voice was lower and more ragged than she would have liked. A testament, if any were needed, that she was desperate for husbandly attention.

When they reached the camp, she was almost frantic in her desire not to be alone. She searched out Cooky and asked him to teach her everything he knew. Puzzled but willing, Cooky took her out onto the desert to show her how to find herbs and wild vegetables for dinner. She was amazed at how many of the weeds she'd taken for granted were lovingly gathered and carefully placed in Cooky's sack.

As they returned and walked past the office car, she heard sounds of things being thrown around inside and stopped. "Wait here," she said to Cooky.

She climbed the steps and looked into Chane's and Steve's office. The bookkeeper, George Rutherford, a thin, graying man with bulging eyes and a pencil-thin mustache, was tossing clothes at a valise propped open on the floor. Rutherford and Steve shared the back half of the car's sleeping quarters.

"Mr. Rutherford! What are you doing?"

"Packing, ma'am."

"You're leaving?"

"Yes, ma'am." His voice quivered; he didn't look up.

"How come?"

"I didn't sign on for this trip to get killed by a bunch of Oriental savages."

"The war's over, Mr. Rutherford."

"For today, maybe, but I know the Chinese. When they've got a mind to fight with one another, they'll fight. Not a stubboner bunch of men anywhere on this earth."

Nothing Jennifer could say would deter him. Finally, she tried another tack. "If you leave, we'll be left without a bookkeeper."

"I expect so," he said, stuffing another shirt into his bag.

"I could take over your job, if you'd train me." It took twenty minutes to convince him, but he finally agreed.

Cooky took over all cooking and cleaning in the Pullman coach. Jennifer spent every available minute with Rutherford, making copious notes, until she felt she understood how the bookkeeping system worked. He wrote out detailed instructions and quizzed her on them. He watched her pay bills and post the transactions to the general ledger and the subsidiary ledgers. He taught her how to keep track of inventory and how to order supplies.

She'd had no idea how much work a bookkeeper did. At the end of each day, Jennifer's head spun with all she'd learned, but she felt more useful than ever before in her life. At night she went to bed weary but pleased with herself. She woke each morning with the feeling that life was wonderful and she was part of it.

As soon as he'd shown her everything he could think of about what might come up, he finished packing and said good-bye.

"I wish you'd change your mind, Mr. Rutherford. Have you noticed how quiet it's been?"

"I'm too old for this, Mrs. Kincaid. I started missing my house and my cat the minute we pulled out of New York, and I haven't stopped. This was just the last straw."

Jennifer asked Tom to escort Rutherford to La Junta.

Chane was due back any day now. She could hardly wait to see what he'd say about her taking over as his bookkeeper.

The crews were laying two miles of track a day. Every morning Jennifer saw new scenery and new weather. She'd never seen such a beautiful sky. But it could change within minutes. It might be clear in the morning, snowing by noon, and clear again before sunset.

All week, Chane had been at the trestle site, miles ahead. Jennifer decided to ride up to the site. She told Tom, and was surprised when he showed up with two extra men, but he didn't look to be in the mood for questions. Birds sang in snowcapped trees along the river, frogs croaked, and a mule brayed in the distance as if it were in pain. The sky was blue and clear. Crusted snow crunched under their horses' hooves.

She first visited the old Basque man and took him a loaf of bread Cooky had baked for him. Then she turned her horse toward the trestle site. They rode through beautiful, wild country. After a time, Tom got restless and rode up close to talk to her.

"Time to turn back," he said.

"Why did you bring two extra men?" she asked, ignoring his suggestion.

"Safety."

"What's changed?"

"Nothing."

"You don't lie well."

"Thank you."

"Now, let's try that again. Why the extra men?"

"My scouts say we're being followed by a band of Indians."

"Good, Tom."

Embarrassed, he shrugged.

Smiling, she kneed her horse forward; they rode in silence for a mile.

"Might be a good idea to stay close to camp," he said.

"I want to ride to the trestle site."

"That's quite a ways."

"I'm not a cripple. I'm a strong, healthy woman."

"I can see that." His eyes flashed a warning at her. She was coming dangerously close to flirting with him.

"What I meant is, I feel strong enough to ride as far as I want to ride."

"I know what you meant. Indians like strong women, too."

She rode until she could see the trestle. Tom came alongside and motioned her to stop. "Men working in water don't wear many clothes."

She'd asked Chane about that. "We use a diving bell," he'd said. "It works on the principle that a cupful of air will displace a cupful of water. When we're working on the stream bed, we put men inside the diving bell, which is like a cup, and we lower it into the water. The air trapped inside is generally enough for them to breathe while they prepare the creek bed for bridge supports."

"Generally?" she'd asked. "Who goes down in this diving bell?"

Chane had turned away. "Whoever needs to."

"You. Right?"

Chane had shrugged. "Sometimes."

"Sometimes? Or every time?"

"What is this? An inquisition?"

Jennifer had glared back at him. His gaze wavered first. "Jennie, I'm here to do a job," he'd said. "I have to do it my way."

Now, Jennifer kneed her horse forward. Tom could either follow or not. She rode down the hill, across a gulley, and up onto the crest of the overlooking hill. Several hundred feet below, the new yellow wood of the trestle glowed softly in the sunlight.

Men swarmed all over it, some raising new wooden beams into place, others working at tasks she couldn't identify.

At the water's edge a group of men stood around one man who looked like he was fishing with a thick rubber hose while another man worked a pump handle up and down.

As Jennifer watched, nothing appeared to be happening to the tube, but they kept watching it as if something would, so she did, too.

A touch on her arm made her look back at Tom. He had drawn his gun. Alarmed, Jennifer looked around for the cause.

"What's happening?"

"Indians," Tom said grimly.

"I don't see any Indians."

"You will."

Tom spoke to one of his men. "Don't let her out of your sight. Get her down and keep her down."

Tom's man started toward Jennifer. Then she saw the Indians—a hundred or more—ride over the top of the hill and toward the men working on the banks of the river below.

"Where's Chane?" Jennifer asked, suddenly afraid for him.

"Don't know." Tom fired a warning shot to alert the men below. The man fishing looked up, saw the Indians, threw down his line, and ran. Another man picked up the line and jerked on it. The man working the pump looked worried, but he just kept working the pump handle up and down. Jennifer recognized Steve as the man on the pump. Where Steve was, Chane could not be far away, but she didn't see him. Men ran for their guns. Others fired.

The Indians swarmed down the side of the hill toward the men scampering for their guns. Shots rang out. An Indian fell. Two Indians dismounted, picked their fallen comrade out of the deep snow, hefted him across the back of a pony, and fled back the way they'd come.

The rest of the Indians converged near the trestle's southernmost end, where Steve was still jerking on the line and pumping the pump handle.

"We picked a hell of a time to come here," Tom growled.

He grabbed at Jennifer's reins, but she saw what he was going to do and evaded him, backing the horse away.

"Do you want to get killed? Are you as crazy as your husband?"

Anger flashed in Jennifer. "I'm fine. Why don't you do something useful instead of trying to take care of a woman not in danger. Hand me a gun."

"My first responsibility is to keep you safe…"

Before she could reply, the sounds of men shouting drew Tom's attention back to the men at the trestle.

The Indians had stopped in mid-charge and were pointing at the water, horrified.

The center of the wide, rapidly flowing river had begun to roil. Tubes seemed to be rising out of the water. One of the men ran over and started pulling on the tubes, hand over hand. At last a shiny metal ball attached to the tubes appeared to float to the surface and head toward the riverbank.

The Indians had halted their ponies in the deep snow and stared wide-eyed as the crown of the ball broke the surface of the water and slowly began to rise out of it. Jennifer saw that the ball with tubes was attached to what must be a diving suit. The man in the diving suit strode to the water's edge and started up the embankment.

Indians watched for another moment, then turned their horses and fled, yipping in terror.

"Well, I'll be damned," Tom muttered.

Jennifer urged her horse forward and rode down to see this marvel at close range. As she reached the river, Steve unfastened the bolts on the headpiece and lifted it off. Just as she had expected, Chane, grinning broadly, burst into laughter.

"I knew this suit would be worth something someday."

Steve laughed. "You should have seen their faces!"

The men howled. But when Chane saw her, his smile faded. Scowling at Tom, he growled, "You let her ride into a pack of Indians?"

Tom looked down at his scuffed boots. "Yes, sir."

Chane snapped his mouth shut. He'd been on the verge of taking the hide off Tom Tinkersley, but he knew Jennie too well. She always did what she damned well pleased. Tom had probably just hung on for dear life—as Chane was learning to do.

Jennie rode closer to him and waited until the men's merriment subsided.

"What is that thing?" Jennifer asked.

"It used to be a gutta-percha diving suit," Chane said. "But now it's a good luck charm against Indian attacks." The men roared with laughter and relief.

"I need to talk to you," Jennifer told Chane. He lifted her off her horse and carried her to a sunny, wind-sheltered place, out of sight of the trestle.

"What now?" he asked warily.

He looked so good to her. She wanted to touch him so badly she ached. Being out in the sun and wind had colored his skin bronze. His black hair was badly rumpled, but his eyes were clear and frank as they looked into hers.

"I hope you don't mind, but I've taken over the bookkeeping."

"What happened to Rutherford?"

Jennifer told him everything that had happened since he left the last time.

"I don't want you stuck with the book work. That's a hard job and a bloody nuisance. You'll get sick of it in no time."

"I don't mind at all. I like doing it."

"It'll get old soon enough," he said, chagrined that her eyes were shining with joy and accomplishment while he was in torment, still so plagued by the very sight of her that he had banished himself to the trestle site. And even there, all he thought about was her.

And she didn't help in the least. Another woman, left alone with so many problems, might have withered and died of loneliness by now. But Jennie was as beautiful as ever, perhaps even more beautiful. And stronger than he'd ever guessed. He had never expected her to step in and give orders in his absence. He'd certainly not expected her to start filling in for men who left.

Over Jennie's shoulder Chane saw Tom Tinkersley gazing in their direction. "Tom's waiting for you. You better get going before the Indians get up their courage and come back."

"You aren't angry with Tom, are you? It wasn't his fault. I—"

"No," he said grudgingly. "I know who's in charge."

Jennie flushed and turned away. Chane let her go.

Tom strode forward, glanced quickly at Chane, then picked Jennie up and carried her to her horse with an easy familiarity. Both blond and slim, they made a handsome couple. An ugly feeling welled up in Chane from some unknown place. He knew his bluff had been called. From now on he'd either have to stay closer to home or farther away.

CHAPTER TWENTY-THREE

Chane returned to the Pullman coach two days after Jennie visited the trestle. That night, Jennie spent a long time in the lavatory. Chane was sorry he'd come back. Everytime she got ready for bed, his mind pictured her taking a bath the way she'd done on board ship. He could see her shapely legs, the curve of her sleek buttocks, the perfect arch of her strong back…

Finally, she came out and padded past his compartment to her own. Instead of finding relief from his imagination, now he envisioned her lying in bed, soft and silky and responsive. Chane lay there as long as he could stand it, then dressed and slipped outside.

He walked twenty paces away from the coach and leaned against a tree. The moon seemed close enough to touch. Almost full, its roundness marred only by a slim wedge off the side, it hung like a silver plate amid a million sparkling stars.

He'd been crazy to bring Jennie along.

The Pullman door opened, and he recognized Jennie's silhouette, with crutches, on the observation deck. She negotiated the steps and swung gracefully on her crutches, straight toward him. He thought about trying to escape, but his pride wouldn't let him.

She stopped beside him and said, "You'll catch your death out here."

"And what about you?"

"I'm not going to try to seduce you, you know," she said, ignoring his question.

"I'm a grown man, for God's sake. Do you think a woman has to *try* to seduce me to stir my passions?"

"Sorry," she said, turning to leave.

"Jennie…"

She stopped. "What?"

"Nothing."

"I know I shouldn't bother you, but I keep hoping…" She turned her face away, but not quickly enough. He could see the silvery snail tracks of tears on her lovely cheeks.

Chane felt such frustration, he levered himself away from the tree. She started angrily back toward the Pullman coach. Although he knew better, he reached out and grabbed her arm. She tried to jerk free, but her strength was no match for his. He pulled her into his arms, and she squirmed with angry resistance. Passions he'd denied for weeks flared, and he caught her hands and kissed her.

He knew he was hurting her, and he didn't care. She smelled of Gillyflowers and tasted as fresh and intoxicating as the headiest wine. Her lips were wet with tears—salty and trembling—as she dragged in a ragged breath and allowed them to part beneath his probing tongue.

Nearly crazed with desire, he kissed her for a long time. He barely realized he had picked her up until he banged his shin on the bottom step of the Pullman coach. Startled back to sanity, he carried her up the steps and lowered her to her feet. "Stay away from me," he whispered, his voice a hoarse croak.

"Chane—"

"No," he whispered raggedly. Without another word he turned and plunged down the steps.

Horrified that he could still want her so much that he'd make a fool of himself at the drop of a hat, he spent the rest of the night in the office car. Toward dawn he fell asleep in one of the upholstered chairs, and awoke with a crick in his neck.

A wire came at ten o'clock that morning from their legislative watchman in Denver, warning that two key legislators were on the verge of withdrawing their support for the railroad. Chane talked it over with Steve and decided to go to the Colorado capital himself.

"Right this way, sir," the porter said diffidently.

Chane followed the black man down the long hall and into a private anteroom. To his surprise, a woman stood up and walked toward him, smiling.

"Latitia," he said stiffly.

"Chane, darling," she said, stepping close to him and lifting her lips to be kissed.

Chane frowned and ignored the opportunity. "I thought I was supposed to meet with a couple of legislators."

"I thought I'd save you the trouble. If we can come to terms, there'll be no need for legislation."

"Are you representing your father?"

"Of course," she said, smiling. "How far have you gotten with the railroad?"

Chane knew her spies always kept her informed of exactly how far they had gotten. "We'll cross the border ahead of you. That's all you need to know."

"So," she said, "you took Jennifer back, after what she did to you. I suppose you realize you've become the laughingstock of New York."

Chane shrugged, but his eyes narrowed icily, and she sensed that she was treading on dangerous ground. "So, has she seduced Tom Tinkersley yet?"

"Is Tom on your payroll, too?"

Latitia laughed, stepped close to him, and put her arms around his neck. "If she hasn't yet, she will. She looks as sweet and innocent as a ten-year-old, but she has the morals of an alley cat." She stopped at the look on his face and sighed. "Well, it's not necessary that you believe everything I say. But it is necessary that you kiss me. I've waited a long time..." She pressed herself against him and whispered, "I love you, Chane. I'll always love you."

Chane was needy. Before his marriage, with one-tenth the motivation, he would have pushed Latitia to the floor and mounted her right there. She was good in bed and very attractive. He had never felt weaker than he did now. She squirmed against him, and the feel of her lush female body pressing against him sent a spear of lust stabbing through him. Tightness, heat, and power filled his loins, but his stubbornness worked whether he wanted it to or not. He grasped Latitia's arms, freed himself, and stepped away from her. "I'm here on business," he reminded her.

"So am I. The business of taking care of you." She stepped close again, reached up, and pulled his head down. Chane could have resisted, but it had taken all his strength to resist the last time. His mind told him that one little kiss wouldn't hurt anything. It might even make her go away. She kissed him, and he realized too late that she knew him too well. She was too good at what she did. The wonderful sensations of power and lust spread through him like a wave, engulfing everything, even his head.

Part of him wanted to push Latitia away, but his body took over. He tore off her clothes and took her in violence and lust and anger. To his amazement, she trembled and cried and begged for more. Seeing her like this, completely undone, he realized that he had probably reached her for the first time. Everything before this had been faked.

When it was over, he groaned and turned away. He felt sick. Latitia must have seen the disgust on his face. She pulled him back so he was facing her. Rage flickered in her eyes, and her lips drew back in a snarl. "How dare you look at me like that," she said, struggling for control. "What a fool you are! Still panting after that bitch who betrayed you! Feeling bad because you've done the same to her. You stupid, stupid bastard! You could have had me."

"Latitia—" he began.

She slapped his cheek hard. Chane pulled on his trousers and stood up. Latitia crouched on the floor where he'd taken her. "You'll be sorry," she hissed, tears streaming down her cheeks. "I promise you that you won't beat us to the New Mexico line. Even if you do, my father will ruin you."

"Your father or you?"

"What difference does that make?"

"And you think Jennie is bad?" Chane asked, turning sharply on his heel.

Chane slammed the door on his way out, and Latitia picked up the nearest object and threw it at the closed door with all her strength. As she looked around for something else to throw, she suddenly remembered this wasn't her room.

She sat down at the writing desk and wrote a note to Jason Fletcher. Her hand was shaking so badly she almost couldn't read the note when she had finished. And she had foolishly signed her name. She tore it up and started over, this time taking more care.

Jason,
    You have been paid well and often for the last few months.
Why have you not done your job? Kill her.

This time she had the presence of mind not to sign the letter. She found an envelope and addressed it to Jason in care of general delivery in the town nearest Chane's railhead.

Then she wrote a letter to Jennifer, telling her in graphic detail that Latitia had just made love to her husband. Only when the letter was in an envelope and carefully addressed to Mrs. Kincaid in care of the Texas and Pacific Railroad did Latitia remember that she was still naked.

Two days after Chane left, a messenger came with a beautifully tooled leather saddle from Chane in Denver. Jennifer had no idea why he'd bought her such an expensive gift. He was a mass of contradictions. But she asked Tom to saddle her horse so she could try it out.

"You don't need to come with me. I won't leave the camp," she said, leaning forward to pat her horse's silky neck. Tom narrowed his eyes at her suspiciously. "I swear," she said, raising her hand.

"All right, but if you get me in trouble—"

Jennifer cut him off, laughing. "I won't."

Men were strung out from the locomotive—sitting dead on the tracks—to a half mile ahead. The roadbed was in every possible stage of completion. Nearest the train, new steel rails gleamed in the sun. Beyond them stretched a wide band of gravel with ties spaced exactly twenty-one inches apart. The sun had melted the snow off the gravel, except in the shady places.

As Jennifer rode her horse slowly alongside all the activity, men carried rails from the wagons that rolled slowly forward through the slush and mud and laid them on the leveled ties. Other crews sprang into place and bolted on the fish plates. Then new crews stepped forward, swung heavy hammers, and placed the spikes. They worked like machines. By the time the plates and spikes were in, yet another crew had laid two more rails.

Ahead of the track layers, a gang of Chinese laborers—swarming like ants over the rough terrain—were cutting a grade through the timber. In baggy coats and round, cone-shaped hats, the Chinese swung sledgehammers, strained against wheelbarrows and shovels, and led teams of oxen pulling scrapers. Behind them a wide band of cleared and leveled earth shone gray in the sunlight. Just ahead of them the rocky, snow-dotted, scrub-and-brush-clogged terrain looked impenetrable.

At first Beaver Targle's men had made jokes about how they were going to have to lay rail right over those tiny little Orientals. But the jokes had stopped as soon as they realized they couldn't lay rails as fast as the Chinese could clear what looked like impenetrable terrain.

A hundred yards ahead of where the men worked, a massive rock blocked the right-of-way. A cluster of Chinese circled the obstacle. Jennifer stopped far enough away not to call attention to herself.

The Chinese appeared to be arguing. Jennifer's horse stamped at the hard snow underfoot, snuffled, and bent her glossy neck to nip at ferns sticking out of the snow. A cold wind tore at Jennifer's hat.

Beaver Targle said something that appeared to end the argument and walked away. Except for one man, the Chinese withdrew from the rock, backed up a good two hundred paces, still circling the rock, and waited. The one who'd been arguing with Targle picked up a bundle of dynamite and headed back toward the rock. He looked back, waved his comrades farther away, and then shoved the sticks of dynamite into different holes until he'd buried all the sticks under different parts of the enormous rock.

He stood up, scanned the surrounding terrain, then struck a match and ran from stick to stick, lighting fuses. When they were all lit, he ran as fast as his pumping legs would carry him toward his comrades.

Jennifer had never seen dynamite explode before, but it seemed odd to her they stayed so close. She thought dynamite was much more fearsome.

The explosions came one after another, so loud Jennifer felt slammed repeatedly by the heavy blows. Her horse reared, almost unseating her. She dragged the mare's head back and clasped her hands over its eyes—a trick Peter had taught her. The horse screamed in fright, but she didn't run. Then the exploded rock began falling to earth in tiny pieces that sounded like hail. A choking cloud of dust obscured everything, blinding Jennifer and stinging her nostrils.

Still controlling her horse, she turned her attention back to the rock, which had miraculously disappeared. As the dust settled slowly, Jennifer was horrified to see injured men screaming and writhing on the ground. Jennifer urged her mare toward the melee. Tom Tinkersley rode up, saw the mess, and shook his head in disgust.

"Where's Dr. Campbell?" she yelled.

"La Junta."

"Send for him now."

Men wailed and talked excitedly. Jennifer dismounted and helped a man bleeding profusely from a cut on his temple. By the time she'd finished with him, other Chinese had arrived. Each injured man had two or three to help him. Jennifer hobbled from man to man, picking rock slivers from stomachs, backs, arms, and faces. Twelve men were seriously wounded.

Kim Wong ran forward, saw her and bowed. "Bad joss. Not look good," he said.

"I've sent for Dr. Campbell."

"White man doctor no good for Chinamen," he said. "We have own doctor. Fix all manner of illness."

"Let's at least get them to the hospital train to nurse them where they have a roof over their heads," she said.

With two men to each jerry-rigged stretcher, Jennifer mounted and led the procession to her hospital car. She knew Chane had told her to stop taking charge, but she couldn't bring herself to leave injured men out in the cold and snow and wind. They needed help.

Ah Ling, the Chinese herbal doctor, ran up just as they reached the hospital car, panting loudly. He was carrying a large black lacquer box hanging by a strap from his shoulder. He deferentially took charge, asking Jennifer to boil pots of water for herbal teas and poultices. Some men were treated and sent back to work. Others were placed on cots.

Jennifer sent for Beaver Targle. "I thought Chane told you he didn't want these men using dynamite."

"He never told me no such thing."

He was lying to her. Jennifer knew it, but she didn't know what to do about it.

One Chinese lad, no more than seventeen or eighteen, seemed on the verge of death. Jennifer nursed him, doing everything Ah Ling told her to do. She bathed the young man's head with cool cloths. She put a tarlike concoction on the sucking wound in his chest to seal it. She gave him sips of Ah Ling's tea every hour. But in spite of everything she could do, his fever soared. He died an hour before dawn.

The Chinese came for their dead comrade and carried him away. That afternoon they buried him. Jennie and Marianne rode down to the grading site. The funeral procession was accompanied by the bang and pop of firecrackers and much flag waving. Men lowered the slim, cloth-bound body into a shallow grave.

Jennifer turned away from the sight, too filled with misery and anger to cry. She found Tom Tinkersley in the cook's shed, sipping coffee. "Send a message to Chane."

"Jennie..."

Startled by his use of her given name, she came out of her misery enough to glance questioningly at him.

"I mean Mrs. Kincaid...No, I don't," he said, running a lean brown hand through his blond hair. "Look, I know this is hardly the time, but..."

Jennifer felt torn between wanting to stop him and wanting to hear what he had to say.

"I guess you could've stopped me from saying this, so I'll say it," he said, a stubborn light in his blue eyes. "Your husband leaves you alone too much. He expects too much. You're a beautiful woman who needs someone who will love her and appreciate her. If you ask me, which you clearly didn't," he said grimly, "your husband is one of the stupidest men I've ever met."

Jennifer stiffened. "My husband is an incredible man who is trying to accomplish the impossible in record time, Mr. Tinkersley. I hope you haven't forgotten who pays your wages."

"Oh, I haven't forgotten anything. And I'm even more convinced now that he doesn't deserve a woman who can be loyal to him under these circumstances."

Jennifer lifted her chin and prepared to fight.

"Your husband avoids you, Mrs. Kincaid. There are a couple thousand men on these crews. Any of them would give his eyeteeth for a woman half as fine as you, and Mr. Kincaid does everything in his power to stay as far away from you as he can. What's wrong with him?"

"How do you know something isn't wrong with me?"

Tinkersley narrowed his eyes and shook his head. "Not possible, Mrs. Kincaid. You're one hundred percent woman, and that's a fact."

"So what else do you know, Mr. Tinkersley?"

"I know that your husband could have chosen a dozen married men to guard you. He chose me."

"And you find that significant?"

"Don't you?"

"No, I don't."

"Liar."

Jennifer felt the heat from Tinkersley's lean body. He was an attractive man, and he was no fool. She felt sudden, hot anger at Chane for putting her in this position.

Chane received two messages when his train pulled into La Junta. The one from Tom Tinkersley was brief:

TROUBLE BREWING HERE STOP MRS KINCAID
NEEDS YOU STOP
TOM TINKERSLEY

The one from Tom Wilcox was longer:

NUMBER ONE DIED THIS MORNING STOP LAUREY
FILED SUIT AGAINST ESTATE IMMEDIATELY STOP

ALL ASSETS SEIZED BY COURT PENDING OUTCOME
PROBATE STOP COULD BE HELD UP FOR MONTHS
STOP NO NEED FOR YOU TO RETURN STOP WILL
HANDLE AND KEEP YOU INFORMED STOP
TOM WILCOX

Chane had no idea what Tinkersley's cryptic message might mean. But he fully understood the one from Wilcox. Latitia had found a way to tie up his grandfather's estate so that money would not be available for the railroad. Fortunately, his grandfather had given him enough gold to keep them rolling down the tracks for a while.

The exchange rate was good, so money was plentiful now, but he knew it wouldn't be by April. In case he couldn't raise the bond money from the local communities, Chane wired his brother Lance in Phoenix for help. If nothing else went wrong, he could probably finish the railroad by making a deal with Lance to meet the critical payrolls in April and May, when they should be nearing Raton Pass.

Chane had meant to spend some time in La Junta buying supplies, but he caught the next train south to find out what was wrong at the work site. Jennie had handled just about anything and everything. He couldn't imagine what sort of emergency would cause her to send for him.

Except for Latitia, his trip had been successful. He'd changed the minds of two legislators who had been on the verge of withdrawing their support for his railroad. He'd convinced several town councilmen into talking their councils into buying railroad bonds.

Five hours after he received Tinkersley's telegram, his train pulled up behind the work train. He saw Jennie draw aside the curtain in her sleeping compartment.

At the Pullman coach, Chane stopped. Jennie crossed the space between them in six flying steps and flung herself into his arms, her tears coming in a torrent.

Chane was too stunned by her reaction to do anything except hold her. She felt like a hummingbird he'd held once. Her slim body was vibrating with emotion. Suddenly he was stung by remorse at what he'd done with Latitia. He felt sick.

Jennifer held on tight to her husband. The feel of his hard body and his snow-chilled skin healed something that had been sick and aching in her for days. She hugged him so tight her arms ached, and still she could not get as close as she wanted.

"I shouldn't have brought you here," he whispered.

"He…He…died," she stammered. "He was just…a…a boy…"

"Who died? What's been going on here?" Chane demanded.

"It was m-my…fault," she said, sobbing. Chane listened in silence as Jennie told him the story about the dynamite. "I should have stopped them. But I didn't know what was going to happen until after it happened."

Guilt piled on top of remorse. He was leaving her alone too much. Now she was taking the blame on herself for everything that went wrong. "Dammit. Where the hell was Beaver Targle?"

"I saw him sneaking away before it happened. I think he wanted it to happen." Overwhelmed with misery and guilt, she covered her face with her hands. Fresh spasms of sobbing shook her.

Tinkersley came out of the telegraph shack, saw them together, and stopped. Chane motioned him forward.

"What the hell happened here?"

Tom's jaw tightened, and Chane noticed something like resentment flaring in the young man's eyes. Chane had the feeling that something had changed while he'd been away. The sick feeling deepened in him, and became almost unbearable. Tom repeated pretty much what Jennie had already told him. When he finished, Chane said, "I told Beaver the Chinese don't understand dynamite."

"He knew," Tom said laconically. "They thought it would just vanish that rock. Hopefully, by now they've figured out that it turns one big rock into a million bullet-sized missiles."

Chane turned his attention back to Jennie, lifting her chin and commanding her to look at him. "You did everything you could have done. It wasn't your fault, you hear?"

Jennifer sniffed, red-eyed. "I should have—"

"No. You couldn't have—you didn't know. It wasn't your fault. It was mine for not being here."

"But I was here."

"You were an innocent bystander who was also put at risk by men who should have known what the hell they were doing. Beaver Targle is the one to blame, not you. Now, lie down, and I'll be back as soon as I can."

Jennie expelled a shaky breath. She started to say something else, but changed her mind and walked toward her sleeping compartment. Chane turned to Tinkersley.

"Where's Targle?" he asked, furious.

"Down by the track layers."

Chane walked down there, found Targle, and hit him in the mouth. Targle staggered backward and fell against two men who couldn't get out of the way fast enough.

"What the hell?"

"You're fired, Targle! Get your things and get out."

"I didn't do a damned thing!"

"You endangered my wife and let a boy get killed."

Looking as if he were trying to decide if he wanted to fight, Beaver cupped his bleeding mouth with his hand. "You owe me for ten days' work."

Silently, Chane paid him from his own pocket. "Now get your gear and get the hell out. In a half hour I'm coming back to look for you. If I find you here, I'll kill you."

Steve had taken to accompanying Marianne into town once a week to shop for Jennifer and Chane. This afternoon they were riding the supply train, and Wendell French, who was one of the saner engineers, took it slow and easy. In spite of having to ride a train, Steve was looking forward to the trip. Marianne was shy and sweet with him. He caught her looking at him a lot. He caught himself looking back at her a lot.

In town they separated to do their respective chores. An hour later, finished himself, Steve went looking for Marianne. He tried the railroad station, since they'd agreed to meet back there.

The stationmaster pushed his green bib eyeshade back on his head and scratched his forehead. "You looking for Mrs. Kincaid's little gal?"

"Yeah."

"I seen her go off thataway with her gentleman friend."

Thinking he probably meant Wendell French, Steve ambled off in the direction the stationmaster had pointed, though he couldn't imagine what Wendell or Marianne would be doing in a wine house. As far as he knew, she didn't drink anything stronger than the tea she shared with Mrs. Kincaid in the afternoons. Wendell preferred beer when he could get it.

Steve stepped into the wine house and waited for his eyes to adjust to the light. Before they had, Marianne left the table where she'd been sitting and walked over to him, a guilty look on her pretty, flushed face.

"Were you looking for me?" she asked so nervously Steve realized something was wrong.

"I wondered if you were ready to leave."

"I'm ready," she said, looking back at the man she'd just left. He was tall and lean with pale blue eyes.

On the walk back to the work train, Steve waited for her to tell him who she was seeing, but she didn't. Finally, he asked. "That your beau?"

"No. That's just Jason."

"Sure looks like a beau," Steve said gruffly.

"No. I knew him to nod to in New York. I don't even like him, but he keeps finding me and hanging around. I was just being nice to him. I don't think he has any friends."

Steve felt disappointed. Marianne was seeing another man. Somehow he'd hoped she was falling in love with him…

Jason watched the two leave. He pondered the news Marianne had inadvertently shared. Number One was dead. Halbertson had hired him on behalf of Number One, so Jason didn't imagine the money from the old man would continue to come. But he was still taking Latitia's money, and he had a plan of his own forming in his mind to do her bidding.

He thought about it from every angle, and he couldn't see any reason on this green earth why it wouldn't work. It would be as easy as eating berries off the vine. He'd take both the woman and the payroll. He'd be keeping his word to Halbertson, just in case that money did keep coming. And the old fart who'd died would still get what he'd wanted. His grandson would no longer be married. He'd be widowed. And free to marry Latitia.

There was nothing at all wrong with his plan. It would make just about everybody happy. Especially him.

Beaver Targle arrived in La Junta just in time to beat the worst of the cold front. He left his horse at the stable and walked to the saloon.

The place was almost deserted. He tramped to the bar and waited. A sallow-faced young man got up off his stool behind the bar and walked toward him. "What'll it be?"

"Whiskey."

The man poured a whiskey for him. Beaver slapped his money on the bar and tossed the whiskey down. "You seen the three men who were fired from the railroad?"

"Yep. Heard 'em, too. Reckon they're not too happy with Kincaid."

"Know where I might find 'em?"

"Heard they're staying at the Prickly Pear Hotel."

"Thanks."

Beaver sent a messenger to the hotel with a note asking the men to meet him behind the livery stable. An hour later Rooster Burnside, Bobo Boschke, and Irish Jim Delaney walked up behind him and stood silent as he continued to throw knives at a paper circle he'd nailed onto the back of the barn.

Beaver hurled three more knives into the circle. They landed less than a half inch apart.

"Damned good knife throwing," Rooster said, spitting tobacco off to the side.

"Not hard when you can see Kincaid's face—" He threw another knife, which landed dead center. "—right there!"

The men laughed. Beaver gathered up his knives and led them away from the barn to avoid any extra ears hearing their business. Once alone, he made them a proposition.

"Against Kincaid?" Rooster asked.

"Damned right."

"Sign us up. What d'ya want us to do?"

"Remember that trestle Kincaid is building?"

"Yeah."

"Well, here's what I'm thinkin'…"

Jennifer rode out to see the old sheepherder and was surprised to find him gone. A young man had taken his place.

"I'm Jennifer Kincaid, and this is Tom Tinkersley. We rode out to see the other shepherd. Do you know where he is?"

The young man looked Irish. He had regular features, friendly blue eyes, big freckles, and coarse blond hair sticking out from beneath a cowboy hat. "He got stomach trouble and had to quit, so the boss sent me out. I got a good stomach. My name's Jim Patrick."

"Nice to meet you, Jim Patrick."

He seemed honest and straightforward. But it nagged at Jennifer. The old man had been so friendly. She couldn't imagine him riding away, even with a stomachache, without saying good-bye to her. She asked Chane about it, and he shrugged it off, saying, "This Patrick may or may not be telling the truth. We'll just wait and see what happens."

Chane hired Ezekiel Jessup as Beaver Targle's replacement. Jessup was an old man now, but he'd cut his teeth on the Union Pacific, which had used Chinese laborers, too. He was short and leathery and plain-spoken. And he seemed to get along fine with Kim Wong, whose crews managed to stay well ahead of the track layers.

With two hundred men diverted from other tasks, Chane finished the trestle in time to greet the arrival of the tracks just after the noon dinner break.

"Lookee yonder," one man yelled. "That stick bridge is pretty as a speckled pup."

Men laughed and added their comments. Reaching the bridge roused a feeling of excitement in everyone. Rails were satisfying to look back on, but not as exciting as this massive structure, almost a quarter of a mile long and towering fifty feet above the creek.

By suppertime the arriving crews had laid tracks across the trestle and half a mile beyond.

Jennifer arrived after the track layers and watched Chane walk the tracks over the trestle. With the setting sun behind him, Chane looked like a toy on the massive structure. She couldn't believe they could do so much in such a short time. It looked like it should have taken years to build such a magnificent trestle. She swelled with pride in her husband.

He came back in such a good mood, he took her across on a handcar just so she could experience it. From above it felt even taller than it looked.

"It feels just like the Brooklyn Bridge."

Chane laughed at the comparison. "Thank you, but I can't take that much credit."

"It's wonderful!"

"It's only a temporary structure. When we reach Raton Pass, we'll come back and build a permanent one, but this will do for a few months. It won't hold up over the long haul, though."

She leaned over to look at the creek below. Chane held her hand to steady her. His hand felt different now, more calloused and even more powerful in the effect it had on her. She glanced back at him. He was looking out over the river, lost in thought. She felt his heartbeat in his hand. It made her own heart beat faster. Chane must have sensed the change in her.

"It's time I got you back," he said, leading her back to the handcar. "It's cold out here."

She'd had no awareness of cold, only the heat and strength from his hand. He lifted her onto the handcar. For one second she thought he was going to kiss her. His eyes met hers, but then they wavered. She thought it a hopeful sign, though.

The next morning, all the railroad crews gathered around to watch the first crossing. Jennifer watched from the observation deck of her Pullman coach, now parked on a newly laid siding.

Locomotive Number 42 chuffed purposefully toward the first major trestle on the new Texas and Pacific line. Many small trestles had been built between La Junta and here, but this was the first to span a major canyon from top to top. Men put down their tools and cheered. She felt such pride in Chane's accomplishment. How many men could build a trestle or a railroad? How many men would even take on such a task?

She felt awed by Chane and wished she could share his moment of triumph with him. Unfortunately, he was riding the locomotive. Three flatcars of cheering men trailed the wood car.

To get a closer look, she hobbled down the steps, mounted her horse, and rode toward the trestle.

As she reached the edge of the canyon spanned by the trestle, someone yelled. The cry was taken up by others—clearly an alarm. Heart pounding, Jennifer scanned the canyon tops for Indians. Finding none, she scanned the riverbanks below and the trestle.

Then she saw it. At mid-trestle a span of tracks appeared to be missing. It couldn't be. Chane had walked those tracks himself only last night. But her eyes were not deceiving her. Number 42 was steaming toward sure disaster at twenty miles an hour with Chane aboard.

CHAPTER TWENTY-FOUR

Chane saw the missing rails and realized there was no way to stop the train in time, but there might be a way to save the men riding the cars behind the wood bin.

Wendell French said the first cuss word Chane had ever heard him utter. Chane glanced over at him and knew he'd seen the missing rails, too. Wendell's face had gone white with fear.

"Break the train!" Chane yelled over the chuffing of the locomotive.

"Break it?" Wendell stared incredulously ahead, his mouth hanging open.

Chane grabbed the emergency brake, pulled hard, then jammed the throttle all the way ahead, and the train broke. He felt the difference in traction when it dropped its load. Grinning, because at least one thing had worked the way it was supposed to, he blew the whistle—a single short toot—to tell the brakemen on the flatcars to brake, if they hadn't already.

"Jump!" Chane ordered, reversing the Johnson bar. He knew he wouldn't be able to stop the train, even with the Johnson bar reversed. He'd given up all hope of stopping when he broke the train and lightened the load, but maybe he could slow it enough.

The fireman didn't wait for a second invitation. He took a flying leap out the open cockpit door.

"Jump!" Chane yelled at his engineer. "That's an order!"

"Nope." The thought of jumping off and leaving the boss on *his* train was not something he could do. In his mind there wasn't anything more shameful than abandoning a perfectly good train. Kincaid was giving him an out. In some folks' minds, the owner was more in charge than the engineer, but he just didn't see it that way. Kincaid paid him four dollars a day. Firemen only got $2.40 a day. Sitting on the four-dollar side of the cab gave him responsibilities a fireman didn't have. To his way of thinking, it was the engineer who said when it was time to jump.

A second later the cowcatcher hit the open place on the rails, teetered for a moment as the leading wheels bit into the ties, and toppled to the right with a great groaning sound.

Chane grabbed Wendell French, who looked too stubborn to save his own life, and jumped to the left with Wendell in tow. The force of gravity, trying to pull them to the right along with the locomotive, was too great. As the cab came up sharply, Chane put all his energy into lunging to the left, and that gave him just enough of an edge to clear the door. As they teetered in the doorway, the locomotive swayed back to the left, tossing them clear before it swayed back to the right and plummeted over the side.

Fortunately for them, the train falling the other way left room on the trestle. Chane hit the trestle and landed on his feet, Wendell on his chest and belly across two overhanging ties. Just as Chane decided they had survived without even getting wet, the thirty-ton locomotive hit the trestle supports two-thirds of the way down and broke them like matchsticks. One minute Chane was standing on cross ties, the next moment the trestle was nosing downward, collapsing to his right. The loud creaking and straining of wood breaking up sounded like a dozen women screaming.

Chane slipped off the side, grabbed one of the cross beams, and wrapped himself around it. Wendell slipped, caught a beam, and hung on. Chane was glad to see Wendell had come alive to the situation. The end supports, which Chane had taken great pains to sink into concrete, were holding. But the timbers, which were only held together with iron bolts, gave out. Now the whole center section of the trestle—thirty feet or more—went over.

Chane rode his beam to the bottom of the canyon. He hit the icy water about ten feet from the locomotive and was driven under. When he came up sputtering, he saw Wendell landing with a splash a few feet from him. Pinned down by the shattered trestle, the locomotive sent up a cloud of steam where the firebox had gone under.

They were both close enough that if the boiler blew they'd probably not live to tell about it. Waiting for the explosion, Chane looked up at the cars he'd cut loose. Wendell had been thrown out into midstream, a perfect target for a runaway car to fall on him.

Fortunately, the rest of the cars had rolled to a stop only feet from the open rail.

The men who hadn't been on the train ran to the edge of the brush-covered canyon and looked down at them. Chane swam with the current to the nearest timber, hefted himself up onto the trestle, and jumped from beam to beam all the way to the riverbank. Looking back at the tangled mess, it seemed a miracle the trestle hadn't fallen on them and pinned them under. The fireman had dragged himself out and stood shivering beside the swiftly running water.

Chane patted him on the back. "You better get yourself into some dry clothes."

Dazed, the fireman nodded and walked away.

Men ran down the bank and stopped beside Chane.

"What happened?"

What had happened looked so evident to Chane he couldn't think what to say for a moment. He glanced over at the man who asked the question. He looked entirely serious and dumbfounded.

"I just dumped fifty percent of our rolling stock into the river."

"How the hell did that rail develop a hole since last night?"

Chane kicked at a piece of the firebox that had landed on the bank near his foot. "Damned if I know. Maybe we'd better post a few more guards."

Chane scrambled up the riverbank and stopped abruptly, about twenty feet from Jennie. The stretch of rocky ground between them looked too hard to negotiate on crutches. But she swung forward as if she didn't see the obstacles. He caught her just as she fell.

"You shouldn't be down here with that foot."

"I thought you'd been killed," she said, panting.

"I might still be. Financially."

"Is it destroyed?"

Chane struggled not to smile. Everything he could see within easy range was certainly destroyed, or as close as it could come with one try. He decided accidents were times when people ran around worrying out loud. He wiped a tear off the sweet curve of her cheek.

"Maybe not," he said. "We'll fish the locomotive out of there, but it's going to take some doing to fix this trestle. I expected to build a few trestles before we got to Santa Fe, but I didn't think it would be the same one over and over."

Jennifer felt numb with cold. Chane was wet from head to foot. His dark hair dripped water down his face. His eyes were bright green from excitement. He'd almost been killed, and he looked like he'd been on a carnival ride. She didn't know whether to be furious with him or to throw herself into his arms and sob.

She reached up and touched his cheek. In spite of just being dumped in ice water, he felt warm. "You need to get out of those wet clothes."

Chane turned to Wendell, who was slogging toward them in waist-deep water. "Did you see that trestle go down? I was hanging on for dear life. You couldn't pay for a better ride than that. It picked up speed about mid-fall and threw me clear, else I'd probably be sucking some of the coldest mud in Colorado."

Jennifer couldn't believe her ears. He had missed being killed by about a foot, and he was laughing about it. Men crowded around them. Wendell French plodded up onto the bank, shivering.

Men patted French on the back and congratulated him on saving some of the rolling stock and a good many lives.

"Wasn't me. I'd like to take the credit, but it was Mr. Kincaid. He told me to break it, but I just stood there with my mouth hanging open. I'll know next time, though."

Jennifer felt weak in the knees. Number 42 had stopped sending up steam. Nosed headfirst into the river, it settled over on its side beneath a tangle of broken cross beams and trestle supports that had fallen.

"Get the crane. We'll lift her out before she starts to rust," Chane said.

"You'll get some dry clothes on or else," Jennifer said grimly.

Chane scowled down at her, then at his clothes as if he had just seen them. He grinned at the men. "You men fish Number Forty-two out of there while we get some dry clothes on."

Men laughed. "That's telling 'im. Good for her."

Chane lifted Jennie into his arms and carried her up the bank to the rocks where her crutches had been abandoned. He sat her down and glared at her wet gown. "Now you're about as wet as I am. Are you satisfied?"

"Not until you've changed."

He picked up the crutches, handed them to her, lifted her again, and carried her up the slope of the canyon toward the Pullman coach they shared. Jennifer felt a twinge of guilt letting him carry her, but the contact felt so good, she would never protest. "Are you limping?" she asked suddenly.

"Do you notice everything?"

"We'll have Dr. Campbell take a look at you."

Campbell examined Chane and joined Jennifer in the parlor area of the car. "He's fine. A bad bruise on that right leg, but it'll heal."

Jennifer asked to view the damaged leg. The bruise had already turned blue. It was just above his knee and looked so bad Jennifer shook her head.

"So, what now?" she asked.

"I think I'll build it stronger this time. An idea came to me as I was flying through the air. Fortunately, we've got two thousand men to do it, since no one's going anywhere until it's done. *And* we're good at it by now. It shouldn't take us long. And we've still got the foundation…"

"Who could have done such a thing? And with us right here?"

Chane scowled and shook his head. Jennifer picked up a towel and wiped water off his face. She had such a light touch that he wanted to just close his eyes and let her take care of him. He was pretty sure Latitia was behind these acts of sabotage, but he didn't want to tell Jennie. Just thinking Latitia's name caused his stomach to lurch. How could he have lost himself with her? "I don't know, but if I catch the scoundrels, they'll be sorry."

Chane dressed, and, barely limping at all, he walked back to the trestle—or what was left of it.

Chane and Tinkersley questioned the men who had stood the last guard duty on the trestle the night before the accident, but learned nothing. No one seemed to have seen anything, and yet the trestle had been sabotaged. In addition to the missing rails, Chane found places where iron bolts had been removed in strategic places. That explained why the whole center section had fallen out that way.

Tom recruited twenty extra men to work in security and told them to stand a twenty-four-hour guard on the trestle. He had them look each other over for about five minutes and told them not to let anyone near the trestle they didn't recognize as a fellow employee.

Chane wired Tom Wilcox for another locomotive to use in the meantime. He put Kim Wong in charge of rebuilding the trestle.

Jennifer found Chane outside by the remuda, cutting out a horse. "Are you leaving?" she asked.

"I'm going after whoever sabotaged my trestle."

That sounded dangerous to her. "Isn't that Tom's job?"

"No, it's mine."

"But he's in charge of security."

"I say who does what around here, Jennie."

"I don't like the idea of you going alone. Indians…"

Chane grinned. "I've ridden alone before."

Jennifer shrugged. He looked so determined and stern, it made her heart race. "I know, but—" The look in his narrowed eyes stopped her. She could imagine him looking at his mother that way if she'd tried to kiss him in public after he'd felt himself too old for that sort of display. "Did you pack some food?" she asked instead.

Chane slapped his saddlebags. "Take care of things while I'm gone, Jennie." His gaze flicked over her, warning her that she'd said enough. He finished saddling his horse, pulled a couple of times on the cinch to tighten it, climbed aboard, touched the brim of his hat, and left without a backward glance.

Jennifer watched him ride away. He'd told her to take care of things. That must mean something. Maybe he was beginning to actually trust her. Maybe he was seeing her value…

Chane rode a large semicircle around the trestle site until he picked up signs of four horsemen. One of the horses had a distinctive rear hoofmark—a cloven hoof. Chane followed their tracks until dark. He felt sure enough of what he'd find that he could have just ridden into Timpas, but he decided not to.

He tracked that cloven hoof all morning. By noon he saw Timpas just ahead.

Chane circled around and came into town from the north, stopping at the livery stable first.

A young kid, seven or eight years old, was mucking out the stalls.

Chane flipped him a silver dollar. "Howdy."

"Howdy, mister." Openmouthed, the kid turned the dollar over and over, admiring it.

"I'm looking for a horse with a cloven rear hoof."

The kid put the dollar into his pants pocket and motioned toward the back of the stable. "Ain't allowed to get involved in no trouble, mister, but you might take a look at that claybank back there."

Chane walked back and took a look at the claybank's rear left hoof. It was the one.

"I could just settle down and wait, or there's another dollar if someone wants to tell me who rode him last."

"Don't know their names, but there's four of 'em staying at the Prickly Pear."

Chane flipped the kid another dollar. "Thanks."

At the Prickly Pear, Chane unsheathed the shotgun and tramped inside. Beaver Targle and the three men who'd quit on Jennie while he was away from camp sat around the potbellied stove, taking turns spitting into the spittoon. They stopped talking at sight of him.

"Afternoon," Chane said.

Beaver Targle looked at the shotgun and stood up. "The hell you say. Didn't expect to see you lollygagging around town. I can understand us out-of-work folks doing it, but not Mr. Highball himself."

"Someone sabotaged my trestle last night. I took a notion to follow the tracks, and this is where they led me."

Beaver Targle's face paled, then flushed with color. "You trumping up some new charge against me now?"

"Thought we'd take a little ride," Chane said, raising the shotgun so it pointed at Beaver. The men still seated looked at one another, then at Targle, who had gone beet red in the face. They slowly came to their feet.

"Out the door."

"Where're you taking us?" Beaver asked.

"Straight to hell," Chane said, waving the shotgun in the direction he wanted them to go.

The four men shuffled outside and across the street to the livery stable. Chane took their guns and knives before he had the boy bring out their horses. Beaver had more knives than any man he'd ever caught.

"We got to saddle 'em," Beaver protested.

"No saddles," Chane said firmly.

They arrived back at camp before sunset. Chane prodded his prisoners up onto one of the flatcars, then climbed up after them. Hundreds of curious men gathered around.

Jennifer hobbled down the stairs and rushed forward to watch. When she saw how stern and purposeful Chane looked, a chill raced down her spine.

He faced the men and spoke loud enough for all to hear: "I followed tracks I found near the sabotaged trestle into Timpas. They led me to these four men. Is there anyone here who has any reason to believe these men are innocent?"

No one spoke up. "Is there anyone here who has reason to believe these men are guilty?"

"Hell, yes! Everyone knows they left here mad," someone shouted. Jennifer recognized him as the fireman who'd been on the train with Chane when it went into the river. "I almost broke my damn neck jumping off that locomotive! I say hang the bastards!"

Other men took up the cry. Chane called for quiet.

"You got anything to say for yourselves?"

Beaver Targle looked out over the sea of angry faces. He swallowed. "I demand a real trial."

"You had it."

Chane turned to Tom Tinkersley. "We'll need four ropes and a stout tree."

Tom and three men got busy preparing the nooses. Other men put the four back onto their horses. Someone remembered an oak tree a few hundred yards from the work site. When the nooses were ready, Tom put them over the men's heads, helped them onto their horses, and headed off toward the oak. Every man in Chane's crew followed.

Jennifer rushed to intercept Chane. "You're not going to—"

"Keep out of this, Jennie. Go back inside."

"I will not."

Jennifer saddled her horse and followed the men to the oak tree.

Tom threw the ropes over a high limb and gave the ends to half a dozen volunteers. They wrapped the ropes twice around the tree trunk and prepared to use their weight to keep the men aloft once the horses were pulled out from under them.

Chane took the reins of the four horses. He looked his prisoners over. They had wilted like cut flowers left in the sun. They realized they were about to die. The full knowledge of it was in their eyes. They'd probably learned their lesson.

Chane raised his hand for silence. The murmuring stopped. Jennifer could hear the crickets, frogs, and birds. It sounded like any ordinary day. The men looked so stunned and listless, her heart went out to them. Her stomach felt like it was filled with rocks. If he hanged them, she would never forgive him.

"Do you have anything to say before we hang you?" Chane asked.

Silence. The silence stretched out. Jennifer hiccuped so loud everyone turned to look at her.

"I have something to say," she said. "They didn't kill anyone. I think you should spare them."

Chane looked from Jennie to the men watching. "Does anyone agree with her?"

A man near Chane nodded. "I know Boschke has a family that depends on him."

"So does Rooster," another man said.

Chane looked at the crowd, softened by the knowledge that these men had families. "I'm personally for hanging them," he lied, "but these men have spoken up for you. I'm willing to commute your sentences, but I'm warning you. If I catch any one of you hanging around my railroad again for any reason, I'm going to hang you higher than a cottonwood blossom."

That night at dinner, Jennifer had to ask him.

"You weren't really going to hang them, were you?"

He'd been planning to hang Beaver Targle, until he saw Jennie watching. He knew he couldn't let her witness something like a hanging. With her soft heart, she'd never sleep again.

"I expect I'll have another chance."

Tom walked in with the mail. "Thanks," Chane said, taking it. He shuffled through the mail, stopping at a letter addressed to Jennie. Something about the handwriting puzzled him. He had a feeling he knew that handwriting. He checked the postmark. Denver. A cold chill raced down his neck. He put the rest of the mail down and reached for a letter opener. It was from Latitia, telling Jennie about the debacle in Denver.

Chane stopped breathing as he scanned the letter, which had obviously been written in a state of rage.

Once he settled down from his shock, Chane couldn't believe his good fortune. Since he'd returned from Denver, he'd paid no attention at all to the mail. The first time he did, he intercepted a letter that could have destroyed him in Jennie's eyes. He searched for a match to burn the letter. Not finding one, he stuffed it into his jacket pocket. He would burn it later.

All that day he kept looking at Jennie and trying to decide what gave him the right to keep something from her that would probably send her back to New York on the next train. It didn't make any sense for him to keep the letter. It belonged to Jennie, but he could no more give it to her than he could have taken a knife and cut his left hand off.

Two thousand men swarmed over the trestle and locomotive. Wendell and his crew took the locomotive completely apart, cleaned the mud and water out of it, and sent a rush order by telegram for the parts that the blacksmith couldn't build on site.

Wendell took advantage of the disaster to paint the locomotive to his own tastes. He painted the running wheels yellow, the stack red, and the cab blue. He beat out the dents and polished the brassworks to a fine patina. He painted a bold *No. 42* in gold with a black border set off in arabesque curlicues. Men took turns admiring it and making fun of it, but Jennifer was charmed by it.

Dr. Campbell took Jennifer's cast off. She was horrified to see that hairs an inch long had sprouted beneath the cast. Her foot smelled like badly soured milk.

She didn't know which problem to tackle first, but she was grateful Chane hadn't been there to witness the hideous sight.

She borrowed Chane's razor and shaved off the offending hairs. Then she scrubbed her ankle and foot with lye soap and finished it off with a bar of lilac soap.

From then on she spent an hour a day exercising her foot. It was a slow, painful business, but it had to be done, to keep the muscles from freezing up any more than they already had. Dr. Campbell checked it once or twice a week. "You're making good progress with that foot. If I'd seen that break on a man, I wouldn't have given him any chance at all of saving that foot for anything except a boot rack. You might dance again after all."

The weather warmed suddenly and turned stormy. Lightning flashed, thunder rolled, and rain poured down for days, stopping all work on the trestle. The river was so swollen that Jessup was afraid to let men go out on the trestle for fear it would collapse under the raging torrent. Occasional trees smacked into it with a resounding crash, but still the foundation held. Work consisted of removing debris from the base of the trestle so it didn't build up and take the bridge down.

Even with all the bad weather, the crews managed to finish the heavily guarded trestle in record time. Chane walked the track and checked the underpinnings for dynamite or missing iron bolts before he let Wendell approach it with the new locomotive.

This time, the train crossed with a little less excitement. Tinkersley stationed guards at each end and ordered them to turn over their guard duty only to men they recognized.

The tracks reached Thatcher two days later, on payday. The residents were in a jovial, boisterous mood. Within minutes after the first work crews arrived in Thatcher, town officials wired La Junta. An hour and a half later the first excursion train from La Junta arrived, loaded with two hundred people and a boxcar full of beer kegs.

The celebrants shook hands with the railroaders. Settlers and farmers who had come into town as word spread rushed forward and manned the kegs. Within minutes, water boys with long-handled tin dippers were ladling the brew for all comers, filling jugs, cups, pails, and even teapots.

Within an hour many men were too drunk to walk.

Chane and Jennie were commandeered by Mayor Ed Hadley and a group of local businessmen who had decorated the tree where the brand-new train station would someday stand with red, white, and blue bunting. People were yelled into silence, and speeches about the arrival of civilization were made all around. Chane declined to speak but was forced into it. He gave all the credit to his grandfather's vision and his work crew's sacrifices. He briefly extolled the hardworking men of all nationalities who cleared the trails and laid the rails.

"Good speech," Ed Hadley said, slapping Chane on the back. "You should run for governor."

Chane laughed.

"You and your wife will stay at our house tonight. You've spent enough time in that little-bitty Pullman coach. I was on one of those once. It's real fine until you get tired of everything being so little."

"Thank you, but we're fine..."

"I won't take no for an answer. We've got a real nice room for you, and my wife's a damned good cook. It'll be a treat for us, and I promise you her cooking will make up for any inconveniences."

Chane doubted that. Very little could make up for being forced to sleep in the same bed with Jennie. He would refuse outright, except Hadley was president of the First National Bank. It was a hole in the wall in Thatcher—literally, as it was merely one desk and a safe in a corner of the mercantile store—but it was affiliated with the First National Bank in Denver, owned by Hadley's brother. The railroad might need a loan before they reached Raton. Chane needed to keep on Hadley's good side.

At sunset the celebration was moved to the schoolhouse, where a fiddler was warming up. Everyone in the county seemed to be there. Jennifer couldn't figure out how so many people could have been assembled on such short notice.

The room smelled like every woman within a hundred miles must have baked either a pie or a cake. As they walked in, Jennifer noticed a pretty young farmer's daughter do a double take when she laid eyes on Chane. Her face lit up and she flashed him a look that clearly said she'd never seen a more attractive man in her life. Chane didn't seem to notice.

Ed Hadley insisted Chane and Jennie start the dancing. "Play a waltz," he yelled at the fiddler.

She had been off crutches for a week, walking gingerly. "You want to risk it?" he asked.

"Of course."

He'd been afraid of that. Chane held out his arms, and Jennie stepped into them as if she had every right to be there. Maybe she did. She was working harder than any woman he'd ever known. She looked as beautiful and fragile as ever, but her actions bespoke a spirit as fiery and determined as any pioneer woman who had ever braved the wilds.

Touching her sparked off an undeniable fire in his loins. Of course, it wouldn't take much. He got erections these days from just pulling up his trousers.

Jennifer wasn't all that sure she should be trying to dance, but she trusted Chane not to step on her injured foot. She felt certain the bone had knit weeks before Campbell had taken the cast off. Her exercises had restored a lot of its flexibility.

Chane held her circumspectly and danced her into the middle of the room. The crowd cheered wildly and loudly.

"You're a hit," he said, his voice oddly hoarse.

"It's your railroad."

Chane didn't argue with her, but he knew it was her. With her shiny blond hair piled high on her head, and her amethyst satin gown bringing out the purple lights in her lovely eyes, she looked like a queen. It seemed the more he avoided her, the more beautiful she became.

The cheers rose to a crescendo, and for a moment she looked like she might cry. Then she lifted her chin and seemed to regain control. They danced in silence. Other couples joined them on the dance floor.

"Are you all right, Jennie?"

"No," she said, lifting her chin. "I saw that pretty young woman making eyes at you."

Chane looked embarrassed. They danced in silence for a moment. Jennifer felt better immediately. At least he still acted as guilty as a husband should. That was worth a lot.

"I'm curious," she said, smiling to relax his guard. "What *did* she say with her eyes?"

His stomach lurched as if she had caught him with Latitia. Chane searched Jennie's face to see where this was leading. But humor sparkled in her lovely violet eyes. "I would never pretend to be an expert at reading what's in a woman's eyes, Jennie, but I *think* she said she'd like to get to know me better."

Jennifer laughed. "If that's all you saw, you're certainly no expert."

They laughed together. After a moment, Jennie looked up at him, something unreadable sparkling in her eyes. "And what did you say to *her* with your eyes?"

"I said—" he paused to add drama. "—'You have *good taste* in men, but I'm married.'"

"You said all that?" she asked, pleased.

"Yes, ma'am. I'm almost positive that's what I said."

"Almost positive?"

"Well, as you said, I'm no expert…"

Jennifer laughed, delighted. She wanted this dance to go on forever, but it ended, another started, and three men tried to claim her.

After the second dance, Marianne waved the men away and walked to the table where lemonade, beer, pumpkin pies, apple pies, corn bread, potato salad, cobblers, and fried chicken had been laid out. Steve Hammond stood next to the table, eating a slice of apple pie.

"Sure, and we finally get to a party, and you don't even ask me to dance."

"I looked for you. But you were dancing with other men."

"And you didn't even rescue me, either."

He knew excuses wouldn't work with Marianne. He stuffed the last bite of pie into his mouth and held out his arms. Marianne slipped into them with her customary frankness and lack of guile. They danced three dances together before a man tried to cut in. Marianne begged off, saying she was too hot to dance anymore. She led Steve off the dance floor and down the railroad tracks.

"Hey, the party's back there."

"Sure, and you think I didn't notice that?" she asked archly, tugging him along after her. They came to the place where the Kincaids' palace car sat on the tracks. She led him up the steps and into the car.

"Oh, it's so much nicer in here," she said. Sounds of merriment from the celebration wafted in the open windows. The music was almost as loud here as it had been at the dance.

Steve started to sit down. "No," she said, pulling him back up. "Don't you think it's time you be kissing me?"

Steve lowered his head and kissed her. But she wasn't content with just kissing. She was squirming her warm body against his and trying to undress him. "Hey," he whispered, "they might be back any minute."

"They won't. I packed an overnight bag for them. They're staying with the mayor and his wife."

"Someone might be back."

"Sure, and it's your job to worry about every single body in the town now?"

"I…"

"Hush, Steve Hammond." She pulled his head down and kissed him again. Slowly, Marianne's irrepressible good humor and her persistent attempts to seduce him worked their magic. His body took over, and he let her lead him into the sleeping compartment reserved for Chane, who almost never slept there.

"I've been wanting to get into a real bed with you for a long time now," she whispered. "I'm tired of laying on the ground and having to keep my clothes on." She pressed him down on the bed and undressed him. When he was fully naked, she began to undress herself. He liked the way she looked right at him while she did it. Heat rose in him. She had a lovely body, full-breasted and narrow-waisted. He liked the shape of her legs and the way her hips tapered from her waist into womanly fullness.

"You're beautiful," he whispered.

"And you're a sight yourself," she said, stroking his chest. "I like a deep-chested man. I like the way your chest drops off like that," she said, trailing her fingers down his chest over his stomach and to his groin. Wonderful sensations followed wherever her hands went. "I like the way your legs are so sturdy and straight, and I even like the shape of your feet." She drew in her breath, then sighed. "Sure, and I think I'll be liking everything."

Steve pulled her down on top of him. "Sure, and I bet you be telling that to all the boys."

Marianne giggled. "And you be mocking me, eh?" She kissed him, and his passion for her took over. They made love slowly and sweetly and for a long time. She was right. It was much better in a bed.

As a precaution, Jennifer sat out every other dance. Chane tried not to keep track of who was dancing with her, but he couldn't help himself. She was the most beautiful woman there. Every man with enough courage asked her to dance.

At ten o'clock Tom Tinkersley approached Chane.

"May I dance with Mrs. Kincaid?"

"You don't need my permission," Chane said, anger rising in him.

"I wouldn't ask her to dance without it, sir," he said, flushing.

Ashamed of himself, Chane led Tom over to Jennie. "How are you holding up? Tom feels like dancing."

Jennifer looked quickly from Chane to Tom. Sudden hot anger flared in her. She supposed from the tension between the two of them that Chane had tracked Tom down and insisted he dance with her. "I'd love to."

"You're in luck, Tom. Be careful of her injured foot."

"I've been taking care of her and her foot for a long time now," he reminded Chane.

Chane tried not to show the slow burn that started in him at Tom's remark. The young man held out his arm to Jennie. She flashed Chane one last look that seemed to condemn him to hell and then smiled at Tom.

In torment, Chane watched them dance. Jennie seemed to be flirting with Tom, but in a way that let Chane know she was keeping track of him at the same time. As if her flirting were for his benefit. Either she knew and was teaching him a lesson, or she didn't know and was actually flirting with Tom Tinkersley.

Either way, they made a handsome couple. Tom had sandy blond hair and a lithe, masculine body. He danced well enough not to embarrass himself. His family in Texas was one of the best in the state. They owned a good chunk of lush grazing land and so many cattle they couldn't count them. Jennie could do worse. The thought caused Chane's heart to sink.

He knew it wasn't fair to ask Jennie to leave him. The only thing he could do was give her the letter he kept forgetting to burn or expose her to eligible men. But he couldn't bring himself to give her the letter, and watching her with Tom was getting to be the hardest thing in the world for him to tolerate. That shameful episode with Latitia had knocked the wind out of him and confused him more than anything else he'd ever done. Suddenly he was not the man he thought himself to be. He didn't know whether he'd ever been. He wasn't sure he knew who he was or what was important anymore. Under those circumstances, how could he make any decisions about Jennie and his marriage? He was plagued with raging jealousy and possessiveness and equal portions of bitter remorse and soul-stinging guilt. He didn't know which to give in to.

Jennifer seemed to be dancing far too close to Tinkersley. That young man would probably have a hard time getting to sleep tonight,

Chane thought. Unless she slipped away with him, which was a definite possibility. The thought filled Chane with jealousy and despair, but he forced himself not to think about it. If she did, she did. It would save him from having to decide.

Tom danced Jennifer carefully around the room. "I haven't seen you dancing much tonight," she said finally.

"The only woman I wanted to dance with was taken."

"Tom…"

"I know. Your husband is watching, and I'm out of line. Well, dammit. *He's* out of line. I can tell every time I get near him that he's mistreating you. He knows it, and I know it, and you know it."

"He has his reasons."

"Oh yeah, I forgot. You killed his mother and his father and his grandparents. Well, hell, I can understand his being upset about that for a while. But, you know, they were gonna die anyway, old as they were. I'd forgive you and get on with my life. Our life."

Jennifer laughed. "If I killed most of your family, you'd no more forgive me than he would."

"Yes I would," he insisted boyishly. "You could kill every one of them, and I'd still forgive you."

The thought was so ludicrous that she couldn't stop smiling. Tom grinned, happy just to make her laugh. He was a good friend. She realized how lucky she was to have him. "Thank you, Tom."

"My pleasure." He was beaming, and she knew that just being with her had made him happy. Just being with him had lightened her mood, at least temporarily.

Ed Hadley walked up and slapped Chane on the shoulder. "Glad your wife's having a good time. Whenever you're ready, we'll show you the way to our house."

"I'll see if she's ready."

The dance ended and Tom returned Jennie to Chane. "Much obliged, Mr. Kincaid," Tom said earnestly.

Jennie's eyes dared Chane to say anything. "You're welcome, Tom," Chane said gruffly.

Chane watched Tinkersley walk away. "He's a good man."

Jennifer started to let that pass, but she couldn't stand it. With one remark Chane had completely wiped away the good mood she'd achieved with Tom. "Oh, is he?"

"Yes."

"Well, I'm grateful for your blessing," she said in a low voice. "Should I just chase him outside and jump on top of him? Or would you prefer I be more discreet?" Rage coursed through her like a fever. She didn't know where it had come from, but it didn't feel controllable. "I don't need a man watching me all the livelong day. I especially don't need a man appointed by my husband so I'll fall in love with *him* and get my husband off the hook."

Chane flushed.

"I'm glad you at least have the decency to feel shame."

"Who said anything about shame?"

"I did. If you aren't ashamed, you should be. He's a perfectly nice young man."

"I want the best for you, Jennie."

His words fell between them like a blade. Jennifer squared her shoulders. "No," she said bitterly. "You're the best for me. You're trying to give me second best so you can go your merry way in peace."

Chane could think of no response that wouldn't make things worse. She was right about his motives, but he didn't feel like the best of anything. He felt like a cad.

Jennie turned and stalked away, her limp gone. He knew she had to get mad enough to make the break. She had to get mad enough to strike out at him, and she was almost there. He just prayed that when she did, he'd have the courage to let her go.

Ed Hadley and his wife intercepted Jennie and brought her back with them to Chane's side.

"Did you have a good time dancing?" Mrs. Hadley asked.

Jennifer lifted her chin and smiled. "Delightful."

Chane cringed. She was in fine form this evening. He would be lucky to survive the coming night.

CHAPTER TWENTY-FIVE

The Hadley house was only two blocks away, but Hadley had a light carriage. They drove the short distance with Chane making small talk with Hadley.

The house was big and comfortable. Their bedroom was dominated by a large four-poster bed and a fireplace on the outside wall. Hadley struck a match to the paper under the oak logs and fanned the tiny flame with a fan.

"The room'll be warm in no time. If you're hungry, there's food in the pantry. Help yourself."

"I could lay out a snack," Mrs. Hadley said jovially.

"No, please," Jennie protested. "I've been eating all day." Mrs. Hadley was a gracious woman who seemed to like Jennie on sight. She carried in an overnight bag Marianne had packed and delivered to the house earlier, poured heated water into the basin on the bureau, and then excused herself.

As soon as the door closed behind her, Jennie took off her coat and tossed it on the bed. Still angry, she ignored Chane and struggled to unbutton her gown but couldn't. Finally, Chane walked over and said, "I'll do that."

He carefully unbuttoned an entire row of eyelet-held buttons. "There." Jennie walked to the mirror, slipped her arms out of her sleeves and pushed the gown down. Chane knew he should look away, but it would have been easier to cut off his hand. In the firelit room, her skin glowed with tawny warmth. A pulse started in his loins.

She stepped out of the gown, then backed up to him again. Chane undid the lacing on her corset and untied the strings holding her bustle in place around her slim waist. Her warm, soft skin seemed to scald his fingers.

Jennie stepped out of her undergarments and left them where they dropped. One didn't drop fast enough. Furiously, she kicked it aside, and strode across the room clothed only in her petal-soft skin. Chane struggled desperately to keep from running his hands across her breasts and down her silky thighs.

She rummaged through the bag Marianne had packed, didn't find what she wanted, and dumped the bag on the bed. "Damn," she said with uncharacteristic vehemence. "I can't imagine why she bothered to send this at all," she grumbled, grabbing her brush angrily and striding to the mirror. She jerked the pins out of her hair and bent forward from the waist to brush the golden cloud.

Chane felt light-headed watching her. To distract himself, he walked to the bed and rummaged through the pile of garments for his nightshirt. It wasn't in the bag.

Now he understood Jennie's expletive. He felt like uttering one himself, but he didn't. He undressed, climbed into the bed, and leaned against the headboard. With Jennie so mad, he didn't feel comfortable lying down. Women had a way of wanting a man's full attention when they were mad.

Jennie finished brushing her hair and stood up, flipping her long blond hair over her shoulders. With her legs spread and her hair fluffed out around her, she was incredibly beautiful and exciting.

She stalked through the mess of discarded garments, stopped at the bureau, and looked over her shoulder at him. "If you were a gentleman, you wouldn't watch."

"I'm not."

"Suit yourself." She wet the washcloth and lathered it with the soap she found on the bureau.

"I intend to," he said. It seemed to Chane that she washed every part of her body two or three times. The firelight gleamed off her wet body, but strangely, Chane suffered less than he'd thought. The sight of her flesh acted on him like a narcotic. The joy of seeing her naked was so satisfying, he forgot everything else.

Too soon, she finished her ritual and toweled herself dry. She stomped across the room, threw back the covers, and climbed into bed.

"You forgot your nightgown."

"I didn't forget. Marianne didn't pack it."

"Mine, either."

Jennie pulled the covers up to her chin.

"You forgot to turn out the lamp," he said.

"I forgot?"

"You were the last one up."

Angrily, she threw off the covers and stalked over to the lamp. She turned the wick down and stomped back to the bed.

They lay in silence for a moment. Jennifer thought he'd gone to sleep. Then he scooted over and pulled her toward him. "I thought—" Jennifer began.

"I changed my mind," he said, stopping any further comment with his mouth. Any other time she would have been thrilled to have him approach her, but tonight she was furious at him for throwing Tom Tinkersley at her. She was too angry to feel anything at first, but slowly, as he continued to kiss her, the anger changed to hunger. It was just like the night of the fire again. Except this time her body was even more desperately deprived and lonely and starved for him. His every touch seemed magnified, vibrating through her and filling her with the sweetest, wildest, most exquisite feelings imaginable.

Chane must have sensed what he was doing to her. His kisses became more hungry and more hurtful, and it was exactly what she wanted and needed.

It was so wonderful to be held by him, to be touched by him, even to be hurt by him. He appeared to be the same man she'd married, but in some indescribable way, he had changed. She felt the difference in the way he touched her, the way he held her, the way he entered her. Before, he had treated her like a goddess. Now he treated her like a woman he'd hired for the night. He showed her no respect, no condescension, and no mercy.

Neither his hunger nor his strength seemed to have any limits. Before the night was over, she did things she had only heard whispers about in the girls' dressing room at the Bellini. He didn't even try to disguise the fact that he was using her to slake a purely physical hunger. And it didn't matter.

He barely finished before he took her again, the last time in a way most women saw as painful and humiliating, but even that didn't matter. She gloried in it, because it came from him. In spite of the pain, or perhaps even because of it, she reached dizzying peaks of ecstasy she hadn't even imagined before. For the first time, she saw her husband not as her lover, but as savage male—dark, primal, and dangerous. She trembled before him, as weak and helpless as any woman prostrate before a conquering warrior.

She felt no shame until he rolled immediately away from her. Then she realized that nothing had changed. He'd pleasured himself, and her as well, but he still didn't love or trust her.

Within moments his breathing told her he was asleep. Still trembling, Jennie lay in confusion, not sure whether she was supposed to see this as progress or not. Maybe this was how it started. Maybe he would go from using her to accepting her and then to loving her again. After tonight anything seemed possible. She'd never thought he would get this far. She fell asleep with that thought still spiraling through her mind.

Chane was gone the next morning when she woke up. She didn't see him for two days, and when she did, he acted as if nothing had happened between them.

Work resumed on the railroad. Two weeks later they had spanned two small creeks and ten miles of track to reach Earle. At each town, they endured the festivities, the beer, the dancing, and the speeches. After each town it took Tom Tinkersley and his crew days to get all the men back to the job site.

March was cold and windy, but not nearly as cold as the winter had been. There were times in the afternoon when it was almost warm. Jennifer oversaw care of the sick and injured, settled disputes, and intervened when injustices occurred. The men were accustomed to seeing her pop up wherever and whenever something went wrong. They much preferred her to Mr. Kincaid, who wasn't half as pretty or one-tenth as patient with them.

The Santa Fe Trail, which ran parallel to the railroad, was busy night and day now that the weather was moderate. Almost any time of the day, Jennifer could look up and see a rider, a lone Conestoga wagon, or a train of Conestogas. Occasionally a freight train of mule or ox teams pulling heavy loads moved noisily past. The trail was heavily traveled.

A blizzard hit the last week in March and brought work to a stop. Men huddled in their sleeping cars, grateful for the wood they'd cut and stored. They had to keep a window open at each end of the car to avoid asphyxiation, and frost formed on the blankets of men sleeping nearest the slitted windows.

During the blizzard, Chane rode the locomotive equipped with a heavy metal snow-plowing shield up and down the track to keep it cleared of snow.

The first night of the blizzard, the sheepherder, Jim Patrick, came into camp seeking warmth. The next morning he found his sheep bleating in fear and pain, many stuck to the icy ground they'd huddled against to keep warm. Chane ordered a crew of men with shovels to cut them loose before they pulled holes in their woolly coats trying to unstick themselves. This was repeated for three mornings. Finally, the icy north winds subsided, the clouds cleared, and the sun came out.

With the blizzard over the first week of April, the weather warmed and men returned to work with a vengeance. Chane said the only good thing about it was that it slowed Laurey down as well. Nights were still icy cold, but days grew as warm as seventy degrees in the sun. Men worked in shirtsleeves. Sounds of sheep bleating were commonplace. A whole new crop of lambs appeared as if by magic.

Chane was more worried about security now that they were approaching Raton Pass. He told Tinkersley to hire more guards and to be ready for anything.

Tom went into the nearest town and came back with four rough-looking men. He led them up to the Pullman coach and called Jennifer outside.

"Mrs. Kincaid, ma'am, I'd like to introduce you to some new additions to our security force." He pointed to a tall, lean sandy-haired man, the obvious leader of the foursome.

"This is Jason Fletcher, my new assistant."

Jason's pale gray eyes failed to match the smile curving his thin lips. Jennifer had a sinking feeling she'd seen him before.

"Howdy, ma'am," he said with a soft Southern accent.

"How do you do, Mr. Fletcher."

"Don't care much for the cold, but other than that, I'm just fine, ma'am."

"You're in the wrong part of the country for a man who doesn't like cold."

He chuckled softly. "Got that right, ma'am. Shore don't know what I was thinking of." His words were right and proper and spoken with respectful demeanor, but his eyes made her uncomfortable. They were as pale as water, and they didn't seem to truly register her presence.

The other men were introduced as Miguel Etchevarria, a small, dark-eyed Basque; Clem Stringer, wiry and lean as catgut; and Jake Blackburn, a soft, pale man with a whiskey tenor voice.

She wouldn't have hired any of them, but fortunately, they weren't her problem. Between bookkeeping and inventory control for the cooks' supplies, the doctor's hospital supplies, and the track layers' supplies, which were the most critical, Jennifer was busier than ever. Anyone who needed or wanted anything came to her first.

Every morning she stopped at the hospital car, labeled the "bed wagon" by irreverent railroaders. By now almost every man working for Chane had been in the bed wagon at least once. Between hospitalizations and paydays, she knew most of them by their first names. Some days she felt certain she went there to get the attention she couldn't from her own husband. Unlike Chane, who had been avoiding her assiduously since that night in Thatcher, the men's faces lit up when they saw her.

This morning she found only six men on the hospital's twenty cots.

"'Morning, Mrs. Kincaid."

"'Morning," Jennifer said, stopping beside the first bed. "How's your back today, Jethro?"

"Comin' along, ma'am. Comin' along. I reckon I'll be leaning on a idiot stick in no time."

Smiling, Jennifer walked to the next bed. "And how are you today, Russell?"

"Better now, ma'am, but I fear I've broke my pick."

The men seemed to search out new ways to say things so she wouldn't know what they meant. "Broke your pick?"

"Coughed a little last night. Plumb discouraged me."

Jethro hooted. "Coughed *all* night last night, he did. Sounding more and more like a lunger."

"I'll get Dr. Campbell to take a look at you. You may need to be sent to a warmer climate. I don't think this cold is good for you."

She felt his head. It was hot and clammy. Consumption was a constant worry with some of the men. They just didn't seem equipped to deal with the damp and the cold.

Jennifer checked the rest of her patients, talked to Campbell about them, and sent Marianne over with a pot of Cooky's hot chicken soup to tide them over until lunchtime.

Marianne was a big help to Jennifer. Cooky was giving her lessons in the kitchen, and she was loving it. Every night at dinner, Marianne pointed out the dishes she had cooked and explained exactly how she'd done it. Now that certain basics had been explained to her, she was a natural in the kitchen.

The Chinese were the most industrious and clever people Jennifer had ever seen. They fished along the banks of the river, even in the rain, and sold fresh fish to the other men. They set up *fan tan* and *pai gow* games and won their money away from them. They baked Chinese cookies and pastries and sold them to whites and Chinese alike for a penny apiece.

Every week, Marianne took a pile of laundry to the Chinese. Most of their customers were non-Chinese who'd rather pay dearly for laundered clothes than wash them. Chane had laughed. "By the time we reach San Diego," he said, "the Chinese will have pocketed all the money we've earned. Then they'll go back to China and live like potentates."

The Chinese had even put together a band. Men with horns and drums and flutes played odd music that Jennifer found she liked. The wind picked up the smell of incense and spread it into every corner of the encampment. The non-Chinese complained at first, but gradually got used to it.

Jennifer had less and less time for riding, but she couldn't resist the new crop of sheep. At least once a day she took a break from her books to ride out to the sheepherder's camp to take Jim Patrick something Marianne had baked and to marvel at the tiny, newborn sheep following their mamas as they grazed on the new grass. She loved their perfect, woolly bodies and their plaintive little bleats, but Tom Tinkersley didn't trust Jim Patrick. He kept a close eye on the young man.

"I imagine you get a little lonely out here?" she asked Jim Patrick.

"Yes, ma'am. I about go crazy at times. If it weren't for you and some of the men I get to talk to every now and again, I don't know what I'd do…"

Chane rode his horse from one work site to another. The train carried timber and ties from the sawmill at La Junta. In the past, on a good day, the tracks were extended southward by two miles a day. As they neared the Raton Mountains, the terrain got rougher and the men clearing the right-of-way labored with greater difficulty and more slowly. They were lucky to lay a mile of track a day, then a half mile.

Trains arrived weekly with loads of rails and other needed supplies. Unfortunately, every load came with an invoice. Jennifer sat down to pay the bills, and this time she didn't have enough money.

That afternoon when Chane came riding in, she met him and took him aside. "We've got a problem."

Chane looked at her skeptically. "We've got lots of problems," he said flatly.

Jennifer ignored the comment. "If we don't do something soon, I'm going to have to start sending our regrets instead of a check."

"Oh, that problem," he said tersely. "All right." Chane strode to the telegraph shack, which sat on a flatcar. Ever since they'd started down the rails, a crew had been stringing telegraph wire. The shack had been moved over so much rough terrain when they were carting it in by buckboard that the nails had shaken loose. Now it leaned to the left.

Chester Sims was asleep at the telegrapher's desk, a wooden door laid over two sawhorses. Chane shook him awake and dictated a message to his brother Lance in Phoenix, telling him to bring whatever he'd managed to raise so far as soon as possible. He turned to leave. "When you get the answer to that, come and get me. I'll be waiting for it."

Chester sent the message, closed up the telegraph office, and climbed down from the flatcar. His stomach was growling with hunger. He walked to the mess car and lined up with others just coming in off the crews.

"Hey, Chester, them wires too heavy for you?" Ed Bailey asked. "Tapping out that one message or so a day getting you down?"

Chester scowled. It was boring enough sitting cooped up in that little rolling telegraph shack without having to put up with men like Ed Bailey. "Not the wires, but sometimes the information I have to carry gets a little weighty."

Ed stopped smiling. It pleased Chester to wipe that smirk off Ed's face. Ed always thought he knew more than anyone else.

"You got some important news?"

Chester didn't, but he hated like the blazes to admit it to Ed. "Let's just say I know things I'd just as soon not know."

"Like what?"

Men stopped talking to listen.

Chester lowered his voice. He knew better than to disclose secrets, but once he got to talking, he couldn't seem to stop just when he wanted to.

"Financial things," he said with heavy stress on the *fi*. Ed Bailey scowled and started to reply. Just then Mr. Kincaid walked up to one of the cooks and stopped to chat. At the sight of Kincaid, men fell silent.

The communal dining car held a long table with a bench on each side. The plates were nailed to the table with one nail in the center of each plate. Chester shuffled up the steps, found an empty bench with a full plate, and ate his dinner in unaccustomed silence. Men with dippers refilled plates on request. Others with coffeepots refilled cups.

Chester liked Kincaid, but he didn't like the idea of his building a road using men who weren't going to be paid for it. Especially since he was one of the men.

His friend, Silas Brough, stopped beside Chester as he was heading toward the sleeping car. Behind them the waiters were getting ready to hose down the plates, tables, benches, and all. Chester was glad he'd eaten in the first shift. He hated sitting on a wet bench.

"What's the matter with you, boy? The cat got your tongue?"

Chester never knew the answer to that. If the cat had got his tongue he wouldn't be able to talk. If it hadn't, it was a foolish question. "What would you do if you knew something important that might or might not be true?"

"Like what?"

"Like suppose Kincaid is broke and doesn't mean to pay us?"

"Well, I'd say a man who knew that would be a damned fool to keep working under those circumstances."

That night a hundred angry men cornered Chane and told him they were quitting.

"You mind if I ask why?"

Most of the men looked down at their shoes, tight-lipped, but one of the German immigrants stepped forward. "Ve hurdt you've gone bust, und ve harn't willing to vork for notting."

"If that were true, I wouldn't blame you. I have every intention of paying for every hour worked." He looked from face to face. "But I'm not going to lie to you. I have a temporary shortage of cash. My grandfather asked me to build this railroad for him, and he gave me startup money, but then he died, and the probate has tied up the money I should have been getting."

Men muttered and looked at one another.

"I've wired my brother in Arizona. He's on his way here with money for the April and May payrolls, but he isn't here yet. I've applied for loans at two banks in Denver. But even with government guarantees, the loans are slow in coming. I realize this sounds like so much smoke, but I swear on the Bible you will be paid in full, every man of you."

"But not this month, right?"

Chane expelled a frustrated breath. "I may have a problem with April."

Men grumbled under their breaths and turned away. Other men had crowded around. Hundreds of men pressed in, trying to hear what was being said.

Jennifer walked up, and the crowd parted for her. She stopped beside Chane.

"What do *you* say, ma'am?"

"You've been paid every month so far. You've been treated fairly. Mr. Kincaid may be having a temporary problem, but I know he'll make good on every dollar he owes."

"That's right," one man said. "He's treated us damned good."

Others agreed.

"So, what'll happen this month?"

Chane looked around at Jennie. Her body slim and proudly held, her profile sharp and clean-cut, she looked like Joan of Arc. A man would have to be a dolt not to believe anything she said.

"Well," she said, looking quickly at Chane. "I haven't discussed this with my husband, but the railroad gets one square mile of land for every mile of track it lays. We're going to end up land-rich and cash-poor. Is there any man here who'd like to buy land with his wages?"

"How would that work exactly?"

Chane flashed an admiring smile at Jennie and explained it. She nodded at critical times. Chane noticed that every time she nodded, another man looked like he was ready to sign up. Finally he ended his speech.

"What do *you* think, ma'am?"

Jennifer looked at the crowd of men pressing around them. She knew almost every one of them by name. "I think it sounds like a wonderful opportunity," she said honestly. "This is some of the most beautiful land I've ever seen. Of course, I've lived in cities all my life…I suppose if you prefer cities to open spaces—"

"Not me!"

"She's right," a man said loudly. Jennifer recognized him as one of the men she'd nursed. There'd been days when she felt sure men got "sick" just to talk to a woman. She couldn't blame them for that. Except for the prostitutes and when they were near a town, she and Marianne were the only ones within miles.

"I'd do it in a minute," she said firmly.

"Where do we sign up?" a man yelled from the back. "That's as good a recommendation as I'll ever need."

Men cheered and laughed. "But what about us with families who're waiting for money to live on?"

Chane looked at Jennie. "We have enough money to meet most of the payroll," she said. "Anyone who needs to be paid either all or part of their pay can have it."

"Good enough for me." It seemed unanimous.

"A month's pay is about as much of a down payment as I'll want to make, though," one man close to the front said.

Chane nodded. "Agreed. By May we should have solved this problem." Either Lance would arrive with the money or his father would return from Europe—unless something was terribly wrong with his mother. That was a possibility he didn't care to dwell on. Hopefully, they were having such a good time in Europe, they'd just forgotten they left him turning on the spit.

Steve recognized Jason as Marianne's beau, and his heart sank a little. He wondered if she'd talked Tom into hiring him. Steve had been on his way to see Marianne, but now he veered off in another direction. She didn't need two men chasing after her.

As the train reached each small town, Chane instituted rail service using backup engines acquired from his father's railroad back East. By mid-April the towns behind them had regular train service using brand-new Baldwin locomotives. Unfortunately, the income from the new service was barely noticeable. And the service had its own costs in employee wages, coal, losses to rolling stock...

Jennifer's head spun with the problems. Shippers didn't ship when they said they would. Sometimes they didn't ship what she'd ordered. Other times they shipped to wrong destinations. Fortunately, she enjoyed untangling messes.

Chane came back from the advance work site earlier than usual. He stuck his head in the door of the office car.

"Jennie, are you going to work all night? It's suppertime."

She looked up and smiled. "Welcome back."

"How's it going?"

"I'm designing a work sheet to keep track of our new payroll system so I don't lose any information."

Chane climbed up into the car and leaned over to look at the new ledger sheet. He reached over and his arm brushed her shoulder. A trembling started in her heart.

"Nice," he said, checking the headings. "Looks like it'll work."

The trembling within grew worse. She knew he was waiting for her to say something, but her mind had stopped working.

Chane knelt beside her, tapped the ledger and looked over at her. The look on her face mystified him. Her cheeks looked unnaturally flushed.

"You're tired, Jennie."

"Am I?"

"I'd say so. You're carrying a full load."

"I like doing it," she said weakly. Having him so near was sending unspeakable longings through her entire body.

"Even so, it's still a load. How's the money holding up?"

"It's not. We got a bill for steel rails today. If we pay it right away, we're going to be short what we need for payroll next payday. I'm encouraging men to sign up for the land exchange, but some of them have to have the money. I've been meeting with the men ahead of time to get an idea of how many need to be paid cash. It's not as good as we'd hoped."

Chane scowled. "If we don't pay the steel bill, there's a good possibility the rails will stop coming, or, worse yet, the rolling plant could fold. Can we make a partial payment?"

"I'm sure he'd prefer that to no payment at all."

"If we have any luck, Lance is on his way."

Steve was miserable. He didn't feel like eating. He let Chane go to dinner without him. A noise at the door caused him to look that way. Marianne leaned against the doorjamb with a plate of something in her hand, a smile lighting up her eyes. The sight of her produced an unaccountable rush of feeling in him.

"Everyone else is down at the mess cars eating. You work too hard," she said.

Steve leaned back and dragged in a breath to uncramp his tired muscles. "I'm not hungry."

"I brought you some blueberry pie. It's the first one I ever made, and Mrs. Kincaid says it's wonderful." Marianne fairly beamed with pride.

Her proud smile caused a slight discomfort around his heart that he didn't know what to do about. Her soft brown hair was loose, blowing gently against her cheek with the evening breezes that came off the river. He'd never seen her looking prettier.

"How come you're not eating?" he countered.

Marianne shrugged. "I don't know. How come you haven't come to see me?"

"Work."

"You used to work and still come see me," she reminded him.

"I thought you had a beau."

The pride and happiness disappeared as if they'd never been there. Her face took on a pinched look of such misery, Steve was sorry he'd brought it up. He couldn't imagine why a woman would keep seeing a man who caused her such discomfort.

"Is that why you haven't talked to me? Because of Jason following me around? He doesn't mean anything to me."

"I'd hate to see how it'd look if he did."

"I don't like him."

"You don't need to explain to me. What you do with Jason is your business."

Tears filled her eyes. "Don't be mean to me, Steve. I hate it when you get mad at me."

"I'm not mad."

"Yes, you are. You know you are." She paused. "Walk with me? Please?"

Steve knew he shouldn't, but he *had* missed her. "All right."

They walked south alongside the Santa Fe Trail toward the railhead. A hundred feet ahead the roadbed had been cleared and filled with gravel. The task would have been easier if they could just run the railroad down the middle of the Santa Fe Trail, but it was in daily use.

"I'd have bet money you couldn't put a railroad through this brush country," she said.

"You'd have counted without a thousand stubborn Chinamen."

"They don't look like they'd be good for anything at all, do they?"

Steve laughed. Marianne leaned against him for a moment, then turned and put her arms around his waist. She felt so good and warm and soft that his mind went blank. She reached up and touched his lips. Then she went up on tiptoe and kissed him. She led him into the thick bushes beside the cleared roadbed and pulled him down beside her. He knelt over her for a moment, but couldn't seem to stop himself. Her skin was so soft and sweet under his fingers.

"Why did you stay away so long?" she asked, caressing his cheek with warm fingers.

"It's a waste of time to court a woman who's making eyes at another man."

"Is that what was wrong with you?" She frowned up at him. "I wasn't making eyes at Jason, nor he at me. Besides, his eyes give me the shakes."

"They do?"

"Sure, and that's not all. The very idea of him gives me the shakes. I really think he hangs around me because of Mrs. Kincaid. I think he's got eyes for her. It's not me," she said with certainty.

Steve chuckled his relief. "Glad to hear that." He was surprised by how much he meant it. A heavy weight that had been pressing on his heart seemed to lift.

Marianne shuddered with the memory of how miserable she'd been without him. She'd thought up all sorts of reasons why he didn't like her anymore. It was such a relief to find out he'd been jealous. She reached up, pulled his head down, and kissed him.

He kissed her back, and she realized how close she'd come to losing him.

"I love you, Steve Hammond."

He hugged her hard. "I love you, too."

"Do you now?"

"Sure, and I guess I do now."

Marianne giggled. "Sure, and you're making fun of me."

"Sure, and I wouldna' be doing that," he teased.

She was so happy she thought she would burst. He kissed her with heat and hunger, and she surrendered completely to his lovemaking, which quickened so many feelings in her, such darkness and sweetness and fire, that she wanted it to go on and on.

Jennifer woke to the strident cock-a-doodle-doo of the camp's loudest rooster. She had half a mind to tell Cooky to use that rooster next. The sky looked blue from horizon to horizon as far as she could see, but waking up made her feel cranky. She turned over and buried her face in the pillow.

Chane was already gone. She must have overslept. Usually she heard him dressing while Cooky and Marianne rattled pots and pans cooking breakfast.

The outside door opened and closed. She thought she recognized his footsteps. Someone knocked softly on the door to her sleeping compartment. "Are you awake and decent?" Chane asked softly.

"Yes." Holding the blanket around her, she sat up.

Chane stepped into the compartment and stopped beside the armoire that faced into the room. His black hair had fallen over his forehead. His sleeves were rolled up, exposing strong, brown forearms covered with crisp black hairs. He looked handsome and solemn this morning. One hand was behind his back.

"What do you have?"

"I found a rose."

It was small and wet and pitiful. Several of the petals were missing and the green stem was bent and thorny. "It's beautiful," she breathed, taking it gingerly from his hand. Her heart pounded against her throat and seemed to swell there.

"I doubt you'd have given that scrawny little bud a moment's notice last year." He had to clear the unaccustomed huskiness out of his throat. "After all, you're used to getting two or three dozen bundles of long-stemmed roses onstage every night."

Jennifer laughed. "I'd forgotten that."

Her life as a ballerina seemed only a dim memory. She searched his face. He seemed different somehow. More open to her. His eyes so intent on hers, so burning, his lips so grimly set, as if he were holding himself back from saying something to her, caused her heart to pound.

This one tiny rose seemed more wonderful than any dozens of roses in the past, because she'd earned this one. It had taken her months. She had suffered more than the whole rest of her life, but she had earned it with her own sweat and determination. She would keep this rose forever. Now she understood why women pressed flowers. If she lived to be a thousand years old, this would be the most special flower she would ever get. Part of her saw it as hopeful that he had given her the flower, and part of her saw it as the end of hope, his way of saying, "I'll never love you again, but I appreciate you."

CHAPTER TWENTY-SIX

They reached El Moro on the last day of April. They submitted to the usual festivities, then work resumed. Jennifer followed the track layers, but Chane stayed behind to build stations, switchyards, and institute freight and passenger service. At every station, Chane's plans called for between five and six sets of tracks to facilitate switching and assembling trains. That took days to build. And the time away from his wife was both agony and ecstasy. He missed her, but he was grateful for the respite from seeing her and all the confusing emotions she aroused in him.

The first day of May, a telegram came from Lance saying he had finally raised the money they needed. Chane appreciated how difficult it had been to bring together $300,000 in a small town like Phoenix. In New York it could be done in ten or fifteen minutes with interbank transfers. In the Arizona Territory, it meant actually gathering the money and transporting it.

Lance's telegram said he was leaving immediately. By a combination of train, stagecoach, and horseback, he expected to reach them in five days.

"What's he like, your brother?" Jennifer asked.

Chane shrugged. "He's big and good-looking, the kind women can't seem to resist."

Jennifer smiled. "He looks like you, then."

"Not really. He takes after Mother. And he's the black sheep in the family. Everyone went into business except him. He became a Ranger..."

"I thought you were a Ranger, too."

"I was, but I got over it. Lance didn't."

"You don't like him..."

Chane scowled. "I love him; he's my brother."

Jennifer shook her head. "I know he's your brother, but I saw a flash of something..."

"No one's perfect."

"It goes deeper than a little imperfection. I sensed something when you mentioned your brother."

Chane expelled a frustrated breath. "I can't hide anything from you, can I? I might as well tell you the truth. Then if you make the wrong decision, it will be on your head. You couldn't claim ignorance."

"Sounds serious."

"I don't know where to start."

"Does this have anything to do with Colette?"

"How did you know about Colette?"

"You told me, remember?"

Frowning, he shook his head. "Six years ago Lance was in love with a woman who was set on by three men, who raped her and beat her. She managed to get back to Lance's apartment and died in his arms. Lance tracked down two of the men and killed them with his bare hands."

"What was her name?" Jennifer asked.

"Lucinda. We were both in Paris about six months after Lucinda was killed. And that's where Colette, my fiancée, fell in love with Lance."

"Oh, no."

"Not on purpose. Neither of them knew the other had any connection to me. From what Colette told me later, she'd seen Lance on the street, flirted with him, and he followed her back to the dress shop where she worked. I guess one thing led to another. One day he drove up to the dress shop in a carriage, took her by the hand, and led her off. Three days later he returned her." He glanced at Jennifer.

Chane had left out a lot, but Jennifer sensed the passion and obsession that must have led to that bizarre behavior. A chill tingled along her spine. Chane watched her closely, as if her response were extremely important. As if she would be judged harshly on it.

"Later, much later, Colette admitted to me that those three days were the wildest, most satisfying experience of her life. She never fully got over it."

Jennifer didn't know what to say. Fortunately, Chane didn't seem to need a response. "She said all Lance had to do was appear, and she'd start to tremble. To his credit—I heard this from friends—he never pursued her. He never courted her. Just every now and again he'd get the urge, appear out of nowhere, and whisk her off for two or three days. She lived for it. She was obsessed by him."

"Did Lance find out she was your fiancée?"

"No. She finally put two and two together and told him."

"What did Lance do?"

"He left Paris immediately. And as far as I know, he never went back. Lance was always a little hotheaded, but he had the good grace to be mortified at what he'd done."

"Did you ever talk to him about it?"

"No."

"Something that important between brothers?"

"Well, he did say once that he was sorry."

"Did you accept his apology?"

The look in his eyes told her he hadn't. "Of course. He's my brother," he said grimly.

Either he'd just lied to her, Jennie thought, or he had no idea he *hadn't* forgiven his brother. "Why did she tell you all this? Didn't she know it would hurt you?"

"She didn't do it to hurt me. After it came out, we talked. I think she told me because she needed someone to share it with. The experience had left her shaken. There was no one else she could discuss it with. I was her friend."

Jennifer puzzled over it for a moment. "It seems odd she didn't know immediately who he was. He had to have told her his name."

"No. He didn't. That was part of the mystery that hooked her into it. He didn't tell her his name, and he wouldn't let her tell him hers."

"How odd." She searched Chane's eyes for some clue. "Well, I'm curious now to meet your brother."

"Curious?" he asked skeptically. "Or intrigued?"

Jennifer shrugged.

"Be warned. I'm less forgiving now than I was then."

"What a dreadful thought," she said, meaning it. The meeting with Lance might reveal even more about her stubborn husband than about his brother.

Jason Fletcher leaned back in his chair and grinned. The money was on its way from Arizona. He had worked out a plan for taking it. He turned the plan over in his mind, looked at it from every angle—it still looked good. They would take the payroll and the woman. She would assure their safe passage to Mexico. Once alone with her, he would be free to do what he needed to do to her. And he'd have all the money he'd ever need. After a while in Mexico, he could give up this life and go back to Georgia, maybe become a gentleman planter. Hell, he could do anything he damn well wanted.

A late blizzard roared out of the Rockies and stopped all traffic for days. Jim Patrick came into camp and huddled in one of the sleeping cars with the laborers. When the blizzard dwindled away, some sheep had to be cut loose from the ground again, but a lot of the young man's sheep got lost, and he either didn't go after them or couldn't find them. Jennifer felt disappointed in him, because she wanted him to track them down and keep them safe. The herd seemed to be dwindling instead of growing, as it had in the early spring.

Lance was overdue because of the bad weather. He was supposed to have telegraphed them from the halfway point on the third and hadn't. Chane was worried about him.

May fifth found them at the base of the Raton Mountains. May tenth was the next payday, and they were broke already. Jennifer had ordered enough supplies to get them to the Pass. They'd have to worry about going farther if they made it that far. She'd learned to fight one battle at a time with their suppliers. So far she'd managed to keep their suppliers from knowing about their financial problems.

Track laying slowed almost to a halt in the rough canyon country. It took days to cut even a narrow path through the rocky, brushy slopes and valleys. The sound of dynamite was commonplace now.

Jennifer's foot appeared completely healed. She could wear shoes or boots again. Campbell had declared her recovered. "You'd do anything to make a liar out of me, wouldn't you?" he'd said, grinning ruefully.

The days were warm now, but that high up the nights were still frosty. On the sixth Jennifer rode the handcar back to El Moro with Tom, Steve, and Marianne. It was a spur-of-the-moment thing to do, because the work train had left without them.

It was hotter and more uncomfortable than they'd expected. About halfway, they stopped to rest and find water. Walking along the creek, Jennifer suddenly realized that she and Tom were alone. Only the sounds of birds overhead greeted her ears as she stopped to listen for the sounds of Steve and Marianne.

"We've wandered away from our party," she said, suddenly self-conscious. Tom had the power to make her dizzy, even from a distance.

She was no longer sure whether it was because she was so needy or he was so attractive.

"Have we?" he asked, his voice husky.

The look in his eyes told her it had not been an accident. She thought he would say more, but instead he pulled her into his arms and kissed her. Jennifer was so startled that at first she didn't respond, but slowly, under the force of his kiss, she felt her body coming alive. His lips were hot and hungry, as if he had been half starved to touch her. She didn't know whether it was his ardor or her own answering ardor, but suddenly she felt a heavy, unwanted throbbing in her belly.

The kiss ended, and he held her close, trembling with the force of his emotion. "I love you, Jennifer. Oh, God, I can't even tell you how much I love you. I want you so much," he whispered.

Jennifer burned with need. Enclosed in the circle of his arms, she wanted him, too. Her body trembled with hunger, and it didn't matter that it hungered for Chane. Tom would do. Perhaps anyone would do. In a daze of desire, she considered his request. It felt so good to be held and kissed and wanted.

"Please, Jennie," Tom whispered. After months of being rejected by Chane, it was a satisfying, heady experience to know that she affected a man so powerfully. She was sorely tempted to accept the comfort he offered. Her mind and body urged her to give in. Tom was tender, loving, and attractive. She enjoyed his company. Chane might never relent. Part of her was tired of the struggle; part of her wanted to give up and just say yes to Tom.

But deep inside she could feel the resistance of her soul, where hope still lived. That part of her wanted to hold out. That part of her believed that she could soften Chane, reawaken the love he'd once had for her. She had no idea if that were true or only a delusion that she was too stubborn to recognize, but it didn't matter. She wanted Chane. She loved Chane. Her body might settle for Tom, but her heart and soul longed for Chane alone.

Her mind flayed her, reminding her that she might lose Tom and not get Chane either, but even that fear didn't matter. Her love for Chane was too strong. Win or lose, she had to stay and fight for what she wanted to the bitter end.

With deep regret that she could not satisfy the burning need in her body or his, she leaned back. "Tom, I can't..." she began, trying to move out of his arms.

"Yes, you can," he said, trying to hold her there. "You kissed me. I felt—"

"It doesn't matter," she interrupted, placing her hands firmly on his chest and pushing him away from her. "I do want you, I can't deny that, but..." She paused, searching for words to keep from hurting him. "I know it seems crazy to you, but I love my husband, and I'm going to stay and wait for him to forgive me. I don't care how long it takes. I have to do it."

His eyes darkened with pain. "He doesn't deserve you."

"Your friendship and your concern have meant a great deal to me, Tom. I thank you with all my heart."

"Jennie, dammit, you deserve so much more..."

"It's time we start back now."

Tom searched her eyes, saw the determination there, and turned and strode back toward the handcar. Jennifer followed. She could sense his hurt and his frustration, but she knew they had said too many words already.

Tom worked the pump that powered the handcar with a vengeance, and no one spoke. Once Marianne glanced over at her with questioning eyes but didn't say anything. Steve looked neither left nor right, but Jennifer could sense his concern.

As they approached the town of El Moro, Jennifer saw Wendell in his locomotive and a man who looked like Chane assembling a train on a side track. Wendell eased the locomotive back and the man stepped out so she could see him better. It *was* Chane. He stepped between two cars, set the pin that would link the two cars together, and then stepped back out as Wendell eased the train forward again.

Watching Chane step between two moving cars horrified her. He shouldn't be doing such dangerous work.

"Why is Chane doing that?" she asked.

Steve shrugged. Tom looked a little sullen, as if he might not answer, but then he said, "Joe Rubosky lost his hand coupling cars this morning. I don't know why Kincaid would think he has to do it. Other men could have done it."

Jennifer knew that train couplings weren't uniform heights from the ground, and sometimes it was almost impossible to put a train together. They had to use hook and pin couplings just to make a connection. A man could easily get crushed or killed between the cars.

"Maybe he's got a death wish," Tom said, suddenly looking more cheerful. Jennifer flashed him a look that took the smile off his face. "Sorry," he mumbled.

Jennifer watched as Chane stepped between the next car and the train Wendell was building. She had waited for Chane to approach her again after he'd brought her that rose, but he never had. He'd thrown himself back into his work as if work alone could save him.

Tom slowed the handcar to a stop. Steve helped Marianne down, and they walked toward the general store. Tom waited until they were out of earshot, then looked from Chane to Jennifer. She started to turn away from the heated light in his eyes, but she couldn't. "Please, Tom."

"No. I love you," he said. "And whether you'll admit it or not, I think I have your husband's blessing to do that."

"Then you've been misled—"

"Like hell I have. He's done everything except tuck us into bed," he said furiously.

Jennifer couldn't think of anything to say that wouldn't make matters worse. She felt the heat from Tom's lean body, and she was still weak enough to be affected by it.

"Don't tell me you haven't noticed," he growled, frowning down at her. "He wants to be rid of you. I love you. Give him what he wants. I may look like a bum, but my folks are wealthy. I can give you a good life, and they'd be tickled to death if I brought you home with me."

Tom glanced up to be sure Kincaid was still busy with the cars he was coupling. "Jesus!"

Tom's brusque comment drew Jennifer's attention back to the coupling operation. Chane was standing between two cars, and the one behind him was rolling toward him.

"Slack running car!" Tom shouted, cupping his hands around his mouth. "*Slack running car!*" he yelled at the top of his lungs.

Chane heard Tom's yell and looked over his shoulder. The car was much closer than he'd expected, and rolling fast. He jumped aside, but his foot slipped. He felt himself going down, saw the shiny steel wheels aimed right at him, ready to separate him from his legs. He jackknifed in the middle and rolled under the train. The first wheel brushed his legs as it flashed past him. The two cars hit with a resounding smack.

The cars stopped rolling, and Chane crawled out from under them, stood up, and dusted himself off. He checked the connection and found the pin had set itself. Shaking his head, Chane waved Wendell forward and walked toward Tom Tinkersley to thank him for the warning.

Wearing a fuchsia gown with white trim, Jennie looked lovelier than ever. Her cheeks were flushed with becoming color. She looked like a woman who had just been kissed. And Tom looked like a man in the throes of love.

"Thanks for the warning," he said, stopping before them. Tom jumped down beside Chane, his eyes hard as steel.

"Don't mention it," Tom growled, reaching up and taking Jennie by the waist to help her down from the handcar. As the younger man touched Jennie, Chane could see his eyes soften visibly. The image of Tom's lean, brown hands on Jennie's slim waist burned into Chane's mind like a red-hot branding iron. He could feel jealousy rising like a filthy, suffocating tide.

He realized Tom was in love with Jennie, and even though this was what he'd thought he'd been wanting, the reality hit him like a fist in the gut.

Tom slowly turned Jennie loose long after he should have, and glanced guiltily at Chane, then back at Jennie. "I guess I better be getting back," he said regretfully. "My scouts'll be coming in any minute."

Jennifer's eyes looked like they needed to say more to Tom, and Chane knew without a doubt that Tom had kissed her, perhaps more than once. He felt sick.

Tom sauntered away, and Jennifer waited until he was out of earshot. "Are you trying to kill yourself?" she asked.

"I thought I just did a good job of saving myself."

"Why is it every time there's a dangerous job to be done, you're right there?"

"Think of the good side. If I get killed, you won't have to sneak around to see Tom."

Rage shot through her, and her hand flashed up and slapped Chane hard across the cheek.

The sting of her hand and the look of fury on her face turned his jealousy into rage, too. He grabbed her and pulled her hard against him. She cried out, but he lowered his head and kissed her, muffling her second scream of outrage.

Her fists pummeled his chest, and even that felt good to him. He relinquished her lips to whisper, "My kisses should be at least as good as Tom's. Cleaner, by rights."

"No!" she cried. "Let me go."

Chane stifled the rest of her cries with his mouth, and once started, he was hopelessly lost. He had ached for her for too long. Even though she was resisting him, her mouth was like a balm that tantalized more than it soothed. Her squirming body was like tinder to his match. He could not get enough of her. He felt crazed by the taste and the feel of her. Slowly, she stopped struggling. He felt her begin to soften, her hands begin to lift. He knew she was only seconds away from embracing him.

Suddenly, a strong hand jerked him loose from Jennie and spun him around. He saw Tom Tinkersley's furious face and then Tom's fist, just before it smashed into his mouth.

Chane's head rocked back. He caught his balance, sprung forward, and brought Tom down. Then he leaped on top of him and began hitting him wherever he could. Tom fought back like a true Texan.

Jennifer screamed. She could see that Chane meant to kill. And so did Tom. She knew instinctively that they would not stop until one of them died. Frantically, she screamed and threw herself on Chane, who had pinned Tom down and was sitting astride him, pummeling him with his fists. She caught him by the neck and tried to strangle him, but he ignored her and continued to hit Tom. Finally, a group of men ran up and pulled Chane away from Tom. The town marshal came running from the train station.

"What the hell's going on here?" he demanded, glancing from Tom's battered face to Chane's bleeding mouth.

"Nothing," Tom said. "Just a difference of opinion."

"Have your differences in your own camp. I won't tolerate any fights here."

Chane and Tom nodded. Tom's face was bruised, his left eye swollen shut. Chane bled steadily from the mouth.

"This happens again, I'll lock you both up, you hear?"

"Yes, sir," Tom said. Chane nodded and pressed his handkerchief to his bleeding lip.

The marshal looked from Tom to Chane to Jennifer and made up his own mind what the fight had been about. She could see it in his eyes, and she felt diminished by it.

The marshal left.

"I guess I'll be resigning now," Tom said.

Shamefaced, Chane glanced at Jennie, then back at Tom. "No. It wasn't your fault," he said.

Under Jennifer's furious gaze, they shook hands. Then Tom headed back to camp with Wendell, and Chane escorted Jennifer to their palace car, which he'd brought there on business early this morning.

When they were inside, Jennifer turned on him. "Why are you blaming Tom? Weren't you the one who pushed us together?"

"Who the hell says I'm blaming him for anything?"

"You tried to kill him."

A man ran up the steps and banged on the door. Chane walked over and opened it. "Mr. Kincaid, there's a man down on the tracks. You'd better come."

"What happened?"

"Don't know. Just keeled over."

Chane shot Jennifer a frustrated glance, then followed the man down the steps. Her opportunity had passed. Chane stayed away from her after that. Jennifer vacillated between wanting to search him out to continue their fight and never wanting to see him again. Her anger stewed in her for days. She could hardly look at Chane, even from a distance, without getting hot. And apparently every man on the crew knew Chane and Tom had fought over her.

She stayed away from Tom as well. She saw by the look in his eye that wasn't swollen shut that he knew he was being avoided.

One day, he stopped by the Pullman coach and knocked on the door.

"I thought you might like to take a ride. It's a nice day."

"No, thank you."

Hurt flashed in his eyes. He looked wan and tired and miserable, a lot like Peter when he was in pain after their parents had been killed. Tom turned away, and she reached out and touched his arm. She couldn't just hurt him without explaining. "I'm sorry," she said. "But I can't ride with you anymore, not after all that's happened."

"Look," he said, "I just thought it might help if you got away for a little while. I'm not going to bite you."

"I know, Tom. Maybe you're right."

They rode up the mountain so she could see where the railroad was going.

Raton Pass was the easiest route over the mountains, and it was an integral part of the Santa Fe Trail. Hundreds of thousands of tons of supplies rolled over the pass every month, and Uncle Dick Wootton received a toll on every wagon. Chane had told her he had no idea how Wootton would take to being put out of business by a railroad. The man could put up a fight or side with Laurey. It was anyone's guess.

Jennifer decided to pay Wootton a visit. Chane might not approve, but she'd just tell him it was a spur-of-the-moment decision, with no time to consult him.

The top of Raton Pass was wide and smooth enough to accommodate six or seven wagons abreast. There was a small toll booth with a full-sized barrel beside it. Jennifer stopped at the booth and the man instructed her to toss her dollar into the barrel.

Several wagons were parked in front of a building with a general-store sign on it. A family of children sat out on the porch, probably waiting for their parents.

Uncle Dick Wootton had built a restaurant and a hotel with a dance floor, which had become a favorite gathering place for young people on Saturday night. Jennifer had heard that young people from the neighboring farms and ranches went there to dance and gaze at the Spanish Peaks bathed in moonlight. Some of the men from Chane's railroad crews rode all the way up there to dance and drink and flirt.

Jennifer went into the store and asked for Wootton.

"Sorry, ma'am, everybody comes through here wants to meet him, he's become such a celebrity over the years, but he's taking a trip to Santa Fe at the moment. Be back tomorrow night, supposedly."

"Thank you," Jennifer said, disappointed.

The ride back was pleasant, but Tom seemed agitated. Finally, he suggested a stop to rest the horses in the shade of a tall pine. He tried to assist her in dismounting, but she waved him away. It felt good to get out of the saddle herself. She walked over to a huge old loblolly pine and leaned against it, looking out over the valley below. Off in the distance she could see the glint of the tracks Chane's crews were laying. Wootton must know they were coming. Folks had to pass the crews on the trail. And no one kept secrets around here. Every tidbit of news was pondered over and discussed.

"Jennifer," Tom said, a frown creasing his brow.

"Yes?"

"I suppose I should apologize for my actions in El Moro, but I can't. I wish I'd killed the bastard."

"Tom, I think it would be best if we start back now."

Tom turned and strode toward the horses. He mounted and started down the mountainside. Jennifer followed. The ride back was quiet and uneventful. Neither of them spoke again.

The Raton Mountains loomed ahead—the railroad's greatest challenge. It would probably take a month or two of hard work to lay rails up the side of the mountain between them and Raton Pass. The grade the surveyors had laid out was an unusual one. They recommended a series of switchback wyes. The train would go up a grade, throw a switch, then back onto another level, then throw another switch and go forward again, seesawing its way to the top. That would avoid the strain of four-percent grades all the way.

Tom Tinkersley and his scouts stayed busy from dawn until

dark almost every day. Jennifer didn't know whether Chane kept him so busy or Tom did it to himself, but he avoided her. His scouting uncovered that Laurey's crew was less than two weeks from the New Mexico border.

Chane had to keep the momentum going. Losing the race to the border at this point was to go broke for no reason. Unless they reached the New Mexico state line, the railroad wouldn't qualify for Colorado's generous land grants that would put them into the black no matter how much red ink they'd spread on paper to get there. This was how he was planning to keep his promises to the men who were working without pay.

Payroll was the tenth of May, but the bank accounts Chane had opened with the gold his grandfather had given him were empty. The funds raised by selling bonds and the loans from various banks were used up as well. They didn't dare miss this payroll. The Chinese weren't willing to take land, because they didn't intend to stay, and Chane needed every one of them to make the assault on the Raton Mountains.

Chane wired his broker in New York and asked him to sell steamship stock in excess of fifty-one percent and deposit the money into his bank account. A wire came back that $150,000 had been deposited. It was accompanied by an apology. Steamship stock was down because of fears raised by the recent sinking of two major steamers during a typhoon.

While Chane was pondering the wire, Tom walked in with the mail. "Thanks," Chane said, taking it.

Tom seemed to be laboring under a powerful emotion. The bruises on his face had faded, but he looked wan and tense. "Excuse me, Mr. Kincaid…"

"Yes?" Chane asked. He'd avoided Tom except when they had business together. But since the fight, Chane had realized it wasn't sane to resent a man like Tom for wanting Jennie. Any man would.

"I'd like to take some time off. I need to go into town on personal business," Tom said, trying to hide his embarrassment.

"How much time?"

"Rest of the day," he said gruffly.

"I guess you've earned it. More than earned it."

"Thanks," Tom said stiffly, turning to leave.

Chane carried the wire from New York to Jennie, who was working in the office car. Jennie's blond head was bent over the general ledger. She had turned into a creditable bookkeeper. No one would have ever guessed it to look at her, though. She was more beautiful than ever. He felt like he was seeing her this way, and actually appreciating her, for the first time. "How many bills do we have outstanding?" he asked.

"Including the payroll on the tenth?"

"Yes."

"About three hundred fifty thousand."

Chane handed her the wire. She read it quickly, then looked up at him, waiting, her beautiful violet-blue eyes clouded with understanding and concern. A rush of gratitude for her help and her caring washed through him.

"Unless Lance gets here in time, we're likely to lose the Chinese."

"But the money is coming. Have you heard anything from Lance?"

"No."

"Meet the payroll on the tenth. Let suppliers wait," she said, leaning back and putting her pencil down.

"If we don't pay our suppliers, they won't send us the next shipments."

"But by then we'll be over Raton Pass," she reminded him. "What about your father?"

Chane wired his father's assistant that he needed $300,000. The answer came right back. It was a short message from his father's secretary, telling him that his father had not yet returned from his trip, and that his assistant was in bed with pneumonia and consumption of the lungs and bowels. The secretary ended the wire saying he would stand by for instructions and do everything in his power to help.

Crane crumpled the wire. He didn't have power of attorney to withdraw funds from his father's bank accounts. The assistant would do whatever Chane asked, but without a thorough knowledge of where his father hid his chestnuts, he might make some wrong decisions that would jeopardize his father's investments. Chane knew there was no way he could second-guess accurately enough to come up with the money they needed by the tenth. If Lance didn't make it...

Chane walked back to the office where Jennie was working. He stopped beside her desk. She looked up at him and said, "I don't suppose you want to hear that we got an invitation to a celebration in Morley on the ninth to officially open the station there." They had been two days ahead of schedule and so had passed through Morley before the celebration could be properly mounted. She passed the invitation to Chane, took the telegram from his hand, smoothed it, and read it.

Chane groaned. He was a little tired of celebrations, but they were an important part of railroad public relations.

Jennie smiled at the look on his face, then sobered and turned her attention to the wire. "I'd give the men a chance to decide," she said after reading it. "Tell them you have a temporary cash-flow problem and that you'll have the money any day. I'll wager that enough of them will stay to give us time to work it out."

Tom rode into town and went directly to the saloon.

"Where can I find Hessie Mae?" he asked the bartender.

"Well, you're in luck, Tom. Since the railroad is going to be near here a while, making its run at the Ratons, she's taken a room over at the Livingston."

That was luck. He'd been afraid, when he heard she'd left the camp, that she'd taken a train out of town.

At the Livingston, he got her room number and went up and knocked on her door. After a moment, the door opened.

"Yes?" she asked, poking her head in the crack.

"'Morning," he began, suddenly embarrassed.

Hessie Mae sized him up and stepped back, smiling. "Why, Tom Tinkersley. I never in my life expected to see you knocking on my door."

Startled that she knew his name, Tom blinked. Up close, she looked nothing like Mrs. Kincaid. He'd been crazy to come here, thinking that just because he remembered this woman as small and blond and blue-eyed, spending time with her would somehow ease his aching heart. Mrs. Kincaid was a sleek and racy Thoroughbred, while Hessie Mae, though attractive in a common sort of way, was a work horse—no match for her at all.

"Come in, come in," she said, stepping back and motioning him inside. She wore only a dressing robe. Her blond hair was pulled back from her face with a red ribbon. Her robe opened, revealing a sturdy leg, pleasingly shaped.

She closed the door and leaned against it, as if she knew he was only seconds from bolting. "Let me guess. Miz Kincaid made up with her husband, and your pore heart is a breakin'."

Tom frowned. "You've got a smart mouth, girl." He didn't like the idea that everyone at the work site knew his business. He'd barely been aware of Hessie Mae, except as a potential problem, and here all this time she'd known far more about him and his business than he'd wanted.

"Yep, and a smart body, too," she said, opening the robe and letting it slip off her shoulders. Her breasts were small and round with pale pink nipples. Her waist tapered into slim, boyish hips. Her pubic hair was thick and gold. Against his will, the fire that had been burning in his loins ever since he'd kissed Jennifer roared into an unmanageable blaze.

Hessie Mae led him to the bed. "A handsome man like you shouldn't be wearing all those clothes. Let's just get you out of them, right this minute."

Jason Fletcher picked up his mail, which consisted only of a letter from his cousin, Latitia. He read it slowly, smiled, and put it in his pocket. This was the third letter he'd gotten from her demanding that he kill Jennifer Kincaid. Something had sure ticked her off. Fortunately, the timing was almost right. As soon as Kincaid's brother arrived with the payroll money, the first pile of cash since Jason and his crew had been working for Kincaid, he planned to take both the woman and the money.

Jason patted his pocket, where he kept all of Latitia's letters, and turned toward the door. As he did, he saw his boss, Tom Tinkersley, walk from the saloon to the Livingston Hotel. Since Jason wasn't supposed to be in town, he stepped back and waited until Tom had disappeared inside. He waited a few minutes more. When Tom didn't come out, he sauntered over to the hotel and waved a dollar bill in front of the desk clerk's long nose. That was a day's pay for him.

"Who'd Tom go up to see?"

The clerk looked at the bill and licked his lips. "That wouldn't be that tall, blond feller, now, would it?"

Jason nodded.

"Hessie Mae."

"She that blond whore that was following the railroad?"

"Yep."

Jason smiled. In order for his plans to succeed, he needed to get rid of Tom anyway. And to relieve his own pressures, which had been building steadily, he could use Hessie Mae, who was slim and blond and blue-eyed, just like Mrs. Kincaid.

"What'd you say that room number was?"

"Two eleven."

"Thanks," he said, slipping him another dollar. "And, if you'll see to it that Hessie Mae and me aren't disturbed tonight or tomorrow morning, here's a few more of these for you," he said, peeling off three fives.

"Yes, sir," the man said, smiling broadly and tucking the bills into his pants pocket.

Jason walked to the saloon and rousted Etchevarria from the arms of a young woman who was about to earn a little money herself. Etchevarria didn't like it, but he followed Jason outside.

"Got a job for you."

Jason told him what to do, ending with, "Wait till you're about halfway back to camp to kill him."

Etchevarria nodded.

They walked around the block and entered the hotel from the back alley. Etchevarria took his place on the steps and waited. Within minutes a door opened and footsteps started down the hallway toward the steps. From his vantage point behind the stairwell, Jason heard Etchevarria's footsteps as he walked to meet Tom, then their voices, which he felt certain were clearly audible to the desk clerk in the lobby as well.

"Kincaid's done sent for you. He's madder'n hell about something."

"He knew I was coming here," Tom protested.

"Well, he didn't say what it was, but rumor about camp is that it's got something to do with Mrs. Kincaid."

"She okay?"

"Fine, as far as I know. Maybe she can't get through the day without seeing your fine, blond head."

"You better watch that mouth, boy."

Etchevarria chuckled. Tinkersley and Etchevarria walked past Jason's hiding place and left. Jason could hear the desk clerk clucking his tongue. Satisfied that the desk clerk had heard and would gladly repeat and probably expand upon the hint of a rumor Etchevarria had started, Jason sauntered outside and got his satchel from his saddlebags. Then he mounted the steps and knocked on Hessie Mae's door.

He would have preferred a more private place, but he wasn't worried. He'd done this enough times that he was fully confident he could ease her through every step without her once screaming or crying out. He'd never met a girl who wasn't scared speechless by the threat of a cut on her face. It never occurred to them that a scream and a cut would be better than dying, probably because they never expected to die. That always came as a surprise to 'em. He had no idea why.

Tom felt like hell. Instead of making him feel better, the episode with Hessie Mae had left a sick feeling in his gut. He was so down in the dumps he rode halfway back to camp without looking up.

Etchevarria rode a little behind Tinkersley. When he figured they were about halfway, he pulled out his gun and aimed it at the young man slouching in his saddle.

"Hey, Tom," Etchevarria said softly.

"Yeah?"

"Turn this way a little."

Tom turned to see what Etchevarria wanted. As he did, Etchevarria fired two bullets into Tom's chest. Tom cried out and fell sideways off his horse.

Etchevarria dismounted, felt for a pulse on Tom's throat, and, finding none, sheathed his revolver.

"Hope it was worth it, boy," Etchevarria said, grinning. He hooked his rope into Tom's belt and dragged Tom's body off the trail so it wouldn't be found before they took the payroll.

The ninth of May was warm and sunny. Blue jays squawked loudly in the trees overhead. About ten o'clock, Chane stuck his head in the open window in front of Jennifer's desk. "I just realized we haven't used every possible solution. How would you like to take a ride into Trinidad?"

"What for?"

"I need to see someone."

"What are you going to do?"

Chane evaded her questions, acting as if revealing the plan would destroy it.

"What about the work crews?"

"Kim Wong and Jessup will keep pushing them toward Raton Pass. We'll be back in time for payroll."

Chane left to see to his men. The locomotive chuffed backward from the work site to pick up the Pullman coach and one flatcar. That didn't tell her much. She gathered up her ledgers and walked to the Pullman coach waiting on the main tracks. She could catch up on her bookkeeping on the way.

Chane clambered up the steps and opened the door. "Ready?" he asked.

Jennie looked askance at Marianne, who nodded.

"Yes," she said.

Chane waved to the signalman. The train rolled forward.

Jason Fletcher leaped aboard. "Where's Tom?" she asked him.

"Don't know, ma'am. He didn't show up at breakfast this morning."

Jennifer frowned. That wasn't like Tom. Other men might get drunk and sleep through breakfast, but not Tom.

The train was picking up speed. Steve grabbed the rail beside the steps and clambered up onto the platform, looking a little pale. "No wonder you're afraid of trains. I would be, too, if I had to get on that way," she said to him.

Steve grinned. He and Chane moved to the table, where they conferred in low tones. Jason squatted on the observation platform, lost in his own thoughts, oblivious to everyone. Marianne started the noon meal. The clatter of pots and pans was barely audible over the rattle and click of the wheels against the track.

Jennifer put her ledgers aside and enjoyed the scenery. This was her first trip over these newly completed rails. The track between Clear Creek Canyon and Trinidad was steep and filled with sharp curves. In places Chane had built temporary switchbacks he intended to replace with deeper cuts, trestles, or tunnels once he had secured Raton Pass.

It seemed so different riding over the finished track than it had crawling slowly forward behind each day's work. The sun was warm. Her foot felt fine. She had no idea what Chane planned to do today. Time was running out, but she trusted him, and she trusted the future. Except for the money shortage, things were finally going right.

She just wished it was Tom squatting up front instead of Jason. She was worried about Tom. He had looked so miserable the last time she saw him. It had hurt her to see him so grief-stricken.

Since then, she had realized just how unfair this had all been to Tom. She wished there was some way to make it up to him without betraying her husband. She realized that wasn't really possible, though. Nothing short of her being in love with Tom would satisfy him. She knew from her experiences with Chane. Nothing but love is acceptable from the beloved.

As the train clicked along the rails, she rehearsed what she would say to Tom the next chance she got, searching for words that would let him know how sorry she was that he'd been put into such an awkward situation and how much she had appreciated his friendship. And how sorry she was that he'd been hurt.

CHAPTER TWENTY-SEVEN

Lance rode into a wide, well-graded road. At places farther south, the Santa Fe Trail was almost impassable. But here it was wide and comfortable. Cuts had been blasted in the mountain and bridges had been built. It was a proper road.

Lance saw a Conestoga wagon on the trail ahead. The curious faces of children peered at him from beneath the arched canvas. A woman held the reins in one hand and a baby in the other, while a boy, maybe twelve years old or so, walked barefoot beside the wagon. A man, probably her husband, rode a horse ahead of the team. He looked to be having an easier time of it than the woman, struggling as she was with the wagon, the baby, and the children.

An hour later Lance passed a team of freighters, two lone riders, and a Mexican leading a pack train of loaded burros. Miles later, at the crest of the mountain pass, Lance saw a small settlement—a blacksmith shop and livery stable, a big white house with a sign on it proclaiming it as an eating and sleeping establishment, and a small building beside the trail with a sign: WOOTTON'S TOLL ROAD.

Lance stopped at the sign and read the smaller print. Wootton apparently had a rate for every type of traffic. The old man in the toll shed next to the trail had beetling white brows and piercing eyes over a big, straight nose and a stern mouth. His straggling white shoulder-length hair was thin on top. He squinted up at Lance. "That'll be four bits."

"Worth every cent," Lance said, fishing into his pocket to bring up a half-dollar.

"Humph! There've been some who didn't think so."

"You must be Wootton."

"Call me Uncle Dick. Everyone else does."

"Do you charge everybody who comes through here?"

"Never charge Indians, posses, or the army. Everyone else pays. Just toss it in that barrel. Sort of a sobriety test. If you can't hit the barrel, you might want to lay over and sober up before you try to ride down the mountain. There's sometimes a band of Arapahoes or Utes waitin' to welcome strays who aren't too alert."

The barrel was a whiskey keg three-quarters full of silver coin. "You ever worry about bandits knocking you on the head and taking off with your silver?"

"Why, no. I've never met a bandit yet who wanted to work that hard. Mostly they just want something light to carry."

"You wouldn't happen to know where I could find the Texas and Pacific Railroad crews, would you?"

"Heard tell they're parked near Starkville, getting ready to launch their attack on the Ratons. That should be something to see! Just bear north and follow the Santa Fe Trail. You can't miss 'em. They make so much racket I can sometimes hear 'em from here."

Lance tipped his hat in salute and rode down the mountain to find his brother and get rid of this money.

Trinidad's switching yard looked capable of handling heavy train traffic. It had a turntable, primitive by New York City standards but quite functional, and six sets of tracks for sidelined trains. It had a maintenance shed for working on locomotives, two of which breathed quietly under the circular roof.

Jennifer had known that Chane was instituting freight and passenger train service as they reached each town, but actually seeing it in operation stunned her.

"When did you buy more rolling stock? I don't remember paying for it…"

"All this was borrowed from my father's railroad. I figured it's the least he can do for us, since he helped get me into this."

The switchyard was busy. One engineer was building a freight train while an assembled passenger and mail train waited on the siding.

It was a tremendous undertaking, and it had sprung up after Jennie had passed through following the track layers. The train was a reality that had already changed the lives of everyone in its path. It was like suddenly seeing the results of all Chane's hours and days and months of work.

"Would you like to spend the day at the hotel? You could do some shopping. You haven't shopped in months…"

"We need every cent to make the payroll tomorrow."

"The payroll is over a hundred thousand, Jennie. The little bit you'd spend isn't going to make a difference. Besides, you've earned a reward. Better take advantage of it. It may be a while before we get back here."

He pressed some bills into her hand. "You worry too much. Take a day off from it."

He and Steve walked with her as far as the general store. "We'll be busy most of the day. I'll meet you back at the hotel by suppertime, if we're lucky."

Jennifer shopped for an hour and then carried her bundles back to the train. She might have shopped longer, but she wasn't accustomed to wearing a corset. Its bony stays were biting into her flesh, and she wanted it off. As she hurried back to the Pullman coach, she saw the door was ajar.

"Marianne!" she called out. "Are you here?"

Marianne heard her name being called, but Jason Fletcher had backed her into Mrs. Kincaid's sleeping compartment. She struggled with him in silence. Jason's hands were a lot stronger than they had looked. And his weight was wearing her out. Now he shushed her. She stopped her hitting and kicking and listened intently. So did he.

"Marianne," Jennifer's voice called out again.

"Tell her to come in here," Jason whispered, pulling his gun and waving it for emphasis. Marianne licked her lips. "Do it!" he gritted, pressing the muzzle to her side and stepping out of sight behind the armoire. She could feel the gun still aimed at her waist, even though it was no longer touching her.

"In here, ma'am!" she yelled, shivering at the thought of him pulling the trigger and sending a bullet into her helpless flesh.

Jennifer walked across the sitting area and stopped at the door to the sleeping compartment. "Marianne, would you unfasten me? These stays are digging into me."

Jason Fletcher stepped out from behind the armoire and pointed his gun at her. "Just do as you're told," he said.

Just then a step sounded on the observation deck.

"Jennie!" Chane yelled.

She looked askance at Fletcher. He nodded, and she called out, "Go away."

Jason lifted the gun as if he were going to bring it slamming down on her head. "You're trying to get yourself killed," he hissed. Jennifer stepped away from him and into the doorway of the sleeping compartment.

Chane walked across the sitting room and almost bumped into her. Trapped between them, Jennifer froze, and Jason pressed his gun into the small of her back.

Seeing Jason, Chane stopped. "What's going on here? What do you want?" he growled.

"Making a citizen's arrest," Jason said, swinging the gun barrel toward Chane.

"For what?"

"For the murder of Tom Tinkersley." Jason reached into his vest pocket and pulled out a piece of paper. He smiled at Chane. "This is a wire from the work site. They found Tom's body this morning about an hour after we left. There are two witnesses who say they saw you kill him."

"That's a lie," Chane said.

"I guess the court can sort that one out," Jason said, moving toward Chane. "Get your hands up. I'd hate to have to shoot you for resisting arrest."

Jennifer watched in stunned silence as Jason marched Chane down the steps and across the station platform.

"What are we going to do?" Marianne asked.

"You go find Steve. I'll gather some things to take to Chane."

Lance reached the work site to find it almost deserted. He found one of the cooks still there, and asked him where the safe was. Fortunately for Lance, it was standing open—mute testimony to how bad Chane's financial situation was.

Lance tossed the saddlebags into it, closed the door, and spun the dial. "Where can a man find a bed around here?" he asked. It had been almost two weeks since he'd gotten a decent night's sleep.

Cooky laughed and led him toward one of the sleeping cars. "This usually full of cranky men, but they run off to Morley. Get drunk 'cause they no get paid."

"Well, their loss is my gain," Lance drawled, limping from sitting a horse for too long. He was sure glad he'd given up rangering.

Jason left his prisoner at the jail and walked back to the train. He could see Jennie moving around inside, like she might be looking for a weapon. He ran the rest of the way, skimming up the steps and throwing the door open. She stopped her frantic search and turned, her face flushed.

He pointed his revolver at her. "Where's Marianne?"

"I don't know."

Jason took Jennie by the arm and pushed her toward the front of the train. They found the engineer sitting on the side of the cab, swinging his legs.

"Get your steam up. We're going to the work site."

Wendell French looked from Jason's gun to Mrs. Kincaid. "You'd better do as he says," she said reluctantly.

Frowning, Wendell stood up and started to fiddle with some of the dials. "Any smart moves on your part, and you're a dead man," Jason gritted.

"I have to turn around."

"I've seen these locomotives going either direction."

"It's easier to see…"

"Forget it."

Marianne found Steve at the general store. She rushed over to where he was talking to a clerk and pulled him aside. "Jason arrested Mr. Kincaid," she whispered.

"What for?"

"For killing Tom Tinkersley. Jason took him to jail."

"Where's Jennie?"

"She's still back at the train."

Steve couldn't imagine what was going on. "I better go see Chane," he said.

Once out of the switchyard, the train rolled along without incident until the town of Morley came into sight. Wendell blew the whistle once to tell the brakeman to apply the brakes, and Jason realized that he was stopping. "What the hell?" he demanded.

"The tracks are blocked ahead. See that train there?"

Jason peered out the window. The train ground to a halt, and to their amazement, a band marched right up to the train. "What the hell is this?" Jason growled, looking at Jennie as if she had somehow caused it.

"Chane and I were invited to the station-opening ceremonies here today. I'd forgotten."

A man in a top hat and a black suit who had been leading the makeshift band stopped before the cab of the locomotive and pretended to knock on an imaginary door.

Wendell stepped forward to see what he wanted. Jason whispered into Jennifer's ear. "If you put up a fuss, I'll shoot holes in some of those younguns over yonder." He pointed to about a dozen very young children who were following the band.

His voice was still polite, but a chill started at the nape of her neck and ran the length of her spine. She nodded her understanding. Fletcher took her elbow and led her to the side of the cab.

"Welcome, welcome," the man said, extending his hand to help her down the steps. Jennifer descended the steps, holding onto his arm. A large crowd had gathered near the locomotive.

As they walked across the station platform, a military band struck up a rousing rendition of "The Battle Hymn of the Republic." A fat man in a stovepipe hat walked over and bowed to Jennifer.

"So glad you could come, Mrs. Kincaid!"

Jason Fletcher flashed a look at her and nodded toward the children playing near the edge of the station platform.

"How dja do, Miz Kincaid. I'm Eldred Withrow, mayor of this fine town. I'm so glad you could make it. Will Mr. Kincaid be along?"

"No. My husband is…working on a problem in Trinidad."

"Well, we'd rather have a beautiful woman any day," Withrow said, taking Jennifer's hand and leading her toward the front of the station, where hundreds of people crowded around. Six soldiers in full-dress uniform stood at attention.

Jason nudged Jennifer in the side. "Oh, Mr. Withrow, I'd like you to meet Jason Fletcher."

The two tipped hats at each other.

"I'm Mrs. Kincaid's bodyguard," Jason explained.

"Yes, I've seen you before," Withrow said, nodding. "In this country it's a good idea to be careful." He turned back to Jennifer. "We're hoping you'll say a few words to the folks here, Miz Kincaid."

Fletcher stopped to smile at one of the little girls and her mother. Jennifer was chilled to the bone. Withrow led her to a chair, where she listened to him go through the formalities of dedicating the new Morley station. Fletcher took the chair beside her and dandled the little girl on his knee. The mother stood in the front row beaming at her daughter.

Withrow had a certain flair for solemn pomposity. He was smart enough to keep his remarks short, although he thanked just about everyone he'd ever known. At last he introduced Jennifer.

She expected to be nervous, but with Jason Fletcher holding the little girl, she chose her words carefully. She thanked the townspeople for their support of the railroad, accepted a gold-plated key to the city, and said she hoped that today's events were only the beginning of a long and harmonious relationship between the town of Morley and the Texas and Pacific Railroad. She sat down to thunderous applause. At last the ceremony was over.

"Will you be staying over with us, ma'am?" Withrow asked.

Fletcher shook his head ever so slightly. "No. I guess not, Mr. Withrow," she said with genuine regret.

Jason took Jennifer's arm and pushed her toward the waiting locomotive. A boy hawking newspapers ran over and waved a paper at Fletcher. "Souvenir edition. Last spike driven to connect Morley to points east!"

Fletcher flipped the boy a nickel and took a paper. "Mrs. Kincaid should have a souvenir," he said, taking her elbow again and urging her toward the waiting train.

It was almost a relief to get back onto the train. Jason forced her into the locomotive. The train that had been blocking their way was gone now, and Wendell had kept the steam up, so they were able to get rolling immediately.

The train picked up speed until it was rolling along at twenty miles an hour. As they neared the outskirts of the work site in good time, Wendell slowed the train to a stop.

Four men who'd obviously been waiting for them dashed out of the brush and ran toward the train. They stopped beside the cab.

"Howdy, boss. We got worried when you weren't on time," Etchevarria said.

"We got stopped by a speechmaker."

Jennifer recognized all of them. Except for Jim Patrick, they were employees of the railroad. Etchevarria, Blackburn, and Stringer, the last security guards Tom had hired. She was especially disappointed with Jim Patrick, whom she now saw as lower than a dog's paws.

Jason motioned one of the men into the locomotive to keep charge of Wendell French. The rest of them walked toward the office car.

"So the money got there, huh?" Jason asked.

"Just got the wire a little while ago." Blackburn slapped his thigh. "He put the money into the safe and fell into a deep sleep like he hasn't slept in weeks."

"He musta been crazy to travel alone packin' that kind of money," said Stringer.

"All them Kincaids are crazy."

CHAPTER TWENTY-EIGHT

Steve examined the wire that had been turned over to the town marshal as proof of Chane's guilt. "This isn't a real telegram," Steve said, handing it to the man.

"The hell you say?" Marshal Turner took the wire and peered closely at it.

"See that?" Steve asked. "I wager if you show that to your telegraph operator, he'll confirm it."

Turner took the telegram and stalked out the door and across the street to the telegraph office. He shoved the telegram at the startled operator and asked, "Did you get this telegram today?"

The man studied the paper for a moment and then looked up at Turner and Steve. "No, sir. That's not one of mine."

Steve let out the breath he'd been holding. "Is there anyplace else in town this could have been received?"

"No, sir. I take the telegrams for the railroad, too."

"Marshal, I want you to release Mr. Kincaid to me," Steve said. "We'll go back to the camp and find out what really happened there."

Turner squinted. "I don't see how I can rightly do that."

"Everyone in the territory knows who Mr. Kincaid is and where he spends his time. I'll personally guarantee that he will appear whenever this matter is set for court."

Turner knew that Steve Hammond was an attorney, and as such, an officer of the court. His career would be on the line if he failed to keep his word. And the railroad was important to this territory. If Kincaid stayed in jail, it might not get built. Grudgingly, he walked to Kincaid's cell and unlocked it.

Jennie and no. 42 were missing. The stationmaster said their leaving had looked forced to him. Chane sent a wire to all points south, ordering them to stop and hold all trains. He directed that they all be searched thoroughly for Jennie. Then he ran toward the tracks, confiscated Engine

Number 6, *The Bruiser*, the most powerful one he owned, from a startled young engineer, and climbed aboard.

In mid-afternoon, Sarah Adair knocked on her new friend Hessie Mae's door. She had seen that good-looking security guard, Tom Tinkersley, go into Hessie Mae's room yesterday, and she wanted to know more about him. Tom was one of the handsomest customers she'd seen in a long time.

No answer. She knocked louder and waited. Still no answer. She tried the door. Maybe Hessie Mae was asleep, though she couldn't imagine how she could sleep through such a racket as the one she was making. Sarah pushed the door open and looked into the bedroom.

"Hessie Mae? It's me, honey."

The room was dim. The window was open. A breeze flapped the shade, which had been pulled down. Sarah pushed the door open wider. Hessie Mae was on the bed, facing her, but her eyes looked kind of funny. They were open, but something seemed wrong with them.

"Honey?" Sarah stepped closer. Then she saw what made her friend's eyes look funny. The pupils were so wide open that the colored part of the eyes had disappeared. Then she saw how pale Hessie Mae looked and that there was a strange pattern on her body. She peered closer and saw what looked like the heads of tacks, as if someone had pushed tacks into Hessie Mae's skin from the middle of her thighs to the tops of her breasts. Blood had welled up around each tack, and in some places had trickled down her body and stained the sheet. The realization hit Sarah between the eyes. She backed away from the body, started to scream, and couldn't seem to stop.

Marshal Davis checked the body, talked to the desk clerk, and sent a wire in both directions, letting every lawman along the telegraph lines know that Jason Fletcher was wanted for the murder of a young woman.

• • •

Within an hour word reached Chane. He was handed a copy of a wire that had arrived just after they left the work site. Chane read it with a sinking heart. The dead woman had to be Jennie, and yet he couldn't believe it.

Jennie couldn't be dead. He was filled with grief and rage. His lungs trembled as if he had taken a chill. It was the darkest moment of his life.

As Chane fired up *The Bruiser*, he was trying to think where Jennie would be, if she were still alive. Jason Fletcher had worked for him for weeks, but the man was a stranger to him. Chane had no idea what motivated Fletcher. Unless...he was after the payroll. If so, he might have taken Jennie to use as a hostage. In which case he might free her as soon as he got the money.

Chane prayed it would be that simple. He would gladly make that trade. Once he had Jennie home safe, he would track Fletcher down and kill him.

Out of breath from running to catch up, Steve swung himself up into the engine cab just as Chane was pulling out. "Maybe Fletcher's going to take the payroll."

"If there is a payroll," Chane said.

The locomotive breathed heavily. A thick cloud of coal smoke filled the air with the smell of sulfurous fumes. "You wait here," Chane said.

"I'm going with you," Steve insisted.

Chane shook his head. "I don't intend to coddle this train with slow speeds. You stay here. That way, if I kill myself and wreck our rolling stock, you can pull things back together."

"You're going to need someone to shovel coal."

"Someone, but not necessarily you." Chane yelled over the noise of the engine.

Steve picked up a piece of coal, threw it into the firebox, and reached for the shovel.

"You're going to regret this decision," Chane said grimly.

Steve scooped another shovelful of coal. "Thanks."

"If you wanted a good scare, I could have paired you up with a grizzly bear."

Steve looked momentarily sick, then he expelled a heavy breath and bent his back to the task of keeping the fire lit. "I reckon you can do as good a job as any grizzly bear. Besides, I'm hoping to keep so busy chucking coal in this box I won't have time to be scared."

Jason sent the other men to the remuda to saddle some horses while he led Jennie to the office car. On the way, she kept hoping against hope that someone would stop them, but there was no one in sight. Either the men were all sleeping or they'd gone into Morley for the celebrations.

"Open the safe," Jason gritted, pressing his knife against her stomach. She gasped with pain as the knife pierced through the layers of clothing and bit into her skin. Jennifer tried to think what Chane would want her to do if he were here.

"You open it right now, or I'll stick this knife in you and keep jerking on it until you'll beg to open it."

Jennifer could tell by the look in his eyes that he would do it. She knelt down and began turning the lock.

Chane reached the work site and slowed *The Bruiser* in time to keep from running it into the supply cars on the tracks. He blew six long notes on the whistle, and waited. What few men were still at the camp ran out and gathered around the locomotive.

"Have you seen Jennie?" Chane asked, leaping down from the train. Steve looked a little shaky, but he leaped down, too.

Cooky wiped his hands on his apron. "No, solly. I heard Missy and security boys come in and then they go. I think mebby something up in Morley."

"The payroll get here?"

"Your brother, he bring money then go sleep."

"Have someone saddle me a couple of horses," Chane yelled over his shoulder. He ran to the office and confirmed that the safe was empty. Then he ran to the sleeping car and found Lance sprawled in one of the bunks with his clothes and boots still on. He shook him awake, and Lance sat up, rubbing his eyes with his forearm.

"Chane! What's the matter?"

"Jennie, my wife, has been kidnapped. They took the payroll."

"The hell you say!" Lance said, lurching to his feet.

"Follow me," Chane said softly.

The horses were saddled and waiting. They rode for an hour, cutting through the canyon to the south. If Fletcher was heading toward the New Mexico border, they might be able to head him off. If not…they might just lose enough time to cost Jennie her life. If she was still alive…

As the day wore on, the sun beat down hotly, and Jennifer swayed in the saddle. In too many places the roadbed was dangerously narrow. It was closed in between sheer rock cliffs on both sides.

On a course that paralleled the small creek, she rode as fast as Fletcher could push the horses through the underbrush. At times it was so thick they had to ride in the creek bed.

A stitch started up in her side. Every movement of the horse aggravated it. After an hour she felt certain she would die of it.

Finally, Fletcher stopped to rest the horses and let them drink from the creek. Jennifer slipped gratefully off her horse and knelt on shaking legs to lift a handful of water to her parched mouth. She drank thirstily, then patted water over her hot face and arms, feeling the sting where the sun had been beating down on her tender skin.

One of the men filled his hat with water and put it on his head, letting the water run down over his face and chest. "Damn! A man's gotta be about three bricks short of a load to ride this hard in heat like this."

"Who'd think it could be so damned hot in the mountains?"

Clem Stringer, silent, dark, and suspicious as always, rode up to the creek. He'd hung back until now, gazing behind them. "There's a rider back there following us."

"What the hell…" Fletcher burst out.

"Coming on right determined, is he?" Etchevarria asked, rising from where he'd laid down on his belly to drink from the creek.

"Considerably determined," Stringer said, taking out the makings to roll a cigarette while the others scowled and stared back at the trail.

Fletcher was the first to speak. "Well, it don't matter. We'll be in New Mexico before he can catch us."

"Miguel, take a look in that spyglass of yorn, and see if'n it's Kincaid or his brother followin' us," Stringer said, lighting the cigarette. "If it's the brother, I heard about that bastard, too. He's even trailed men into Mexico and brought 'em back dead."

Etchevarria took out a spyglass from his saddlebags. He threw a rope over a high limb of a nearby lodgepole pine, tied one end around his chest, under his arms, and yelled for Stringer to hoist him up so he could take a look-see.

For a moment he spun in circles, then caught the tree trunk with one leg and anchored himself. He scanned the terrain in all directions, then raised the glass and focused on something. Jennifer held her breath. He scanned the countryside in the opposite direction, then motioned for the men to let him down.

"Don't see nobody out there. There's no posse coming from the direction of Morley, either. With that big celebration on, I doubt the sheriff'll be able to pull anything together before noon tomorrow."

"We'll be long gone by then," Stringer drawled. "If we angle off and leave the creek, we can hit into New Mexico, where we'll be safe. I have hideouts in them Santa Fe mountains no lawman kin ever find. Not even your hotshot Kincaid."

Hope of rescue died in Jennifer.

As Jason hurried them toward the border, the pain in her side grew worse. Sunset came early in the mountains. A sky full of flaming orange and red clouds streaked with purple signaled the end of her first day of captivity.

She rode doubled over in her saddle. The pain struck like lightning, without warning, and she ached in a hundred places. Her gown was in tatters from snagging on brambles and branches. Her face stung from them as well.

At last Fletcher called a halt. Jennifer slipped down and lay on the ground. She'd thought herself in good shape after six months with the railroad crews, but she felt half dead.

Jim Patrick walked over and offered her his canteen. She felt such disappointment in him. Her eyes must have showed it because he flushed and could no longer meet her gaze. She took a few swallows of water and passed it back to him. "Thank you."

"My pleasure, ma'am."

He was still soft-spoken and polite. He had such a guileless look of Irish good humor that she wondered what twist of fate had driven such a friendly young man into a life of crime.

"I guess this explains why you lost so many sheep."

"Yes, ma'am."

Stringer was obviously a hardened criminal, but Jim Patrick was little more than a boy.

"We'll rest here for an hour. The horses need it," Fletcher said. He grabbed a rope off his saddle, walked over to Jennifer, and grabbed her arm. He jerked her to her feet and pulled her along behind him. Jennifer flashed one look back at the men watching him tow her away. They avoided her eyes, even Jim Patrick.

Fletcher dragged her to a small clearing and threw her on the ground. "You've been more damn trouble than a dozen women."

He grabbed her right arm and started to wrap the rope around it. Jennifer hit him with her left fist as hard as she could.

"Damn you!" he yelled, drawing back his fist and smacking it into her jaw. Lights flashed in her head. As he drew back to hit her again, Jim Patrick came flying out of the bushes and landed on Jason's back. They tumbled over. Jason struggled free of Patrick, grabbed the gun out of his holster, and shot the boy in the chest. Jim blinked in disbelief and fell backward.

"Now see what you caused," Fletcher said, grabbing Jennifer's arm and dragging her even farther away from the other men. Fear and defiance sparkled in her eyes. He found himself in a box canyon and stopped. Ordinarily this would not be good. But with no one pursuing them, and some time to spend with the woman, it was right handy.

He shoved Jennie toward a pile of pine needles. She still had a little fight in her, but he knelt beside her and unsheathed his special knife from his boot. She cowered away from him, but he leaned close to her, stroking it on her throat.

"Do you know what this is?" he whispered. "It's a special kind of knife. All I have to do is stick it in you, and you'll bleed to death. It's like a siphon. Has a hollow center so the blood just keeps draining out of you."

Fear and revulsion made Jennifer cringe away. His hand twisted in her hair, holding her against the knife.

"It's not that painful, actually. You'd be surprised at the girls who thought they weren't hurt that bad, 'cause it probably don't hurt much— once you get used to having it in you. But it just keeps bleeding you and bleeding you."

As he talked Jason realized he wasn't going to be able to stop himself. He needed to kill her now. He probably wouldn't need this woman for their escape. They'd travel easier without her.

Jennifer tried to back away from him, but he tightened the rope around her hands and wrapped the other end around the trunk of a small tree, then pulled it taut until her arms were stretched behind her head. Jason sat on her hips and thighs, immobilizing her legs. Frustration at her helplessness filled her with rage.

His pale, opaque eyes smiled into hers as if they were co-conspirators. He held the knife up so she could admire it. It had no handle. It was made of steel, but it looked more like a hollow reed, pointed and razor-sharp at one end, gradually getting bigger until it was the same size as the tube attached to it. At the sight of the knife, so shiny and lethal, her insides writhed with fear.

Jennifer realized, without knowing how she knew it, that in spite of his soft Southern drawl and his polite manners, he had killed Tom Tinkersley and he was going to kill her.

Jason saw her fear and liked it. He lifted the knife up to her throat and smiled at the terror that filled her eyes. An answering jolt of lust shot through his body, so strong he was almost immobilized. He'd waited too long for her.

To cover his inability to move, he talked. "What I do is, I make you swallow this tube and then I tape it to your neck so it won't come back out. It's a little miserable, but you'll do it, because I have some good little incentives to help you along…"

Jennifer remembered the newspaper article saying that Bettina's body had been riddled with carpet tacks from her thighs to her breasts. Revulsion and terror almost overwhelmed her. She struggled to get free, but her hands were tied too tightly, and Jason was too heavy.

"Then I push this tiny little razor-sharp knife into the vein in your throat, and when the blood comes out of your vein it follows this tube into your mouth and down into your stomach. It'll be a race to see whether you bleed to death before your heart stops."

Jennifer's stomach lurched. If she'd eaten anything at all in the last few hours it would have come up then. He was insane. Terror caused a cold sweat to break out on her body.

"You killed Bettina," she said, horror growing in her.

"Was that the one in New York?"

Jennifer nodded.

"It's time to swallow the tube now."

She shook her head.

Jason grinned and took out a small sack and hefted the weight in his hands. "I usually save these until after the girl is dead, but you've been so much trouble to me…"

CHAPTER TWENTY-NINE

Chane's horse caught a hoof in a hole and went down. He flew over the horse's head and landed hard. Lance reined his horse and dismounted to kneel by his brother's side. Chane was bleeding from a cut on his forehead. "You okay?"

"Yeah, I'll live, but I think my horse broke his leg." Chane checked the leg—he was right. Regretfully, and frustrated that he couldn't seem to do anything right, Chane shot the suffering horse and climbed up behind Lance.

They rode in the direction of the New Mexico border, still tracking the kidnappers. Frustration almost overwhelmed Chane. Jennie's life was in danger, and he was floundering around like a beached salmon. If Jennie died...The thought was too horrible to contemplate. His mind veered away from it. And his rage and frustration increased.

The sun was hot, and they didn't spare themselves or the horses. Chane felt dizzy, and blood kept trickling down his forehead. Lance forced the horse up a ridge and rode along the rim for a long time, watching the canyon below for any sight of Jennie and her abductors.

Finally, near sunset, Lance motioned Chance to look down. Way below, in a small box canyon, a man knelt over something that might be a woman. Two others in a small clearing about a hundred yards away were lying on the ground as if taking a rest. Chane recognized them as Stringer and Etchevarria, Fletcher's sidekicks.

The sight galvanized him into action. He slid off the horse, lifted his rifle, took aim, and shot six times. When silence fell again, the two men lay dead or dying. He had spared only the man near Jennie. He couldn't risk sending a bullet in that direction for fear of hitting her.

Lance blinked and shook his head. Now he understood how his brother had become such a feared lawman. He didn't waste time on civilized niceties like trials.

Fletcher heard the gunfire, but he couldn't tell what had happened from where he was. He untied the rope around Jennifer's wrists, jerked her to her feet, and held her in front of him. He separated the knife from the tubing, slipped the knife into his boot, and tossed the tubing aside. Grabbing his gun out of its holster, Jason kept turning around like a man on a spit, trying to see where the bullets had come from. "Stringer!" he yelled. "Etchevarria!"

No answer came.

"Answer me, dammit!" Fletcher yelled.

"Now we negotiate," Chane said, turning to Lance.

"This is what I want *you* to do…"

Lance nodded as Chane started away on foot. But he stopped and turned back. He knew he was wasting precious time, and Jennie's life hung in the balance, but this had been preying on his mind. "About Colette…"

Lance scowled.

"In case I don't make it back, I forgive you for that."

"I figured you already had."

"Well, I hadn't. But now I do." Lance shook his head. It amazed him that Chane could worry about that at a time like this. Chane slipped out of sight.

Lance counted to twenty and yelled, "Your men are dead, Fletcher."

"You shoot again, you bastard, and this woman's gonna be dead, too!"

"Hold your fire! I want to parlay," Lance yelled.

Jason jerked the woman toward the place where he'd left the others. At the clearing, he saw the dead men and cursed.

"Fletcher! We've got you surrounded. Let Jennie go."

"Go to hell!"

Jennifer strained to recognize the voice of the man yelling at Fletcher. She desperately wanted to believe it was Chane, but it didn't sound like him. She'd know Chane's voice even if he tried to disguise it.

"Throw down your gun."

"You throw down your guns. Or I'm going to shoot this woman! I can put a lot of bullets in her before she dies!" Fletcher yelled, tightening his grip on her and pressing the gun against her temple. "I'm going to count to three. You better start throwin' 'em out here. One! Two!"

"My guns are down."

Fletcher grinned. "You see how much he loves you?" he said to Jennifer. Then he yelled, "Everybody! Three!"

"I'm alone. And my guns are down."

The sky was turning dark blue with approaching nightfall. Seconds ticked by. Lance glanced at his watch. Five minutes since Chane had left.

"You better not be lying! Anybody fires a shot at me, and this woman dies," Fletcher warned.

"My guns are down," Lance said flatly.

Fletcher held the woman in front of him like a shield and pushed her forward. "Stand up so I can see you."

Slowly Lance stood up.

Fletcher took aim, and Lance dropped and rolled to the right. Dirt spanged up behind him. He reached the rock he'd been aiming for and crouched and ran, hoping Chane was where he could do some good.

Jason forced the woman up and onto his horse and leaped on behind her. That way if the bastard shot at him, he'd hit her first. He rode toward the rock, firing at where he expected the man to be, but when he got there, the bastard was gone. Jason scanned the bushes nearby, but he didn't find him. He wasn't worried, though. The man was unarmed and running for his life. He probably wouldn't stop till he got back to the work site.

Jason decided to take all the horses in case he needed them. No sense leaving anything behind. He unhobbled the horses and led the string away. He set a fast pace, and quickly broke out of the scrub forest and onto a wagon trail. There was no pursuit in sight, and Fletcher was pleased with himself. "Dad gum, my luck is holding today!"

He reached around and squeezed Jennifer's breast. "You must be my lucky charm."

Jennifer jerked away. He chuckled. "You ain't got that much, anyway—"

A volley of gunfire made the horses scream and paw the air. Fletcher clawed for his gun. Jennifer grabbed his gun hand and held onto it. "You bitch!" He clubbed her with this other hand, but Jennifer held on tight in spite of the battering she was taking.

A dark form loomed out of the darker shadows, grabbed Fletcher by the waist, and pulled him off the horse. Jennifer almost went down with them, but she managed to hang onto the horse's mane.

The two men rolled on the ground, each straining to get control of the gun. Even in the semidarkness, Jennifer recognized Chane. Joy and relief washed into her, along with the fear that Jason might kill him.

Fletcher tried to force the gun down against Chane's head, but Chane grabbed his arm. They rolled over again, straining against one another, panting. The gun went off. Someone yelled. For a moment neither man moved. Jennifer's heart felt as though it had stopped in mid-beat. Then, slowly, Chane disengaged himself and stood up. "On your feet," he growled at Fletcher.

"You shot me, you bastard."

"Apparently not bad enough to shut you up. Get up!"

Fletcher struggled to his feet. Lance ran up and grabbed Fletcher by the arms. Jennifer felt faint. And so glad to see Chane alive that she could barely think. He walked over to her and looked her up and down, searching for wounds.

"Are you all right?" he asked.

"Just scared. Are you—"

"I'm fine."

Chane grabbed a rope off Jason's saddle and fashioned a noose. He place it over Fletcher's head and around his neck. "Turn away," Chane said to Jennie. "You don't want to watch this."

"Yes, I do," she said.

Chane looked at her oddly, but he figured after what she'd been through, she was entitled.

Lance forced Fletcher up onto a horse, while Chane threw the rope over a tree limb and tied it to the trunk. Lance took the saddlebags with the payroll off Fletcher's horse and placed it on his own. Then he went through Fletcher's personal saddlebags and came up with a small packet of letters.

"Wait a minute," he said to Chane, who looked impatient to get on with the hanging. Lance opened one of the letters and read it.

"Look at this," he said, passing it to Chane.

It was a short, unsigned note to Jason. It ended, "Kill her." Chane recognized Latitia's handwriting instantly. The note was in the same handwriting as the note she'd written to Jennie—and reflected the same rage.

"You've been working for Latitia Laurey all this time, haven't you?" he asked Fletcher.

"Go to hell," Jason growled.

Chane shuffled through the other letters. All of them were in the same handwriting and signed by Latitia. He stuffed the letters into his pocket and turned back to Fletcher, who was now gray-faced with fear. "You were the one following Jennifer in New York, weren't you?" Chane asked.

"Go to hell."

Jennifer realized he *was* the one, and that she should have known it right away. Tall man. Pale blue eyes. "He killed Bettina, too," she said. Jason sneered.

"And Tom Tinkersley, and that young woman at the hotel." Chane said. "It's going to give me great pleasure to remove this piece of garbage from the land of the living. Got any last words to say, Fletcher?" Chane asked.

"Go to hell!"

"You try it first. Let me know if you like it."

Chane led the horse out from under Fletcher.

The killer kicked a few minutes, looking for something to ease him, then went still. Jennifer didn't look away until she felt certain Jason Fletcher was dead. Chane walked back to her side. For a moment they just looked at the man dangling there in the dusk.

The silence stretched out. Chane's mind went blank. He had wanted to find Jennie alive so bad he couldn't remember anything else. And here she was, alive. He wanted to pull her into his arms and hold her, but he couldn't. All he could do was stand there, frozen.

She seemed as immobilized as he. Fortunately, Lance took charge and got them all on horses. They made it back to the work site in two hours. It was deserted and quiet as a tomb. Jennifer was so tired she couldn't get off her horse. Chane lifted her down and carried her to the Pullman coach. He had figured out what he wanted to tell her, but she was already asleep.

The next morning Chane received a message from what was left of Tom Tinkersley's security network that the Denver and Mexico crews were within two weeks of the New Mexico line, and that hired thugs were massing in Morley to keep Chane away from Raton Pass until Laurey's crews had reached the New Mexico line.

When Jennifer came limping out of her sleeping compartment, Chane told her the bad news.

"So how do we stop them?"

"I don't know. Most of the men quit last night. We missed payday, remember?"

"Men can be rehired," she said. "I can't believe you'd just give up."

"Just give up? I'm only one man, two if you count Lance. But I don't see what right I have to get him killed."

"Well," Jennifer said hesitantly, "it seems to me that if you had a crew up there and they were grading the roadbed when Laurey's men arrived..."

Chane scowled. He might be able to round up a couple hundred men and get them up there before morning. Except he had no idea how Uncle Dick Wootton would react. Uncle Dick was friendly enough on the surface, but he might just be pleased that Chane was going to be stopped from replacing his toll road with a railroad track.

"It's worth a try," he finally admitted.

"I can help," Jennifer said.

"No, you've been in enough danger for a lifetime. I order you to stay out of it," he said grimly. Jennifer took some hope from the fact that he didn't relish her being in danger.

Chane left for Morley to recruit as many men as he could, and Jennifer went looking for Kim Wong.

At three o'clock in the morning Chane led his crew up the mountainside. The sky was darker now than it had been all night. The moon had slipped over the horizon, leaving the mountainside darker than the inside of a tomb. The tall trees added to the darkness. One of the men following Chane stepped in a hole and cursed. Except for that, only the sounds of their footsteps on the cold ground broke the stillness.

The cold up here was biting. Chane carried a shotgun. Every man with him had some sort of weapon, even if it was only a road-grading tool. Lance wore two guns and carried a shotgun as well.

Fewer than a hundred men had agreed to come with him. The rest of the men were too hungover from the festivities in Morley to walk, much less scare away armed, determined men. The Denver and Mexico line couldn't have picked a better time for a confrontation.

Chane had promised his men an extra week's pay and a chance to keep their jobs, which had been the deciding factor. If Laurey's crew took the pass, the Texas and Pacific was as finished as it would get.

They passed a Conestoga wagon that had pulled to one side of the trail for the night. A pale face parted the canvas and peered out at this small army of men trudging up the hill.

Near the top, the wind blew even harder and colder. Men grumbled about the icy winds. The little settlement Wootton had named after himself finally came into sight. A light burned in the window of the toll shed. Chane motioned his men to wait. He and Lance walked toward the light. Before they reached the shed, a white-haired man stepped outside, lantern in hand.

"Well, so it's to be you, is it?" His white hair was frizzed out around his head as if he'd just gotten out of bed.

Chane stopped. "'Morning, Mr. Wootton."

"I tell everyone to call me Uncle Dick."

"Chantry Kincaid," Chane said, extending his hand.

"'Mornin' t'all of you," Wootton said, turning and picking up a shovel from the side of the cabin. "Brought my shovel with me."

Chane scowled. He couldn't imagine what the old man was going to do to him with a shovel. If the stories were true, he was richer than Midas. He could easily afford a gun.

"Well, where do we start?" Wootton asked.

"Start what?"

"Why, gradin' the roadbed for your railroad. I've brought my shovel."

"You mean…you're going to help us?" Chane asked, startled.

"Help you put me out of business? Why, yes, I am. I've worked here long enough. It was so lucrative that I'da been crazy to just walk off and give it up. But with progress comes change, and I'm ready for it. I think I'll take me to San Francisco and see what all's new since the last time I was by that way. There's a whole world out there I haven't seen in years."

Chane stuck out his hand. "That sure makes my job easier and more pleasant."

Wootton shook his hand, then Lance's. "I wouldn't get too excited about winning yet. I 'spect we're in for a fight when the Denver and Mexico crews reach here. I got no use for them varmits. Especially that Beaver Targle who come up here to bribe me into signing that Denver and Mexico right-of-way agreement. If they're all like him, they're crooked as sidewinders, and I think they'll fight like 'em, too. I reckon you ought to know that."

"Shovels weren't the only things we brought."

Wootton looked from man to man. "I see that. Well, it's a straggly crew at best, but I'm sure you brought all that would come. Let's get to work. We wouldn't want those Denver and Mexico crews to think we're lollygaggers. I've heard there are some hard cases amongst them. I hope you've brought plenty of bullets."

Lance grinned at Chane. The old man had spirit.

Chane spread the crew across the mouth of the pass. The men raked at the cold, hard ground to keep warm. They looked pretty puny spread out like that. Chane looked at Lance, who shrugged. "Maybe they won't come today. By tomorrow we could get enough men rounded up and sobered up…"

The eastern sky turned gray in the gathering dawn. Before many minutes had passed, sounds of men approaching could be heard over the sighing of the wind in the pines.

Chane walked to the front of the crew and took his place. Lance followed and stood shoulder to shoulder with his brother and Wootton. The men behind Chane pretended to work at grading the roadway.

Jennifer watched Chane and the small band leave, and wished she'd gone with him. She was a nervous wreck from waiting to hear from Kim Wong. She'd sent him into town hours before to try to get the Chinese to come back, but he hadn't returned. They should be here by now—if they were coming.

The night was a cold one, even for the Colorado mountains. She turned out the lamps and sat in one of the upholstered chairs, gazing at the stars and being glad she was alive. She'd been closer to dying today than ever before in her life. Knowing that made life more precious—and Chane more precious. He'd made tremendous sacrifices to save her. And he'd killed the men who took her. That must mean something.

The camp was deserted, except for her. She may have dozed. She woke with a feeling of falling. Something had startled her. Panicked, she looked around, searching for the cause.

In the distance she saw moonlight flash against something shiny. She stood up and walked to the window. In the Santa Fe Trail next to the freshly laid rails she saw hundreds of men walking up the hill toward the pass. It had to be the Denver and Mexico crews.

Chane had left with fewer than a hundred men. This looked like five or six hundred. They walked by as quietly as they could, but the sound of so many feet hitting the hard earth made an ominous, unsettling sound.

The sky was pale gray when the Denver and Mexico crew saw the Texas and Pacific crew and stopped. A few curses were followed by silence as men waited to see what their leaders were going to do. Finally, Beaver Targle and a man Chane recognized as Frank Edgerly, Laurey's construction superintendent, stepped forward.

"You aren't fooling anyone with this charade, Kincaid. You haven't laid a piece of track within a mile of here."

"Neither have you, Edgerly. Close don't count in poker or railroading. Either you've got an ace or you don't. As you can see, we beat you to the pass."

"Had a little trouble getting your boys out of bed, did you?" Edgerly asked, looking at the scant force opposing him. "I reckon we can take this pass."

"Nothing wrong with your ability to count, but you might be overlooking important details. The men in the back might live to tell about this clash, but I suspect anyone standing this close to the front is going to get ventilated by this shotgun, if trouble starts. Does Laurey pay you enough to get killed for him, Edgerly?"

Edgerly glared at Kincaid and then Wootton. "Have you chosen up sides against us as well?" he asked Wootton.

"Yup. I didn't appreciate your man Targle coming here to try to bribe me into signing that right-of-way agreement."

Beaver Targle looked belligerent and ready to fight. "We'll let you boys get on back to your work site. I expect you'll want to start packing things now that you've finished your railroad," he said.

"We're claiming this pass," Chane said, raising the shotgun into position.

"You're a fool, Kincaid. This isn't even your railroad. You'll be dying for something your grandfather didn't even live to see."

Chane knew it was true, but somehow he'd gotten attached to the idea of finishing this railroad the way his grandfather had planned it. He wasn't willing to give that up, even if he was outnumbered five to one.

Beaver Targle raised his shotgun and pointed it at Chane. Other men on the Denver and Mexico crews did likewise. Chane had second thoughts about getting his men killed for what might be nothing. Many could die, and he could still lose. The Denver crew had more guns and more men to hold them.

"I'll give you another chance to clear out, Kincaid."

Before Chane could respond, a murmuring started at the back of the Denver crew.

"Hold it!" a familiar female voice yelled from behind the Denver crew.

Frowning, Edgerly and Targle looked over their shoulders to see what was happening. Startled men murmured and turned.

Chane watched in amazement as Jennie, with the help of two Chinese men, clambered up and stood on a rock beside the trail looking out over the opposing factions. In a white coat, with her pale blond hair fanned out around her, she seemed to sparkle with ethereal brightness in the predawn air. Facing the east, her clear skin picked up the light and magnified it. She looked for a moment like an avenging angel. From around her and behind her, hundreds of Chinese bearing spears advanced on the Denver crew.

Chane grinned. Somehow Jennie had gotten the Chinese back and armed them with the spears she'd bought months ago. With their shaven crowns, and their spears drawn back, poised to let fly, and their faces set in belligerent frowns, the Chinese looked ferocious.

Instinctively, the Denver crew backed away from them.

"They aren't fighters!" Edgerly yelled to reassure his men. "Stand up to them."

"Like hell!" Chane yelled. "These Chinese are some of the most savage fighters I've ever seen. They're worse than Indians. And they'd rather gut a man than shoot him," he said, making it up as he went. "They've been a problem ever since we started this railroad. Trying to keep them from fighting…it almost can't be done. They'd rather fight than eat."

"You're bluffing, Kincaid," Edgerly said, sounding less confident. And Targle knew Chane was right. The Chinese looked small, but they were fierce.

Jennifer's troops hissed and spat and shook their poised spears. The Denver crewmen nearest them edged back.

"Hope you can still count, Edgerly. It'd be a shame to get caught between us with our shotguns and a thousand angry Chinese armed with spears and knives. Like you said, this isn't even your railroad. You can't ask these men to give up their lives for nothing, as badly outnumbered as you are."

Edgerly flashed Chane a look to see if he was lying. Chane faced him down. Edgerly shook his head. A look of disgust replaced the disbelief. He walked back to his crew. "Let's go, boys. We've got here too late."

Grateful, the men turned and started down the mountain. Men behind Chane laughed and slapped one another on the back. Beaver Targle was hanging back.

Chane ignored him and walked over to help Jennie down from the rock. He reached up, and Jennie stepped forward to meet him. Just as she did, Targle reached into his jacket and something shiny flashed through the air.

Jennie saw it and flung herself at Chane, knocking him off balance. She could see the knife coming at her, but she couldn't do anything else after she'd used all her strength to push Chane out of the way. There was no time. She saw it arcing end over end and then straightening out at the very last moment. It seemed to wait for a split second until Chane's body fell past, and then it embedded itself in her side.

Chane hit the ground, and Jennie followed. Lance raised the shotgun, but he was too late. One of the Chinese dashed forward and ran a spear through Beaver Targle's chest. Targle staggered backward, clutching at the spear, and fell.

Other Chinese crowded around to form a shield between the enemies and their fallen leader. Lance ran over and knelt beside Chane, who was holding Jennie. She was conscious and alert in spite of the knife in her left side.

"Jesus!" Chane said, feeling more helpless than he'd ever felt in his life.

The look of distress on his face warmed her against the cold seeping into her bones. "Don't be upset. I think I did this all by myself," she said, smiling that she finally had his attention. "We beat them, didn't we? We beat the Denver and Mexico line to the New Mexico border. It's all going to work out just fine."

Blood was spreading out around the knife. Her eyes blinked and closed. She lay so still, so pale, that his breath caught in his throat. Fear almost swamped him. In a panic, he turned to his brother. "I think my wife is dead."

CHAPTER THIRTY

They fashioned a stretcher from two-by-fours and a bolt of fabric from Wootton's store. Chane was too stricken to think. Wootton sent a runner to find Dr. Campbell, while two men carried Jennie down the mountain. Chane strode alongside her, mute with terror that she might die.

Dr. Campbell met them on the run and had them set her down right there so he could examine her, then he just shook his head and asked them not to jar her too much.

"Aren't you going to take the knife out?" Chane croaked.

"Hmmm." Campbell walked him a short distance away from her and said, "I don't think I'll take that knife out just yet. Sometimes the shock of removing it suddenlike—" He paused and frowned as if he wished he hadn't started on that line of reasoning. "—well, it's a jolt to the system. She's a healthy young woman, but I just don't want to take any chances until I get her back to the hospital car."

Chane had never felt more terrified in his life. Rage almost overwhelmed him. It was illogical, but he was furious at her for getting hurt.

They reached the work site in an hour. The longest hour Chane had ever survived. At the camp hospital, Campbell spent what seemed like forever preparing his surgical tools. Lance sat in a chair a few feet from where Jennie lay on the operating table. Chane paced from Jennie's side to the end of the car and back again, each time hoping for some change in her condition. She remained asleep or unconscious, her face pale, her lips blue. They had piled on blankets to try to keep her warm, but her skin felt cold to the touch.

Dammit, Jennifer! If you die, I'll never forgive you. Please, God, don't let her die. His mind swirled with promises, but they defied articulation. At last Campbell seemed ready. He reached for the knife protruding from Jennie's side. Chane stepped close to watch. Campbell straightened and shook his head. "This is going to be nerve-wracking enough without you standing there breathing down my neck. Why don't you wait outside?"

Lance took Chane by the arm and led him away. Chane wanted to protest, but he felt too weak to do anything except trudge along beside his brother.

"I killed her," he whispered.

"She's not dead, and she'd be real upset to hear you talking like that," Lance said, leading him away.

A lifetime passed. Chane could almost feel his hair turning white. He'd never known such agony before. If Beaver Targle were still alive, he'd have roasted him over an open fire. Suddenly, he realized how Lance must have felt when Lucinda was murdered. She had died in Lance's arms, and he had gone out and killed two of the men with his bare hands. Now, in the face of Jennie's injury and possible death, he understood how Lance could have taken the law into his own hands.

At last Campbell opened the door and stepped out.

"How is she?" Chane asked, dread almost choking off his ability to talk.

"Got the knife out without killing her. It's not as bad as I feared. It was stuck pretty tight in that rib, but that's probably what saved her. I broke the rib getting it out, or it was already shattered. But it only took a few stitches to close the wound. She's going to hurt for a while, but I don't think she's got any internal damage. Still, infection's always a possibility when you break the skin. Only time will tell."

Lance staggered to a bed and fell asleep. It had been almost two weeks since he'd had any real rest. Chane pulled up a chair and sat wanly by Jennie's side.

She woke a few hours later, and Chane was holding her hand. Her eyes blinked open and slowly focused on his face.

"Is everyone okay? I had a terrible dream…"

"Everyone is fine. Except you."

"You're not just saying that, are you?"

"No. You saved the day by bringing Kim Wong's men, and then you saved me." Part of him wanted to tell her that he loved her and had been devastated by her injury, but he couldn't. Part of him was beginning to understand how she could have been unfaithful, because he'd made the same mistake himself, but he still couldn't get the words out.

He truly wanted to forgive her, but to do it, he'd have to trust her completely—or he'd have to love her at his own risk, without regard for his own safety and well-being. That would be like lying on a railroad track and trusting her not to run the train over him. He wanted to, except she'd already run the train over him once.

Or he'd have to find a way to feel that his mistake cancelled out her mistake. That didn't sit well with him, either. If she hadn't made the first one, he'd never have been in such a state that Latitia could have gotten to him the way she had.

He realized with frustration that he couldn't live with Jennie, and he couldn't stand to live without her. He'd seen what hell looked like when he'd thought Jason had killed her. Now he felt trapped in a life he couldn't live.

Vaguely, he knew there was something wrong with his mind—something that stopped him from forgiving and moving forward—but he had no idea what it was. This was the mind he'd always had. It used to work properly. But ever since Jennie had betrayed him, it had been oddly out of kilter, and he had no idea what to do about it.

He feared she would die from despair over his inability to forgive her. And still, he couldn't bring himself to say anything. The part of him that could have told her how he felt wasn't the part in control of his mouth. His inability to communicate terrified him and frustrated him and filled him with guilt, but none of that mattered.

Jennie looked at him, waiting for him to speak. Her eyes were soft and beautiful and asked so damned little that he could feel himself bleeding inside. He looked down, and she knew nothing had changed. She didn't appear angry about it, though. She just closed her eyes and slept again.

He sat for an hour beside her bed, too immobilized to do anything else. When the gong for the noon meal sounded, he trudged out of the Pullman coach and walked to the telegraph shed. He sent a telegram to Tom Tinkersley's parents in Texas to tell them the sad news that their son had been killed.

That afternoon, they buried Tom in a sheltered, level place on the side of the mountain. Jennifer had no business being out of bed, but she insisted on being carried there. Filled with regret and sadness, feeling as bad as if her own brother had died, she cried quietly and bitterly the whole time.

Alarmed that Jennie was making herself sicker, Chane cut the ceremony short and took her back to the Pullman coach.

"Were you in love with Tom?" he asked finally.

Jennifer opened her eyes and sniffed back tears. "No. I feel awful because he was a decent, respectful, deserving man, and we treated him in the most awful way…" Tears flooded her eyes, and she had to gulp back sobs. "I am so ashamed of the way we used him."

Chane nodded. At least they agreed about that.

He stayed by her side until she cried herself to sleep, then he went outside to check on the work crews. Most of the men had come back. Hammers rang out against iron. Men dropped ties and rails into place, and the sounds echoed down the mountainside.

That night Jennie developed a fever, and Chane's fear increased. He stayed by her side, fed her water and beef tea to keep up her strength, and put cool, wet cloths on her forehead. But she lay still as death, and Chane panicked at the thought that she might not recover. Instead of loosening the words stuck inside him, Jennie's sudden turn for the worse added to his rage. He was furious with her for taking the knife that was meant for him.

Her fever rose and fell. Three days passed with agonizing slowness. Chane died a thousand deaths. Finally, on the morning of the fourth day, she opened her eyes and seemed lucid for the first time. And Chane finally allowed Lance to lead him off to bed, where he collapsed and slept the day through.

It was a beautiful day. Birds sang noisily overhead. Sunlight filtered through the pine trees. A cooling breeze took the edge off the sun, high and hot overhead.

Lance and Chane rode up and witnessed the laying of the rails at the base of Raton Pass. On the way back to the base camp, Lance said, "Well, I'll be leaving tomorrow."

"Why so soon?" Chane asked.

"I'm going to Dodge City to meet Angie. She's working on a picture book of that little metropolis."

"When you finish there, bring her back with you. I think Jennie would like your Angie."

"I'm sure she would, but I don't *bring* Angie anywhere. She comes and goes as she pleases."

Chane nodded. Complacent women probably didn't exist anymore. The memory of Jennie, spear in hand, standing on that rock like Joan of Arc, flooded over him. She had been magnificent. She'd also saved a lot of men's lives.

Lance received a letter from Angie when they got back to camp. He read it in silence, grinning a few times, and laughing outright once. Then he folded it and leaned back in his chair.

"How's your wife?" Chane asked, chafing at the need to think up polite questions, when he burned inside with a fever that felt like it was killing him.

Lance grinned. "Mouthy, intelligent, stubborn, beautiful, hot-tempered, sweet, bitchy, sensuous, wise, interesting, talented, and mouthy. Definitely mouthy."

Chane scowled. "Sounds like you miss her."

Lance gave a deep sigh. "I never thought I could miss constant turmoil as a life-style, but I do. She's been gone a month now, and I'm real sick of not having her around." He smiled proudly. "Likes Dodge, she does. Feels it's in its heyday now, but on the verge of a big decline. She's excited about catching it while it's still going strong."

Chane realized that although he loved his brother, he was ready for him to leave. Lance's contentment only turned the knife in Chane's heart.

Jennie could feel her strength returning. Chane looked like a man in torment, but he still didn't say a word to her about his feelings. She didn't blame him, though. Before, she'd been angry and impatient, but now, strangely, she was content to sleep and rest and wait.

Jennifer's recovery was going so well that she decided to accompany her replacement bookkeeper on payday. The men were in a jovial mood. Chinese and whites joked with one another in a way they never had before. In the past they'd formed two separate lines, Chinese in one, non-Chinese in another. Now they formed one line, Chinese and non-Chinese intermingled. She was so happy to see the men and to receive their happy smiles that she would have stayed to the end, but after only an hour or so Chane came and led her back to bed.

"Are you trying to kill yourself?" he demanded angrily.

He seemed angry so often that she was getting used to his being out of sorts and just ignored it. "I'm fine. What's that?" she asked, noticing the telegram in his hand.

"Good news for once," he said. "Tom Wilcox discovered that Simone left New York shortly after we did. Apparently, she's gone to join your brother, wherever he is."

"Thank goodness," she said. It was the first proof he was still alive. "Do they know where she went?"

"No, but her mother told a neighbor they were going out West. So, we know two things. Your brother is alive. And Simone is probably with him."

"Maybe he'll write. Would his letter reach me here?"

"It should. There's more. In the course of the investigation, Wilcox offered a reward for any information about your brother. The reward flushed out a woman who remembered the Van Vleet name. She claimed that her former, live-in friend, Edgar Noonan, was flashing some big bills about a year ago. They got drunk one night and he told her he'd eliminated a couple of problems for a rich and powerful woman. He mentioned Latitia Laurey and the Van Vleet name."

Jennifer's heart dropped. Chane caught Jennie's arm to support her. "Latitia hired Noonan to kill your parents."

"My parents? Why in the world?"

"Tom thinks, after more research, that it was a lovers' quarrel."

Jennifer's face turned white. "But I knew about all of Reginald's affairs. Everyone knew."

"Apparently, Latitia wanted to keep this one secret, and she wanted it badly enough that she would kill for it."

Shaken, Jennifer took Chane's hand and gripped it tight. He waited a moment and continued. "Now for the good news. The lawsuit has been settled against my grandfather's estate. We'll have all the money we need to finish the railroad. The Colorado legislature has unanimously approved the land grants we earned, and the Commodore has filed for bankruptcy protection."

"But what's going to happen to Latitia?"

"Well, the witness we found—the woman—isn't too reliable, so we have no real evidence there. I sent the letters we found on Fletcher to Tom Wilcox. He said he turned them over to the district attorney, but not to hold our breath. The Commodore has a lot of influence in New York, where she'd have to be tried. She may or may not be punished, since you didn't die. But at least we've neutralized her."

"But you're not happy," Jennifer said softly.

"Of course I am," he growled.

"Well, I'm happy for you," she said, searching his face.

Chane started to say "for us," but he couldn't. The words caught in his throat. "There's more. I wired Mr. Halbertson and told him everything that had happened. He wired back today and confessed that Number One had hired Jason Fletcher."

"Your grandfather!" Jennifer said, astonished. "But why?"

"To keep me from marrying you."

"But he didn't."

"No." Chane didn't know how he felt about this latest news. His grandfather had probably meant well, but he'd almost gotten Jennie killed. Knowing Fletcher had been in New York as well and had undoubtedly been following Jennie—and that she'd told him and he'd ignored her—filled him with shame.

Fletcher and Latitia had been trying to kill Jennie all along, and Chane had ignored her comments about his enemies, refusing to believe that he had any. He'd made a lot of mistakes himself—Latitia being the biggest one. He knew he should forgive Jennie, but something still stopped him. And that, too, was a cause for rage. He seemed consumed by it.

They reached the Pullman coach in silence. Jennifer took a nap, and Chane went back to work. When she woke up, Cooky had prepared a feast. He told her that Chane had ordered it, because it was Mr. Lance's last night with them.

Jennie put on one of her prettiest gowns, the amethyst one she hadn't worn since the celebration in Thatcher. She wondered if he'd notice.

Lance looked crisp and handsome in one of Chane's suits. Even Chane had taken special pains with his appearance. He looked slimmer and tougher than he had six months ago, and he smelled of the bay rum aftershave he'd worn when she first met him.

Steve and Marianne joined them, and Jennifer could tell by the way they kept sneaking looks at one another that there was likely to be another celebration soon.

Chane opened a bottle of wine, and Lance made a toast to Jennifer's full recovery and the railroad's success against amazing odds. After dinner they sat outside. Marianne and Steve took a walk, holding hands. It was nice to see them so obviously and happily in love.

The unusually warm evening was one of the most beautiful she'd ever seen. There was a medley of birdsong, and crickets and frogs provided a perfect background harmony to the sounds of the laborers playing cards, doing their household chores, and settling down for the night. Fireflies flickered on and off in the distance.

Jennifer was so hungry for good times like these, she'd learned to cherish them even while they were happening.

At bedtime Jennifer, Chane, and Lance walked toward the Pullman coach. Jennifer saw a baby lamb that had strayed a little too far from the herd. "Oh," she said, "Maybe I should take it back to its mother."

Chane laughed. "Its mother will find it."

"Are you sure?"

Chane grinned. "As sure as I am that you'll find some other small, helpless creature to worry about."

Lance nodded. "I understand completely," he said ruefully. "In the spring, life becomes unbearable for Angie. I guess every woman who wants a baby goes through that. It must be hell. I can tell she can't help herself. She just starts collecting little living things…"

Surprised and caught off guard by Lance's amazing conclusion, Jennifer glanced at Chane. He clamped his jaws and looked away.

"We had a bed for you inside," Jennifer said. "I feel terrible that you're sleeping somewhere else."

"I don't want to embarrass myself by snoring in front of my beautiful sister-in-law," Lance said, smiling at Jennifer. She knew it was because he didn't want his presence to keep them from making love, now that she was well. But she had no hopes in that direction. It was obvious Chane hadn't forgiven her.

"You're very gallant," she said.

"Just smart. I'm trying to keep all my shortcomings to myself. Angie may kick me out, and I wouldn't want word to have gotten around."

They reached the Pullman coach.

"This is good-bye," Lance said. "I've packed my things and I'll be leaving early in the morning. I gotta go see what that woman's doing. I expect they'll have a petition started to get Angie out of town while they still have a decent hellhole there."

"I'm looking forward to meeting your wife."

"And she you. You don't need to get up to see me off. I'll just walk my hoss down the tracks to the first station I run into."

"You'll do no such thing," Jennifer insisted. "We'll send a work train into Starkville. You can catch a train from there that'll take you into Dodge."

Chane nodded. It was settled.

Lance went off to his own bed. Chane nodded to her and went to his sleeping compartment. Jennie went to her lonely bed and cried herself to sleep as silently as she could.

Jennifer got up early the next morning to see Lance off.

"If Chane doesn't shape up, you keep me in mind," he said. "I'm always about six minutes from being thrown out myself," he drawled, leaning down to hug Jennifer good-bye.

"I'll do that," she said, sorry to see him go. He was soft-spoken, and one of the finest men she'd ever met. And he had a humanizing effect on Chane.

That afternoon, the work crews tackled an enormous rock that squatted in the middle of the right-of-way. Chane went up in one of the baskets to place dynamite for blasting. He set the dynamite, capped it, and lit the fuse. She kept waiting for them to lower him down, so he could find cover, but the basket kept swinging there.

Below, men yelled and fought with the equipment, and Jennifer figured out that the rope-and-pulley arrangement wasn't working. For a tense moment she watched Chane hanging there beside the lit fuse while the men struggled to free the twisted rope that was keeping the pulley from working. When she could contain herself no longer, she yelled out, "Put out the fuse!"

Chane heard Jennie, but he knew there was no urgency yet. He craned his neck back to see if they were going to be able to clear the lines in time. He had two minutes before the dynamite blew.

"Put out the fuse!" she yelled again.

Chane waved her away.

At last the men cleared the lines and lowered him down to the ground. They all took cover behind one of the enormous rocks dotting the mountainside. Seconds later the dynamite blew.

When the explosion was over, and only the dust cloud remained, Jennifer ran across the intervening space. "You could have been killed," she said furiously, holding her side, which had begun to ache.

"And you could tear something open and die," he growled, standing up to brush dust off his clothes. "I was watching it." Anger sparkled in his eyes.

"You were watching the fuse burn toward the dynamite!"

"I knew what I was doing," he said grimly. It was obvious he didn't appreciate being yelled at in front of his men, who had suddenly gotten busy enough to pretend they weren't listening.

"I did, too," Jennifer said, turning to stomp away. She thought about their problem all the rest of that day. She felt it was no accident that he'd almost killed himself.

No matter what she was doing, her mind kept going back to that. Finally, she knew what she had to do.

Jennifer put aside her ledgers and went to the palace car to pack. She didn't know why, but suddenly she knew it was over. Chane was stuck. He couldn't go forward, and he couldn't go back. Only she had the power to release him, and to do that she had to give him up.

Marianne was away, so Jennie sent Cooky to the storage car for her trunks. While he was gone she started going through all the closets to gather her things. In Chane's closet, she noticed that one of his frock coats had a spot on the sleeve. She pulled it out to give it to Cooky so it could be cleaned. Automatically, she went through the pockets. In the top right inside pocket she found a letter. She started to place it on his nightstand, but she noticed that it was addressed to her. Puzzled, she opened the letter and read it.

It was from Latitia Laurey. She had to read it three times before her mind would accept it. Then she sat down on Chane's bed and let its message sink in. Her mind felt entirely blank for a long time, then it formed an image of Chane and Latitia naked together, kissing and making love. The tears started, and then the pain came. It started slowly, building to such intensity that she knew why Chane could never forgive her. Nothing in her life had ever hurt like this. She felt sick in every cell of her body, sick enough to die.

She staggered to her bed and just lay there for a long time, crying and praying for death. Anything would be better than this terrible pain. Cooky returned with the first trunk, and she realized she wasn't going to be lucky enough to die, so she got up and began to pack.

Through the window of the Pullman coach, Chane saw Jennie moving around inside. He walked up the steps and opened the door. She didn't turn to greet him, even though he stamped his feet on the small throw rug in front of the door. Jennie had a trunk thrown open on the sofa and was carrying things to it. He walked over to watch her pack. His heart sank at the sight of her clothes and possessions going into the trunk.

"Are you leaving?"

Jennifer stopped, her back to him. "It's time."

"Time?"

"You've reached the Pass. It'll be easy sailing from here, and my foot is healed now. It's time to get back to work before I forget how." Her voice sounded muffled by pain. This was what he'd thought he *wanted* to hear. Except now he *was* hearing it, and it didn't feel like liberation. It felt like a weight crushing his chest.

"You know, I had a hard time forgetting or forgiving you for what happened with your dance partner..."

"Yes, I know."

"I told you I'd never be able to forgive that, and that I don't give any woman two chances at me..."

"I know, and I understand."

"Well, I just wanted to tell you that I might have been a little bullheaded..."

"No, you were right."

"A little *too* bullheaded..."

"You were entitled, and you were right. You see, I found the letter from Latitia—"

"Jesus." He cursed himself for forgetting to burn the letter.

"I was in so much pain that I realized why you can't forgive me, why you'll never be able to forgive me—"

"Jennie—"

"I know now that you're right about fidelity and trust. I accept it."

Chane reached out as if he would touch her. Jennifer flung his hand away. "Don't touch me. It's too late for touching and making up. I've been wrong about everything. I was even wrong about being wrong. I didn't make a decision to cheat on you. It just happened. I thought Frederick was my friend. I believed the terrible things he was saying about you. I'm not even smart enough to pick decent friends, or recognize lies when I hear them."

She threw one of her gowns into the trunk and stalked back into her sleeping compartment. She grabbed another gown, wadded it up, and threw it at the trunk. "I didn't mean to cheat on you, Chantry Kincaid. I thought you had killed my brother. I was punishing myself for ever marrying you."

She grabbed another gown and threw it. The gown missed its mark and landed on Chane. He carried it back to the closet. Jennifer grabbed it out of his hands, wadded it up, and threw it as hard as she could.

"Leave my gowns alone! I don't want your help!"

"Jennie, we need to talk."

"It's too late! You don't trust me, and you never will. You'll just blow yourself into a million pieces someday, and everyone but me will wonder how a smart man like Chantry Kincaid could have done such a stupid thing."

"Chane! Chane!" A familiar voice from outside caused Chane to stop, turn, and peer through the window.

Jennifer glanced around Chane's broad shoulder. A tall, still handsome, elderly man and woman stood on the ground, peering up toward the Pullman coach.

"My parents," he said grimly. "Can't this wait until after they leave?" he asked, lifting the trunk and carrying it into her sleeping compartment. "I'm sure they won't stay long."

Jennifer wanted to leave now, while she had the courage, but it would be too awkward with them just arriving. She checked the mirror. Her hair was combed and her face clean. That was the most she could hope for today. Nothing else had gone right.

Chane put the trunk down and faced her, his eyes dark with pain. "Jennie, I promise you that what happened with Latitia was an act of blind desperation. She forced herself on me. Even so, I behaved like an animal, and I've never been sorrier about anything in my life."

"And you still couldn't forgive *me*—"

"I don't know what the hell's wrong with me, but I am trying my best to get over it," he said, his eyes pleading with her. "Please stay."

His parents walked up the steps and stopped at the door. Jennifer braced herself. Chane walked to the door and opened it. "Mom. Dad. Come in. Come in."

CHAPTER THIRTY-ONE

Their first meal with his parents was one of the most strained Chane ever remembered. He was glad to learn his mother's health problem had cleared up and that both his parents were healthy and happy. But he wished they would just leave so he could get back to his argument with Jennie, who surprised him by being absolutely enchanting to his parents—and enchanted by them. She especially liked his mother, who was being equally charming and saying all the right things.

Radiant and possessive, his mother smiled frequently at his father, who seemed to swell with pride every time she looked at him. She was either touching him or adoring him with her eyes. His father was more subtle, but it was apparent they were very much in love. It almost hurt to look at them. Chane wished he could ask his parents for the secret to their happy marriage.

A week went by, and the elder Kincaids showed no sign of leaving. They appeared content to watch the work progressing, to take long walks in the daytime, and to sit on the observation deck of their luxurious Pullman coach in the evening, holding hands until bedtime.

Jennifer told Chane she wanted to leave, but he was no help. "Wait, Jennie, please. They'll be gone any day now."

Ten days after they had arrived, they were still there. Chane's crews were well over Raton Pass and starting down the other side. The surveyors had laid out another series of zigzag switchback wyes to make the descent gradual enough.

That night, Chane fished into his pocket and handed Jennifer a letter. She unfolded it and looked at Tom Wilcox's signature. Hoping for news of Peter, she read quickly.

The letter explained many things, but the only thing it said about

Peter was that they hadn't found him yet; Wilcox was still looking.

However, it also said that the letters Derek Wharton had "found" and pinned so much weight on—from Chane about the proxies, and from Reginald about the bankruptcy—were forgeries planted to throw suspicion onto Chane. Wilcox's staff had petitioned the bankruptcy judge into calling for an inventory of the Van Vleet estate, and they had discovered in excess of $4,000,000 in assets. Tom said that the Van Vleet attorney, Ward Berringer, had been hiding assets and systematically plundering the estate. Tom felt certain that a thorough audit could sort it all out. In time, the entire estate and its value would be restored to the heirs.

"Then Peter and I are not bankrupt!"

"No. Far from it."

It took a moment for the actuality of wealth to sink in. "As soon as I have cash available to me, I want to repay you for all of the money you expended in paying our debts."

"No."

"Yes. I need to do that."

"That's water under the bridge, Jennie. And I don't need your money. My grandfather left me with more money than I can ever spend, unless I decide to build another railroad. Besides," he said, his voice lowering into gruffness, "it pleased me to pay your debts."

For a moment, Jennifer thought Chane was going to say more. He shook his head and stood up to walk toward his sleeping compartment. "Good night," she said softly.

"Good night."

The next day, Elizabeth Kincaid invited Jennifer to walk with her. The day was so beautiful, the warm sun and clear air so invigorating, they walked up the side of the mountain almost to the top. With the camp below, they sat down to rest. The men looked like ants swarming over the fresh cut in the earth.

"I'd like to ask a personal question," Elizabeth said.

Jennie shrugged. "All right."

"A *very* personal question."

Jennifer flashed a quick look at her mother-in-law. Elizabeth's blue eyes were friendly and loving.

"All right."

"What happened to cause the estrangement between you and Chane?"

Jennifer leaned down and picked up a pinecone from the matted pine needles underfoot. Chane would not appreciate her sharing their private business with his mother, but she could see no reason not to. The marriage was over. In spite of all that had happened, Chane couldn't forgive her. "I disappointed him. I guess I betrayed him, and our love."

"How?"

"I thought Chane had had my brother beaten. I was confused. I did the unforgivable. I gave in to the advances of another man."

"You've been wonderfully candid with me, Jennifer. I want to thank you for that. I hope you don't think I was prying with my questions?"

"You may ask anything you like. I have nothing to hide. The only man in the world whose opinion matters knows everything and can't forgive me."

"He's a Kincaid, all right," Elizabeth said grimly.

Elizabeth could not get the conversation with Jennifer out of her mind. That night when she and Chantry were in bed in their own parlor car, she turned to her husband. "Dear..."

"Hmmm?"

"I want you to tell Chane about our problem."

"What?" he growled, his eyes blinking open in astonishment.

"I want you to tell Chane about our problem."

"Dammit, woman, I'll do no such thing."

"If you don't, he and Jennie will divorce shortly."

"Go to sleep. You shouldn't be meddling in those young people's lives. If they divorce, they divorce."

"But she's a wonderful young woman. I love her."

"You love everyone."

"Chantry, please."

"No. I'd feel like a fool."

"Better you should feel like a fool than those two lovers should part."

"I can't imagine where you get the idea that hearing about our problem would make a hill of beans of difference to Chane. He knows what he's about. He's built a fine railroad and beat the Commodore. My father would have been proud of him. He's got guts. You don't appreciate your son. That young man can do anything."

"Except make his wife happy. Are you going to tell him?"

"No."

In frustration, Elizabeth turned over and closed her eyes. Kincaid men. They should be tortured periodically by professionals.

Chane had decided his parents were going to stay forever. His mother had apparently fallen in love with Colorado and with Jennie. They took long walks every day. At times it seemed a strategy on Jennie's part to stay out of his way. At first he had avoided her. Now she avoided him.

Just as he had decided not to worry about their staying, his parents announced at dinner that they would be leaving the next day. Chane looked quickly at Jennie to gauge her reaction.

Jennifer looked down at her plate. The food no longer seemed appetizing to her. Her heart beat harder and faster. She glanced up. Chane's eyes were dark and searching. She looked away to control the trembling that had begun in her midsection. After the Kincaids left, she would have no choice but to pack and leave, too.

"Jennie, love..." Elizabeth said, with the same tenderness Chane had used in the old days, when he had loved her. A flush started deep inside Jennifer and crept up to her cheeks. Panic seized her. She felt as though she were about to cry in front of everyone.

"I didn't mean to startle you, dear..."

"You didn't, I was just—"

"You look lovely, startled. I was just wondering if you might like to come with us?"

"Come with you?" Jennifer panicked. "To New York?"

"Yes, dear. You could do some shopping and come back in a month or so. It would give you a chance to meet members of our family you didn't meet when my son rushed you off to the wilds of Colorado. Actually, you could both come. Almost anyone could take over as superintendent now."

Chane pushed his plate away. "I can't leave the railroad now. A thousand things can still go wrong, but Jennie might enjoy a vacation."

Jennifer put her napkin on the table. Chane looked guilty. Perhaps he had put his mother up to this to ease her out quietly, she thought, so he wouldn't have to deal with her.

"Why, yes, I guess I could," Jennifer said. She waited for Chane's response, but he merely looked from her to his mother and down at his plate.

Elizabeth clapped her hands in enthusiasm. "Wonderful, my dear! Can you be packed by tomorrow morning?"

That seemed much too soon to leave. Jennifer felt sick. "Yes, I'm sure I can."

"Good! What fun we'll have. I haven't shopped in New York for months."

Disgusted about something, his mouth twisted with chagrin, Chantry Two shook his head. "I'm surprised there's a shop still open, considering your absence. The economy must be stronger than I thought."

Elizabeth leaned over and kissed her husband. She looked delighted with the way things had worked out. An ache started in Jennifer's chest. By this time tomorrow she'd be on her way to New York. At least she wouldn't have to travel alone or on those hard wooden seats. The Kincaids' parlor car was one of the most luxurious she'd ever seen.

Chantry Two took Elizabeth aside as soon as he could arrange it. "Lizzy, dammit, whatever possessed you to ask that young woman to come with us? You know damned good and well if she goes, she won't come back."

"That's right."

"Well, why on earth—"

"Your son is as stubborn as you are. She might as well go back to New York in comfort."

"If you'd left her here, they might have worked it out."

"Not a chance. They've had months to do that."

Chantry shook his head in disgust. "You did this to force me to talk to him, didn't you, Lizzy?"

Elizabeth opened her eyes wide in innocent indignation. "I wouldn't dream of doing such a thing," she said, walking away from him. Then she turned and fixed him with a piercing look. "I know how stubborn you are. You'd let your son lose that wonderful young woman, and you wouldn't raise a finger."

"You're not going to blackmail me into a thing," he shouted after her.

"It couldn't be done, Chantry Kincaid. I know that better than anyone."

"Damnation!"

• • •

Jennifer sat by the open window. The night was relatively warm for the mountains. The scent of pine reminded her suddenly of the atrium at the Bricewood East and happy moments with Chane. The Kincaids had retired to their parlor car. Chane had excused himself and walked toward the office car. Cooky walked from the kitchen and bowed to her.

"I finish dishes, Missy Kincaid." He bowed again and touched his forehead. "Good night, Missy Kincaid."

"Good night, Cooky. Thank you."

Alone at last, Jennifer pulled out her trunk and started to pack. She felt worse than she'd ever felt in her life. Chane was just going to let her go. He wasn't going to try to talk her out of it. She felt too dispirited to be angry. She figured out what she would wear tomorrow, then took her other gowns down, folded them carefully, and placed them in the trunk.

Elizabeth was in the lavatory getting ready for bed. Chantry Two stepped back outside and leaned against a tree trunk, hesitant to call it a night. Inside his son's Pullman coach, Jennifer was packing. Lizzy blamed him for that, but he wasn't about to tell his son about their problem. Lizzy had been wrong to put him in this spot.

The crunch of gravel underfoot caused Chantry to pull back into the shadows. As he watched, his son slowed his step, paused, and peered longingly at the window, watching his wife packing her gowns.

"Go to her, son," Chantry Two wanted to tell his son. "Tell her it doesn't matter. Tell her that only love matters. Dammit, it's obvious to me and your mother that you love her. Why the hell isn't it obvious to you?"

Chane had paused so long, Chantry thought his son had turned to salt. "Go to her," his mind fairly cried out. "For God's sake, boy. She's your wife. Women make mistakes, too. Where the hell did you get such a stubborn streak?"

Now, Chane turned back toward the office car and entered it. Chantry waited a long time for him to come out. Finally, he walked to the office car and looked in. Chane was sitting alone in the dark.

"Would you like to take a short walk, son?"

Chane stood up. His parents would be leaving tomorrow. He'd forgotten that, in light of Jennie's leaving. It might be his last chance to visit with his father. "Yes, sir."

They headed up the tracks. In silence, Chane walked the ties the way he had in Texas, as a child walking to school. Somehow, walking them beside his father made him feel young and foolish. He stepped off to the side and walked in the gravel, which was noisier and more difficult. His father continued to walk the ties.

After a while Chantry Two sat down on a rock beside the rails to rest. Night birds warbled in the brush.

"So, why is your wife leaving you?"

Chane kicked at a rock in front of his foot. He couldn't believe his father would ask such a question, especially after his mother had been the one to instigate it. It puzzled him into silence. Also, he hadn't thought his father would understand the significance of Jennie's leaving. He didn't like the idea of telling his father his and Jennie's business. He felt certain that if their roles were reversed, his father would never tell.

Chantry Two expelled a heavy breath. "Lizzy was right about you," he said heavily. "You're too damned stubborn for your own good." He paused a moment and then plunged ahead. "Your mother almost left me six months ago. But thanks to your willingness to take over this project, I was able to talk her out of it."

Chane picked up a pinecone and ripped off one of the scales. "Why did she want to leave you?"

"Found another man. Thought she was in love with him."

Chane couldn't believe his father was telling him this, as if it were just any fact.

"I don't think he was as good in bed as I am, though."

Chane coughed. His father looked over at him. "Have I shocked you, son?"

"No, sir," he said, lying manfully.

"Well, you're married now. I guess you're old enough and experienced enough to take life straight. Your mother had an affair this past summer. I'll spare you the details. It's enough to say that we talked, and I asked her to give me another chance."

"Give *you* another chance?" Chane asked incredulously.

"I hadn't been spending nearly enough time with her. She got so damned lonely, she was easy prey for a man who was smart enough to see what a beautiful and charming woman she is."

Chane was too stunned to reply.

"We went to the Mediterranean and spent the last few months getting to know one another again."

"*You* didn't do anything wrong," Chane protested.

"The hell I didn't. She was so starved for attention, she was looking for it anywhere. It didn't take me long to realize that all the money I've made couldn't begin to make up for the loss of her. She's a fine woman. I've been a lucky man, but not nearly as lucky as I'm going to be in the future."

Chane felt as though he'd been kicked by a horse. His mother had had an affair, and his father had forgiven her—not only forgiven her, but begged her to take him back.

"I can see you're a little shocked."

"Yes, sir." He was more than shocked. He felt like a house with the load-bearing walls ripped out.

"Well, I was, too. I thought all a man had to do was be a good provider, and a woman could continue to love him. Well—" He laughed and continued. "—I was sure wrong about that. I almost lost one of the best women God ever made."

"I can't believe you took her back. I mean…after she had an affair…"

"Son, the secret of a successful marriage is in knowing what to remember and what to forget. We've each had something to forgive now."

"Each?"

"Yes, I'm ashamed to admit it."

"What did she have to forgive?"

"You promise me this won't go any further?"

"Yes, sir, of course." Chane could not imagine anyone he could tell this to.

"A few years ago I allowed myself to be seduced by a beautiful young woman." He expelled a heavy breath and shook his head in chagrin. "I blush with shame at the thought of it. If I didn't think you needed to hear this, I probably wouldn't admit it even now."

"Go on."

"Beautiful, but as unscrupulous as they come. My God, what a fool I was…"

Chane ripped another scale off the pinecone and waited in silence.

"I didn't find out until later that she was having an affair with my son."

"Your son?"

Chantry Two nodded. "Your brother."

Chane sat there dumbfounded for a moment. He had no idea what his father was trying to tell him. "Lance?"

"That's right."

"You had an affair with—"

"Lucinda."

Minutes went by while Chane tried to get his mind to think about these new developments, but it wouldn't. It seemed completely blank. "Did Mother know?"

"She found out when Lucinda died. Women just seem to have a way of knowing some things. Maybe she looked at Lance and looked at me and saw we were having the same reaction. I don't know. She came into my office one day and told me she knew. It was almost a relief to be caught."

"What did she do?"

"Nothing right away. But this past summer I guess that old pain and anger that had been festering in her so long just couldn't be ignored any longer. Or maybe she was just tired of me working such long hours and ignoring her."

They sat in silence for a long time. "Ready to go back?" his father asked.

"Yes, sir." But neither of them moved. Chane stared at the lights of the camp below. In the stillness he heard men laughing, talking, eating, probably playing cards. His mind seemed entirely blank.

"How do you decide about a woman?" Chane asked finally. "I know how to judge men, but women..."

His father sighed. "Women take more time. Because they aren't finished yet when we get them. The secret, if there is one, is to give a woman complete freedom and watch what she does with it.

"A woman can no more hide what she is than a man can. If she's a good woman, she'll blossom into something damned fine, as your mother has done. If she's not, she'll just sort of slip away from you."

Chane could feel himself crying inside. Finally his father continued.

"You can't put too much store in mistakes, because everyone makes 'em. You've got to look at the whole package, decide if it's something you want to invest in, and go from there. Aren't any perfect women, or men, either, for that matter."

"What if a woman—" His throat almost shut down with the effort to get the words out. "—betrays her husband?"

"I don't know what 'betrayal' is, exactly. I know what bad judgment is, though. A man has to expect a little of that. Life is hard, and it comes at us too fast sometimes."

He sat in silence for a moment. Then, almost as an afterthought, he said, "To be real, love has to be unconditional. It's not worth much to love someone before you've seen their flaws. If I were making an important decision, I'd judge a woman by her intentions and what she wants for herself, her husband, her family. And what she does. Anyone can talk a good fight, but it takes guts to actually live it."

Lying in her lonely bed, Jennifer waited for Chane to come to her. At the very least she expected him to say good-bye. But he didn't even come back to the parlor car to sleep.

At first she cried. Finally, the tears passed. Then she realized she didn't really have to leave, unless she wanted to. She knew she could tell Elizabeth she'd changed her mind. Chane would let her stay.

That felt much better, but then she remembered how Chane had lit the fuse on that stick of dynamite and just hung there in the basket beside it, waiting to see if they were going to get the lines untangled in time to pull him up before the dynamite blew. He was getting more reckless, not less.

She wept again. Finally, she wiped her tears and walked to the window to look out. The stars were so bright, she felt she could reach out and touch them. To her surprise, she realized that she would hate to leave this beautiful land and go back to the stifling city.

For the first time, she realized that loving Chane had opened her to loving life itself. Life had taken on meaning and purpose. Her world looked bigger and brighter now. She had passed all the tests this rough land had thrown at her. She had done it with all the honesty and energy she could muster, and somehow, without realizing it, the struggle had connected her with her own soul and that of the man she loved. Life here felt good and right. She could even forgive Chane for making love to Latitia.

Looking out at the dark shapes of the construction camp reminded her how satisfying it had felt to win at Raton Pass. In that one moment before she was stabbed, she'd felt better than ever in her life. Winning at the Pass had been the culmination of their combined hopes and dreams.

Chane should have been uplifted, too, but he hadn't been. He was still stuck in the past, still as likely to kill himself as ever, maybe more so. She felt cheated and let down by him and his unwillingness or inability to let go of the dead past and forge a new, shining future.

But in the same breath she realized she had sown the seeds of her own pain. Maybe her whole life had prepared her to sow them. The original guilt had been hers. If she had loved and trusted him at the outset the way he'd loved and trusted her then, this couldn't have happened.

She realized that as painful as her betrayal and its consequences had been, it had taught her some valuable lessons. And in the process, Chane had been revealed as a very fine man, one she would give anything to love and be loved by. He was honest and loyal and strong. He was a man she would like to work beside the rest of her life, but she couldn't have him, because to keep him, she would have to destroy him.

Even that despair passed. The sky was growing lighter now. With approaching dawn came her darkest moment of all. She had morbid fantasies of a doomed future. She could see herself dancing and living alone for the rest of her life. What had once seemed a wonderful prospect now looked like death to her.

Fortunately, she remembered again that she didn't *have* to leave. For a time that thought buoyed her. But eventually even that brought its own bitterness. Chane really would find an honorable way to kill himself. His wound had been as deep as his love. He suffered not from stubbornness, but from scar tissue, which was not willful at all. He was as much a victim of his injury as he had been of his love.

Struggling, she managed to get past the bitterness. Finally, at dawn, she realized that love was not about possessing, about having. It was about giving and letting go. Chane couldn't change, so she had to. The only way to save her husband's life was to leave him so he could make a new life without painful reminders of her and what she'd done to him.

At last she dressed herself and finished her packing. Hopefully, she would be strong enough to leave gracefully. She hated the thought of crying again.

"Jennie."

Chane's voice was so near she jumped. She hadn't heard him come in. Heart pounding, she turned to face him.

"I didn't mean to startle you."

"Well, you did."

"Sorry."

An awkward silence stretched out. Finally, he spoke. "I guess I can't talk you out of leaving."

"I guess not." *I guess I can't talk you out of leaving* was just a way to let her salvage some pride. If she had no pride at all, she could remember that and tell her friends he'd asked her to stay, but she'd refused.

"It's a long, hot trip this time of year."

"Thank you for your concern, but I guess now is better than summer, which is coming early, I think."

"Jennie…"

Chane's eyes reflected misery and confusion. It hurt her to see him so confused, but it reinforced her decision. If she didn't take charge of this mess, they would spend the rest of their lives almost loving each other.

She took his hands in hers and brought them to her lips to kiss them. "Don't be sorry, Chane. I know you were right about everything. If I had my life to live over, you would be the only man who *ever* touched me. I love you so much it makes me ache all over to think about leaving you, but I'm going to...for both our sakes."

"Is this another one of those favors women do for men?"

Jennifer smiled at his pained tone. "No. This is a blessing in disguise. I'm freeing you from your promise. It was wrong of me to hold you to it. I did it out of selfishness. I realized how much I loved you, and I wanted to win you back. I now realize I wouldn't have been able to stand what I did to you if our places had been reversed. Now I just hope you can rebuild your life. I want you to be happy."

"What about you? What will you do?"

At one time she'd thought art was the be-all and end-all, but the control and craft it took robbed life of all spontaneity. She'd grown to appreciate living life one day at a time, facing whatever needed to be faced, taking risks, playing herself instead of a role written by someone else.

But it made no sense to tell him all this. It would just sound like she was giving him an opening. He might feel obliged to take it. "I'm a good dancer. My foot is fine now. I'll rest awhile until this heals," she said, touching her rib. "And I'll always be proud of what we did here. It was a wonderful experience. I thank you for that. I'll never forget it. Good-bye," she said huskily, blinking back tears. "I think I'd better go find your mother and tell her I'm ready in case they're waiting for me." She gripped his hands hard and let them go.

Jennifer turned away and stepped blindly outside to see a surprising sea of men surrounding the Pullman coach. She hadn't noticed them come up. The crowd stretched back forever. It looked like over a thousand men.

Steve Hammond stepped forward. "Mrs. Kincaid. These men asked me to speak for them. They've heard you're leaving, and they're upset. They want to know when you'll be back."

Sudden tears had to be blinked away. "I don't know, Steve. I..."

The look in her eyes must have told him too much. He took off his hat and ran tobacco-stained fingers through his dark hair. "Well then, I guess we were right to fear the worst. I hope you'll forgive me, Mrs. Kincaid. Every man here has fallen in love with you, myself included." He swallowed, unable to continue. Men nodded and looked embarrassed.

"We're sorry to see you leaving. If you ever have an opening in your life for a thousand men or so..."

Jennifer half laughed and half cried. He looked so miserable, she reached up and hugged him.

"Thank you, Steve. You've been a wonderful gentleman. All of you. Thank you for everything."

Listening to Steve Hammond, who had never done anything like this before in his life, Chane hurt so bad he thought he might die of it. Jennie waved to the men and turned away. They watched her for a moment, then slowly turned to go back to work. Chane had never seen Jennie looking more beautiful or more composed. She looked warm, loving, and vibrantly alive.

Jennie stepped inside, looked quickly around the parlor for anything she'd left, and closed her trunk. The loud click of the trunk closing resounded in him.

The weight he had carried for months lifted and was gone. He didn't know if he should trust it or not, but words were forming and wanting to come out of his mouth without even a rehearsal in his head. "Jennie..."

She turned back to face him. She wiped quick tears off her cheeks, and in that instant she was the most beautiful woman he'd ever seen. "I just realized I don't give a damn if you slept with the entire dance company...as long as you don't do it again. As long as you don't ever leave me."

Jennifer searched his face. "You don't mean that."

Chane tried to decide if he did mean it. This was a new experience for him. It felt like he meant it. "Yes, I do."

"How do you know you can trust me?"

"I know you better now than I did six months ago. Before, you were trying to keep being a ballerina, and that confused you. I watched you enough these last six months to trust that once you set your heart on something, no matter what it is, you'll get it. You never lied to me. Even when you should have. I trust that. Maybe I was confused, too. Maybe I didn't realize that life isn't as perfect as I'd like it to be, or that I'm not as perfect as I'd like to be. But I don't think I'll survive if you leave me."

The intent light in Chane's eyes roused hope in Jennifer. "So what are you trying to say, Kincaid?"

"I'm asking you to stay with me."

"As what?"

"As my wife."

She stepped into his arms and tilted her head back to look into his eyes. "Your *what* wife?"

"My beloved wife."

Something opened in her chest. Her blood seemed to run more freely. "Your completely reinstated, beloved wife?" she whispered.

"Yes."

She detected no hint of wavering in his eyes. "Can you promise me that you will never again let the memory of my mistake come between us?"

"Yes. If you promise not to let my mistake come between us." His voice was firm.

"How do you know you can do that?"

"Once I give something up, it's gone."

"Your iron will works both ways, does it?"

"Yes, ma'am."

Chane pulled her closer into his arms and held her tight. He kissed her for a long time, putting such intensity into it, she lost track of everything except how much she loved him. His kiss made her knees go weak. It was filled with love and hunger and fierce longing. At last he relinquished her lips, but his arms continued to hold her close. He buried his face against her hair. "When I thought Fletcher had killed you, I got a glimpse of hell. Life became unbearable."

"Why didn't you tell me?" she asked.

"I knew that I still loved you and I'd never stop, but I couldn't bring myself to tell you."

"What if—"

Chane stopped her questions with his mouth. He kissed her long and tenderly. Then he lifted her into his arms and carried her to his sleeping compartment. He put her on the bed and closed the curtains.

"Chane, it's broad daylight. What if your parents—"

He ignored her protests. There was only one way to bridge the rift between them. His warm hands freed her of her gown, and he lowered his head to kiss her breasts, her throat, her mouth.

"Chane," she breathed. "You're torturing me."

"You've driven me crazy for months, you heartless little wench." His lips resumed their teasing of her flesh, and ripples of ecstasy quivered through her.

"I've watched a thousand men fall in love with you," he whispered against her breast. "I've lain in my lonely bed aching for the smell of you," he said, pressing his nose against her skin and inhaling. "For the feel of your skin," he said, caressing her body from her throat to her thighs. "For the taste of your mouth," he said, kissing her deeply. "Wanting you with every fiber of my being until I almost lost my mind," he whispered. "Now, you, my sweet little tormentor, must suffer," he said, his voice gruff with passion.

His strong hands moved to her hips. His lean fingers pressed into her soft belly, sending waves of fiery sensations coursing through her body. Trembling with need, Jennifer remembered a conversation they'd had on his ship. She opened her eyes and smiled dreamily up at him. "Will ye be killing me, sire?"

"Aye, wench, in my own way," he whispered, lowering his head to kiss her belly, and then work his way down her body. She cried out and writhed beneath his heated kisses. At first, her hands tried desperately to pull his head up. But slowly, the sensations overwhelmed her, and she relaxed and allowed him to do as he pleased. When she stopped struggling, he moved up and caught her hair at the back of her neck the way he'd done so long ago. A spear of heat shot through her now as it had done then. A moan of pure need tickled her throat.

"Look at me, Jennie," he whispered.

"No." She didn't want reality to intrude on the wonderful sensations rippling through her love-starved body. But curiosity made her open her eyes. His handsome face was only inches from her own. The look in his eyes was one she would treasure for the rest of her life. It was one of power and masculine purpose. His hand tightened in her hair, pulling her head back and increasing the response that had already devastated her.

She cried out her need and her surrender. Only then did he enter her. Her body responded wildly. The sensations he'd started and now controlled turned fierce and heated. It was different from the way he'd made love to her in New York and even different from the way he'd taken her in Colorado. Somehow, the love and adoration of the former were now strengthened by the fierceness and power of the latter. She felt loved and wanted and protected and cherished.

She had waited so long for this change in him. At first, she couldn't believe it had actually happened. But slowly, the warmth of his mouth on hers, his hands on her body, his heat and hardness inside her, dissolved all doubt. Her heart opened the way it had that first time he made love to her. Her bliss was almost too exquisite to bear.

In spite of the strength of her arousal, tears of deep happiness streamed down her cheeks. Chane kissed them away while his strong hands stroked her and held her. She marveled that at last the miracle she'd been praying for had happened.

Chane brought her to peak after blazing peak, and when it was over, they lay close together, listening to a mockingbird overhead, singing first like a thrush, then like a Rocky Mountain jay.

Jennifer glanced over at Chane, and the sharpness of his profile reminded her of the many times he'd turned away from her. "It won't work," she whispered. "You'll forget your promise. You'll stop trusting me."

Chane rolled over and covered her body with his. He gazed intently into her eyes. "I promise you I've learned my lesson," he whispered.

"How do I know you really mean it?"

"I had a talk with my father last night that curdled my fine Kincaid blood. I'll never be able to reach that same level of blind intolerance again."

"What did you talk about?"

"Women and life. That's all I'm going to say, but I realized I didn't know anything about either one before."

Jennifer laughed. She knew his parents well enough to realize that Elizabeth had somehow prevailed over her husband.

Chane pulled her against his chest and buried his face in the Gillyflower fragrance of her hair. "I love you, Jennie. This has been the most miserable six months of my life. I thought I'd die a thousand times..."

"You deserved to. If there was any justice at all..."

Chane laughed. "You heartless little wench." He pulled her on top of him and swatted her bottom. Out of sheer bullheadedness he had almost lost Jennie. Thanks to her determination to win him back, she'd given them a chance to forge a truer, deeper relationship than the one they'd lost.

Chane kissed her forehead, her nose, and finally, her lips. Then he cupped her face in his hands, and stared deep into her violet eyes. "I love you, Jennie." He breathed a deep sigh of contentment. "I've learned to have tremendous respect for you in these last few months. I married a girl, and I've watched you grow into a wonderful, awe-inspiring woman before my eyes. There were times I could have knelt at your feet."

"You should have," she said, straining upward to kiss his bottom lip. Then, suddenly serious, she said, "I love you, too, Chantry Kincaid."

Chane kissed her, and she felt overwhelmed with love for him. He came into her again, and even though he'd made love to her only moments before, her body seemed to catch fire and burn with the love that had never stopped and never could.

THE LADY AND THE LAWMAN

Life on the Western frontier in the 1880s is filled with risks and danger—a fact Angie Logan quickly relearns upon arriving back at her family's Arizona ranch, home from college back East. To help quell the riots against Chinese immigrants that have settled in Durango, Angie relies on her education and wits in appealing to the governor for assistance. The governor sends help in the form of Lance Kincaid, a charismatic gentleman who became a ranger to avenge the murder of the woman he loved. While working to resolve the current upheaval, Lance catches the trail of the murderer. Nothing will stop him from catching the killer and bringing him to justice, except perhaps Angie, the mysterious woman who looks eerily like his lost love.

THE LADY AND THE OUTLAW

Leslie Powers has every reason in the world to hate Ward Cantrell, the devilishly handsome outlaw who kidnapped her. Instead she finds herself head-over-heels in love with him. When prompted by the sheriff to testify against Ward, Leslie firmly states that she was never Ward's hostage. Now a free man, Ward courts his way through the young ladies of Phoenix society, appearing to seduce them with wanton abandon. Leslie believes he is a rogue and worse, but she can't get him out of her mind or her heart. She's seen behind his mask and knows there is more to him than meets the eye; something in him has captured her heart.

ADOBE PALACE

After the deaths of her parents, Samantha Forrester was raised with the Kincaid children. She fell in love with Lance Kincaid as he protected her from childhood bullies. Now they've both grown up and Lance has married another. When the devilishly charming Steve Sheridan rides into Samantha's life, she sees her chance to build the house of her dreams, save her son's life, and claim Lance's heart for her own. But life doesn't always go according to plan, and fate will take them all on a journey as wild as the land they live on.

AFTER EDEN

Teresa Garcia-Lorca was raised as the favored daughter of "El Gato Negro," the infamous Mexican revolutionary. She lived in sheltered bliss until the day the truth of her paternity comes out, and her former "father" becomes furious. Teresa and her mother are forced to flee for their lives to escape El Gato's murderous rage. Her only hope lies in the home of her biological father, Bill Burkhart, but nothing could have prepared her for the treachery of gringo/white greed. Her new-found father's bastard daughter, Judy Burkhart, has had everything—and every man—she's ever wanted. Her indulgent world shatters when Judy learns she's been disinherited in her father's will. She and Teresa must learn to fight for all they have lost—and only one of them will end up with the man they both love.